Greaves saw that the door had been jemmied open. The little flat was crowded with people; he had to push past uniformed figures to get into the bare living room where Chief Inspector Asher was waiting.

'Hello, Bruce,' Greaves said.

'Colin,' Asher replied. 'I've been expecting you.' He gestured across the room. 'Well, there it is. I've done all the usual. I'll leave you to get on with it.'

Greaves stood alone now, aware of his own breathing, and forced himself to put aside emotion. A detached manner was necessary if he were to protect his own sanity. The sight before him was as terrible as any nightmare could devise.

Michael Molloy began to work on newspapers after an Art School training, and was apppointed editor of the *Daily Mirror* in 1975, later to become Editor-in-Chief of Mirror Group Newspapers. He is the author of six novels, including *Sweet Sixteen*, which preceded *Cat's Paw* and introduced the characters of Sarah Keane and Colin Greaves.

Also by Michael Molloy
available from
Mandarin Paperbacks

Sweet Sixteen

Michael Molloy
CAT'S PAW

Mandarin

A Mandarin Paperback
CAT'S PAW

First published in Great Britain 1993
by Sinclair-Stevenson Ltd
This edition published 1994
by Mandarin Paperbacks
an imprint of Reed Consumer Books Ltd
Michelin House, 81 Fulham Road, London SW3 6RB
and Auckland, Melbourne, Singapore and Toronto

A CIP catalogue record for this title
is available from the British Library
ISBN 0 7493 1453 2

Printed and bound in Great Britain
by Cox & Wyman Ltd, Reading, Berks

Prologue

This was the part she liked least of all: waiting for a new one to arrive. When they had a face it became somehow more acceptable, even if they were ugly she could make them fit into one of the fantasies she had devised; but the anticipation of a new client was always disturbing. There was nothing to focus on; and therefore too much scope for her imagination. Then came the terrible fear that this time, this one would hurt her. She didn't mind if their urgency made them rough, she was a strong girl and could easily cope with an over-zealous lover; but she had heard that some men liked to beat women for pleasure, scar them, break teeth and bones. The thought made her reach up and touch the fine contours of her features for a moment. She had waited so long to finally buy the face she had always dreamed of, the thought of it smashed to a pulp caused her throat to constrict and a sudden lurching convulsion deep in her entrails.

On the glass-topped coffee table before her was a neat line of white powder she had prepared. Quickly she leaned forward and, holding a delicate glass tube, inhaled the snowy substance. The rush of exhilaration came instantly, causing her to throw back her shoulders and sigh with relief.

Then the doorbell sounded with a harsh unmelodious rasp. Rising from the pink velvet sofa, she glanced down at her evening dress. It was pale tan silk that exactly matched the colour of her skin. With a small thrill of pleasure she remembered that it had cost a little more than her mother earned in three months.

Yes, it was all worth it. Confidently she walked towards the door and the cat ran ahead of her, a silver bell tinkling on her collar.

CHAPTER
ONE

Monday, October 26 3.10 p.m.

In sudden anger, Brian Meadows, the editor of the *Gazette*, turned to his desk, put down the two glasses of brandy he carried, and with a spasmodic shudder, tried to claw between his shoulder blades, like a murder victim attempting to remove a dagger. The cause of his discomfort was twofold. The first was his haircut; that morning he had suffered one of his infrequent visits to the hairdresser, and despite careful instructions, the barber had clipped his hair shorter than he wanted it, and allowed some tiny particles to work their way inside his collar. Consequently, he had suffered the sensation that an army of ants were attacking his backbone all day. Meadows was not a particularly vain man. He bought his suits off the peg and carried a bit more weight than perhaps he ought, but he was secretly proud of his usually full, flowing head of hair.

The second reason for his mood was the conversation that had just taken place at the lunch held by Sir Robert Hall, Chairman of London and Overseas Communications PLC, the company which controlled the *Gazette*. The other guests had been Geraldine Miller, a junior cabinet minister, whom Meadows had known slightly since they had been at Oxford together, and Jeremy Blakestone, who had come to prominence in recent years as the chairman of a charity he'd founded called HAND. Meadows had taken an instant dislike to Blakestone, who affected the speech patterns and dress sense of an ageing rock star. He had also lectured them for the past two hours, on the plight of the under-privileged, in a manner which suggested that he was the only member of society with sufficient compassion to grasp the problem.

Meadows – bored by Blakestone's endless flow of irritating jargon – had consumed impressive amounts of the Château Lafitte served in Sir Robert's private dining room, and towards the end of the meal allowed his thoughts to drift away from Blakestone's numbing monologue.

Gazing at the storm clouds framed by the wide windows behind Sir Robert's chair, he let his mind return to an afternoon – many years before – when he'd sat in a dingy rehearsal hall and watched with feigned indifference as Geraldine Miller, perfect in the role of Juliet, had filled his callow heart with hopeless longing.

His attention was jolted back to the room, when Sir Robert turned to him and said imperiously, 'Something must be done. Don't you agree, Brian ?'

Sir Robert was a small man in his early fifties, who kept his chin permanently thrust forward as if he were expecting a sculptor to suddenly begin modelling his profile. 'Certainly,' Meadows replied firmly, and without the faintest idea of what course of action he had just committed himself to, glanced hopefully towards Geraldine Miller, who smiled slightly and came to his rescue. 'I'm positive an article in the *Gazette* would

2

be effective,' she said in a low voice. 'It could go a long way in alerting the parents to the appalling dangers their children face when they leave home and take to living rough on the streets of London.' Now fired with enthusiasm, she continued, 'I'm sure you're aware, Sir Robert, there's only so much we in government can do – without limiting the individual's freedom of choice. That's why charities such as HAND play a vital role in guiding the naïve and unwary. In cases like this the role of the press can be especially helpful.'

Meadows picked up the cue effortlessly. 'We'll be on to your office this afternoon.'

'Great, Brian – now, get your main man to, kind of, interface with Tony Glendowning on this one,' Blakestone said earnestly. 'He knows the streets – where it's at, that sort of thing.' Meadows winced inwardly at this fresh assault upon the language, but he managed a smile. Blakestone then turned to Sir Robert. 'And can I ask one more favour, Bob ?'

Sir Robert's little head inclined slightly, and Meadows was suddenly reminded of a child seated in a high-chair. Because the chairman of the *Gazette* was small in stature, Meadows knew that beneath the fine linen tablecloth touching the floor, his feet were resting on a Victorian lap-top writing desk.

'Tony's taken a lot of stick from the press,' Blakestone said, holding up a hand. 'So OK, he was busted on a drugs rap himself, and his old man was supposed to have pulled strings,' Blakestone now wiggled his index fingers. 'But I quote: "I'm clean now." So let's keep his name out of the piece. I know his old man would be grateful.'

Sir Robert inclined his head again. Lord Glendowning was a man of great power; such a request on his behalf was perfectly reasonable.

'It shall be done,' he answered, and his remark seemed to signify the end of the occasion. But as they rose from the table, Blakestone asked Sir Robert if he could spare a few more minutes in private, so Meadows offered to escort Geraldine Miller to her car.

While they waited for the executive lift, Meadows tried not to stare at her splendid figure. It was fuller now than in the slender days of their youth, and the long blonde hair that had once floated around her face was plaited and coiled about her head. The part of Juliet would no longer seem appropriate, but it was evident from her regal bearing that she could manage Cleopatra with ease. Although decisive enough in his professional duties, Meadows was usually rather hesitant with women, but on a sudden impulse, probably caused by a surfeit of wine, he asked if she would care for a final brandy before she departed.

'Why not,' she replied. 'But I must find a loo first.' Her smile brought another rush of longing from the past.

When they entered his office, Meadows poured the drinks and indicated the door to his private bathroom. Having managed to scratch his back with a ballpoint pen, he now stood awkwardly, all previous boldness spent, feeling once again like the gauche undergraduate he had been at their first meeting. When she emerged, Meadows caught the scent of an expensive perfume. 'Thank you for rescuing me,' he said as he handed her the glass. 'I owe you more than this.'

'It was the least I could do,' she laughed. 'After all, I did instigate the lunch and I could see how bored you were.'

Meadows noticed the faint lines about her eyes. Nature had been gentle to her in the time since their earlier days. She was still the same fair-haired beauty, and marriage to one of the richer men in Britain had obviously helped to ease the passage of the years. 'What did you think of Mr Blakestone ?' she asked.

Meadows sipped some brandy. 'Interesting,' he replied thoughtfully. 'It's rare to meet someone who is so completely satisfied with themselves.'

4

She laughed again. 'You should try politics. Self-satisfaction is endemic.'

'Why does he wear those dreadful clothes at his age?' Meadows asked. 'And that accent and vocabulary. It was like listening to a demented disc jockey. I read the library cuttings on him before lunch. You know he claims to have gone to Harrow?'

Geraldine sat down on one of the sofas near his desk and Meadows was slightly surprised by her lack of urgency. In his experience, junior ministers were generally in a hurry and harried from appointment to appointment by an accompanying civil servant who acted like an apologetic sheepdog. It was unusual for her to be alone today.

'That's part of the HAND approach,' she answered. She patted the place next to her. Meadows sat down, and she continued: 'Blakestone insists that all their employees dress casually and speak the language of the kids they're trying to help. It's all a question of relating. Street cred, he calls it – part of understanding the problems of youth.'

Meadows finished his brandy and, seeing that his guest was still in no hurry to leave, poured another. 'I think I prefer the Salvation Army,' he said with another sudden convulsion caused by the tormenting hairs inside his shirt. 'And I prefer the uniform.'

Geraldine sat deeper in the sofa and glanced towards the windows that overlooked the Gray's Inn Road. The dark clouds had thickened and her mood seemed to alter, matching their deepening gloom.

'None of it really matters,' she said quietly. 'Blakestone's organisation is only papering over the cracks. Society is breaking up. Most of the next generation won't know what it's like to belong to a real family.'

'Isn't that a bit apocalyptic?' Meadows asked. 'People are still getting married.'

5

'And divorced,' she said quickly.

Meadows didn't look at her when he asked the next question. 'How are you and Charles ?'

Geraldine spoke briskly. 'Still married – but he's living with a twenty-year-old receptionist during the week. Sometimes we spend a few hours together on Sundays.'

'I'm sorry.'

Geraldine made a dismissive gesture with the hand that held her glass. 'That's not for publication, of course. Charles still likes to keep up appearances. Sometimes I think he relishes my job more than I do.' She touched Meadows's hand. 'What about you – didn't you marry someone terribly glamorous, an actress, wasn't she?'

'Valerie and I were divorced – oh, five years ago.'

'Did you have children ?'

Meadows made a concealed attempt to scratch himself while he answered. 'One, a boy – full grown now. He disappeared into the Alps with a pair of skis three years ago. I know he's still alive, he writes fairly regularly for money.'

Meadows felt the warm pressure from her hand and heard a new softness in her voice. 'So we still have something in common.' Her tone altered. 'Why do you keep shifting about like that? You were doing it all through lunch.' There was suddenly the smack of firm government in her voice.

Meadows explained the reason for his discomfort, and she was still laughing when his secretary buzzed on the intercom to ask if he was going to attend the features conference.

'Tell Mr Brooks to take it,' he instructed carelessly, the brandy causing a renewal of his earlier boldness.

'You don't seem to be pushed for time,' he said, watching her mouth on the rim of the brandy glass; the smile she gave him made the pulse at his temple tick.

'I told my people to clear my diary,' she answered. 'After this lunch, I had intended to go to the country for a few days.'

6

Meadows noticed the careful phrasing of her last sentence. Was an option being presented – or was the brandy overheating his imagination ? He tried to think of something subtle to say, words that would convey his deepest desire but at the same time not make him look a fool if she was simply making small talk. All he could come up with was, 'The weather doesn't look very promising.'

She glanced towards the window again. 'No, it won't be much fun. I miss Oxford sometimes. Do you ever see any of the old crowd, our group I mean?'

Meadows looked into his glass. In his recollection, they had belonged to quite separate groups that barely mingled at the edges, but he let it pass. 'Not really,' he said. 'Lewis Horne, occasionally – and Guy Landis. But I wouldn't say we keep in touch.'

'Touch,' she repeated. 'Such a beautiful word.' And she squeezed his hand with such deliberation he could not fail to read the signal. But still he hesitated.

'This job, it's pretty full-time – there's always a lot of problems ... ' he let his voice trail away and with sudden resolve made an awkward attempt to kiss her. To his intense relief, she did not back away, but responded with equal enthusiasm. Then she stood up and held out her hand: 'At least I know how to cure one of your problems,' she said.

'How?' Meadows replied in a barely audible voice. He realised he was on the edge of fulfilling a fantasy; the prospect suddenly daunted him. But Geraldine Miller was in full command. She nodded her head in the direction of the bathroom. 'We can use the shower to wash away those hairs.'

Meadows stood up, his head now swimming from the wine, brandy and Geraldine Miller's musky perfume. In the outer office, the editor's secretary looked up as the small red light above the door flicked on, signifying that he was not to be disturbed.

Monday, October 26 4 p.m.

Superintendent Colin Greaves sat at the kitchen table of Sarah Keane's Hampstead house, studying the property pages of the local newspaper while she prepared vegetables at the sink. Although it was a Monday, Sarah had a day off from her work as a reporter on the *Gazette* and Greaves had arranged his own duties so they could spend some time together, but so far the day had not been a success.

To the people who knew them, they appeared a well-matched couple. Both looked younger than their actual ages, but it was more than superficial appearances that made their relationship successful. Similarities that they recognised in each other created deeper bonds than most people realised.

Both were deeply reserved, and slow to respond when confronted by the uninhibited. They concealed this aspect of their characters with careful manners, so that their entire personalities seemed understated to many of those they encountered in daily life, where their jobs constantly involved meeting new people. This reserve was not the result of indifference – in truth, they were deeply concerned about other people – but they found it impossible to display the depth of their feelings until they were absolutely sure they would not encounter rejection . When that wall was breached they committed themselves completely – and their friendship, once given, was as sound as granite.

Each possessed a deep sense of humour that could surprise or disconcert the unprepared. Sarah's was mischievous, which sometimes puzzled those who expected her to be in a constantly serious state of mind. Since boarding school, Greaves had developed a razor-edged wit that had been honed at university and dried like bleached bone in the harsh reality of police work.

Other factors that drew them together were the differing circumstances of their previous marriages. Sarah had been widowed suddenly almost two years before, and the shock of losing Jack, a television reporter, had had a profound effect on her. When Greaves had first met her, she had only just emerged from the grief and returned to work after an absence of seventeen years.

Greaves's wife had divorced him some years before at the time when he was working for the Hong Kong police. The reason was still so deeply painful to him that Sarah sometimes wondered if it would ever heal completely. His children, a boy and a girl, had drowned in a boating accident and his wife never forgave him for the tragedy.

They had found each other at a time when each had thought the kind of relationship they now enjoyed would never be possible again, and both were secretly fearful that it was too good to last. Tentatively, they had already decided to marry some time in the undecided future. For the time being they lived together, but the location they had settled on was causing a certain amount of friction. Finally, the previous week, Greaves had raised the subject of moving to a new home but Sarah was clearly cool about the idea.

The half-grown golden Labrador that sat between them sensed the strained atmosphere and glanced anxiously at each of them in turn as if hoping a friendlier relationship would develop. Sarah turned from the sink with a colander of peelings and almost tripped over the dog, who shuffled under the table and collapsed with a sigh of distress.

'Have you finished with the paper?' Sarah asked.

Greaves pushed it towards her without answering and she tipped the contents on to the open pages.

'I don't think we'll ever find another house you want to live in,' he said. 'Is there any point in searching further?'

Sarah sat down next to him and dried her hands with her apron. 'It isn't just me, Colin,' she answered. 'The children have grown up in this house. It means a lot to them. You never had a

9

proper home as a child, so I know it's hard for you to understand. But moving is supposed to be one of the most stressful events a family can experience … Emily is just coming up for her A levels and the boys … '

Greaves smiled ruefully. 'Not the boys, they'd be happy moving to a mud hut in Borneo.'

Now Sarah smiled. She had to admit that her twin sons did lack some of their sister's sensitivity. She reached out and took his hand. 'Do you still want to marry me?'

Greaves looked down at the slim wedding ring she wore before he answered. 'Of course I want to marry you, and I want to take care of your children – but I think it will be … difficult in this house.'

'What's so wrong with it?'

Greaves shook his head. 'There's nothing wrong, it's … ' he held up both his hands. 'It's charming, delightful and full of character … it's just – '

'The house where Jack Keane's widow lives,' she interrupted. Greaves let go of her hand and picked up one of the potato peelings. 'It's not only that. I don't resent the fact that you loved your first husband. It's just that sometimes I feel like a stranger here. Everything has its proper place. If I move a piece of furniture, even the poker in the fireplace, I find it put back where it was before, as though I'd moved the exhibits about in a religious shrine.'

Sarah thought for a time. She glanced out of the window to watch the storm clouds coming from the west and then back to this new man she loved. His use of the term 'religious shrine' seemed apt, somehow. When she had first seen him, his long face, with the flesh pared to the bone, and his cropped, greying hair had put her in mind of a painting of some medieval saint. Even now, when he smiled he still possessed an air of melancholy.

'If that really is the case,' she said finally, 'you must blame

10

me – not Jack.' She looked around her. 'Every stick of furniture, each knife and fork and piece of bedlinen you see, the ornaments, pictures, the pots and pans and rugs in the hall were all chosen by me – and given their place.' She paused and raked a hand through her short, dark hair. 'Darling – Jack lived his life out of a suitcase. If you're looking to find his ghost don't start here – try the offices of Thomas Cook. Jack was so used to living in hotels he'd put his shoes outside the bedroom door at night.'

He looked up, and was about to answer when the telephone rang. Sarah picked up the receiver, then held it out to him.

'Greaves,' he said with an apologetic glance. It was Detective-Sergeant Nicholas Holland. 'Sorry to bother you today, sir,' he said. 'We've got a murder, a bad one.'

'Where?'

'The Brent River estate. I thought you'd want to know because of the location.'

'How long has the body been there?'

'Looks like most of the day. Half the local population have been in for a look.'

Greaves rubbed the crease between his eyebrows and then glanced at his watch. It was just after 4.30, and nearly dark:

'Christ, and it's only been reported now.' He turned towards Sarah. 'Right, I'm on my way.'

'I've sent a car for you. It should be there any minute.'

When he returned to the table, Sarah was staring down at the advertisements for houses that were now part obscured by the peelings. 'I'm sorry,' she said. 'Did you want to keep this?'

Greaves shook his head and took her in his arms. 'No, put it on the compost heap.'

The Labrador, relieved by the reunion, emerged from beneath the table wagging its tail, and then ran to the front door at the sound of the ringing bell.

Monday, October 26 5.05 p.m.

The rain that had threatened all afternoon began to fall in torrential sheets, drumming on the corrugated iron roof of the dusty little public hall that lay in a side turning off Camden High Road. Cat Abbot, a younger and better-dressed figure than the rest of the packed audience that sat in the dim light, leaned forward to hear the words that emerged from the woman, who was slumped in a wickerwork armchair on the small platform. Before she had entered the trance she had told them of her spirit guide, Homa, and for some time she'd been delivering messages to people in the hall, spoken in the deep masculine tones of a long-dead Egyptian scribe.

'Now, I have a message from someone called Alfie who lived at the time of your Great War,' the voice said in sonorous tones.

'That's for me,' an elderly lady, seated two chairs away from Abbot, said in a matter-of-fact voice. Abbot shifted uncomfortably on his canvas and tubular metal chair, and listened while the spirit guide passed messages of reassurance.

' … Alfie says do you still have the picture of Mum and Dad at the old house?'

'Yes,' the old lady replied, and there was a sudden, hard crack of thunder. The woman on the platform sat up and slowly shook her head.

'I'm sorry,' she said in her normal, Welsh accent, 'but the storm is proving very disruptive. Homa says he is returning to the land of the dead. I'm afraid the seance must end for today.'

The people in the hall nodded their understanding and shuffled to their feet, buttoning their coats in preparation for the weather outside. Abbot, who was not wearing a raincoat, remembered with relief that he had managed to park his car directly in front of the entrance. The other members of the audience began to file from the hall, but Abbot waited for the woman on the platform, who was now talking to an old man in a brown overall, who appeared to be the caretaker of the premises.

'Next Monday, same time, Bert,' she said in a cheerful voice and she stepped down to face Abbot.

'Doreen Clay?' he asked, holding out his hand. 'My name is Raymond Abbot, I'm a reporter with the *Gazette*, I telephoned you earlier.'

She took his hand and held on to it longer than was usual for a handshake, but Abbot didn't mind. Although she was a trifle short and no longer youthful, Doreen Clay was a fine-looking woman. Cat noted the trim figure, dark red hair and olive complexion. She had a full mouth, which showed small, very white teeth when she smiled, and her slanting eyes were greenish brown. There was another quality to her that Abbot could not place, but he felt it like the heat emitted by an electric fire.

'Raymond,' she repeated softly, 'but they don't call you that, do they?'

'Most people know me as Cat,' he replied with slight surprise.

'Cat,' she said. She cocked her head to one side as she looked up at him. 'That's unusual. How did you come by that?'

'It's a long story.'

'Well we've got all night,' she said with another smile. 'I'm free now.'

Cat was beginning to feel happier about the job. He had not expected someone so attractive. He was about to suggest going for a drink, when the pager in his jacket pocket began to sound. He took out the little electronic device and read the message: COME BACK RIGHT NOW, CONWAY.

'Problems?' Doreen Clay asked.

Cat nodded. 'An urgent call to return to the office.' He looked at his watch: 'Look, I don't know how long this will take, may I make another appointment for tomorrow?'

She thought for a moment. 'I won't be free until after seven, you could come to my house.'

'Where do you live?'

'Just around the corner. If you've got a car you can drop me off. Then you'll know the address.'

'That's very kind of you, Mrs Clay.'

'Miss Clay,' she said, taking his arm, 'but you can call me Doreen.'

Twenty minutes after leaving the house, Greaves's car was heading south along the North Circular Road, through a grim industrial landscape of peeling factories and bleak, featureless storage depots. Even the forlorn stretches of semi-detached houses they occasionally passed seemed defeated and abandoned to the deadening roar of juggernaut traffic. Coming from the quiet leafy streets of Hampstead, it was like entering another country.

Once past the Welsh Harp Reservoir, where a handful of suburban yachtsmen sailed brightly painted dinghies against a backdrop of slate-grey water, the car turned into a series of slip roads flanked by shabby Victorian houses. After a time they passed a vast, green-tiled public house that stood on a corner like a monument to a previous civilisation. Then the car entered the grim acres of the Brent River estate.

Even in the air-conditioned interior of the car, Greaves thought he could feel the brooding malevolent atmosphere that now lingered about him like mist. Outlined against the darkening sky, the estate looked as if some gigantic child had grown tired of a game with building blocks and carelessly left them scattered, to rot in the surrounding wasteland. Through the darkness to his left, the car's headlights momentarily illuminated a group of children scrambling about the carcass of a burnt-out car that had been abandoned on one of the wide expanses of packed mud that had been intended as lawn.

In the days of certainty, a quarter of a century before, the Brent

River estate had been presented to the world as a beacon of hope for those who had been deprived and brutalised by the harsher inequalities of life. There – the jubilant planners announced – amid soaring tower blocks and placid parklands, racism and despair would finally be eliminated. New generations, freed from the chains of the past, would demonstrate that all men and women were equal and that only environment shackles the human heart. And so – accompanied by fanfares of publicity – a rich mixture of families, taken from north London's varied ethnic ghettos, were transported to their new Jerusalem.

But reality refused to conform to the fantasies presented by the architects and planners. The lifts did not work; and people found no sense of companionship in the bleak concrete corridors of the towers. The young, guided by a new philosophy preached by false prophets, were taught to believe that desire alone deserved reward. When it did not materialise they grew increasingly bitter.

Gradually the darker side of nature prevailed and instead of reaching for the expected sunlight, the majority – leaderless and abandoned – gradually sank into despair, and allowed a lawless few to recreate the rank and fetid undergrowth of a jungle.

Tin-pot local demagogues still poured out the same rhetoric about society being to blame. But for those cowed inhabitants, who still struggled for a decent life amid the broken lifts, burnt-out flats, landings defaced with graffiti and stinking with urine, only one reality proved certain. The meek shall inherit the Brent River estate; and the savage shall make their life hell.

Greaves knew the chief among the savages well; they had met in another place, years before. Now their hatred cut deeper than the usual relationship between policeman and criminal. There was no sense of detachment: the feelings Colin Greaves and Danny Doyle held for each other were like some ancient tribal blood feud, bred in the bone. To each of them, the other's very existence was like an acid that ate into his soul. Greaves understood that such obsession was as dangerous to himself as it was to the object of his loathing, but logic could not guide him in this matter and he knew he would risk his own life to see the other die.

It was dark now, and floodlights set high on the towers bathed the rubble-strewn courtyards in a harsh, bluish light. A uniformed constable directed Greaves's car. He could see parked rows of steel-grilled police vans that contained reinforcements clad in protective gear. Such precautions were always necessary. Any strong police presence on the estate was taken as a provocation to riot, and to confirm this possibility Greaves saw a sullen crowd of youths at the edge of the police tapes when the car drew to a halt. About half were black and half white, but the two groups did not mingle.

Greaves got out of the car and looked up at the dark sky and, as if his prayer had been answered, rain began to lash down. A jagged fork of lightning momentarily bathed the estate in white light. The crowd began to disperse as Detective-Sergeant Holland, who had come to greet Greaves, led him up the dank stairway to the second-floor landing of Green Tree House. Holland was a powerful young man in his late twenties, with blunt, handsome features, who looked less formidable when he smiled.

Greaves stopped for a moment when they reached the balcony and said, 'Who's on this one?'

'Chief Inspector Asher,' Holland replied.

'Could be worse,' he said softly. Greaves held a special brief to operate outside usual police procedures and this was often resented by the more conventional members of his profession.

'The body is in a flat that was unoccupied and boarded up,' Holland explained as they walked on. 'The electricity was cut off so we've had to use mobile lights.'

Greaves saw that the door had been jemmied open. The little flat was crowded with people; he had to push past uniformed figures to get into the bare living room where Chief Inspector Asher was waiting.

'Hello, Bruce,' Greaves said.

'Colin,' Asher replied. 'I've been expecting you.' He gestured across the room. 'Well, there it is. I've done all the usual. I'll leave you to get on with it.'

Greaves stood alone now, aware of his own breathing, and forced himself to put aside emotion. A detached manner was necessary if he were to protect his own sanity. The sight before him was as terrible as any nightmare could devise.

Beneath the broken windows, the naked body of a young woman had been seated on the bare boards of the floor, legs stretched out towards him and back upright against the wall. The girl was slim with a well-developed dancer's body. But the pale, coffee-coloured skin had been systematically burned. Not in a random fashion, but in a careful pattern of circles and parallel lines that covered the torso and limbs. Greaves knew that the instrument used for this obscenity had been a heated poker and that the mutilation had taken place while the girl was alive. To complete the horror, she had been decapitated and the head placed between her open legs, hands resting on the crown of long silken hair. The sightless eyes were still open and seemed to stare at Greaves, as if appealing for him to perform an act of charity that would put an end to her agony and humiliation.

Monday, October 26 5.35 p.m.

Despite his encounter with Doreen Clay, Abbot's mood had sunk to one of near depression as he crawled through the storm-bound traffic that clogged Gray's Inn Road. Recently he had begun to have an increasing presentiment that ill-fortune was about to befall him. Although he still managed to hold on to his job with the *Gazette*, he sensed that things had begun to slip. At the age of forty-seven he was not exceptionally old for a general news reporter, but he had noticed that the younger members of staff were now getting his share of the bigger stories. He had no illusions about himself, knowing that most newspapers carried people who were prepared to handle the grubbier aspects of the business, and he had long ago traded self-respect for job security. But even that niche was starting to feel threatened. The job with Doreen Clay was an indication of his present standing in the office. The features department had needed some back-up material for a series they were preparing on extra-sensory perception and the news editor had loaned him, as one might an old lawnmower. Now he was being called in, no doubt to deal with some dank, irksome corner of the garden. Some job that was beneath the brighter stars on the paper.

Abbot had first begun to feel sorry for himself some years before, when he had accepted the fact that he was not the hero of his own life story. In his heart, he knew that position would always belong to Jack Keane. From his first days on a local paper, Abbot had cast himself in the role of someone who would do the dirtier jobs. But Jack Keane had always been the stuff of *Boy's Own Paper*: fearless, handsome, acclaimed for defending the rights of ordinary people against the big battalions of the rich and powerful. The bastard could write, as well. Even when Jack had been killed in the Middle East, Abbot had felt envious. Especially by the memorial service held at Saint Bride's, and the wake that followed in El Vino's. For Jack Keane, even death had been a party. Cat Abbot knew that in his own case, even if invitations were passed out, no one would come.

Frustration boiled within him as the traffic slowly edged nearer the entrance of the *Gazette* building. 'One big break,' he said aloud, and he banged the steering wheel with both hands. 'That's all I need – just one big break.' As if in partial answer to his prayer, a sudden gap opened in the traffic and he roared forward and turned into the vanway of the scruffy grey stone building.

George Conway, the news editor of the *Gazette*, watched Cat Abbot approach and wearily prepared himself for the wrangle he knew was inevitable. Despite his heavy frame and broken-nosed profile, Conway was not an unfeeling man, and on this occasion he knew he was handing out a lousy job, even for Cat Abbot. It probably made him even sharper than usual, when the reporter stood before him: 'No arguments, Cat. This is an editor's special, so don't give me any grief,' he began.

Abbot's heart sank. Now he knew just what a stinker it was going to be, but he made an effort for form's sake. 'I'm due off at six, George,' he said as pathetically as possible. 'I'm going to a golden anniversary dinner, it's been booked for weeks. My Uncle Ted and Aunt Dolly, it'll break their hearts if I'm not there.'

'Send them a kissogram on the firm,' Conway replied. 'All leave has been cancelled.'

Cat sighed, the fight almost gone from him. 'What is it?' he asked.

Conway looked down at the piece of paper before him. 'There's a lad called Tony Glendowning, from the charity HAND coming here at seven o'clock to pick you up. You're to go to King's Cross station with him and observe how he saves runaway kids from the clutches of the low life who hang about there, preying on the innocent. But don't mention Glendowning's name under any circumstances. I want you to file by midnight, so we get it in plenty of time for the last edition.'

Cat looked at him in disbelief. 'You've got to be kidding,' he said. 'That bloody story has been done to death. Christ, we had a whole series on it in the paper two weeks ago. The readers will think we're fucking balmy.'

'Listen to me,' Conway said in a low voice. 'The chairman wants this story. You know he never reads the paper, so how was he to know we did it all weeks ago.'

Abbot stood his ground. 'Why didn't the fucking editor tell him, that's supposed to be his job, isn't it, stopping the paper from looking as if it's run by cretins?'

Conway continued in the same soft voice: 'Because he likes being the editor, and if he points out in front of important guests that the chairman has an IQ that's barely in double figures, somebody else may get the job nearest his heart.'

Conway stood up and placed a meaty hand on Abbot's shoulder. 'Now come along, bite on the bullet. I'll buy you a drink in the Red Lion until this lad shows up.'

Abbot realised that Conway was making an effort to show sympathy. The two men had never really liked each other, but this was a gesture of goodwill and Cat thought it might help to shore up some of his falling stock with other members of staff. 'OK,' he said with a sigh. 'I'd better go and sign off with Jimmy Bedford first.'

Abbot walked to the far end of the newsroom, where the features department was located, and stood before a desk in the corner. Bedford was peering myopically at a computer terminal.

'You're supposed to rest your eyes every couple of hours when you're using them things,' Abbot said.

'How the fuck would you know,' Bedford replied without looking up from the screen. 'You've never written anything that's taken two hours.' He looked up. 'Where's the copy?'

Abbot gestured towards the news desk: 'I've got a special for the editor. Straight up,' he added, when he saw Bedford's look of disbelief.

Bedford glanced at Conway, who nodded affirmation. 'So when will I get my stuff?'

'I'm seeing her again tomorrow night.'

Bedford returned his attention to the screen. 'All right, but don't let me down.'

Cat was about to leave when he remembered the rain outside. There was an old mackintosh hanging on a coat rack next to Bedford's desk. 'Can I borrow this?' he asked.

'Take what you like,' Bedford replied dismissively.

When they entered the bar across the road from the *Gazette*, they found Fanny Hunter holding court. It was unusual to see Fanny in a pub; the star columnist of the *Gazette* rarely socialised within the precincts of the office except at Christmas time.

'Have some champagne,' she called out, and Abbot realised he would not have been included had he not been in the company of Conway. It had not always been so, Cat remembered. There had been a time in the distant past when he and Fanny had been more than friends.

'What's the occasion?' Conway asked, accepting a glass.

Fanny reached out and hugged a slender girl with a bubbling mass of bright red hair to one of her formidable breasts. It was like seeing a forest elf being captured by the Queen of the Amazons. 'Our little Pauline is going to get married,' she announced in a voice raucous enough to be the envy of sergeant-majors. Fanny Hunter was the daughter of a Smithfield meat porter, and she liked the world to know it.

Pauline Kaznovitch disentangled herself from Fanny's jangling jewellery and raised her own glass in reply to George Conway's toast of congratulations.

'I thought you Women Libbers didn't believe in holy wedlock,' Cat said when his own glass was filled.

'He's from Poland,' Pauline replied icily. 'A lifetime of communism has made him a convinced Catholic.'

'I thought you were a communist.'

Pauline turned away from him, saying, 'No, I'm a socialist.

21

That's something completely different.'

'Well it's a good job he's a Catholic, because he won't be wearing any Polish French letters. They're so full of holes a tribe of pygmies drowned in the Congo when they tried to use them as waterwings.'

Pauline had turned her back on him now, but Cat persisted. 'Here,' he said to the onlookers. 'Do you know how to tell the bride at a Polish wedding? … she's the one with braided armpits.'

Although he was ashamed a moment later, the remark made George Conway laugh.

Fanny nudged him and said in a stage whisper, 'Talking about braids, did you hear about Brian Meadows and his afternoon guest?'

Conway shook his head. 'I knew he was tied up, but I don't know who with.'

'Tied up, eh. Maybe that's what they were doing. I hear she likes it a bit on the rough side.'

'Who?' George asked.

'Mrs Charles Miller,' Fanny said with another nudge. 'Otherwise known as the Right Honourable Geraldine Miller, junior minister of the bedchamber.'

'She's a goer, is she?' Cat interjected.

Fanny nodded. 'Apparently there hasn't been a star fucker like her since Nell Gwynn.'

'Lucky old Brian,' George said.

The time passed quickly in the festive atmosphere, and Cat enjoyed himself, until George Conway tapped him on the shoulder and pointed to a young man with a ravaged face who stood at the doorway looking around the bar.

'I think your date's arrived,' he said, not unkindly.

CHAPTER
TWO

Monday, October 26 5.40 p.m.

Colin Greaves stood on the landing outside the flat and watched the falling rain caught like flashes of silver by the lights shining from the tower blocks around him. Perhaps, he thought, it was time for another flood, like Noah's, that would wash the world clean. Odd, unrelated noises came from the mass of humanity packed densely about him: the blare of televisions; music, from various sources, mingled in discord. A couple argued nearby, their rising voices ending with the crash of breaking glass; a motor car roared into life, wheels squealing on wet asphalt; a dog barked and another answered.

There was the sound of footsteps behind him, and Paddy Gibbon, the pathologist, a thickset man in early middle age, came and stood beside him. As always, he was smoking. 'They're bad for your health, Paddy,' Greaves said softly. Gibbon didn't smile; he was used to the remark.

'Danny Doyle's work?' Greaves asked.

Gibbon nodded. 'It looks like it. She was tortured and killed elsewhere and the body brought here. This was where she was decapitated.' He spoke dispassionately; they both wore the mask of duty. 'Quite a professional job. The surgery, I mean.'

'Doyle used to be a butcher,' Greaves said.

'Used to be?' Gibbon replied.

Greaves turned to him. 'I mean, that was his job when I first knew him.'

'He wouldn't have come here, Colin,' Gibbon said. 'Others do that work for him, from what they tell me.'

'I know,' Greaves answered and he watched the spark of light from the cigarette Gibbon threw curve away from the balcony into the night.

'You'll get my report later,' Gibbon said as he walked away.

'Goodnight, Paddy,' Greaves called after him. The doctor raised a hand in farewell.

'I'll see some of the people who've given statements now,' Greaves said to Holland who now came and stood beside him. The sergeant pointed along the landing. 'We're using one of the empty flats.'

Greaves followed him and a few moments later he stood in an empty room lit by a single bare light bulb. There was no furniture, and the room smelt like an animal's lair. The first person shown in by Holland was a thin old woman with straggly grey hair who blinked in the light. She wore bedroom slippers and a pink nylon housecoat she clutched about her.

'Mrs Ryan, sir,' Holland announced. 'She lives next door to the flat where the girl was found.'

'Thank you for helping, Mrs Ryan,' Greaves began. 'Tell me, did you hear any odd noises today, or see any people who came into the flat next door to you?'

The woman shook her head; it was quite clear that she was terrified.

'Are you sure, Mrs Ryan?' he continued as gently as he could. 'The walls are very thin.'

She mumbled something.

'What did you say?' Greaves asked. 'Will you repeat that?'

'I had the telly on all day,' she said in a trembling voice.

Greaves knew it was hopeless. He gave a slight indication with his head and Holland took Mrs Ryan gently by the shoulders. 'Come on, love,' he said. 'Why don't you go and make yourself a cup of tea.'

The black youth who entered next stood before him with thumbs in the pockets of his fawn-coloured trousers. His soft leather jacket was zipped to the throat.

'Delmer Bladon, sir,' Holland said. 'He was on the landing when the first officers arrived.'

Greaves could tell that Delmer was nervous but determined not to betray his feelings.

'What time did you arrive at the flat, Delmer?' Greaves began mildly.

The youth sucked his teeth and shrugged without answering. Greaves allowed a little menace to enter his voice. 'You were found at the scene of a crime, Delmer. We haven't got any other suspects.'

The youth held out his hands. 'Look at me, man, would I cut off any heads in these clothes?'

'So you saw the body?'

Delmer looked up at the ceiling. 'Everyone saw the body, man, this place been a peep-show all day.'

'But you didn't come until this evening?'

'I was at work.' He noticed Greaves's surprise. 'That's right, man, work.'

'Where?'

'Marcel, Robbins and Mead, they're an advertising agency in Marylebone High Street.'

'We'll check.'

Delmer's shoulders slumped slightly. 'Look, I only just got the job. The police start asking questions, I'm out of there.'

Greaves nodded. 'Don't worry. We'll be discreet. You can go.'

Delmer hesitated and looked at Greaves. He said nothing but the appeal was in his eyes.

'Good luck with the advertising profession,' Greaves said. The boy left and Greaves could hear a whining female voice raised in protest: 'I keep telling you, I don't fucking know nothing, this is a bleeding waste of time.'

The slim young woman now shown into the room was dressed in grubby jeans and a T-shirt stencilled with the face of Mick Jagger. Her pretty face, surmounted by a riot of pink spiky hair, was spoilt by a sulking pout. The hand that held a cigarette was stained with nicotine and the nails were bitten down to the quick. When the door had closed behind her she straightened her slouch and stood before Greaves, who looked at her carefully before speaking. 'How are you, Constable Woods?' he asked eventually.

'Not bad, sir, considering.'

Greaves smiled sadly. 'I know, it's a rotten place to work. How is Alistair?' he asked. WPC Janice Woods and her husband, a detective constable, had been living undercover on the estate for the past seven weeks.

'He's getting to know some nasty people, sir. But nobody really trusts us yet.'

Greaves raked a hand through his hair. 'What can you tell me about this business?'

Janice Woods spoke with a softer accent now. 'We live in the next block, we got a buzz about three o'clock that something had happened over here. We hung about in the crowd, listening. The line we got was that a small white van, with three men wearing balaclavas over their faces, arrived just after three. They carried a rolled-up carpet. They jemmied open the flat and dumped the body. Afterwards the carpet was doused with petrol and set on fire. Forensic have got the remains. Alistair took a walk off the estate and called the local nick. I hung about here so that I'd get pulled in.'

'Nothing else on the men who carried the body?'

She shook her head.

'Did the victim live on the estate?'

'Nobody claims to have known her. But the message was clear to everybody. Don't try anything with the Doyle family. Oh, Alistair heard a rumour in the local pub. He got it from his pusher. The word is, there's another gang trying to cut in on Doyle's territory. They're supposed to be from Northern Ireland too.'

Greaves thought for a moment. 'Any names?'

She nodded. 'The pusher told Alistair not to buy anything from McNally.'

Greaves did not want the girl to see that the name had registered with him. 'Does Danny still come to see his sister?' he asked, changing the subject.

'Yes, every Wednesday night and Sunday. The whole family meet in the Three Castles.' This was the green-tiled pub that stood near the entrance to the estate.

Greaves looked up at the naked light above them. 'Usually these monsters venerate their mothers. In the case of the Doyles, they have to make do with Lily,' he said softly, more to himself than WPC Woods. Then he glanced at her. 'Have you noticed how often a matriarchy produces vipers in the male line?'

Woods shrugged. 'Lily must be the only human being who actually likes this garbage tip,' she replied. 'She's like the queen beetle in a dung heap.'

'Have you actually been inside her flat?' Greaves asked.

'Oh, yes. We had to get permission from Lily before we were allowed to squat on the estate. She lives on the ground floor of

27

Twyford House. Two flats have been knocked through, although I doubt if the Doyles bothered with planning permission. The inside is incredible, all the fixtures and fittings come from Harrods. The locals say it's the only thing that Danny Doyle ever paid for. No blacks are allowed to live in her block and it's the only tower on the estate where people don't bother to lock their doors. All the residents have to be approved.'

'I thought Danny got on with blacks, uses them in his organisation?'

'That's the strange thing,' Janice Woods said. 'Danny says he's signed a peace treaty, like some bloody private country. Separate but equal. Christ, they're giving up apartheid in South Africa but it's alive and well on the Brent River estate. And the black gang leaders go along with it. They say it's good business. The story is: last year a black kid, a stranger from south of the river, walked into one of the flats and helped himself to a video recorder. The Doyles tracked him down and brought him back here. They made two black pimps throw him off the roof. Nobody ever called us.'

'What's supposed to have happened to the body?'

Woods looked around the room for somewhere to deposit her cigarette end, shrugged at the squalid surroundings and dropped it on the floor.

'They say that the bodies Doyle doesn't want found go to the abattoir he owns in Kilburn. They get mixed in with the offal that goes for dog food.'

'Does Doyle still operate in the same way on the estate?' Greaves asked.

Janice Woods lit another cigarette before she answered. 'Yes, he uses local labour to push drugs, here and all over north London. But he gets his muscle boys and pimps from elsewhere. There are no major drug dumps here, at least as far as we can find out. Everything is in cells, nobody knows where the chain leads to.'

Greaves nodded. 'He learned that in Belfast. Before he emigrated. What drugs are you two supposed to be using?' Woods took a plastic bag from her pocket and handed it to Greaves. 'I'm on pot and Alistair heroin. He flushes it down the toilet, but he hates making the needle marks on his arms.'

Greaves glanced at his watch. 'You'd better go, I've already kept you longer than the others.' He paused and then said, 'You're doing good work here. I hope it doesn't take much longer.'

'Thank you, sir,' she replied, then she let her shoulder drop into her previous slouch.

Greaves waited for a time before he left the flat. The rain-washed air smelt clean after the stench of the landing.

'Where to?' Holland asked when they got into the car.

'To the Yard first, but don't dismiss the car. After that I want to go to the Circle of Shamrock Club,' Greaves replied. 'It's time to see Danny again.'

As the car moved forward, a shower of stones smacked down on the roof. The driver slowed down and Holland made a move to open his door, but Greaves held out a restraining hand: 'Don't bother, Sergeant,' he said softly. 'You might as well go chasing after moonbeams out there.'

Monday, October 26 7.04 p.m.

Cat Abbot had buttoned the old raincoat to the throat against the driving rain, but the young man who walked beside him seemed to ignore the weather. Cat glanced at him from time to time. His face seemed oddly familiar.

'What did you say your name was?' Abbot asked eventually.

'Tony Glendowning,' he replied in a cultivated voice. This time the name clicked.

'Lord Glendowning's son?'

'That's right,' he replied when they stopped at a crossing on the Euston Road. Ahead of them was the sleazy grandeur of King's Cross station. Reflected lights shimmered in the wet roadway and the air was thick with the scent of fried onions.

In the heavy rain the occasional wrecked human being would shuffle past and mumble a request for spare change.

'So this is the community work you were supposed to do instead of going to nick?'

'It was,' the young man replied. 'I do it voluntarily now.'

The traffic swished to a stop and they began to cross to the station. As they walked on, Cat remembered that there had been a lot of publicity when Glendowning, the only son of a prominent member of the government, had been charged with possessing drugs, and further controversy when a jail sentence had been commuted to compulsory community service.

'This chap Blakestone,' Cat continued. 'What's he like, good bloke is he?'

'I think he's a totally bogus, self-seeking shit,' Glendowning replied lightly.

'Isn't he supposed to be some sort of trendy?' Cat asked. 'Every time there's a big pop concert, he's up there on the platform at the end, trying to put his arm around Elton John.'

'That's right,' Glendowning replied. 'But my father remembers him from Oxford and says he was frightfully pukka then, although nobody was quite sure which college he was at.'

'Why do you work for him if he's what you say?'

Tony Glendowning had stopped now and he looked over Cat's shoulder while he answered. 'I think Blakestone is personally appalling, but that's a matter of taste. The organisation actually does a lot of good, and he founded it. No one can take

30

the credit for that away from him. His methods all sound phoney, but they work.' He now looked his companion in the face: 'After all, look what it did for me.'

'What was your problem?' Cat asked.

Glendowning scratched one hollow cheek that had been pitted by acne scars. Despite the disfigurement he was extremely good-looking, with a mop of jet black hair which had been plastered to his skull by the rain. 'Oh, the usual thing,' he said lightly. 'I had too much money and no talent or application. The classic pattern of the wastrel – as my father used to tell me.' He looked around him again. 'I've actually helped some of these poor bloody children. I suppose they realise I'm just like them.'

'Except you're going to inherit an Elizabethan manor house and an income of about a million quid a year,' Cat said quickly.

'But that's the only difference,' Glendowning answered with a smile. He looked at his watch. 'It's a bit early yet. The nasties don't usually come crawling out until later. Let's go and have a drink.'

They found their way to a depressingly sordid bar on one of the platforms. When they entered, Glendowning turned to Cat: 'Scotch all right?'

He nodded his agreement and Glendowning smiled at the barmaid. 'Two large malt whiskies, please. From the second bottle on the left.'

'How's your drink?' Glendowning asked when Cat had taken his first swallow.

'Fine,' he replied. 'Why?'

'My great-grandfather invented the stuff. That's where the money came from.'

Cat raised his eyebrows. 'I thought your lot came from the landed gentry of Norfolk.'

Glendowning shook his head. 'That's my mother's family; all they had left was a crumbling house and a great deal of snob value. Great-grandfather bought his title from Lloyd George and his wife from the Seddens, who, incidentally, I am supposed to take after.'

Abbot shook his head. 'Christ, money can buy you anything.'

'Can't buy me love,' Glendowning replied.

'Don't believe that,' Cat replied morosely, 'it's just words in a Beatles song. They didn't live in a yellow submarine either.'

'Can you remember the Beatles?' Glendowning said wistfully. 'That must have been a great time.'

Cat slightly resented this reminder of his age. 'Only John Lennon is dead, you know. You can go and see Paul McCartney any time you like.'

'No, I mean the Sixties.'

Cat swallowed the last of his drink and said nothing for a moment. The local paper in Walthamstow – where he had spent his youth – had been a long way from the King's Road, but time had shaped the past into a happier place than he had actually experienced. Now – like most of his generation – his memories of the Sixties were bathed in a rosy haze. Recollections of miniskirts and Mini cars; willing dolly birds and endless parties came into his head. But had it been like that? He'd met his wife in 1968 at a Young Conservative dance he was covering for the local paper. There hadn't been any drugs or flower power on that occasion, nor had free love been as readily available as social historians would have the modern world believe.

Judy Lawson was the only daughter of Councillor Lawson, a man of solid reputation, and owner of a thriving travel business, located in the High Road. For Cat, it had been ambition at first sight. He cut a presentable figure in his hired dinner jacket, and he knew how to use a public school accent, so Judy accepted his invitation to dance. To be fair to his wife, it wasn't just her expectations that Cat desired. Although Judy was not a great beauty, she was vivacious enough to seem attractive, and she had flawless skin, the colour of cream.

Three more dances and Cat asked her father if he could escort his daughter home. Cat could see that Mrs Lawson didn't like the look of him, but Daddy, who had been at the bar all evening, smiled a blessing.

They parked in a side street on the way home, and Judy demonstrated that although intercourse was out of the question, anything else he could think of was permitted. Eighteen months later they were married, and two years later they had a daughter.

'Let me tell you what the Sixties were really like,' Cat said. And he began to weave together all the folk lore he could remember. One thing everybody who knew Abbot agreed upon: he could tell a wonderful story. The reason this skill had been developed to such a pitch was that Cat had found it necessary, throughout his life, to talk his way out of the seemingly endless supply of corners into which he painted himself.

Tony Glendowning listened, enthralled, as Cat told of nights when he had caroused with the legendary figures of Rock. Being there; when Lennon and McCartney got the idea for a song, pulling birds with the Stones, wrecking hotels with Mad Moon. It was a pastiche of other people's lives, but the young man seemed to want to believe it. He kept urging Cat to tell him more, but eventually Cat grew bored.

Sensing his lack of interest, Glendowning consulted his watch: 'Most of the normal people will have gone home now. Let's go and take a look.'

They left the bar and as they walked along the platform Cat probed deeper into his companion's background.

'Where did you go to school?'

'Eton.'

'Well that must have been nice for you,' Cat said, 'rowing up and down the Thames with flowers stuck in your hat.'

'We only did that one day a year. I disappointed my father once again by failing to get into Pop.'

'What's Pop?' Cat asked. He knew the answer but was seeking a verdict from Glendowning.

33

'A sort of club where you wear fancy waistcoats and order everybody about.'

'It sounds like being in the government,' Cat said.

'Exactly,' Glendowning replied as they reached the main concourse.

His prediction had been correct. The station was now like some great animal carcass crawling with human maggots.

'The rain's brought them all inside,' Glendowning said. 'The pimps usually do their business on the pavement.'

Abbot looked around him and was actually shocked by the scene with which he was confronted. Although his own paper had written about it, he had not bothered to more than skim the pages and the significance had passed him by. He was not prepared for the squalor he now witnessed.

'Where do you start?' he asked.

Glendowning gestured to him to keep moving while he answered. 'As I told you, Jeremy Blakestone devised the technique, or to be more precise he borrowed it. We use the Triace Theory.'

'What's that?'

'It was the official policy used by the French to treat their wounded during the First World War. Very logical, very Gallic. You divide the casualties into three categories: fatal, bad and light. You concentrate on the lightly wounded with all your resources so you can get them back into the line as quickly as possible. In our case, normal life.'

'So how do you divide this lot?'

Glendowning nodded slightly in the direction of a group of menacing blacks who were marshalling flocks of prostitutes about the entrance and directing them to the areas they were to patrol. The women were of all types and of a wide degree of physical attraction, from the plain and matronly to a few who were very young and startlingly beautiful.

'Pimps and whores are in the fatally wounded category,' he said softly. 'So are the drunks and lunatics. The badly wounded

34

are the kids who've been here for a few weeks. Some are already rent boys, and some of the girls are selling it occasionally, but not really on the game – yet. They get a look about them after a time. It doesn't take long to recognise. The lightly wounded are the kids who are brand-new to the scene. They've got a bewildered look, as if they've gone for a day to Frinton and let go of nurse's hand. Sometimes we can get to the kids who have been around for a while, but it's easier with the fresh arrivals.'

For the next few hours, Abbot stayed with Glendowning while he moved about the station. Some of the young people he talked to already knew him and responded in differing ways. One or two with sullen indifference, but a few times his interest in an individual's plight seemed to spark a glimmer of gratitude. All accepted small sums of money and some took the card printed with the address of the HAND hostel nearby.

'What happens when they get to the hostel?' Abbot asked eventually.

'They get a shower, something to eat and a clean bed for the night. The place is strictly supervised. So they're safe there. Some hostels are no better than this place. That's why they prefer sleeping rough. If they want it, there's counselling. If they respond and we think they're the right type, we send them on to selected hostels in the country.'

Abbot had enough for his piece. 'I'm going to work on my notes and get a cup of coffee,' he told Glendowning. He made his way to a café on the concourse and sat at one of the Formica tables littered with discarded cardboard containers. He laid the damp mackintosh on the seat beside him and was soon absorbed by his work, when a voice made him look up. 'Mr Abbot, it is you, isn't it?'

Cat was surprised to see an attractive, well-dressed young woman, carrying a cup of coffee, smiling down at him. As far as Cat could recollect, she seemed to be a complete stranger.

'You don't remember me, do you?' she said in the same friendly voice.

'I'm sorry … ' Cat said, half rising from his chair.

'I'm Jill Slade. We met on holiday, oh, goodness it must be eight or nine years ago. I made friends with your daughter, Debbie. It was in Majorca.'

Vague memories stirred of a dark-haired little girl who had been in the same hotel. He seemed to recall she had been with an elderly woman.

'You were with your grandmother,' he said.

Jill Slade sat down at the table. 'Actually she was my foster mother. She's dead now.'

'I'm sorry,' Cat said automatically.

The young woman shook her head. 'I'm quite used to being an orphan. Tell me, how is Debbie?'

Cat realised with slight surprise it had been nearly two years since he had seen her. 'She's fine,' he replied. 'I don't see much of her now. My wife and I are divorced. The last I heard Debbie was going to get married.'

'Really, I am too,' the girl said, and she sipped some of her coffee. 'Damn, no sugar.'

'I'll get you some,' Cat offered. He went to the counter where the cashier was exchanging words with a drunk who was bothering her. When he returned to the table, Jill Slade was gone.

'Did you see a girl sitting here?' he asked a weary-looking black boy who was stuffing rubbish from the tables into a plastic sack. The youth shook his head. Cat hesitated, then picked up the old raincoat and walked out on to the concourse. There was no sign of the girl, or Glendowning. He looked about him for a few moments more, then decided to make his way back to the office. It had stopped raining by now, so he carried the old mackintosh slung over his shoulder, the way Jack Keane would have done.

Monday, October 26 8.07 p.m.

Greaves stopped the car halfway down Bow Street, Covent Garden and led Sergeant Holland to a modern office block faced with dark red brick. On the ground floor, huge windows, tinted dark blue, were set in the fabric of the building and a wide row of steps led to an entrance hall. Automatic doors opened as they approached and a wave of warm air and soft, taped music enveloped them as they crossed the threshold.

The lobby of the Circle of Shamrock Club was decorated in tasteful shades of dove grey and dusky pink, and there were little shamrocks woven into the carpet. At a long, bleached wood table a uniformed security guard sat beside a fit-looking young receptionist who wore a track suit that matched the colour scheme. Small television monitors were set around the walls so that there were no blind spots. A row of lifts faced the desk and next to it, wide doors led to the basement.

'Yes, gentlemen, may I help you?' the girl asked with a professional smile.

'We've come to see Mr Doyle,' Holland said, showing her his warrant card.

'Which Mr Doyle do you wish to see?'

'Danny,' Greaves said.

The girl lifted a telephone and a few minutes later another girl, similarly clad in matching track suit, emerged through the swing doors from the basement.

'This way, gentlemen, if you'll follow me,' she said.

The girl led them along wide, bright corridors thronged with young people. Despite the air-conditioning, there was a strong scent everywhere, composed of sweat, resin and rubber. They passed squash courts where desperately cavorting figures thrashed hard little balls against the walls, rooms full of earnest young men exercising oiled bodies with gleaming pieces of machinery, and a vast hall, filled with women in training clothes, who were performing a violent sort of dance to loud rock music. They turned again and now passed steam rooms, Turkish baths, saunas and massage cubicles. The girl finally stopped at a door marked PRIVATE. She knocked and a voice called out, 'Come in.' Smiling again, she gestured for them to enter but did not accompany them past the door.

The room they entered was bigger than Greaves expected, about twenty feet square. The lighting was very low and the furniture modern: chrome and softly padded leather the colour of tobacco. One wall was entirely tinted glass and looked into a brightly lit swimming pool where satisfied club members splashed in the water. But no sound penetrated the room.

Danny Doyle stood barefooted on the thick, cream-coloured carpet, looking into the pool. Thin and swarthy, with lank black hair, he was wearing a soft, white towelling robe and drinking from a long glass that appeared to be filled with blood.

'Superintendent Greaves,' he said in the harsh, nasal accent of Belfast. 'I'm just having a glass of juice after my sauna. Will you join me?' He held out the glass: 'Oranges. I have them specially imported from Seville because I like the colour.' His smile revealed a row of perfectly capped teeth. Greaves could remember when they had been broken and jagged, like the mouth of a shark.

'One of your girls has been found murdered and mutilated on the Brent River estate,' Greaves said flatly. 'I want you to come and identify her.'

'Jesus, what's the world coming to?' Doyle replied. 'But why would you think she's anything to do with me? You know I'm a businessman, Superintendent.'

'Get dressed, Doyle, there's a car waiting downstairs.'

'This is a waste of time,' Doyle persisted. 'I don't know any murdered whores.'

'I didn't say she was a prostitute. Why should you make that assumption, Danny?'

38

As Greaves spoke, the door had clicked open behind them and a figure, almost as tall as Holland, came and stood beside Doyle. Although the double-breasted suit he wore was expensive, his wide, powerful frame made him look like a schoolboy dressed in the clothes of an adult. The pudgy face and mop of curly blond hair did not appear impressive, but the eyes were different ... They stared at Greaves unblinking, the colour of soiled ice.

'Did you have any luck, Fergus?' Doyle asked softly, still looking directly at Greaves.

'Not yet,' the bulky figure replied in the same accent.

'You're acquainted with my brother?' Doyle said in the same easy fashion.

Greaves did not bother to answer. 'Get dressed,' he repeated.

'Should I call Congreve?' Fergus Doyle asked, naming the solicitor who acted for the brothers.

'I don't think that's necessary,' Danny Doyle replied. 'I won't be very long.'

Seated next to him in the back of the car, Greaves could smell Doyle's cologne. The tall, thin figure was now dressed in plain, well-cut, conservative clothes. His hair was styled in the fashion of older generations and oiled flat to his head. The long, narrow face and dark, hooded eyes bore no resemblance to his brother at all. Doyle was quite relaxed, and whistled softly as they approached the morgue.

Paddy Gibbon accompanied them to the room where the body lay waiting for him to complete his post-mortem. Greaves watched Doyle's face when the sheet was pulled back. There was no flicker of expression on his face. He simply shook his head: 'Never seen her before in my life.' Greaves looked at Holland. 'Take him out,' he said. When they had left, Greaves and Gibbon stood in the corridor.

'Anything for me to go on?' he asked.

Gibbon lit a cigarette. 'I haven't opened her up yet, but there are a couple of things. She's wearing a wig, it's woven into her own hair. And I'm pretty sure she's had plastic surgery, a nose job. I've already told Forensic.'

Greaves folded his arms and leaned back against the green-painted wall. 'That's more than we had with any of the others.'

Several bodies had been found on the estate over the years. It had been Doyle's way of reminding everyone of who ruled. Greaves straightened up again and bid Gibbon good-night.

When he reached the street again the rain had stopped. Holland was waiting in the car. When Greaves sat back in the upholstery he could still smell cologne. 'The Yard,' he told the driver, and opened the window to let fresh air blow away the scent of Doyle.

Fergus, who had picked up his brother, sat bolt upright behind the wheel of the Mercedes as they headed back towards Covent Garden.

'So where's that bloody disc?' Danny Doyle said after a time.

'That fucking girl working in the office must have taken it,' Fergus replied. 'We think she lives with a boyfriend.'

'We've got to get that back,' Danny said quickly. 'It's the only fucking thing the Dutch want to buy from us. They've offered five million dollars. Find the boyfriend.'

Danny Doyle chewed thoughtfully at a callous on his left thumb, but the grisly nodule of flesh slid easily beneath his smoothly capped teeth. Sometimes he missed the old jagged edges.

Tuesday, October 27 12.45 a.m.

Brian Meadows could not remember when he had last been in a better mood. Even the delay by the Night Editor in answering his call did not cause its customary irritation.

'Corby,' a voice snapped eventually.

Meadows recognised one of the night editor's assistants.

'Brian Meadows,' he said. Instantly the tone changed. 'Yes chief,' the young man said. He was not yet on first-name terms with the editor.

'Anything happening?'

'Everything quiet. No changes except the Abbot piece. I've put it on a box at the top of page five, where the panda pictures were.'

'What's the copy like?'

'Better than I expected. I would've liked to have given it more space. I didn't know he could write like that.'

'That's always been Abbot's trouble,' Meadows said lightly.

'Do you want the first editions sent to you, chief?'

'No,' he replied, 'I'm moving about a bit more. Good-night.' Meadows replaced the receiver on the table by the bedside and turned once again to face Geraldine Miller.

'Did you mean it, about moving about a bit more?' she asked. He smoothed the rumpled bed about them. It was the first time he had lain between silk sheets. 'Certainly,' he replied. 'Unless you've got a late-night sitting or something.'

Tuesday, October 27 1.10 a.m.

Greaves finally left his office later than he intended. He sat in silence throughout the journey to north London. When he was close to his destination he told the duty driver to drop him at the turning into Sarah's road. The car drew away and he walked beneath horse chestnut trees that still shed rainwater from the recent storm. Across the gardens, lights glowed from a few windows. The red-brick houses with their white stone trim reminded him of Christmas cakes decorated with icing. Christmas soon, he thought, autumn always seems to go so fast. A ginger cat padded towards him and turned suddenly, to dart beneath a garden gate.

The sense of peace and tranquillity in the quiet street seemed absolute, the time he had spent on the Brent River estate now part of a distant past. Sarah's house was in darkness except for the light in the porch. He let himself in with a latchkey and walked as softly as he could to the kitchen. On the table was a small earthenware pot and a note in Sarah's neat hand: 'Put this in microwave for five minutes. Eat and then come to bed.' Beside it was another sheet of paper. The handwriting was less well formed than Sarah's: 'Dear Colin, please settle a bet between me and Martin. Did Britain have a war with China over opium? I remain your obedient servant, Paul Keane.'

Greaves placed the pot in the microwave oven as instructed, then went to the telephone extension that hung on the wall. His call was answered by an Irish voice with a Belfast accent. In the background he could hear an old familiar tune, 'The Black Velvet Band'. Speaking with the same accent as Danny Doyle, he said, 'Is Robbie McNeice in the bar?'

'Who wants him?'

'His cousin Ian.'

There was a delay and then a Scottish voice said, 'Christ, Ian is that you?'

Greaves continued in the same accent. 'Who else? Listen, I'm over for a few days and I met a fella who told me some of the boys we used to play cards with at Doogan's might be in town.'

'You heard right,' the voice answered. 'I'm working on getting another game together right now.'

'Well, don't forget me, Robbie,' Greaves said and he hung up. When he turned Sarah was standing in the doorway. He had not heard her bare feet on the tiled floor.

The timer on the microwave sounded and she took out his food. 'I knew you spoke other languages,' she said. 'But I didn't know you did accents as well.'

Greaves sat down and she placed the food before him. He stirred the casserole with a fork for a moment. It smelt delicious, Sarah was a good cook. He looked up at her: 'If I tell you something, will you promise me it will remain a secret?'

Sarah sat down opposite him and waited in silence.

He ate a mouthful of the food and then began. 'When we first met, you read a file on me, remember?'

Sarah nodded, and he continued: 'It didn't tell you everything. There was a year of my life missing. The file said I came back from secondment with the Hong Kong police and went straight to the Yard.'

Sarah nodded but didn't speak.

'That wasn't strictly accurate. From Hong Kong I went to Rio de Janeiro.'

'Why?'

Greaves stirred his food for a moment, then looked up. 'To establish a new identity. In three months, I became a writer and academic called Peres Hothca. When I left Brazil, I spent six months at the university in Lisbon. Then I went to Belfast.'

'And what did you do there?' Sarah asked, watching his face carefully.

'I went about the business of Peres Hothca, I was supposed to be writing a history book on the persecution of Catholics, the IRA were quite keen on the idea. They encouraged the local population to co-operate with me. It was excellent cover.'

'I don't suppose that many English policemen speak fluent Portuguese,' Sarah said.

Greaves ate another mouthful, then laid down the fork.

'People here think Northern Ireland is an ideological guerrilla war between Catholics and Protestants. It's much more complicated than that – surreal, in some ways. Of course, the IRA and the Protestant para-military groups are dedicated to their different causes, but at the edge they shade into gangsterism. Private organisations that rob banks and run protection rackets for their own benefit. The Catholics and Protestants both have them. It was decided that the worst two were to be eliminated. I was to provide the information on Danny Doyle's Butcher Boys and another undercover officer, the man you heard me speaking to on the telephone, was to infiltrate the Protestant gang called the Book, run by a local warlord called David McNally, who was also a big bookmaker.'

Greaves stopped speaking and Sarah could see that he was preoccupied with memories.

'Were you successful?' she asked. Greaves rubbed the crease between his eyebrows. 'I don't know, I've never really been able to judge the results by any normal yardstick.' He could see that she was puzzled by the statement.

'I cracked Doyle's organisation wide open, but then he was given immunity from prosecution because he turned informer on the regular IRA. They still don't know that. Doyle had to get out of Belfast, so he came to London and set up business on the Brent River estate. That was nearly eight years ago. Since then he's thrived: mostly in prostitution and drugs. But he's also used the money to start a successful chain of health clubs, and he owns an abattoir in Kilburn. Now I hear that McNally has come over as well, and he's set up in opposition to Doyle. He may get sloppy now with pressure on him from McNally. If I can get Doyle for murder in England his immunity won't work.'

Sarah had heard something in Greaves's voice that she had never detected before. 'Why do you hate this man so much?' she asked.

He looked at her. 'He hates me as well.'

'Why?'

Greaves now spoke more slowly. 'The night we broke his gang, he'd taken one of my informants – a girl. I knew where the Butcher Boys were holding her: in a garage. We arrested Danny and Fergus first, then we were to go on to find her. But I was too late. When I got there, I found Doyle's youngest brother, Liam. I shot him dead.'

'Why did you kill him?' Sarah asked; and when he answered she could see his pain like an open wound. 'Liam Doyle had a woman's hat pin in his hand. He'd stabbed the girl to death – through both of her eyes.'

CHAPTER
THREE

Tuesday, October 27 7.41 a.m.

In the first light of the day, Jeremy Blakestone glanced at his wrist-watch when he saw that he'd reached the northern tip of the Nursery in Hyde Park: it was at least fifty yards from the point he'd usually reached by this time on his morning run. Breathing easily in the chill morning air, he increased his pace to compensate, and let his mind return to the pleasurable problem he had wrestled with since he had set off, forty-one minutes ago: the final seating plan for the HAND-OUT ball, which was to take place that evening at the Hilton hotel. The late inclusion of Sir Robert Hall and his wife Lady Amanda, who was the daughter of an earl, had created a minor difficulty, but he had solved it in Rotten Row. Instead of going for a squeeze, he would create an entirely new table that Sir Robert could host. If it included Lord Blakestone and Viscount Warley, he wouldn't feel slighted. And he could fill the other places with a few more titles, he had a spare baronet and a floating dowager duchess. Christ, Sir Robert would be in a state of complete bliss.

At one minute before eight o'clock, he reached the headquarters of HAND, which was located over a Chinese restaurant in Queensway. Three of the rooms also served as his flat, but he had to pass through the main office to get to them. Although it was early, his secretary, Vanessa Drake, was already at her desk and the scent of freshly brewed coffee permeated the scruffy room, which was furnished by Oxfam and littered with heaps of dusty papers. 'Morning,' she bellowed, as if calling a greeting to one of the tenants on her father's estate. She was dressed in a Laura Ashley frock that made her look like a chintz-covered sofa, but, as her mother always said, her heart was in the right place.

'Not quite so loud, darling,' Blakestone said as he lowered himself into the chair opposite her and sipped some of the coffee she had poured.

'Geraldine Miller's already called,' Vanessa said in a more sedate tone. 'She says she can come now, and may she have a spare ticket for somebody called Meadows?'

'Did she, now?' he replied thoughtfully. 'So the country has been cancelled and she's found a meadow in the heart of town.'

'I say,' said Vanessa, impressed, 'that's jolly clever. I must remember to tell Mummy.'

'Don't you utter a word, you wretched child. All you hear in this office is absolutely confidential. By the way, did you remember to take my dinner jacket to the cleaner's?'

'It's in your wardrobe,' she called out as he made for his own rooms.

Brian Meadows would have been surprised had he listened to the conversation that had just taken place, not by the remark about

48

himself, but by the language and pronunciation employed by Blakestone when he talked to his secretary. Blakestone conducted his life according to the company he kept at any given moment. Before the public, he always styled himself in the fashion of a pop programme presenter, and that was how he had chosen to be with Sir Robert Hall, but in private, and with genuine members of the aristocracy, he reverted to the language of his childhood.

Blakestone had not used Received English with Sir Robert the day before, because he was a shrewd judge of character. In the first moments with his host he had realised that the little man was cunning, single-minded and, outside his own narrow field of expertise, extremely stupid. Had he spoken in the language he used with Vanessa, Sir Robert would have become suspicious; he would have thought Blakestone was pandering to him, and Jeremy Blakestone knew that those who sought to please Sir Robert were instantly categorised as lesser breeds. In future he would drop the accent slowly and the fellow would never notice.

Fifteen minutes later he had showered and was sitting at the desk opposite Vanessa. She handed him a large wad of Polaroid snapshots pinned to fact sheets, and he began to sort through the weekend's batch of youngsters that had been culled from the mass of human detritus littering the streets of London.

Tuesday, October 27 11.30 a.m.

Detective-Sergeant Holland slept late that morning. He had neglected to set his alarm clock the night before and his mother had allowed him to slumber on, convinced that he worked too hard. In her view, if he was still sleeping, he needed the rest.

Mrs Holland never missed an opportunity to cosset her son,

to compensate for the punishing hours demanded by the job. Although some of his friends thought it odd that Nick Holland, at the age of twenty-seven, should still wish to live with his parents at their semi-detached house in Putney, few would care to accuse him of being tied to his mother's apron strings. His impressive physique ruled out such careless remarks, and his sheer size, in itself, was a sort of statement of warning.

The reasons why Holland stayed in Putney were simple. He got on well with his parents, who were both retired grammar school teachers, and they never interfered with his private life. There was little opportunity for home entertainment in his line of work, and the two girls he saw on a casual basis both had pleasant flats of their own. Sometimes he daydreamed about comfortable, clubbish quarters, closer to Victoria, but in his experience, most of his unmarried friends lived in the sort of squalor he had been grateful to give up when he'd left Bristol University with a second-class honours degree.

Besides, he'd have missed his dog, Jacko, a springer spaniel, which had been given to him on his twelfth birthday by his two elder married sisters. Although the dog was getting on in years now, Holland still enjoyed taking him for walks. He'd missed their usual stroll through Putney Common that morning, Jacko had gazed reproachfully at him when he had hurried from the house.

Greaves had been fretful when he'd reached the office. God knows what time he'd arrived. Holland knew his superior was an insomniac which made his times of arrival erratic, but Holland was invariably there by 9.30, however late he had worked the night before. Others, who did not know Greaves, often asked Holland how he could stand working for someone who seemed so remote. They usually got some noncommittal answer, so few of his colleagues (including Greaves) ever suspected that Holland actually hero-worshipped his boss.

He'd first encountered the Superintendent when he'd come

to lecture Holland's intake of recruits at police college. Greaves's contribution that day had been to recount the breaking of an assassination gang in Hong Kong. He told the story with such vivid precision it had become suddenly clear to Holland, halfway through the lecture, that although he had scrupulously described every stage of the operation in the third person, all of the crucial detective work had actually been performed by Greaves alone, even though another senior officer had been promoted because of the successful outcome of the operation.

Holland checked later and found that his suspicions had been correct. From then on he had watched Greaves's career carefully, and when, in the fullness of time, Greaves had been given a special brief that required the services of a detective-sergeant, Holland had jumped at the chance to volunteer for the post. In the end he had been the only applicant, because policemen were often deeply conservative and suspicious of anything new, imagining the prefix 'special' might describe a ladder of promotion that led to nowhere.

But Holland had never regretted his decision for a moment, and in the two years they had been together, Holland had come to realise that Greaves was the exceptional human being he had suspected. Others spoke of him as being arrogant, because of his mordant wit and careful manners, but Holland knew that Colin Greaves was the only human being he'd ever met who seemed entirely without personal vanity: it was yet another quality he admired and sought to emulate.

Now he directed the driver to stop at a vacant parking meter in Harley Street fifty yards from the number he wanted. After the storm of the evening before the weather had changed, it was a bright morning with a slight chill to the air. Holland walked briskly to the address written on the large photographic envelope he carried and pressed the bell on the entry system. Immediately a squawking, disembodied voice said: 'Can I help you?'

The sergeant leaned closer to the louvred box set in the wall beside the door frame. 'My name is Holland. Mr Berkley is expecting me.'

There was a buzzing sound followed by a click and he pushed open the large black painted door. Holland had never visited any of the consulting rooms in Harley Street before and he was expecting something rather grander than the dingy corridor that he entered. Gloomy steel engravings lined the walls of the narrow entrance hall and a worn carpet lay on the marble floor. But there was nothing plain about the young woman who stood smiling in a doorway. 'Hello,' she called out, and when he stood before her Holland saw that, despite the low heels she wore, the top of her head reached his eye level and Holland was eight inches taller than the minimum requirement for entry into the Metropolitan Police.

Instinctively, he liked everything about her: the wide blue eyes, high cheekbones, snub nose and generous mouth. She held herself well, back straight like a model, but she had the body of an athlete. Here was a woman he could hug without fearing the consequence of snapped ribs.

'You're Nick Holland, aren't you?' she said, and smiled again when she saw his surprise. 'I'm Lucy Patterson, I used to watch you play rugby for the Met four seasons ago. My brother, Clive, was in the same team.'

'He never mentioned you,' Holland said.

'Oh, I was only seventeen then and thin as a rake. Clive always said I had shoulders like a wire coat hanger.'

The sergeant looked at her splendid figure and thought how quickly the world could change.

'Clive left the Met, didn't he?'

'Yes, he transferred to a village in Hertfordshire when he got married. This way,' she indicated. 'Mr Berkley is in here.'

A voice called, 'Come,' at her knock and Holland found himself in a large, sparsely furnished room. Net curtains hung at the tall sash windows, diffusing the bright sunlight and causing the surroundings to seem even bleaker. There was an examination table in one corner, next to a changing area that was screened off, and under the window an ugly old desk that appeared to be carved from coal. The carpet on the block-wood floor was as threadbare as the rug in the hall. Porridge-coloured walls were hung with a few amateurish watercolours in cheap wooden frames and an ancient, hissing gas fire made the room uncomfortably warm. A tired-looking young man in a dark three-piece suit was standing at the desk. He held out his hand for the envelope as Holland crossed the room.

'I understand you spoke with Superintendent Greaves about the purpose of my visit, sir,' Holland said as he handed it to him. Berkley nodded and pulled out the large coloured portrait of the murdered woman.

'This photograph was taken after the girl was dead,' Adrian Berkley said after a cursory glance.

'That's right, sir.'

The young man began to massage the back of his neck as he studied the photograph. Holland noticed that he had a large mole on his left cheek, which had been turned from him when he entered the room. 'Strange how you can tell the spark of life has gone, even in a photograph,' Berkley said while he continued to study the picture. 'I suppose that's why people believe in the soul.'

He handed the photograph back to Holland. 'Superintendent Greaves is quite right in his assumption. I do have a pretty good idea of how she would have looked before her nose was altered. So what's the next stage?'

Holland placed the picture back in the envelope. 'If you can come with me, I'd like to take you to a studio in Marylebone where they've got special equipment. Under your direction an artist will be able to alter the picture and recreate an image of how the girl used to look.'

'Retouch it, you mean?'

53

'Something like that.'

Berkley looked at his watch. 'How long will this take? I'm due to start operating in Chiswick in a couple of hours.'

'You should make your appointment with time to spare, sir,' Holland reassured him.

It took only a few minutes to reach the mews off Baker Street where the studio of Direct Artists was located. One of the partners, who introduced himself as Les Travis, was waiting for them in a tiny reception area. He was a cheerful, middle-aged man in a baggy suit and a tie that was all the colours of a rainbow.

'Of course we're delighted to co-operate with the police,' he said to Holland as he showed them into an air-conditioned basement. The atmosphere was hushed and heavy with the ozone created by computers. In the dim light they were introduced to a young man called Spike, who wore jeans, an open-necked denim shirt and a heavy beard. He sat at a console of controls before a large, expensive-looking piece of equipment with a built-in display terminal. Spike told them it was called a magic paintbox. It reminded Holland of a cinema organ and the young man looked to him as if he would be more at home behind a horse-drawn plough than a sophisticated piece of twentieth-century technology.

But when he began to operate the machine, it was clear that Spike was a master of his craft. Quickly, he scanned the photograph into the equipment and the face of the girl flooded on to the screen. Then, with Berkley seated beside him, he used an instrument called a light pen to alter the image, recreating the features as Berkley described how he thought the girl had once looked.

Holland now understood why the word 'magic' was included in the title of the machine. The effect was startling. There was no semblance of retouching; the features of the altered face looked perfectly natural. While Spike worked, he explained the capabilities of the magic paintbox to Berkley, who seemed equally fascinated.

'It's quite wonderful,' he said after a time. 'I had no idea this sort of thing existed. With this equipment I would be able to show people exactly how they would look after surgery.' He turned to Les Travis, who still hovered near them. 'I'd like to call you tomorrow to discuss business, if that's convenient?'

'Certainly,' the partner replied with satisfaction. 'I'll be here all day.' He produced a card and Berkley slipped it into his waistcoat pocket with a smile of thanks.

Holland had been right in his promise to Berkley. It did not take long; the work was soon completed, and well within the hour the surgeon was on his way to Chiswick, while Holland headed for Scotland Yard with a photographic transparency of the recreated face. During the journey, he thought about Lucy Patterson, and tried to imagine how he would improve her features. It didn't take him long to decide he would leave them exactly as they were.

Tuesday, October 27 3.55 p.m.

Although it was late in the afternoon, Sarah Keane was going to the office. She had worked at home for most of the day, on a story about a woman who had made a fortune out of herbal cosmetics. Now she was now going in to the *Gazette* to file her copy. She could have telephoned it from home; but her daughter, Emily, wanted to go into town to buy some textbooks for her A-level curriculum, so she decided to take her.

'Don't you ever get tired of the same streets?' Emily asked her mother as they drove along Chalk Farm Road. Sarah did not answer until she had passed a milk float that was slowing the traffic. She was always a careful driver, but today she was paying extra attention because she was using Colin Greaves's beloved Riley, as her own car was being serviced.

'How do you mean?' Sarah asked, and just then a bright-red hatchback swung out to overtake her. Two young men were in the car and as they passed, the one in the passenger seat called out an explicit sexual invitation to them both.

'He probably thinks you're my sister,' Emily said as they watched the car roar ahead of them. 'All my friends say you look too young to be my mother.'

Sarah couldn't help feeling pleased, but she could not accept that there was any sisterly resemblance between them. Emily was slender with long, floating brown hair and her skin was pale and translucent. Sarah was also slim, but her figure was more pronounced, and her breasts were fuller than Emily's would ever be. Sarah's hair was thick and tended to grow like a bramble bush if it wasn't cut short, and where Emily's features were as delicate as bone china, Sarah's were shaped in chiselled planes, almost sharp-edged in their definition. Even so, the offer from the young man was in some ways flattering. She sometimes found it hard to realise that she would be thirty-nine at her next birthday.

'What did you mean by being tired of the same streets?' Sarah asked again.

Emily gestured about her: 'North London – all these buildings you pass every day. I would've thought it gets you down sometimes.'

'Where would you like to live?'

Emily looked up into the clear sky. Although it was quite cold, she had insisted they drive with the hood down.

'Oh, somewhere along the river,' she said dreamily. 'A Thames backwater with willow trees at the end of the lawn.'

Sarah remembered that the parents of Emily's boyfriend, Ric Daggert, had a motor cruiser and the previous Sunday they had taken them on the river between Richmond and Maidenhead.

'So you'd like us to move?'

Emily glanced quickly at her mother's profile. 'I wouldn't want you to move completely, I was thinking of a weekend cottage. After all, you and Colin could afford another place after you're married.'

Sarah was suddenly intrigued by the simplicity of her daughter's suggestion. It still came as a slight surprise to her that Greaves had money. Wealth was not usually associated with policemen, and he did not flaunt his riches. I wonder if he'd settle for a compromise? she suddenly thought.

'The twins think Colin's family made their money in Hong Kong from the opium trade,' Emily said, starting a new line of conversation.

'I don't think so,' Sarah replied. 'They were in banks and shipping but Colin's father was a civil servant.'

'The twins know that. They say the bank bought the opium in India and the ships transported it to Hong Kong. They think Colin's father probably went into the civil service to make it easier for the family to get import licences.'

'The boys have been watching those videos of *The Godfather* again,' said Sarah, and she glanced about her to check the flow of traffic. 'Now where is it you want me to drop you?'

'As near to Dillons book shop as possible.'

Sarah signalled and switched to the inside lane. 'I might as well go down Gower Street and take you all the way,' she replied. The traffic wasn't as bad as she expected.

When she finally arrived at the newsroom of the *Gazette*, Sarah checked in the tape room to see if there was any post. Then she walked slowly to her desk while she opened two promising-looking letters, but they turned out to be handouts and she dropped them into a wastepaper basket. When she'd first returned to the paper, after such a long absence, this walk through the long, open-plan newsroom had terrified her. Everything had changed so much from the bustle of her early days.

Strangely enough, it had been the quiet that she had found so daunting. Carpet on the floors and the introduction of computer terminals had altered the atmosphere of newspapers entirely. Now there were rumours that the offices were to be transferred to the new headquarters of LOC PLC, somewhere in Docklands. Sarah did not relish the prospect, she liked the shabby character of the Gray's Inn Road, as did most of the staff of the paper, and the journey would be more complicated. Still, she wouldn't be a new girl any more, or, to be strictly accurate, a new old girl.

As she progressed along the newsroom, she saw Fanny Hunter approaching. 'Who do I have to fuck for an early edition of the *Evening Standard*?' Fanny called out, like a bookie touting for business on a racecourse.

A messenger who was distributing an armful of the papers to various executives hurried to offer her a copy. 'Thanks, Ted, ' she said with a wink to the messenger, and paused to lean against a desk while she scanned the front page.

'I see your boyfriend's up to his armpits in blood and guts again,' Fanny said as Sarah passed. 'It says here the girl's on the game; anyone he knows?'

'Surely you'll be able to help him with his inquiries, Fanny,' Sarah replied without breaking step. 'It says on your column that you're "always at the heart of the matter".'

When Sarah reached the reporters' section she found Cat Abbot basking in an unusual degree of attention. It was one of the small burdens in her life that her own desk was located in such close proximity to Abbot. While she turned on her computer terminal to check for any messages, she could hear his loud conversation with Gates and Sinclair, two of the other reporters.

'Apparently Meadows wanted to put it on page one, but those berks on the back bench crammed it on to five,' Cat said airily. 'Still, the chairman was pleased. Alan Stiles gave me the word that they talked of nothing else in the morning conference. So I'll probably be doing a few other specials for him in the future.'

'You jammy sod,' Sinclair said enviously. 'I worked on the last series we did about King's Cross for three fucking weeks, and you get a bloody herogram from Meadows for one night's work.'

'Feast your eyes,' Cat said with satisfaction. And he gestured to the screen of his terminal, where two sentences glowed from the green-tinted screen: CAT ABBOT'S STORY ON RUNAWAY CHILDREN IN THE LONDON EDITION WAS AN EXCELLENT PIECE OF INVESTIGATIVE JOURNALISM. HE IS TO BE CONGRATULATED. BRIAN MEADOWS.

'What do you think of that, Goody Two-Shoes? Congratulations from the editor and in black and white,' Cat said, and he leaned forward to prod Sarah with a ballpoint pen.

Sarah did not turn round. 'Actually it's green on green,' she replied. 'But accuracy was never really your strong point, was it Cat?'

'The only thing green around here is you,' he shot back. 'Green with bloody envy. Christ,' he said, turning to Sinclair and Gates. 'Women can't stand anyone else being successful. It's bred in their hormones.'

'Genes,' Pauline Kaznovitch corrected him. She had come to stand by the desk and overheard his last remark. 'Breeding is determined by genetic inheritance, not hormones.'

'The bloody sisterhood of envy,' Cat exclaimed. 'Here's another one with her claws out. I think I'll go and get a drink.'

'Better leave it until you've visited Ralph Stratton,' Pauline said. 'I've just come from his office. He asked me to tell you he wants to see you right away.'

A sudden chill descended on Abbot. Ralph Stratton was the managing editor, a bleak man who dealt with the administration of the newspaper. Once, long ago, he had been a journalist, before the corrosive acid of business efficiency had entered his bloodstream.

'What the fuck does he want?' Cat asked plaintively.

Pauline smiled. 'You're the one who's writing about extra-sensory perception, you tell me.'

'I suppose I'd better give the bastard a few minutes,' Cat said as he pulled on his jacket. He turned to Gates and Sinclair. 'I'll see you in the Red Lion.'

The managing editor was located on the floor above the news-room, in a corridor of boxed glass offices. Abbot knocked and entered a room which was as characterless as a paper bag. Except for a row of cactus plants that grew in little pots on the window-sill, there was very little sign of life.

Stratton, a thin, balding man, as grey as the metal desk he sat behind, was studying a pile of papers. When he looked up, pale expressionless eyes fixed on Abbot from behind gleaming wire-rimmed spectacles.

'Sit down,' he instructed in a dusty voice. 'I shall be with you in a moment.'

Cat sat in an upright chair before the desk and watched as Stratton made tiny marks with a red fibre-tipped pen on a sheet of expenses. After a time, he placed the pen before him with careful deliberation, sat back in his chair and raised both bony hands as if he were going to pray. Instead he touched lips that were pursed in disapproval.

'Have you ever heard of a spectroscope, Abbot?' he asked finally.

Cat's mind was a blank, but he felt a pounding pressure in his head, which was normally induced by running quickly up a long flight of stairs. 'Can't say as I have,' he replied in a croaking voice. Suddenly his throat was very dry.

Stratton reached into a drawer and produced a wad of bills, which he threw on to the desk. 'These were attached to the last expenses you submitted.'

Stratton extracted one from the paper clip that held them

together and held it up for a moment. 'This one is from the Sitar Indian Restaurant in Acton High Road. I suppose you remember it?'

Abbot shifted uncomfortably. 'You know how it is, Ralph. That story was a long time ago.'

Stratton leaned forward and looked at the bill: 'July 21, to be precise. Although nothing appeared in the paper.'

'What about it?'

Stratton touched his lips again. 'I have reason to believe this bill has been altered.'

'What makes you say that?' Cat asked with as much innocence as he could muster.

Stratton leaned forward and when he spoke, it was as if Cat could see nothing but his large yellowish teeth. 'Because of the seventh item. The word written here is "poppadoms" and the restaurant seems to have charged you £21 for the amount ordered.' Stratton sat back again. 'Which must lead me to the conclusion that the Sitar Restaurant serves either the most expensive Indian food in the United Kingdom, or that the bill has been altered.' Stratton paused again, and Cat gazed numbly at the cacti. 'If the latter is the case such an alteration will become evident when we examine the document with a spectroscope,' Stratton finished with a decided note of triumph.

There was now a silence, during which Abbot was tempted to say, 'Can I have another 10,000 cases taken into consideration?' He often found that panic could bring on an attack of frivolity. But instead he brought into play a ploy that he had long ago arranged for just such an eventuality. 'Ah, I can explain that, Ralph,' he said with authority. 'I was working very closely with the police when I submitted that bill. Spending a lot of money entertaining a certain officer who was helping me with a big story.'

'Go on,' Stratton said.

'Well, he didn't want his name on my expenses because he

was giving me stuff his chief inspector would not have liked mentioned to the press. I'd promised not to put his name down, so I just made up some phoney bills to cover it.'

'What was the name of this policeman?' Stratton asked.

'Detective-Sergeant Reg Glover. Do you want me to get him on the phone?'

Stratton nodded. 'Yes, I'd like to speak to him.'

Abbot dialled the number of Savile Row police station and asked to speak to his contact. After a few minutes a voice Abbot didn't recognise came on to the line: 'I'm afraid Reg Glover took early retirement in February,' the voice said. 'I understand he's living on the Costa del Sol now. May I help you?'

'Thanks,' Abbot said in a subdued voice. He replaced the receiver and looked up at Stratton. 'He's out at the moment, I'll have to try later.'

'I see,' Stratton said frostily. 'Well I shall go ahead and have the bill examined in the mean time. Perhaps you'll contact me when your policeman is available for a conversation.'

Cat trudged from the building in the direction of the Red Lion. Suddenly, after the glories of the day, his life had become like an hour-glass once more, with precious little sand left to run. 'One break,' he said towards the heavens above Gray's Inn Road. 'Just one bloody break.'

Gates and Sinclair were waiting for him at the bar. The bright morning had now turned to a gloomy twilight. It looked as if it might rain again. When he took the beer Gates offered, Cat saw himself reflected in the window. Portrait of a drowning man, he thought, and he raised the glass to himself in a silent salute.

Nothing demonstrated Fanny Hunter's importance to the *Gazette* more than the fact that her weekly column was allowed to go to press at six o'clock on Tuesday evenings for publication the following morning. As a general rule, all pages that did not contain news or sport had to be finished by lunchtime so that the production desks of the paper were clear to handle breaking stories. But Fanny had won the concession that her last item could be written late enough to give it real 'news' topicality. Nonetheless, this week she was pushing her dispensation to the limit and the features sub-editor who processed her copy was beginning to sweat.

'If the paper's late, it'll be my bloody head on the block, not God Almighty Fanny Hunter's,' Ted Bolt complained to Fanny's secretary, Jackie, while he hovered about in the outer office, as if his presence would encourage Fanny to deliver the last item for her page with greater urgency.

'Just stick your head around the door and ask her how it's coming?' he wheedled, after a few more minutes.

Usually she would have ignored any such request, but Jackie had a special relationship with Ted. They lived quite close to each other in Ilford and for the past four months, two or three times a week, Jackie had stayed late in the Red Lion, waiting for Ted to drive her home. As her parents went to bed early, Jackie would ask him in for a cup of coffee, and after a few minor protests, allow him to make love to her on the sitting-room sofa. As yet, neither of them had removed more than a minimum of clothing, but Jackie thought it still constituted an affair, so she was prepared to make a sacrifice for her lover, as she now thought of him.

'Honestleee, you'll get me shot,' she whispered, but she slowly opened the door and put her head into the room. Fanny Hunter did not take her eyes from the terminal. 'Fuck off,' she said tonelessly.

Jackie withdrew her head. 'She doesn't want to be disturbed,' she said softly.

Ted Bolt raised his arms as if the weight of the universe

pressed down upon him. 'Well, I've done everything I can,' he said in a martyred voice, and stalked from the room. Jackie felt a flutter of excitement at his demonstration of histrionics; she knew how he would need comforting later in the evening.

Meanwhile, Fanny sat hunched in concentration, her mind whirling like a kaleidoscope as she pondered a way to harm Colin Greaves. It wasn't that she disliked him personally, it was just that Fanny loathed Sarah Keane, and she always operated on the principle: My enemy's friend is my enemy.

The reason for Fanny's hatred was well known in the office. Many years before, when Jack Keane had still been a reporter on the *Gazette*, he and Fanny had had an affair. But Jack had chosen to stay with Sarah, and Fanny had never forgiven the slight. It still rankled, and whenever Fanny could, she attempted to even the score with Sarah.

Finally a first sentence came to her and she began to type: So a prostitute is found murdered on the Brent River estate. So who cares? Certainly not the police, it seems. But I wonder if the same indifference would be shown by investigating officers if the dead woman turned out to be a friend of Princess Di? Fanny sat back with a sigh of pleasure: the rest would be easy and it would allow the subs to put a picture of the Princess of Wales on the page, which was always good for business.

It was just before six o'clock when Brian Meadows stood before the mirror in his private bathroom, adjusted his bow tie and checked his general appearance. His evening shirt was a little tight for comfort, causing a slight bulge to overhang his waistband, and the collar cut into his neck uncomfortably. He reached under the bow tie and undid the collar button. Not bad, he thought, but he needed to lose a few pounds. Perhaps he would start swimming in the mornings. The RAC club had a pool and a Turkish bath. It should be easy enough to join and the company would pay the fees; they already took care of his subscription to the Garrick Club. He left the bathroom and found Corby, the assistant night editor, standing in front of his desk holding a layout.

'Page one, chief,' the young man announced, his voice full of enthusiasm.

'You're early,' Meadows said as he took the scheme from his hand.

'This is the best stuff we've got,' Corby answered. 'The pictures issued by the Yard of the dead girl are cracking, they make a good contrast with the car competition and the policy leader.'

Meadows switched on the television in the corner of the room, then glanced at the layout. In the space next to the seal was a box proclaiming: 'Your chance to win six fabulous new cars'. Beneath were two pictures of the murder victim either side of a caption with the heading: DO YOU KNOW THIS GIRL? then a short leader with a bold headline: FOR GOD'S SAKE GIVE A HAND.

Meadows looked up from the page layout to see the same two pictures displayed on the television screen. It was the first item on the six o'clock news. Corby followed his gaze and said, 'That's how we always beat the telly. No one will be able to remember their faces when they just flash them up on the screen like that. The readers will really be able to study them in the paper.'

Meadows smiled, since both of them knew in their hearts that Corby's words were meaningless bravado, but they also knew that similar conversations would be taking place in the offices of their competitors. Tomorrow morning the front pages of all the national tabloids would look pretty much the same.

Meadows held on to the page for a moment and said, 'I'm going for an early drink at my club and then on to the HAND charity dance at the Hilton. I'll be on the chairman's table. The publicity department have arranged for copies of the first edition to be delivered there at midnight. Enough for all the guests to see how the *Gazette* is backing HAND, so for Christ's sake make sure, whatever happens, the leader stays on page one.'

'Right, chief,' Corby replied. He held out his hand for the layout.

'OK, let it go,' Meadows said with a slight sigh. 'At least we've got the car competition and the leader to ourselves.'

Corby walked from the office with a swagger: he was really showing them how he could shine in the absence of Reg Stenton, the night editor. Meadows was all right but, Corby thought, a little slow, not much snap left there. It was all a question of age.

CHAPTER
FOUR

Tuesday, October 27 6.25 p.m.

Cat Abbot stood in the Red Lion and glanced at the clock; it was nearly time to keep his appointment with Doreen Clay. The saloon bar was crowded now – there was a sprinkling of office workers and secretaries from other businesses in the area, but mostly with staff from the *Gazette* building. Cat scanned their faces. He recognised people from the various departments – circulation, publicity and advertising – but none well enough to join the groups they stood within. As his eyes flickered from school to school, he thought how much the Red Lion had changed in recent years.

Once the landlord had done a thriving trade with the blue-overalled production workers who had also pressed, shoulder to shoulder, at the bar. But they had all gone long ago. Banished to satellite print-works in Docklands, when the technological revolution swept through Fleet Street and finally destroyed the once awesome power of the print unions. The place was more like a wine bar now, with carpets and fancy bits of fake Victoriana cluttering the walls. It was funny how everyone still said they worked in Fleet Street: the offices of the *Gazette* were exactly three-quarters of a mile from El Vino's. The reporters had measured it for a walking race that George Conway had won on a late summer evening years ago.

The good old days, Cat thought, and he pretended for a moment that they had been happier times. Perhaps one more, he told himself, and then off to see Doreen Clay. But when he glanced at his companions, it was clear that none of them was going to buy. They had all stood their rounds at least twice, while Cat had managed to escape putting his hand in his pocket except for the purpose of jingling his change. Cat had one golden rule when drinking in the office pub: avoid buying a round whenever possible.

The techniques he employed were simple. First, always make sure you don't finish your drink before anyone else in the school, thus eliminating the need to utter the dreadful words: 'What's everyone having?' The class of people who drank in the Red Lion were likely to order anything: champagne; large whiskies; double vodkas; even bottles of expensive mineral water, a drink that Abbot particularly resented paying for.

Secondly, when it inevitably comes to your shout: go to the lavatory. On your return, switch the group you're with and begin a passionate discussion – preferably on some controversial aspect of office politics – that will include you in a different round.

Moving about in this fashion, Cat often found that he could go for most of the night without buying a drink. But this evening was an exception; there was only one journalists' school in the bar and now they were beginning to openly demand that he buy them a drink.

'Come on, Cat,' Sinclair urged. 'Get 'em in.'

'I'd like to, lads,' he said regretfully, 'but I've got a meet in Camden Town.'

Followed by jeers of disapproval, he started to leave the bar when a voice shouted, 'Telephone call for Abbot.' Cat returned to the bar and picked up the receiver, pressing the palm of his hand against his free ear to cut out the noise.

'Abbot,' he shouted above the din.

'Mr Abbot, it's Jill Slade,' a clear voice said. 'Do you remember me? We met again last night at King's Cross station.'

'I remember,' Cat shouted. 'What happened to you?'

'I had to leave in a hurry, but I must see you again – it's very urgent.'

'How about tomorrow?'

'It has to be tonight.'

'I can't make it, I've got an appointment in Camden Town.'

'This will only take a few minutes, and it's on your way. I'm at Mornington Crescent,' the girl pleaded. Then she added, 'There could be a lot of money in it for you.'

Cat paused. The conversation with Stratton came back to him, causing a sudden shiver of fear. There would be no redundancy payments if he were dismissed for fraud. A lot of money sounded attractive. 'Give me the address,' he said, and took out his notebook.

It was dark and it had started to rain as he drove along the Euston Road, but Cat felt comfortable enough in the warm fug of his office car. Frank Sinatra sang of lost love and filled him with a pleasing melancholy. Sinatra had known bad times, he told himself, but he'd seen the bastards off, ' … dreams broken in two, made like new, on the street of dreams … ' he sang along to the tape as he approached the address given to him by Jill Slade.

It wasn't hard to find. The house was on the corner of a newly restored Georgian terrace, crisp in its fresh coat of white paint and trim with iron railings. Slums a few years ago, he told himself, now selling off at greatly reduced prices to those yuppies who'd survived the Eighties. The words of the Sinatra song returned. This had certainly been somebody's Street of Dreams, probably a property developer's. There was plenty of room to park. Ahead of him, through the rain, he could see two groups of men. One of them was being supported by his companions.

Pissed, he thought, as they got into two cars. A large dark saloon pulled away, followed by a smaller BMW. Cat locked his car and then hurried to the doorway of Number 1. It seemed to be the only one that was occupied. Lights shone through the cracks in a shuttered window as he approached the front door, but there was no response to his knock. And when he rapped with the heavy brass ring the door swung open slightly. Cat knew something was deeply wrong before he entered the hallway. His first instinct was to leave, but curiosity overcame his misgivings. So instead he walked on down the narrow, white-walled corridor, his footsteps sounding on the bare, polished boards. The lighted room was on his left with the door ajar.

When he entered, it took a few moments for him to comprehend the scene that confronted him. His first impression was of the feathers that gently stirred everywhere in the chaos of the little room. Then he saw the body of Jill Slade sprawled on the ruins of a sofa under the window. She had been shot in the chest at close range, the force of the blast throwing her head and arms back as though she were frozen in a moment of careless abandon. The shot, Abbot guessed, had been fired through a cushion to muffle the sound. It was the feather stuffing that had spread about the room. Abbot also saw that the killer had been searching for something, judging by the wreckage. Books were pulled from the shelves and the upholstery of the furniture ripped open. Then he saw the words that were written in blood, smeared on the wall next to her: UNFAITHFUL BITCH.

70

Cat felt a moment of deep compassion for the girl who lay before him, and the memory of her playing with his own daughter long ago suddenly filled his mind. Two little girls, shrieking with delight as they splashed each other in a Spanish pool. Then another realisation hit him: the potential of the story. He had this all to himself, an exclusive! One that handled properly could restore his ailing fortunes and knock the awful figure of Ralph Stratton off his back. Careful not to disturb anything, he backed from the room and stood in the corridor. He looked down and saw that his own wet footprints had mingled with others. There was nothing to connect him with the place. Think, Cat, think! he told himself.

Then it came to him, and his entire body seemed to be fired by the sudden inspiration. Pieces of an idea whirled for a moment in his mind and then fitted together as if he were seeing the parts of a jigsaw puzzle arranged by other hands. The audacity of the plan almost made him falter as he stood in the doorway and checked the deserted street. After a quick wipe of the door knocker with the sleeve of his coat, he hurried into the rain.

'Let my luck hold,' he prayed as he slipped into his driving seat. On his way to Camden Town, he remembered the car that had been pulling away as he arrived. What the hell was it? Something foreign and expensive, anyway it was black, or maybe dark blue.

A few minutes later Cat entered the one-way system that fed to the right after Camden High Street and found the road where he had dropped Doreen Clay the night before. She answered the door of her little Victorian house and he glanced about him. A staircase led up from the narrow hallway and on his right were doorways leading into two little rooms. At the end of the corridor there would be a kitchen. All of the floor was covered in the same pale tan carpet, the woodwork white, and the walls painted a warm orange. There were framed reproductions of Impressionist prints on the walls. It seemed very normal for the residence of a mystic. 'Isn't the weather awful,' she said brightly. 'Would you like a cup of tea? I've just made a pot.'

Cat followed her into the kitchen and accepted the offering. It was served in a delicate bone china cup.

'Let's go into the parlour,' she suggested and they walked to one of the little rooms, which seemed to be filled to overflowing with furniture that glowed with polish. All of it was old, bought in the Thirties for a larger house, Cat guessed, apart from the expensive electric fire that she now switched on. Doreen sat down on a small chintz-covered sofa under the window and, kicking off her shoes, drew her feet under her. Cat chose one of the upright chairs placed around a table in the centre of the room. There was hardly space to sit because of the upright piano. He liked the clean smell of the rooms. In his years as a reporter, he'd met people who seemed fastidious enough, but when you visited them in their homes it had been best to avoid sitting on anything. His own mother had been excessively house-proud and despite the cramped surroundings they had always lived in, she had insisted everything be 'neat as a new pin'.

Cat sipped some of his tea and glanced at the artificial logs flickering in the fireplace. Then he looked quickly away and studied a china figure on the top of the piano. He was keen to proceed with his plans, but he did not want to seem over-anxious.

'Is everything all right?' she asked. 'You seem a little upset.'

Cat smiled quickly. 'Just a bad day at the office. I'm fine now.'

'So tell me something of yourself,' Doreen said, after another brief pause.

Cat took a sip of his tea, then placed the cup in its saucer. 'There's not much to tell, really. I'm a reporter on the *Gazette*, divorced with a grown-up daughter, they live in Spain now and I live in Notting Hill.'

'That's a bit short,' she said with a laugh. 'What about your mam and dad?'

'I never knew my father,' Cat said after a moment. 'He died when I was small. I come from a big family – four brothers.'

'So there were five of you for your mam to look after?'

'Seven originally. The two eldest were killed in the war.'

Doreen sat up a little. 'And your dad, was he from a big family?'

Cat nodded. 'He was Irish, from Dublin. There were ten of them. Three girls and he was the youngest son.'

'So you're a seventh.'

'Sorry?' Cat asked.

'The seventh son of a seventh son.'

'I suppose I am, I've never thought about it. Why?'

'Oh, nothing,' Doreen said. 'There's an old superstition that you're supposed to be, how shall I put it - lucky.'

Cat smiled. 'I can't say as I've noticed.'

'Did things ever happen to you?' she asked, and he could hear the interest in her voice. 'Odd things that you couldn't explain?'

Cat thought for a time. 'Only once I can think of,' he answered.

'Tell me about it.'

'You know I told you my nickname is Cat?'

'Yes.'

'It used to be Cat's-Eyes. The reason they called me that was because I once did a story about something I saw, but it all happened in pitch darkness.' He stopped for a moment to see if she was smiling, but Doreen's expression was quite serious. 'The other reporters took the mickey out of me something rotten,' he continued. 'And when my boss found out it all happened in the dark, I nearly got fired. So that's why they called me Cat's-Eyes.'

'But you really saw it happen?' Doreen said.

'I don't know,' he replied. 'I felt as if I did at the time.'

73

'And this big family of yours, do you still see a lot of each other?'

He shook his head and suddenly felt a slight sense of regret. 'No, I haven't seen any of them for years – not since my mother died.'

Doreen got up and went to the kitchen to fill her cup again. It was only a few yards away. 'So how can I help you?' she called out.

Cat relaxed a little. 'We're doing a feature on clairvoyants – you know the sort of thing: out-of-body experiences, astral projection, hypnotic regression to past lives, mediums who go into trances like you do. I'm writing a piece on what the actual sensation is like. If there is any difference in the physical being of the person who is actually having the experience.'

'So what do you want from me?'

Cat felt he was on the verge of a triumph. 'The trance you went into the other day,' he answered, making sure there was no excitement in his voice. 'Did you know what was going on around you when it happened?'

Doreen entered the room and sat on the sofa again.

'Oh, yes,' she said cheerfully. 'That wasn't a genuine trance.'

Abbot felt a bitter stab of disappointment. 'Not genuine?' he repeated forlornly.

'Oh, dear, no,' Doreen answered. 'It was just for those old dears who come to the Institute, I tell them what they want to hear, it makes them happy. I don't want to go upsetting them with a proper seance, you never know what's going to come out. So I invented my Egyptian for them.'

'How do you know I'm not going to print this?'

'But you're not, are you?' Doreen said with gentle conviction.

'Can you go into a proper trance?'

'Yes, but it's very tiring.'

'And do you know what's going on around you then?'

'I haven't got the foggiest notion. It's a complete blank to me when it happens.'

Cat took a deep breath. It was as he had hoped, and he knew she was telling the truth. 'Will you do one for me?'

Doreen thought for a time. 'Are you sure?' she asked at last. 'People sometimes hear things they don't want to hear.'

'I'm sure.'

Doreen was silent for a while and then she got up and pulled the heavy curtains behind the sofa. Squeezing past him, she took a large, smooth, blue-coloured stone from a drawer in the sideboard. She placed it in the middle of the table.

'Turn the big light off, then come and sit opposite me and hold my hands.'

Cat did as he was instructed. Now the only light was from a small lamp on the piano.

When they clasped each other across the table, Doreen Clay stared down at the stone and began to take deep, audible breaths. This went on for some time until Abbot became aware of the loud ticking of a clock on the mantelpiece. Just as his attention was beginning to drift away, Doreen gave a sudden convulsive jerk and pulled her hands away from his. As she did so, Cat felt a sensation like an electric shock pass through his body. Doreen now slumped back in her chair, head tilted forward on to her chest, her hands still resting on the table. Cat reached out to touch her hand: it felt as cold as ice.

There was silence for about a minute and then Doreen Clay began to speak with the voice of an old woman. At first, Cat did not understand the language at all. He reached for his notebook and craned forward. After a moment he recognised a few words. It was German, a language he had been taught at school. Concentrating as hard as he could he scribbled in longhand. The voice seemed to alter in strength, as if the old woman was at varying distances. As he came to the place in his notebook where Jill Slade's address was written, it faded away completely. His pen hovered momentarily, and at that point Doreen Clay woke up and began to massage the back of her neck.

'Well, did you get anything?' she asked.

Cat looked down at his notebook. 'An old lady, I think. She spoke mostly in German.'

Doreen laughed. 'That's a new one.'

'Don't you speak German?' Cat asked.

'Not a word.' Cat looked at his notes again and slowly began to translate:

'More bodies … near the forest and the field of the three horses … two tribes of the same blood. The one from the East fights both … he is right about the gun … ' Cat looked up. 'There was more, but I couldn't quite get it. Then there was a sentence in English and an address.'

'An address,' Doreen said, 'that's unusual – where?'

'Number 1 Caulfield Terrace.'

Doreen looked on a little bookshelf next to the fireplace and produced an ABC street guide of London. 'There's only one Caulfield Terrace, that's in Mornington Crescent. What else did the voice say?'

Cat looked down at his notebook to avoid her eyes. 'Jill Slade lies dead …'

Doreen looked unconcerned and got up casually to go to the telephone.

'Who are you calling?' Cat asked with sudden concern.

'I've got a friend at the local police station, a sergeant, his wife is interested in my work. He'll get one of his lads to look in on Caulfield Terrace.'

'You don't seem too bothered.'

Doreen smiled. 'Well the problem is, you see, the girl could have been lying there a hundred years ago. The spirits don't keep the same time as us.'

Somebody answered at the other end. 'Sergeant Payne, please,' she said, and then: 'Hello, Jim, it's Doreen Clay here. How are you … and Pat … mustn't grumble. Listen pet, I know how busy you are but I was wondering, could you do me a favour? ... I just got a message from the other side and I think there may be trouble at Number 1 Caulfield Terrace ... that's right ... could you get someone to pop in to make sure everything is all right? ... Yes, just to put my mind at rest ... that is good of you. Love to Pat.'

She hung up.

'I think I'd better go round there as well,' Cat said. Doreen put the stone back in the sideboard and followed him into the hallway.

'Hang on,' she said, 'I'll just get my coat and come with you.'

Cat looked at his watch when they got into the car. There was still plenty of time to catch the main editions, he thought with suppressed excitement. Maybe even the first.

Tuesday, October 27 9.55 p.m.

Colin Greaves looked up from his desk as Sergeant Holland entered his office carrying a piece of paper. 'Any reaction to the television pictures yet?' Greaves asked.

'Plenty of calls, the usual nutcases, and one or two that could be genuine, but this is interesting,' he held up the sheet of paper. 'A positive ID on a girl called Jill Slade who's been found murdered in Mornington Crescent.'

'Same style as the other?'

Holland shook his head. 'No, but she worked as a secretary for the Circle of Shamrock Club.'

Greaves rose from his chair. 'Who's on the job?'

'Chief Inspector Amhurst.'

'Fred Amhurst, he's a good man.'

'Yes, sir.'

Greaves got up quickly. 'Let's go and take a look.'

'There's just one thing. A reporter from the *Gazette* was at the scene almost as soon as our lads.'

'Sarah?'

'No,' Holland looked at the paper again. 'A man called Abbot; it seems he's got a clairvoyant with him as well.'

Greaves had heard a great deal about Cat from Sarah. 'That sounds like him,' he said grimly.

Greaves's car was waved down by a uniformed constable when they arrived at Caulfield Terrace but he recognised Greaves immediately and raised the tape across the narrow roadway. Already carloads of reporters and television vans were spilling across the turning.

'The tip-off merchants must be working overtime,' Holland said, referring to the press contacts throughout the police force who sold information to the media.

When they entered the house Chief Inspector Frederick Amhurst was standing in the hallway, talking to his sergeant. He looked up in surprise. 'Hello, Colin. What brings you here?' he asked with a hint of hostility. 'This isn't gang warfare.'

'I don't want to get in your hair, Fred,' Greaves said soothingly. 'But this might be connected with my investigation.'

'I don't think so,' Amhurst replied. 'It looks pretty straightforward to me – crime of passion, I'd say. Come and take a look.'

As Cat had found, it was possible to view the entire scene from the doorway. Amhurst pointed into the room. 'The girl was killed with a small-gauge shotgun. He used a pillow to muffle the sound. There's no sign of the weapon.'

'Who's "he"?'

Amhurst stood back. 'I think it's the man who lives here with her. We found a couple of letters addressed to Christopher Webb, and clothes in the wardrobe upstairs. The gun was his, there's a couple more up there.'

'Any luck on the computer ?'

Amhurst shook his head. 'No licence, no name. We tried. There's nothing else. No personal papers or anything. It looks as if they just moved in. There's no sign of him.'

'Any leads ?'

Amhurst shook his head. 'We tried the estate agents, their board is still up on the other properties in this terrace, but there's no one available until the morning.'

'So what do you think happened ?'

Amhurst gestured towards the room. 'You can see the words on the wall. The way the place has been turned over. I think he suspected her of having it off with somebody else. Maybe he found the evidence – pictures, letters, who knows. Anyway he topped her and had it away. Don't worry, we'll find him.'

Greaves stood with his hands in the pockets of his raincoat and continued to look into the room. 'I know you will, Fred,' he said after a time. 'By the way, what's all this about a clairvoyant ?'

Amhurst wiped his face with a beefy hand. 'Now, that is odd. A sergeant at the local nick got a call from a woman he knows called Doreen Clay. She lives around here, well known in the community. Does fortunes, that sort of thing. She swears she got the information about the murder in a seance she was giving for a reporter on the *Gazette*. A bloke called Cat Abbot.' Amhurst held out his hand and rocked it from side to side. 'He's a bit iffy, I hear, but the sergeant swears that Doreen Clay is as straight as a die.'

'Where are they now ?'

'Giving statements at the local nick, but Abbot's had plenty of time to get in touch with his paper.'

'I think I'll pop round for a chat,' Greaves said. 'Thanks, Fred.' He was about to leave, but paused. 'You did say she was shot with a small-gauge shotgun ?'

'That's right.'

'Where did he keep it ?'

'Gun locker. Upstairs, first room on the left.'

Greaves climbed the stairs and found a metal gun cabinet with the door swung open. There were two other shotguns in racks: an old-fashioned sporting piece with a broken hammer and a 12-bore Winchester pump-action shotgun. He looked in the bottom of the cabinet. Tucked in the back was a half-filled box of 12-bore cartridges. There was also an empty box that had contained small-bore ammunition and a handwritten receipt. Greaves examined the sheet of paper for a moment, then put it back in the cabinet. 'Let's go and see Mr Abbot now,' he said to Holland.

Frank Corby sat on the back bench, wishing he was experiencing a bad dream rather than the reality of the telephone call he was now conducting with Peter Kerr, the chief crime reporter.

'I know it's fucking Cat Abbot,' Kerr shouted in exasperation. 'But I'm telling you his story stands up. This bloody clairvoyant Doreen Clay did tell him where the body was – and the name of the murdered girl. I got it from one of the coppers I know who's working on the job. It all checks out.'

'But we've got a policy leader on the front page,' Corby said miserably. 'The editor instructed me not to touch it.'

Peter Kerr sat in his office car, near Caulfield Terrace and spoke on a mobile telephone. It was the first day of his new diet and his temper was a little frayed because he had eaten only a small cheese salad at lunchtime.

'Well ring the editor and tell him we've got a story that will knock the shit out of the rest of Fleet Street. Good God, man, this is the real thing, not some bloody waffle from the chairman.'

There was now almost a whine in Corby's voice. 'Don't you think I've tried? Nobody knows where he is. Once the dancing started at this do at the Hilton the chairman fucked off with all the other big-wigs. The waiter says that Meadows vanished ten minutes later.'

Kerr thought for a moment. 'Listen, get the news desk to ring Annie's bar in the House of Commons. Geoffrey Walker, the political editor, should still be there, ask him to call me on this number.'

Kerr slammed down the telephone and sat watching the wet street in front of him, imagining what it would be like to be eating a double hamburger. Then his telephone rang.

'Walker here, old boy,' said a fruity voice.

'Geoffrey, Peter Kerr here, I need a big favour.'

'Speak and it shall be done.'

'Have you heard a rumour from Fanny Hunter that Meadows is having it off with a certain lady politician?'

'Such words have reached my ears,' Walker replied after a moment's hesitation. 'Why?'

'Meadows has gone missing from some charity bash at the Hilton. Do you think he could have popped out for a quick one?'

Walker thought for a moment. 'The geography would make such a thing possible. Half Moon Street is only a stroll away from the Hilton.'

'Do you know her well enough to ring her there and see if she's got Meadows banged up? It really is urgent that he rings Corby.'

'Say no more, old boy,' Walker said with a dry chuckle.

Taking another sip from his glass, Walker picked up the receiver he had just replaced and, waving reassuringly to Geraldine Miller's cabinet colleague, with whom he was having a quiet drink, he dialled her private home number. The telephone was answered after a longish pause and Walker thought he could detect a catching of breath on the junior minister's part.

'Geraldine, my love, it's me, Geoffrey. Still working? Look I know you'll be going to this bash at the Hilton later. If you should happen to see my esteemed editor there, please ask him to call back bench urgently, there's a dear.'

Walker hung up and rejoined his guests. 'Another satisfied customer,' he said jovially. 'Same again ?'

Still paralysed with indecision, Corby could hardly bring himself to pick up the telephone when it rang, in case it brought more bad news. 'Back bench,' he said weakly. Confidence flooded back when he heard Meadows's voice. 'Tell me what's going on,' the editor said in calming tones; he could tell Corby was badly rattled.

Corby began to babble out the situation. ' … and Peter Kerr assures me it all stands up,' he said when he had finally explained his dilemma.

Meadows did not speak for a time and eventually Corby said in a timid voice: 'I could drop the puff to the car competition, put in a cross-ref to an inside page ?'

'No,' Meadows replied. 'We've spent a quarter of a million on television advertising, it'll have to stay where it is. Put the faces of the murdered girl on the top of page two. They'll have to go in black and white, switch the leader into a double-column box under the seal and reduce the headline to 36 point. That should leave you enough space to splash on Abbot's story. Let that run as long as it makes, turn it on to page two, under the pictures of the dead girl if necessary.'

'What shall I do with all the stuff about Romania ?'

'Drop it.'

Corby was making frantic notes.

'Got all that ?'

'Yes, chief.' He paused. 'It's a pity about the murdered girl pictures, they look great in colour.'

'Not to worry,' Meadows said casually. 'They've all seen it on television.'

*   *   *

Greaves decided to talk to Doreen Clay first. She was not what he had expected. When he entered the interview room she looked up and stared at him intently. Usually people kept their eyes down after an initial glance, but she got up and shook hands, holding on for just a bit longer than was usual.

When they were seated at either side of the table Greaves said: 'Tell me, how long have you known Mr Abbot ?'

'Since yesterday,' she replied, quite relaxed.

'How did your meeting come about ?'

'He rang me to arrange an interview. I told him to come along to one of my seances. We were going to talk afterwards but he was called away. We made another appointment at my house this evening, he came there soon after seven o'clock.'

'And what happened then ?'

'I demonstrated a deep trance for him.'

'And that's when you told him about the dead girl at Caulfield Terrace ?'

Doreen smiled. 'Well, strictly speaking it was somebody else who told him, I was just the medium.'

'And has this … person ever spoken through you before ?'

'I can't say, Superintendent. When it happens I'm not aware of what's going on.'

Greaves exchanged glances with Sergeant Holland, who stood silently beside them. 'Tell me, what's your impression of Mr Abbot ?' he asked lightly.

'He's been badly directed.'

'In his work, you mean ?'

'In his life,' she replied firmly.

'I don't understand.'

Doreen Clay folded her hands on the table and looked at each of them before she answered. 'Raymond Abbot has very powerful psychic abilities, but he doesn't know it. I felt it the moment I touched his hand. His problem is, he's gone through life being someone he shouldn't. Something forced him as a child to take the wrong path and so his life has been in chaos. I've met others like him before. I should think the people he works with find him a very disruptive influence.'

'How do you mean?' Greaves asked. Despite his scepticism, he was beginning to be intrigued by Doreen Clay.

'He releases elementals and they like to cause mischief; arguments between people, things get lost, misunderstandings occur.'

Greaves remembered Sarah's accounts of mishaps in the office when Abbot was around; she called it 'The Cat Factor'.

'And you knew all this just by touching his hand?'

'Yes.'

Greaves had to smile. 'That must be a very useful ability, Miss Clay. I wish that I possessed it.'

'Oh, but you do, Superintendent, everybody does to some degree, only we like to call it intuition, or even hunch. But we all know the truth about certain situations instinctively. Sadly, we in the West have pursued only scientific reasons for everything. You must have found different attitudes in the East. After all, you were born in China.'

Greaves looked at her sharply. 'How did you know that?'

She smiled once again. 'I felt it in your hand.'

'Have you ever had anything like this happen to you before?' he asked.

Doreen shook her head. 'No, but then I've never met Mr Abbot before. He's as much to blame.' She stood up. 'You're finished with me now, aren't you?' Greaves nodded and Holland showed her out of the room.

'What do you think?' Greaves said when he and Holland were alone.

'I don't know,' he replied. 'I believed her – at least I think she was telling the truth … I mean, I think she believes what she was saying herself.'

'So do I,' Greaves replied. 'Well, let's hear Abbot's story.'

* * *

84

Greaves was also surprised by Cat. As with Doreen Clay, he had expected someone quite different. From Sarah's accounts of his behaviour, he'd anticipated a seedy man with dandruff and scuffed shoes. Abbot was much more distinguished. His thick grey hair was brushed back from heavy, handsome features and his carelessly knotted bow tie and well-cut, dark blue suit gave the effect of an actor playing the part of somebody important. Only his shifting eyes failed to impress.

'How did you come to choose Doreen Clay for your feature, Mr Abbot ?' Greaves began.

'One of the office drivers told me about her, the family live in Camden Town. His mother goes to her meetings at the Institute,' Cat answered easily.

Greaves was interested in Abbot's voice; it was lighter than he had expected, with a London accent. But Greaves had a good ear for languages and he thought he could detect traces of some other influence.

'And Jill Slade, you've never heard of her before ?'

'Never.'

'May I see the section of your notebook where you took down the words spoken by Doreen Clay ?'

Cat folded it back at the page and handed it to him.

'This isn't shorthand, it's mostly in German,' said Greaves.

'I never learned shorthand very well,' Cat replied. 'I can get by.'

'Read me what it says,' Greaves said. He watched Cat carefully while he listened to the translation.

'Do you know any other languages ?' he asked when Cat had finished.

'Latin.'

Greaves slid the notebook back to him. 'Take this down,' he said, and he spoke at conversational speed. '*Haud facile emergunt quorum virtutibus opstat res angusta domi.*'

As Greaves finished, Cat slid the book across the table again and Greaves glanced down. It was as he had dictated it.

'Where did you go to school, Mr Abbott ?' Greaves asked, with genuine interest in his voice.

Cat mumbled a name, as if he was ashamed of it.

'Where ?' Greaves asked, missing the words.

'King William's.'

'Were you a boarder ?'

'Until I was sixteen, then I left.'

'Why didn't you stay on ?'

'There weren't many kids from Walthamstow there, I was lonely.'

'You were a scholarship boy ?'

Cat put the notebook back in his pocket. 'My father was a fireman, he was killed in 1945. Later on, they sent me.'

Greaves stood up. 'Thank you very much for your help. You can go now.'

When Abbot had left, Holland shook his head. 'There's something funny there.'

'I know,' Greaves replied. 'Maybe we should have shaken hands with him.'

When they left the station it was still raining. As they got into the car, Holland said, 'What did that Latin you asked him to take down mean ?'

Greaves thought for a moment. 'Difficult indeed it is for those to emerge from obscurity whose noble qualities are cramped by narrow means at home.'

'That's rather apt,' Holland said, 'considering you didn't know about his background when you dictated it.'

'I suppose it is,' Greaves replied thoughtfully. 'Play me the tape where he translated the German again.'

Holland found the section on a small cassette player he carried and they listened once again to Abbot's voice. 'More bodies … near the forest and the field of the three horses. The one from the

East fights both … he is right about the gun … ' Greaves repeated
to himself as the car took him towards Hampstead.

CHAPTER
FIVE

Wednesday, October 28 6.07 a.m.

Before dawn, the people who lived at the top end of Paignton Street in Camden Town were awakened by a curious phenomenon. Bright lights flickered against their bedroom curtains and the occasional sound of shouting voices disturbed their rest. Mrs Edith Warmon, who lived at Number 11, a sprightly widow in her late seventies and a light sleeper, was the first to peep through her snow-white curtains.

When she saw a group of people milling about in front of Number 13, which was illuminated by mobile floodlights, her heart leapt. In her confusion, she was momentarily reminded of the Blitz, and a flood of memories returned. 'I'd better make some tea,' she told herself, and headed for the kitchen.

Arthur Pritchard, who lived at Number 17, had been the first to make contact. He'd risen well before the crowd had swelled to its present dimensions, so had not yet been disturbed by unaccustomed noises. Arthur was used to having the streets pretty much to himself when he was on early shift, but when he entered his little front garden on this particular morning, a bright light cut through the darkness and shone in his face. He found himself blinking at an aggressive young man, dressed in an expensive sheepskin coat, who was thrusting a microphone in his face: 'Good morning, sir. I'm from breakfast television, tell me, do you know Doreen Clay who lives at Number 13 ?'

'Yes,' Mr Pritchard replied, quite relaxed now he realised that his interrogator was not the mugger he had expected.

'And what is your name, sir ?'

Mr Pritchard knew the form; he had seen many such inter-views broadcast and he suddenly felt pleased that his turn had come to speak to the nation. 'My name is Arthur Pritchard and I'm a guard for British Rail.'

'And what do you think of this morning's story about your neighbour ?'

'What story ?'

The young man thrust a copy of the *Gazette* into his hands and Mr Pritchard was bewildered for a moment. He read the puff for the car competition and then part of the leader before he reached the main headline:

EXCLUSIVE: CLAIRVOYANT
TELLS GAZETTE MAN WHERE
TO FIND MURDER VICTIM

'Well, all I can say is, this is a surprise,' Mr Pritchard answered, still not absolutely sure of the question's meaning.

'Can you tell us anything about Miss Clay, sir ? How long has she lived here in Paignton Street ?'

Mr Pritchard tried to recall what he knew of his next-door neighbour, and was slightly irritated to realise it was very little.

When he daydreamed about being interviewed on television, the questions always concerned problems that were of great moment to the nation. Somehow he now felt cheated. But he had a go ...

'About ten years, no, tell a lie, nearer twelve. It was just after our Karen left school ... so that would be ... yes ... twelve years ago in June.'

'And is Doreen Clay a good neighbour ?'

'Oh, yes. To tell you the truth we were glad when she moved in.'

'Why was that, sir ?'

Arthur Pritchard looked surprised at the question. 'Well, she's white, isn't she, even though she comes from Wales. When old Mrs Wilson died we thought blacks would buy the place. Not that I've got anything against 'em, mind. But you like to live with your own kind, don't you ?'

The young interviewer said a silent prayer of thanks that the footage wasn't going out live, then asked his next question. 'And tell me, Mr Pritchard, have you ever noticed anything strange about Miss Clay, anything that would give an indication of her strange powers ?'

Pritchard scratched his chin in contemplation and a voice called out: 'Tell him about her finding our Roger that time, Arthur.'

The interviewer turned towards a stout woman who was standing just off camera. To his astonishment he saw she was wearing an extravagantly padded, lime-green suit and a wide, matching hat that were more suitable for Ascot than a cold, wet, pre-dawn morning in Camden Town.

'I take it you are Mrs Pritchard ?' the young man said.

'That's right, Molly Pritchard.'

'That's a splendid outfit, Mrs Pritchard.'

'Do you like it?' she said. 'I bought it for our Karen's wedding.'

'And you say that Doreen Clay found your Roger when he went missing ?'

'That's right.'

'And where did she find him ?'

The camera and lights had now swung on to Mrs Pritchard, who was half turning her face to present what she considered her most flattering angle.

'Hiding in a pipe behind her garden shed,' said Molly, in a voice she hoped conveyed sufficient drama. 'We'd looked everywhere, I can tell you; I was going crazy. Mind you, he's always like that when he needs a bath. Arthur always says he's a boy and a half.'

The young man, who'd begun to feel that the interview was entering another dimension of sanity, was reinforced in his suspicion when an old lady, wearing a dressing gown and carrying a gaily hued umbrella, suddenly thrust a cup of tea into his hand. 'And where is he now ?' he asked faintly, after nodding his thanks for the refreshment.

'Well, he was in bed with our Karen.' Mrs Pritchard turned away and bellowed: 'Karen! Did Roger sleep with you last night ?'

'He's here, Mum,' a voice shouted back.

Now filled with an apprehensive dread that he was about to reveal some sordid example of inner-city incest, the young man turned, as the camera and lights swung to the garden gate of Number 17, revealing a sallow girl who wore a raincoat over her nightdress and held a wriggling Jack Russell terrier in her arms.

By the time these first interviews were concluded, many more members of the media had arrived on the scene and the Pritchard family now found themselves pressed for further comment by representatives of the world's press and television. Other neighbours, anxious to co-operate, were sharing their reminiscences of Doreen Clay, and Edith Warmon passed happily among the crowd dispensing tea. But there was no answer to the repeated knocks on the door of Number 13.

Wednesday, October 28 7.02 a.m.

Colin Greaves was dressed and had been on the telephone non-stop since the first call he had made woke Sarah up just after six o'clock. When she decided to rise at seven, she found her three children, still in their night-clothes, grouped around the kitchen table, reading the morning edition of the *Gazette*. 'This story is fantastic,' Martin, the elder of the twins by three minutes, said. 'Do you know Cat Abbot, Mum ?'

'Very well,' she replied while she made a pot of coffee. 'And fantastic is the correct word for most of the stories he's involved with.'

'It's like something from a horror movie,' Paul added. 'Remember the video of *The Dead Zone* ?'

'I shouldn't take all that too seriously,' Sarah warned in motherly tones.

'It's in your paper,' Emily pointed out. 'Are you saying it's not true ?'

Sarah folded her arms and chose her words carefully. 'No, we try to print what we hope are the facts, but sometimes the whole truth doesn't emerge until later.'

'So you think this Doreen Clay may be a fake ?' Paul asked.

Sarah continued in the same noncommittal vein.

'Colin doesn't think so, he talked to her last night. But Cat Abbot might have not got the story quite straight.'

'Colin talked to her ?' Emily said.

Sarah reached for the coffee pot. 'Yes, he told me all about it when he came in late.'

'Wow!' the boys exclaimed together, and they made for the bedroom, where Greaves was still talking on the telephone.

'He doesn't want to be disturbed,' she called out after them.

'Don't you believe in psychic phenomena ?' Emily asked, now they were alone.

Sarah picked up her coffee and held it in both hands before glancing at her daughter. She now wondered what the underlying question was going to be. Emily was a chess player, and complicated opening gambits were a common approach when she wished to raise a delicate subject.

Psychic phenomena! Sarah thought, pawn moves to King four. 'I suppose I must,' she replied cautiously. 'In a way it's the basis of our religion.'

Emily continued to look down at the paper as she formulated her next move. 'So you still think of yourself as a Catholic ?'

'You know the saying,' Sarah said lightly. 'Once a Catholic … ' but she knew the game was already over.

'Then how can you go on living with Colin, if you know it's a sin ?' Emily asked lightly.

Sarah turned to refill her cup, really to allow herself enough time to give her answer some thought. 'I know the Church considers it a sin, darling,' she replied finally. 'But in my view it isn't such a big one. Colin and I talked about it a lot and we decided this was the best way. If we're happy together, after a while we will get married.'

'So you think it's all right to make love to someone even when you're not married ?'

Damn! Sarah thought, so it's about her and Ric Daggert, not me and Colin.

'No,' Sarah said with more firmness than she intended. 'Because I commit an act which I know to be a sin it doesn't mean I approve of others doing the same, neither do I wish to encourage them. Remember your sins are between you and God. What other people do or believe doesn't come into it.'

Emily closed the paper slowly and stood up to go. 'That's what I was trying to explain to Ric last night.'

'I thought Ric was a Catholic.'

Emily smiled suddenly, in a very womanly fashion. 'He forgets sometimes – when he's with me.'

Greaves came into the kitchen and found Sarah gazing moodily into her coffee cup.

'What's up ?' he asked.

'That girl has just been running rings around me on the subject of sin,' she replied.

'*Nemo repente fuit turpissimus*,' he quoted, filling his own mug of coffee.

'What's that ?'

'Juvenal,' he said.

'What does it mean ?'

'Ask Cat Abbot.'

'Abbot,' Sarah repeated, 'how would he know ?'

Greaves kissed her on the top of her head. 'Like your daughter, still waters run deep in Cat Abbot. Actually it means: No one ever reached the climax of vice in one step.'

'Show-off,' she said. 'By the way, may I use the Riley again today?'

'I can run you in if you like, Nick Holland is on his way to pick me up. We're going to Hertfordshire.'

'Why?'

'They've found out where Christopher Webb may be. His parents live near a village called Weyden.'

Sarah considered his offer: it was early to get to the office, but she had things she could do. There were several letters to answer and she liked the peace of the newsroom before the first shifts arrived.

'If I come with you, I'd better get a move on,' Sarah said. 'Can you hang on for half an hour?'

'Better that than risk the Riley,' he answered.

Wednesday, October 28 8.14 a.m.

To Sarah's surprise, George Conway was waiting for her when she reached the office. Usually the only people about the news-room in the early morning were the tape-room staff, sorting mail, as well as Nigel Potter, an old reporter who slept next to the news desk on a camp bed in case a story of earth-shattering dimensions should break during the hours before dawn. But today, George was the boy on the burning deck. He waved to her as she approached her desk.

'What's this, George, thrown out of the house again?' she greeted him.

Conway had a difficult relationship at home. He had recently gone back to his second wife, or was it his third? Sarah had difficulty keeping track.

'I've been here since seven o'clock. Meadows is bouncing about like a ping-pong ball at a youth club rally.'

'The young don't play ping-pong any more, George,' said Sarah. 'They think it may spoil the look of their trainers.'

'Don't bandy words, just go into the editor's office. I'll follow you there in a few minutes,' he said softly.

'Why?'

'Just do it,' he hissed. Puzzled by his clandestine behaviour, she did as she was ordered.

The editor's secretary, who usually controlled access to Meadows with the authority of a border guard, was not yet on duty in the outer office. So Sarah knocked and entered.

Brian Meadows sat with his feet on the desk, speaking on the telephone. He indicated that she should take a seat, and she waited while he continued his call.

'It was entirely my decision to alter the layout of the leader, Sir Robert,' he said patiently. Glancing at Sarah, he raised his eyebrows to the ceiling. 'Yes, I thought the occasion justified it.

I've already spoken to the circulation department and they confirm we have a sell-out … Yes, Sir Robert … Well I don't really think it's because of the leader, splendid though it was. All our telephone calls indicate it was the story about the clairvoyant. It's not just the British press, the whole world is following the *Gazette* on this one … Of course I shall keep you informed, as always … goodbye, Sir Robert.' He banged down the telephone and swung his chair round to face Sarah.

'Is it really a sell-out?' Sarah asked politely.

Meadows held both hands palm upwards and shrugged his shoulders. 'It ought to be. If it isn't then I no longer know anything about the newspaper business.'

'But you just told Sir Robert … '

Meadows smiled benevolently, 'The chairman only believes what he wants to believe. A few days ago he announced that our circulation was rising, so I just confirmed his opinion.' He swung his feet from the desk and rubbed his hands together. 'Now, has George told you what this is about?' he asked, and Sarah thought she could detect a new dynamism about Meadows, despite the yawn he now attempted to stifle.

'No, he just told me to come straight in here.'

Meadows slapped the desk top impatiently. 'Well, we'd better wait till he arrives. No point in going over it twice.' He glanced around the rather spartan room that was decorated in pale wood, insipid fawn carpets and tweed-covered furniture the colour of dust.

'What do you think of this office?' he suddenly asked.

'It's a little modern for my taste,' Sarah replied.

Meadows slapped the desk again. 'Exactly my view,' he said with the same enthusiasm. 'Actually, a friend of mine is going to give me a hand redesigning it. She thinks something in leather and dark wood, a few mementoes, photographs and bookshelves, that sort of thing.'

'It sounds splendid,' Sarah replied, remembering it had been exactly like that when she had first worked on the paper many years before.

'Yes,' he said slowly. 'I like the sound of it too.'

Conway now entered the office with an apology for being delayed. 'Has the editor told you about the job?' he asked her.

'No, you tell her now, George,' Meadows said quickly. Sarah's gaze darted to each of them in turn. Whatever it was, she had a sudden feeling she wasn't going to like it.

'We want you to work on the clairvoyant story with Cat Abbot,' George said after a noticeable pause.

'Please don't do this to me,' Sarah said quietly.

'We need you, Sarah,' Conway said pleadingly.

She shook her head. 'Abbot and I have no … empathy,' she replied. 'We never have been able to get on. It won't be for the good of the paper. Please … pass this cross to broader shoulders than mine.'

'You're the best person for the job, Sarah,' Meadows said with a harder edge to his voice. 'We need someone who won't be bamboozled by Abbot. Someone with integrity who won't attempt to put any extra spin on the story.'

'So you want me to go and act as a minder for Cat Abbot, a sort of moral conscience of the paper?'

'Someone to soothe doubts away when Cat starts filing ex-clusive stories dictated to him by … Napoleon or Elvis Presley,' she continued softly, 'because he will, you know.'

'Actually I'm more concerned for the reputation of Miss Clay,' Meadows said rather pompously. 'She is single, you know. It would be better if we had a woman present as well.'

'Why not send Fanny Hunter!' Sarah suggested, a note of hope in her voice. 'She's a much bigger name than me. The readers would love it.'

Conway and Meadows exchanged glances. 'Well, actually, it was Fanny who suggested you,' Meadows said with a slight cough.

98

'So she's turned it down?'

'Not exactly. In fact she was very frank. She told us that she and Abbot had an affair once and it could be embarrassing if any of the gossip columns got hold of the story that they were sharing an hotel room.'

'That was ten years ago, it's ancient history,' Sarah said.

'Since when has that stopped a diary printing a story?' George interjected.

'I don't want to order you to do this, Sarah,' said Meadows in his most sincere voice. 'But I would consider it a great favour – both to me personally and to the paper as a whole.'

She knew there was no escape now.

'Very well, if you put it like that, how can I refuse?'

'Splendid,' Meadows said briskly.

'Where's Cat now?' Sarah asked.

The two men exchanged glances. 'Actually,' George said sheepishly, 'we haven't the faintest idea.'

Wednesday, October 28 10.55 a.m.

Even in the finest weather, Weyden was not an attractive village. Now, in the seeping rain, it looked deeply unappealing to Greaves as the car slowed down on entering the outskirts. The last rustic cottages that had once clustered around the ugly grey-stone church had been demolished at the turn of the century and replaced with yellow-brick houses that had aged to the colour of old teeth. The elm trees that had once broken the skyline were all gone, leaving a curious naked roughness to the landscape, and the general drabness was not enhanced by a dribble of pebbledashed council houses, verged with strips of scrub grass, which ran from the arterial road to a row of shops facing the wire-enclosed playground of the local school. Shouting groups of children swirled about on the wide expanse of wet asphalt when Sergeant Holland got out of the car and entered the general store that also served as a post office.

He waited while an old woman paid for her groceries, then asked the surly man at the cash desk the whereabouts of the local policeman's house. He directed Holland to one of the yellow houses on the green and when the car stopped before it, Holland suddenly knew who would answer his knock.

'Well, I'll be … Nick Holland!' Sergeant Clive Patterson exclaimed when he stood at the open doorway in his shirtsleeves.

'Hello, Clive,' Holland replied. 'This is a week for coincidences, I met your sister yesterday.'

'Lucy?' he said. 'How come?'

'I called on her boss, he's been helping us.'

'Who is it, Clive?' a woman's voice with a country accent called out.

'It's an old friend of mine, Judy,' Patterson replied, and a young woman appeared beside him. Until that moment, Holland had not been able to understand why Clive Patterson had chosen to live in such a deadening backwater. But Judy Patterson answered all his unspoken questions. Even in a sweatshirt and jeans, her hair tied up in a scarf, she had the sort of looks for which most men would forsake kingdoms, never mind Streatham, where Patterson had last been stationed before he departed from the Metropolitan Police.

They shook hands and Holland remembered the impatient figure sitting in the car. 'Look, this is work, Clive. Do you know a family called Webb that lives somewhere about here?'

'Colonel Webb?' he replied. 'Sure, Hanger Cottage. Wait a minute, I'll get my tunic and take you there.'

'This is Sergeant Patterson, sir, we used to play rugby together,' Holland said when they reached the car.

100

'Sergeant,' Greaves acknowledged when Patterson got into the seat beside the driver. Patterson gave directions and when they were clear of the village Holland said, 'So how do you like it out here in the sticks, Clive?'

'It's not so bad,' he replied. 'The village is a bit grim but there's some pretty countryside. Judy would prefer it in town, but her mother is an invalid and we look after her.'

They drove on and Holland gave a bare outline of the reason they were on Patterson's patch. After a time he leaned forward: 'Take this turning on the right and follow the lane all the way up the hill, until you come to a wood, then take the first turning on your left.'

'Is there a field by the Webbs' cottage, where horses graze?' Greaves asked.

'That's right, sir,' Patterson replied. 'Mr Leighton, the big landowner around here, keeps his three hunters in the meadow. Do you know it?'

'No, just a guess,' Greaves replied, keeping his eyes on the road ahead.

The cottage lay on the side of the hill where the wood gave way to pasture enclosed by thick hedgerows. It was a remote spot, peaceful in the gentle rain that continued to fall.

'Stop here,' Greaves instructed, when they saw a red BMW parked in front of the cottage. Holland noticed that the driver's door had been left open.

'Watch where you walk,' Greaves said as they got out of the car. Holland looked down at the muddy pathway.

'Follow me and tread in my footsteps,' Greaves said. He led them through the long undisturbed grass at the verge and then on to the gravel where the BMW was parked.

'Oh, Christ,' Sergeant Patterson said quietly when they drew level with the open door of the car.

The body of a young man sat in the front seat with a shotgun jammed between his knees. His right hand was covered in dried blood. Greaves noticed that it had congealed around the strap of his wrist-watch. The blast of the gun in his open mouth had blown away the back of his head.

'Do you know him?' Greaves asked.

Patterson nodded. 'Chris Webb. His parents live here.'

Still walking carefully, they entered the cottage. The bodies of Colonel and Mrs Webb lay amid the chaos of the little living room. Like the house in Mornington Crescent, Hanger Cottage had been ransacked. There was another message written in blood on the whitewashed wall by the fireplace:

THEY HID THE TRUTH. NO ONE LOVES ME.

'What would you say happened here, Sergeant Patterson?' Greaves asked in almost a conversational tone, after they had checked the bodies for any sign of life.

Patterson looked at Greaves, who still stared at the message smeared on the wall.

'It seems as if Chris Webb was looking for something his parents hid from him,' he answered. 'Then, when he couldn't find where it was, he killed them both. It looks as if he wrote that message on the wall and then turned the gun on himself.'

Greaves continued to study the words next to the fireplace. 'See if the telephone works,' he said mildly. Holland did as he was told.

'It does, sir,' he replied after a moment's examination. 'It was only pulled from its socket.'

'You know what to do,' Greaves said. 'I'm just going outside for a bit.'

He walked to the back of the property, across the wet lawn to a wooden gate that separated the cottage's garden from the meadow. At his approach, three horses, a chestnut and two bays,

102

snuffled towards him. Greaves held out the apples he had taken from a bowl in the kitchen and the horses edged closer.

When they had taken the gift, Greaves looked up towards the clustered trees: ''Twould blow like this through holt and hanger When Uricon the city stood: 'Tis the old wind in the old anger, But then it threshed another wood,' he quoted softly to the nuzzling bay that searched his hand for more tit-bits.

'And who may you be?' a commanding voice suddenly called out, and Greaves looked towards a tall figure who strode towards him along the line of the hedgerow. The upright old man was dressed in a waxed shooting coat; an Irish setter nosed ahead of him. Greaves also saw that he carried a small-bore shotgun in the crook of his arm.

'Police, eh?' Gerald Leighton said when he had examined Greaves's identification and introduced himself. 'What's going on?'

'I'm afraid there has been a tragedy here, sir,' Greaves explained. 'The Webb family have all been killed.'

'Killed?' the old man said, but there was less shock in his voice than was usual from members of the public. Greaves guessed that sudden death had not been unfamiliar to him in the past.

'How did it happen?' the old man asked. 'It doesn't seem possible.'

'Did you know them well, sir?' Greaves answered, avoiding the man's question.

'Of course I did,' Leighton said sharply. 'They were very old friends of mine. Vivian Webb and I soldiered together.' He shook his head in disbelief. 'We were going shooting, this morning.'

'Just you and the colonel?'

'No,' Leighton answered. 'Christopher was taking a day off from the City. He was coming too.'

'What were you going to shoot?'

103

The old man looked at him in bewilderment for a second. 'Pigeons. Why?'

When Gerald Leighton had departed, Greaves walked back across the lawn and saw that Holland had come out to stand beneath the glass-roofed shelter of a patio at the rear of the cottage.

'What do you think, sir?' he asked.

'Christopher Webb didn't kill anyone, it was definitely someone else,' Greaves replied. He waved towards the figure of Gerald Leighton, who was now halfway across the meadow.

'And he confirmed it for me.'

'How?'

Greaves reached up and brushed his hand along a branch of wistaria that grew against the wall of the cottage. 'Yesterday afternoon, Christopher Webb bought a box of four ten cartridges from a gunsmith in the City. I saw the bill in his gun cabinet. But there was also a 12-bore pump-action shotgun in his collection. The ammunition for that was out of sight. If he were going to commit mass murder, a man familiar with guns would have chosen the Winchester.' Greaves broke a leaf from the wistaria and examined it for a moment before he continued.

'No – Webb intended to go pigeon-shooting today, not kill his girlfriend and parents. The people who did it grabbed the first gun and ammunition they came to. Webb would have known where the ammunition for the Winchester was.'

He touched Holland on the shoulder. 'Stay here, Nick, and make sure they go over everything carefully, I'll see you back in town.'

'OK, sir. Everyone is on their way, it shouldn't take long. Oh, before you go, there's something Clive wants to tell you.'

'Yes, sergeant,' Greaves said, looking at the young man keenly when he joined them on the patio.

'It's just about Chris Webb, sir,' he said hesitantly. 'There's something wrong about him writing that stuff on the wall.'

'That's because he was left-handed,' Greaves said.

'That's right, sir,' Patterson said, surprised. 'I've played cricket with him in the village team, but how did you know?'

'He wears his watch on his right wrist,' Greaves answered.

'Someone else put his hand in his parents' wounds and guided his hand on the wall.'

Holland had been optimistic when he said the work involved would not take long. The Hertfordshire police did a thorough job on the cottage, determined to show the man from Scotland Yard that they were not country bumpkins. In the early afternoon a television crew turned up and a photographer and reporter from the local paper. Holland kept out of their way: he did not want to signal that it was anything other than a local story. Every inch of the grounds was combed, and the whole cottage dusted for prints. The killers had been highly professional. There was nothing to mark their presence, except a small section of tyre imprint in the muddy drive, which a detective constable spotted just as it was growing dark.

'The Webbs drove a little Ford,' Patterson confirmed. 'It's in the garage.'

The examining officer crouched beside the impression and said, 'Well, I'll bet a pound to a pinch of shit that this was made by a Jaguar, and a big bugger at that.'

'When will you be sure?' Holland asked.

'In a couple of hours. Where will you be?'

Holland looked up at the darkening sky. 'It depends how long it takes me to get back to London. What's the train service like?'

'Tell you what,' Patterson suggested. 'Why don't you stay over with us? They can ring you at my place.'

'No, I don't want to put you to that trouble, Clive,' Holland said.

'It's no trouble, Judy will enjoy the company. We can have supper and sit up over a few jars.'

Holland went back to the cottage and rang Greaves. 'There's a possible tyre print, sir,' he said. 'But it's going to take a while to confirm the make. Do you mind if I stay up here for the night? Sergeant Patterson has offered to put me up.'

Greaves looked down at the pad before him where he had been making notes. 'No,' he replied. 'There's nothing developing this end. The Doyles have a solid alibi for their movements last night. They were at the opening of a new restaurant in Soho. It even seems genuine.'

'They're a bit like that cat in the poem,' Holland replied. 'The one who's always somewhere else when anything happens.'

'I didn't know you were a T.S. Eliot fan, Nick,' Greaves answered.

'I can't say I am, really. He's a bit obscure for my taste. It was strange about that field with the horses – and the stuff about the gun. You couldn't call it coincidence, could you?'

'Not really,' Greaves agreed. 'But if the spirit world is trying to communicate with me I wish they'd just ring instead of taking complicated detours through Doreen Clay.'

Holland laughed. 'Ours not to reason why ... '

Greaves sighed. 'The actual quotation is: "Theirs not to reason why",' he answered.

'I didn't care for Tennyson either, sir. See you in the morning.'

Greaves smiled when he hung up. He was deeply fond of Nick Holland; one day soon he must try to tell him so.

A squad car dropped them back in the village. Judy Patterson was in the kitchen when they entered the house. She was wearing a dress now and her dark hair was loose about her face.

'I see you've tarted yourself up,' Clive said. Holland noticed that they had kissed more warmly than most married couples.

106

'I thought we might have guests so I bought two bottles of wine as well. You've been a long time, what's up?'

He told her about the Webbs and Holland could see that she was genuinely upset; this wasn't some senseless tragedy that appeared on the six o'clock news. To Judy Patterson it was about her neighbours.

Patterson took a can of lager from the refrigerator and held it up to Holland, who nodded. They walked into the living room with their drinks and sat down in easy chairs each side of a log fire, which crackled cosily and threw a pleasing light over the room.

'Anyone want me while I was out?' Clive called to Judy.

'Mrs Lawrence,' she replied. 'She says is it all right to do the kids' road safety lecture next Wednesday?'

Clive raised his beer to Holland. 'You can see how high the stress factor is around here.'

'Oh, and your sister rang,' Judy said. 'She sends her love.'

'What did she want?'

'She wondered if she'd left a blue sweater here last time she stayed.'

'And did she?'

'Yes,' Judy replied, appearing at the doorway. 'Funny that, because I was thinking about her after you'd gone and she suddenly rang.'

'That often happens in our family,' Clive said as Judy appeared again, carrying two plates. 'Get to the table,' she ordered.

'Now you'll see why I married her,' Clive said with a wink.

'Where's your mother-in-law?' Holland asked when they were seated.

Patterson pointed to the ceiling with a fork. 'Bedridden,' he replied, and reached out to pour some wine.

'I could drop that sweater off for you,' Holland suggested when Judy joined them.

'Well, if it's no bother,' she replied, 'it'll save making up a parcel.'

After supper they sat by the fire and the men talked of their days of glory on the rugby field until Judy announced she was going to bed and leaving them to it. The telephone rang as she was kissing Patterson good-night.

It was the call Holland was expecting about the tyre impression. 'It was a Jaguar,' Patterson said, 'and one of the big buggers, just as the lad thought.'

He poured them another beer. 'It must have cost them a packet in petrol to get up here, those things only do a few miles to the gallon.'

Patterson's words triggered the same thought in both their minds. He snapped his fingers as Holland sat upright in the easy chair.

'It's worth a try,' Holland said quickly.

'What's worth a try?' Judy asked, curiosity about the call preventing her from going to bed.

'A visit to the garage on the way to the motorway,' Clive answered.

'Oh,' she said wearily, 'I thought you were still talking about rugby.'

The girl sat enclosed in the floodlit glass booth of the garage, on a lonely stretch of the arterial road out of Weyden. When she unlocked the door the sound from her cassette player pounded rock music over the wet countryside.

'Were you on duty last night?' Holland asked, his voice loud to rise above the sound of the music. The girl nodded.

'Did you happen to serve a big Jaguar at any time?'

She nodded again. 'Yes, there were three men in it.'

'Did you notice anything about the men?'

The girl turned off her cassette. 'Not really.' She thought for a moment. 'He was old, forty-odd and he had a funny accent, not from around here. He bought a lot of petrol. The car must have been nearly empty.'

'How did he pay?' Holland held his breath while she thought.

'By credit card,' she said eventually.

'Do you still have the docket here?'

'Oh, yes,' she replied, 'we hardly do any cash business so they only bother to collect twice a week.'

She sorted through her receipts and produced the counterfoil.

'That's it,' she said.

'Are you absolutely sure?' Holland asked.

'Certain,' she replied, 'I remembered the amount of money. It only costs a tenner to fill my car.'

Holland looked at the girl with a wide smile of appreciation. She was thickset and dark, with hair cropped close to her head, not his type at all, but he still wanted to lean forward and kiss her.

CHAPTER
SIX

Wednesday, October 28 10.25 p.m.

George Conway stood at the back bench, looking over Frank Corby's shoulder, and read aloud the main headline on the proof of page one that he was studying: 'HORROR AT HANGER COTTAGE.'

Corby glanced around at him with a frown of annoyance. 'The copy's a bit bloody thin on this one,' he said in a carping tone. 'And we had to take the picture from the television screen.'

'Tell that to our revered chairman,' George replied briskly. He was in no mood to put up with complaints from Corby, whom he considered to be of severely limited talent. In fact, George had been known to refer to Corby as a 'reputation burglar' and there was no greater transgression for an executive in George's eyes.

'What does the sodding chairman have to do with it?' Corby continued, pushing his luck. 'The news desk is in charge of getting stories.'

'He instigated the budget cuts that caused us to sack all the district reporters,' a new voice said. 'We were lucky to catch up on this one at all. Good work, George, by the way – any sign of Cat Abbot?'

It was Brian Meadows speaking. He had come up on Corby's blind side to reach out and pick up the proof of page one.

'Not yet, Brian, but we're still trying.'

'Good,' he said in a preoccupied voice. Corby shot a re-proachful glance at Conway, who was smiling as he picked up a selection of pictures from the desk. They showed the scenes of police activity at Hanger Cottage that afternoon.

'No, no,' Meadows said quietly as he read the picture caption. 'The word "hanger" in this context has nothing to do with hanging people, it denotes a wood on the side of a hill.' He handed the proof to Corby. 'Put that right next time.' Then he looked up at the newsroom clock. 'I'm just on my way out for a while. I'm not sure of my movements, I'll give you a ring later.' Smiling again at George, he turned and walked swiftly away.

'Christ, I wish he wouldn't creep up on me like that,' Corby said. 'I could have been talking about him.'

'Did you say these were taken from the television screen?' George asked, still holding the batch of pictures.

'That's right,' Corby answered, and began to make the editor's correction on the page-one proof.

'They're very good quality,' George said. 'Why don't they have those lines on them like you usually get?'

'It's done with a new piece of equipment, computer enhance-ment or something. Like they do with the pictures from outer space.'

'How does it work?'

'How the fuck should I know,' Corby replied irritably. 'I don't even understand how a television works.'

George continued to browse through the photographs. Sud-denly he stopped to study one of the figures in the background.

112

He walked over to the picture desk and held it under a large magnifying glass that was mounted at a work station. After further examination, he looked up and saw that Sarah was still at her desk. He moved towards her just as she was banging down her telephone.

'That's it, George,' she said wearily as he approached. 'It's nearly eleven o'clock and Cat Abbot is nowhere to be found. I'm going home.'

'Have you tried his own place?'

'Constantly. The opposition have been doorstepping it all day. As I told you, no sign.'

'Take a look at this,' he said, holding out the picture. Sarah gave it a cursory glance. 'I saw that on television.'

'This figure here,' Conway persisted. 'Isn't that Sergeant Holland, the one who works with Colin Greaves?'

Sarah looked longer at the grainy picture. 'It could be,' she said finally.

'What the hell is he doing out in the sticks?' Conway said and walked back to the news desk.

'Have we got any more copy on the Weyden murders?' he asked Sinclair, who was working as an assistant.

'A bit. There's agency stuff coming in now.'

'Does it say what the family were shot with? There were no details earlier.'

Sinclair called the copy up on his terminal and after a short search read: 'A police spokesman said: the murders were committed with a small-gauge shotgun ... '

George massaged his broken nose with thumb and forefinger. 'So was the one at Caulfield Terrace. What's Greaves up to?' he said softly. He turned to look towards the reporters' desks, but Sarah had already gone.

Wednesday, October 28 10.35 p.m.

Greaves was asleep. But his dream was as vivid as any reality. His wife and children waved from a small boat that sailed gently on a sea dancing with light. He called out to them, but no sound came, and on the horizon he could see dark storm clouds rolling closer. The telephone's ring jerked him awake. He sat blinking in his office, where he had stretched out in an easy chair for a few minutes to read his letters. The image of his wife and children remained for a moment, and the familiar feeling of panic, then he remembered that his dream was part of a past life; his children were dead and his wife married to another man in another country. Rubbing his aching eyes, he lifted the receiver and listened while Nick Holland told him of his success at the garage.

'Andrew Muir of Belfast,' he repeated, when Holland had told him the address on the credit card counterfoil. 'Good work, and thank Patterson.' He looked at his watch. 'We won't be able to do anything more tonight, I'll see you here in the morning.'

He looked down at the wad of unopened letters and decided to read them at home. Greaves never carried a briefcase, so he stuffed the assortment of mail into a large brown envelope, rang down for a car and left the building.

The journey to Hampstead irritated him; the cross-town traffic was heavy, even at this time of night, and slowed by the rain. When the driver dropped him he paused for a while to look over his Riley, which was parked in the roadway outside Sarah's house. He hated leaving it out in this weather. It should be in a garage covered with a dustsheet, he told himself. A few more months' constant exposure to the elements and the chrome and bodywork would begin to suffer. As he walked along the garden path he saw that Emily and her boyfriend, Ric Daggert, stood in the dark recess of the unlit porch.

'Good evening, Mr Greaves,' Ric called out as he walked towards them.

'You two look like waifs sheltering from the storm,' he replied.

'We're sheltering from those two idiots in there,' Emily said. 'They're playing some awful game. It's been driving us crazy. Please make them stop, Colin.'

Greaves was surprised by the request. It was the first time he had been asked to exert any kind of authority in Sarah's family and he found it curiously pleasing.

'What kind of game are they playing?' he asked.

'I don't know,' Emily replied, 'but it's maddening.'

'Oh, by the way, Mr Greaves,' Ric interjected, 'my dad says you can park your car in our garage if you like. There's plenty of room.'

Greaves felt his spirits lift another notch. He looked at the youth, making up his mind about something, and then came to a decision. 'Can you drive, Ric?' he asked.

'Yes, sir. I passed the test two months after my birthday.'

Greaves reached into his pocket and produced a set of keys. 'How would you like to take her there now? … I can't bear to see her in the rain any longer.'

'Me drive it?' the youth answered, in a tone that suggested Greaves had just offered him a prize beyond the dreams of avarice.

Greaves nodded. 'You know how to use a car with a clutch, I take it?'

'Oh, yes,' Ric replied.

'I'll come with you,' Emily said quickly.

'How will you get back?' Greaves asked her.

'I'll bring her,' Ric said.

'Won't that defeat the idea of driving home? It's raining.'

'I'll take a mac,' Emily said.

Greaves watched them pull away with a moment of misgiving and then entered the house. There was a strange silence considering the twins were about. When he tried to open the living-room door it wouldn't budge and he could hear the sound of suppressed giggling.

'What's going on?' he called out.

'Knock, knock,' a voice called out, 'now you say: who's there.'

'Who's there?'

'Cath.'

'Cath who?'

'Cath O'Dray, the Irish television star.'

Greaves tried the door once more and the voice shouted 'Knock, knock!'

'Who's there?' Greaves said, remembering his part.

'Lindsey,' the voice replied.

'Lindsey who?'

'Lindsey Doyle, the Irish cricketer.'

Greaves had to force his laugh. He didn't associate the name of Doyle with anything humorous. The boys let him pass the door and the dog wagged his tail in greeting. The room looked as if a party of drunken sailors had used it for a dance.

'Didn't Mrs Page come today?' Greaves asked.

'Yes,' Martin answered. 'She left a note for Mum in the kitchen. Something about needing another mop head.'

Greaves looked around at the chaos. 'I'll give you a pound each if you tidy up before Sarah gets home,' he said, knowing it was a poor solution. Really he ought to insist that they clear up their own mess. But the bribe worked.

'I bet you didn't have to do housework when you were at school, Colin,' Paul said when they had set about the task.

'I didn't live in a house,' Greaves answered. 'Anyway you're wrong. They still had fagging in my day. I had to make beds, dust, prepare tea. And suffer the lash if it wasn't done to my housemaster's satisfaction.'

'Did you like your schooldays?' Martin asked.

116

'Yes, I think so, on the whole,' Greaves replied after a moment of reflection.

'Aren't you sure?'

He sat on the sofa, still in his raincoat, and thought again. 'You can't always be certain about the past when you get to my age,' he said after a time. 'Sometimes the unhappiest memories fade away and you're just left with the good days, so you imagine you were enjoying yourself, but when you think deeper you realise things were really pretty awful.'

'So you weren't happy?'

'About half and half, I suppose. That's not so bad an average.'

'So you didn't use to sob into your pillow at night?' Martin asked. 'You toughed it out?'

Greaves nodded. 'Boarding school is all right for some. I didn't mind it – others suffered a bit more. It depends on the individual. I was lucky – my school work was passable, and I was good at cricket.'

'Did you know of anyone who had a really bad time?' Martin asked.

'Yes, when I was up at Oxford I made friends with a boy who was a year older than me. We'd been at the same school but he was in another house so we'd never really known each other. When we discussed it, he told me he'd hated every day. But I didn't recognise the place he described at all. It was as though we'd existed on different planets.'

'That's pretty much what it's like for us and Emily,' Martin said. 'She loves school, it's sickening.'

'I think I'd like boarding school,' Paul said.

'Me too,' Martin added.

'You'd like to go?' Greaves asked, incredulous that any child would want to leave home, given the choice.

'Yes,' Paul said. 'It sounds like a laugh. And they've stopped fagging now.'

Martin made an exaggerated coughing noise. 'Talking about

fagging, how's that?' he said, sweeping his hand around the tidied room, and bringing it to a stop, palm up under Greaves's nose.

He fumbled for the coins, and then flipped them in the air. Both twins took their bribe like trout rising for a fly.

'I'm turning in,' Greaves said. 'Before the day costs me any more. You go up too, your mother will skin you for being up this late.'

He made his way upstairs and walked to the far end of the L-shaped corridor, to where he and Sarah had made their new quarters. When he had moved in, he had insisted that they buy a new bed and sleep in a different room from the one Sarah had shared during her first marriage. It was also necessary to have his own telephone line; and he had brought a few pieces of furniture from his previous home: a desk; a reading lamp; three landscapes, painted by his grandfather who had been an accomplished artist; a brass-bound military chest and a leather sofa. Luckily the room was large, but sometimes he felt he had started life anew in a bedsit.

He showered quickly, then sat in his dressing gown before an electric fire. He had just begun to open his letters when he heard Sarah calling she was home. A few minutes later she flopped down on the sofa next to him. 'How are you?' she asked after a fleeting kiss of greeting.

'Never better,' he replied, preoccupied with his mail.

'Can I get you anything, some food?'

He shook his head. 'No thanks, I had a sandwich earlier.'

'Me too. I think I'd like a drink, though.'

Greaves looked up. 'In that case, I'll have a large brandy, if you're going downstairs again.'

She took longer than he'd expected. When she returned with the drinks she sat next to him and said, 'There's something I want to raise with you, when you have a moment.'

'And I with you,' he replied, holding the last item of mail. It was a lavender-coloured letter that didn't bear a stamp.

'What would you think of us buying a weekend place,' she began, 'somewhere on the river?'

He thought for quite a while. 'Sounds all right to me,' he said finally. 'What would you think about the boys going away to school?'

Sarah put down her glass and stared at the electric bars of the fire. 'You want to send Martin and Paul to boarding school?' she said softly, but he could hear dangerous undercurrents in her voice.

'I don't want to send them,' he said hastily. 'They just told me they wanted to go.'

Sarah's hostility was instantly translated into guilt. Am I such a poor mother my children want to leave home? she asked herself. Or was it bringing another man into the house? Someone, they imagined, who had replaced them in her affections.

Greaves watched as she got up quickly and walked along the corridor to the boys' room. She had left the door open, so he could hear the mutter of distant conversation. When she returned, she picked up her drink and sat beside him again.

'Well?' he said.

Sarah sipped a little more of her wine. 'They said they wouldn't mind going if it was in Hampstead and the dog could go too.'

Greaves laughed, and as he opened his last letter three Polaroid snapshots slid from the envelope and into his lap. Two of them showed an adolescent girl in a leotard, the third was a portrait of the same girl. The features looked familiar: it was an almost exact image of the face Berkley had reconstructed on the magic paintbox.

Silently, he passed the pictures to Sarah and took the accompanying letter from the envelope.

The sheet of paper had a printed heading: The Fairway School of Dance and Drama, 19 Hope Parade, Acton W3. It was dated the same day. Greaves began to read it aloud: 'Dear

Superintendent Greaves, I saw from this morning's paper you are in charge of the search for the murdered girl. Enclosed are some pictures of one of my ex-pupils, Polly Weaver. Polly left us the summer before last. I know her mother returned to the West Indies, Jamaica, I believe, and I understood, at the time, that Polly had gone with her, but her picture is so like the one in the newspaper, I felt it was my duty to send it to you. Yours sincerely, Georgina Hemp. Headmistress.'

'That sounds like a break,' Sarah said. 'I wish my luck would turn.'

'What's the problem?' Greaves asked.

Sarah began to undress. 'I can't find Cat Abbot,' she said ruefully. 'It's almost humiliating.'

Wednesday, October 28 11.45 p.m.

The band played 'Dancing in the Dark' and Cat Abbot buried his face in Doreen Clay's fragrant hair as he guided her around the dance floor in the restaurant of the Savoy Hotel. At their table, an attentive waiter had poured the champagne, and the music was soothingly romantic. The only slight note of discord about the entire affair was Doreen's firm insistence on separate rooms, otherwise he was in a time warp of contentment.

'Are you sure your office will pay for all this, Raymond?' she asked when the music came to an end and they crossed the floor to sit once again. The previous night, when he had booked them into the hotel, Cat had explained that it was necessary to take refuge at the Savoy because her house in Paignton Street would be under siege as soon as the rest of Fleet Street saw his story in the *Gazette*. A statement that had been confirmed by the early news broadcasts. Throughout the day, although they had not stirred from the premises, he had lavished attention on her. The services of a hairdresser and a manicurist had been commanded, flowers delivered, and Cat had shown her how to send for all the toilet and make-up articles she had required. At his insistence, she had ordered practically a new wardrobe from the hotel's shops, but she wasn't an acquisitive person, and the sudden lavish and unaccustomed lifestyle had caused her more concern than comfort. Still, she couldn't resist a certain wide-brimmed hat.

'Of course I'm sure,' he assured her, while he sipped some of the champagne contentedly. 'We do this all the time with big stories.'

'I can hardly believe all this is happening,' Doreen said. 'The only posh thing I've ever done before was go to a dinner and dance held by Freemasons in Cardiff.'

'Get used to it,' Cat said grandly. 'This is only the beginning. With me handling you, it'll be stardust all the way.'

'Do you really enjoy this sort of life?' she said uncertainly.

'How do you mean?'

Doreen glanced at her bare shoulders for a moment as if she expected to find something had settled on them. 'Champagne, servants bringing you everything. You know what I mean, never having to lift a hand for yourself.'

'Doesn't everybody?' Cat answered, and he gestured around the room. 'You don't see many unhappy faces in here.'

'But are you happy?'

'I've never been happier in my life,' he answered, but as he uttered the words, he saw a stocky figure standing up at a table on the far side of the dance floor and gesturing to Cat that he should follow him from the restaurant. It was Brian Meadows; seated at the table from which he had risen was a striking blonde who looked vaguely familiar to Cat. Murmuring an excuse about the bathroom, he reluctantly complied with the editor's signal.

They walked in silence to the foyer of the hotel and Cat looked longingly at the revolving door. A few more paces and he could

121

be free; out into the night, the surly bonds of responsibility cut once more. And if he kept running …

Brian Meadows had taken a large cigar from a handsome leather case. He said nothing while he carefully trimmed the end and made sure it lighted to his satisfaction.

'Now, Mr Abbot,' he said in a pleasant enough voice, 'will you tell me just where the bloody hell you've been all day?' Although Meadows spoke gently enough, the real threat was in the use of 'Mr Abbot'. Cat had known Meadows for many years, since the editor had been a reporter on one of the quality papers, and usually they were on first-name terms – on the rare occasions when they spoke to each other these days.

'Thank Christ I've bumped into you, Brian,' he answered. Cat had no idea what he was going to say, he simply allowed his brain to slip into automatic pilot. 'I've been looking for an opportunity to contact the office all day. Do you know, this is the first time she's let me out of her sight.'

'I take it you're referring to Doreen Clay, if that is Doreen Clay seated at your table?' Meadows asked. As Cat watched the drifting curls of blue smoke from the cigar that now seemed to bind them together, suddenly he was inspired. 'That's right,' he answered. 'I've spent the entire day trying to persuade her she should tell the *Gazette* her story – but she just doesn't want to know. Says she couldn't stand the publicity, she just wants a quiet life, doing what she's always done. She seems to have become obsessed by me. She really is the most extraordinary woman. Normal as your average housewife to talk to one minute – but a mass of neurosis when you get to know her. Every time I tried to use the telephone she threatened to walk out. Finally she agreed to come down here tonight. I think I've just about persuaded her to give us her story. But I'm still not sure.'

As he spoke, Abbot could feel all his grandiose plans slip away. Since last night, he had been dreaming of signing Doreen up under his own personal management. Then holding an auction for the world rights to her story. Visions of global television deals, book contracts and lucrative personal appearances had raced through his head. But one brush with authority had brought him to heel. Meadows nodded at Abbot's ramblings; it sounded convincing enough to him. He was deeply familiar with the reluctance shown by most members of the British public when they were dealing with newspapers.

'How much have you offered her?'

Cat held out his arms. 'She doesn't want money. She says she just wants things to be like they were before the story.'

'Do you think you might be able to sway her?'

Cat's mind was an empty vessel. A thought – which did not seem his own – filled it. 'I think a woman might help, someone she could trust,' he said.

Meadows was pleased. It had been his idea to use Sarah Keane on the story; now his instincts appeared to be confirmed. He took another pull on the cigar and smiled. 'I agree, Cat.' His manner was one of a fellow conspirator. 'What name are you using here?'

'Henry Higgins.'

Meadows smiled again, 'And I suppose she's Miss Doolittle?'

'No, Pickering, actually.'

'Excellent.' Meadows put his arm on Cat's shoulder. 'Tell me, would Miss Clay mind if I introduced my companion?'

'I don't think so, but she is a bit shy.'

'You do know who she is, my guest,' Meadows said as they returned to the restaurant.

'Of course,' Cat replied, although he still hadn't the slightest notion.

'Bring her over,' Meadows said when they parted at the dance floor.

Cat sat at his table once more and leaned towards Doreen. 'I've just bumped into my editor. He wants to meet you.'

Doreen looked across the floor and saw Meadows raise a hand in acknowledgement.

'Oh, he's with Geraldine Miller,' she replied. 'I like her.'

'Geraldine Miller,' Cat repeated with momentary interest, then, 'Oh, there's just one thing. I told him you don't want to do any articles. I said you're not interested in publicity.'

'That's right,' Doreen answered. 'I'm not.'

'You're not?' Cat said in sudden panic. All the time he had been plotting the various ways he could best exploit Doreen to his advantage, it hadn't occurred to him to consult her about his plans.

'No,' she said. 'If you try to use the Gift for your own advantage it turns against you. I'm happy as I am.'

Cat now felt as though he were riding on the crest of a tidal wave. At some point it might dash him on a rocky shore but for the moment his head was still just above water.

'Come on,' he said, 'let's go and drink their champagne.'

Geraldine Miller was a rational, intelligent woman with an impressive degree from Oxford University – and she was entirely captivated by the supposed powers of Doreen Clay. As soon as they were introduced, she insisted on altering her seat so they sat side by side and immediately plunged into a conversation that the two men could not overhear. It was evident that the two women had established an instant rapport.

Sisters under the skin, Meadows thought as he watched their heads inclined towards each other. No doubt discussing the old mysteries women had shared in ancient times. He allowed himself a little smile. It was a relief to see that she had a weakness for this clairvoyant nonsense; it somehow made her seem more human, or was it vulnerable. Geraldine had proved a formidable companion, and the demands did not cease after the exhausting sexual encounters they had enjoyed in the last few days. Her mind was as honed as her body, and after several years of editing a newspaper he had become unused to having his opinions challenged – except by Sir Robert, and he didn't count that.

Constantly boasting that he was self-educated, the chairman did not really have a grasp on any subject, merely a set of prejudices that he had acquired, like the social graces of others that he had imitated over the years.

The band leader announced an interval from the music and it was easier for Meadows to hear the women's conversation.

'So where did the gift come from?' Geraldine asked.

'My mam, and I suppose her mam too. They were well known in our village for helping people. One of my nieces has it a bit, she can find things.'

'And you never married?'

Doreen laughed. 'Yes I did, his name was Owen Jones, we kept a sweet shop and tobacconist's in Cardiff. Funny thing, when I was married to him, nothing ever used to happen at all. I was like a telephone that had been disconnected. The day he left me it all came back like the post piled up on the doorstep when you've been on holiday. That's why I call myself Miss. The least said about Owen the better.'

'Why did you come to London, Miss Clay?' Meadows asked.

'Have you ever been to Cardiff?' she replied with a smile.

'Yes, once for a day.'

'Well, there's your answer. If one day was enough for you, think what four years was like.'

Meadows realised she had a point. 'Cat tells me you aren't interested in earning any money with your gifts,' he continued.

'That's not quite right,' she said and the two men exchanged glances. 'Mind you, I already earn a bit of money, that's how I make a living. But if I was to try and make a fortune it would go away again ... or worse.'

There was a pause and after a thoughtful pull on his cigar, Meadows said, 'Supposing you donated your fee to charity?'

Doreen nodded. 'Yes, that would be all right,' she said happily. 'But I don't want to become too famous. Can I do it anonymously?'

'Well, your name is already known, but we don't have to reveal how you look.' He tapped his cigar in the ashtray. 'In fact, it could be rather effective.'

Geraldine looked at her watch and Meadows picked up the signal. 'Well, all good things must come to an end, I suppose. I think we'd better be going. It really has been delightful meeting you. I look forward to the first article, Miss Clay. We can discuss the details tomorrow and draw up a contract.' He signed the bill that had been skilfully presented and they said good-night.

'Nice to meet you,' Doreen said, 'and I look forward to working with the lady you're putting on the story.'

'Well, I thought she was wonderful,' Geraldine said in the car as they headed for Half Moon Street.

'She was charming, but I'm still not convinced,' Meadows replied. 'Still, it will make an excellent series for the paper and HAND will be glad of the money.' He laid his head back against the cool leather upholstery and suddenly remembered he had not mentioned Sarah Keane to Doreen. Abbot must have, he told himself, but had he told Abbot? He must have. He closed his eyes in an effort to catch a brief nap.

Thursday, October 29 12.16 a.m.

The bar of the public house in Kilburn High Street was packed with people. They were crammed four deep at the counters with barely room to move between the crowded tables, except for one corner, close to the door leading to the street, where Danny Doyle, his brother Fergus and two other men sat. Their backs were against the wall around one side of a circular marble-topped table. The atmosphere in the rest of the bar was warmed by the heat of so many bodies and thick with tobacco smoke. But near the Doyle table it seemed cooler. The two men who sat with Danny and Fergus were also brothers. Terence and Patrick Brady were both redheads; with lumpy muscular bodies, paper-white skin and slack-mouthed faces, they might have appeared comical were it not for their eyes – which had the dead, expressionless quality of sharks. The Bradys had known the Doyles every day of their lives: played in the same streets, gone to the same schools, fought the same enemies. They had known no other loyalty than the one demanded by Danny. That was sufficient for them.

On a small stage in the opposite corner the floodlit figure of a girl in a tight miniskirt urged the swaying crowd to join her in the last chorus of 'Fields of Arran Rye'. The other customers roared out the words and when the singing came to an end, the girl left the stage and wormed her way through the audience to stand at Doyle's table.

'Are you going to buy me a drink, Danny?' she asked. He inclined his head towards the bar. 'Tell Desmond to give you what you want.' The girl hesitated for a moment, but a jerk from his head sent her on her way.

No one spoke until Doyle said, 'So McNally got to her first?'

'That's right,' Fergus answered.

Doyle raised the glass of whiskey to his lips and took a long swallow of the burning liquid without taking his eyes from the singer, who now stood at the bar looking back at him.

'Do you think they got the package?'

Fergus shrugged. 'Who knows.'

'We fucking soon will,' Danny said flatly, 'if the organisation starts falling apart.'

'Let's go after them,' Fergus said in a sudden urgent voice. 'We can hit all the bastards in one go. There's only about half a dozen of them in London, we can wipe them out.'

Doyle shook his head. 'I don't want a war over here. Not if I can help it. A dead whore, that's one thing. Too many bodies and the shit'll hit the fan.'

A youth in a leather jacket and jeans pushed among the crowd holding out a collection box. 'For the lads and their families,' he chanted monotonously in a flat London accent. Everyone gave, but when he reached the Doyle table he veered away. Fergus reached out to hold his arm, and put a £20 note in the box. 'For the lads,' he said with a smile.

Danny glanced up as two young men entered the bar. Both wore raincoats and were laughing at a remark made in the street outside. Without pausing, they turned towards the corner where Doyle sat and started to raise their hands in unison. But Danny and Fergus had begun to move before the semi-automatic pistols they held were levelled to the firing position. Danny threw a glass in their direction, and for a vital split second the men flinched from their aim. It was time enough for the Doyle brothers. Heaving on the edge of the heavy marble table so that it crashed forward, at the same moment they snatched for their own guns that were taped beneath the surface.

The first of the intruders' shots was high: the 9mm round drilled a neat little hole in the engraved glass window above Danny Doyle's head. The second hit the marble table-top at an angle of fifteen degrees. It flattened the bullet and absorbed so much of the impact that after deflecting there was only enough force in the spent round to give a bruising blow to Terence Brady's shoulder.

Danny and Fergus were now also armed. Before the intruders could fire another round, Danny and Fergus had returned the fire. To the shocked spectators in the bar, their shots sounded as one.

Danny took the man to his left. His first round smashed into his target's sternum and the impact of bullet hitting bone threw the man backward to crash against the open doorway. The shot from Fergus's pistol passed through his opponent's throat, severing his spinal column and causing the man to collapse like a puppet parted from its strings. The bullet continued on its flight, gouging a deep furrow in the plastered wall before lodging in a mahogany window frame.

The two brothers did not hesitate. Pausing only momentarily to stoop at the bodies and to fire another round into each of their victims' heads, they walked quickly to the counter through the parting crowd. A flap in the bar was lifted and they vanished into the living quarters of the pub. Seconds later they were in an alleyway at the rear, where a Ford Escort was parked. They had reached the Finchley Road, at least a mile away, before Fergus spoke. 'Now shall we hit the bastards?' he muttered. Danny, who was driving, had stopped at a set of traffic lights. He shook his head. 'No,' he said slowly. 'Remember the old saying: Ladybird, ladybird fly away home, your house is on fire and your children will burn.' He turned and looked at his brother. 'We go for their families – in Belfast.'

CHAPTER
SEVEN

Thursday, October 29 2.44 a.m.

Greaves clicked awake as if someone had turned a switch in his head. The room was very warm and bathed in the glow from the electric fire which was still burning at full power. The sound of Sarah breathing came in gentle counterpoint to the ticking of the carriage clock on the old iron mantelpiece, which now began to softly chime the quarter-hour.

He knew it would be some time before he slept again. Raising himself on one elbow, he looked down at Sarah who lay naked, curled towards him, having kicked away the duvet. He got up and, after putting on his towelling robe, he switched off the fire and covered her. She turned and muttered in her sleep. The warmth of the room had made him thirsty. Soundless on the thick carpet, he eased open the door and padded along the corridor.

There was a dead-of-night stillness about the house as he

descended the staircase, but when he passed the living room a line of light reflected in the polished wooden floor of the hallway. Someone had left a lamp burning, he told himself. He opened the door but before he was fully into the room he heard the sound of movement, and was just in time to see Emily and Ric frantically disentangling themselves on the sofa. His embarrassment was tempered by relief when he noted they were rumpled, but both fully dressed.

'I'm so sorry,' he said apologetically. 'I just came down to make a cup of tea.' He closed the door quickly and moved on to the kitchen. Still feeling rather foolish, he sat at the pine table, waiting for the kettle to boil and a few minutes later he heard the front door click. Then Emily entered the room.

'Ric says good-night,' she said, and he could see from a sideways glance that she was fully composed.

'Sorry I disturbed you,' he replied. 'I didn't know you were still up.'

'That's all right, Colin,' she answered in a forgiving voice. 'I was glad of the interruption.'

The kettle began to boil and making a gesture for him to remain seated, she made two cups of tea and sat down at the table. 'Can't sleep?' she asked.

'That's right.'

Emily flicked her hair so that it fell over her shoulders. 'I have that trouble. It never seems to bother Mum. No matter what's happening, she can always sleep.'

'I've noticed.'

Emily raised the mug to her lips and then changed her mind and set it down again. He could see she wanted to say something. 'What's on your mind?' he asked gently.

She glanced up at him and smiled. She was such a pretty girl, he felt a sudden lurch in his stomach at the memory of his own lost daughter.

'Do you mind if I ask you a question?'

'Fire away.'

She looked down again and fiddled with the handle of the mug. 'Boys – ' she began almost reluctantly, 'do they always want to make love?'

He decided this needed a plain answer. 'Yes,' he replied firmly. 'Boys always want to make love.'

'Why?' She raised a hand. 'I mean, I have … well, feelings too. But Ric says I can't love him as much as I say if I won't … well, you know.'

Greaves now wished he was deeply asleep, or on Mars, anywhere but facing Emily at this moment. But he also knew it was necessary to answer her honestly. 'It's all to do with a man's nature,' he said carefully.

'Do you mean "mankind", or men alone?'

'Just men – we are different, you know, don't get equality mixed up with it.' He paused, attempting to marshal his thoughts. 'All human beings have drives that are programmed into us as part of our biological make-up. The sex drive is about the strongest, obviously, because that's how we perpetuate ourselves as a species. Some scientists say the need to keep the human race going is the explanation for all our actions – that all living things have similar programs.'

'Do you believe that?'

Greaves smiled. 'I think we're a bit different from viruses and chickweed.'

'But men and women have the same drive?'

'Up to a point, but there are other factors we've developed to hold those desires in check, so that we only release them at the appropriate time.'

'Religion, you mean?'

'Not exactly, although religions have often incorporated the ideas into their dogma.'

'Explain.'

'It's to do with the social contract.'

'I thought that was about politics.'

'Yes, but it goes deeper than that. When human beings began to live in tribes they evolved certain behaviour patterns that are fairly common all over the planet.'

'Such as?'

'Well, the idea of the family. And that concept became the basis of all civilisations. So when a young man desired a certain girl, he had to prove that he could provide for her before taking her from her family. Sex had to go hand in hand with responsibility. She in turn had to fulfil her part of the bargain. Together they owed a further loyalty to the tribe, which would protect them in times of trouble. Breaking the rules of the family offended the whole tribe. Hence the social contract.'

'So are you saying sex without responsibility is the end of civilisation?'

Greaves smiled. 'No, that's too simple. Mind you, it was true when people lived their entire lives in little communities. That's why the punishment for transgression was so severe. Nowadays – at least in this country – it's only considered a minor infringement.'

'But how about families? How can they survive if the husband and wife make love to anyone they fancy – or people have all the freedom they want?'

'I don't think they can. But in modern society, the need for a family has become separate from the desire for sex, and a lot of people don't think they go together any more.'

'But you do, don't you?'

Greaves drank some of his tea, which was now growing cold, before he answered. 'I'm old-fashioned – quite a lot of people still are.'

Emily stood up and suddenly leaned over to kiss him on the cheek. 'Thank you,' she said. 'I'm glad you don't think it's all coming to an end. Good-night.'

He sat for a time, wondering if his words had made any sense.

Then he touched his cheek where Emily had kissed him and thought for a moment of the Brent River estate, where people existed on the very edge of civilisation.

Thursday, October 29 10.33 a.m.

Brian Meadows was almost late for his morning conference. His deputy, Gordon Brooks, who was about to take the meeting, stood up hastily when Meadows entered the room. Moving from behind the desk, he took his customary seat on the sofa next to George Conway.

Instead of his usual greeting, Meadows nodded curtly for the conference to begin and Conway started to read out his news schedule. The first item was about the public house killings in Kilburn High Street.

'More murders,' Meadows interrupted grumpily. 'That's all we've had this week, murder after murder. The paper's getting to be like some tabloid rag in prohibition Chicago.'

'We only cover them, Brian, we don't commit them,' Conway said sourly. He had been in the office until after one in the morning and was feeling decidedly hungover.

'Of course we have to cover them,' Meadows replied irritably. 'But we don't have to relish them. Let's look for the brighter side of life as well.'

'Item number two,' Conway said grimly. 'This is brighter. A crowd was watching two penguins fucking at the zoo and a woman leaned forward so far over the pool to get a good view, she fell over the wall and broke her leg.'

Meadows did not join in the laughter. Instead he glanced down at his copy of the schedule and noticed that George had actually promoted this item from the bottom of his list. It was an old habit of news editors to leave their audience with a smile. George ran through the rest quickly, and the other department heads read their own schedules dead-pan, without further comment from the editor. Then they gathered round his desk to study the dummy of that day's edition.

Meadows skipped through it quickly and handed it back to Jimmy Bedford, the features editor. 'Leave a space for a big puff at the top of the page.'

'What for?' Bedford asked.

'I'll tell you in good time,' Meadows said shortly.

The executives exchanged glances: the editor's prevailing mood did not bode well for the rest of the day. He dismissed them with a nod, then called out: 'George, bring Sarah Keane in right away.'

George nodded and left the room in silence. Meadows got up from his chair and looked from the window into Gray's Inn Road. His present disposition matched the sullen light of the morning. His private line rang.

'Meadows,' he answered bleakly.

'I'm sorry, darling,' Geraldine Miller said quickly. 'It was a silly argument. Please say you forgive me.'

His spirits soared.

Peter Kerr was waiting for Conway when he reached the news desk. 'I need more help, George,' he said.

Conway nodded: Kerr didn't have to explain. He glanced towards the reporters' desks. 'Take Bradshaw and Prior, and ask Sarah to come and have a word with me.'

'Any sign of Abbot?' he asked when she stood beside him.

'Nothing,' she replied. 'I've tried everywhere I can think of – twice.'

'Well, we'd better go in and get a bollocking from Meadows, he wants to see us both.'

Sarah looked at him in surprise, George rarely swore. 'Bad night?'

'Actually it should have been good,' he said as they walked the length of the newsroom. 'We did a pretty fair job on the Kilburn shootings for the last edition. Not that the editor noticed.'

'Why don't you ever go home, George?' Sarah asked with sudden concern. She was deeply attached to Conway. 'Other news editors take nights off, you know.'

Conway grinned. 'I do it so that lovable little rascal, Alan Stiles, never gets a chance to shine,' he answered, naming his deputy, who was universally loathed in the office.

'Watch out,' he said before he knocked on Meadows's door, 'he's in a foul mood.'

'George – Sarah,' the editor said expansively when they entered the room. 'Good of you to drop in.'

'You sent for us, Brian,' Conway said cautiously.

'Of course I did. And you, Sarah. How are you getting on in your search for the elusive Mr Abbot?'

'Nothing, I'm afraid. The earth seems to have swallowed him up.'

'Really?' Meadows continued playfully. 'You should have come to me.'

'Well, it really isn't my place to bother you with the problem, Mr Meadows.' Sarah was at her most reserved, and bewildered by the editor's mood of bonhomie after George's warning.

'Call me Brian,'

'You know where he is, don't you?' George said quickly.

Meadows was lighting a cigar. 'Umm,' he replied between puffs. He leaned forward and buzzed his secretary. 'Jean, ask Mr Trottwood to come and see me, please.'

Still waiting expectantly, Sarah and George watched Meadows as he sat back in his chair and grinned at them: 'They're at the Savoy. I had a drink with Cat and Miss Clay last night.'

'The Savoy!' George exclaimed. 'I'll kill the weasel when I get my hands around his throat.'

Meadows shook his head. 'No, you mustn't blame Abbot, he's played the whole thing very well. It seems Miss Clay was deeply reluctant to have anything to do with the press. If it hadn't been for her attachment to Cat, we would never have got her story.'

'She's attached to Abbot?' Sarah asked incredulously.

'It seems so,' Meadows replied.

Sarah made no further comment; the thought of being attached to Cat was about as appealing as snagging one's clothes on a barbed-wire fence.

'You mean he's giving her one?' George asked with brutal candour.

A pained expression passed fleetingly over Meadows's face, and in that moment Sarah realised that for all his years in journalism, a prudish streak remained in the editor's make-up.

'Certainly not,' he replied. 'Separate bedrooms and all that sort of thing. Miss Clay appears to be a woman of moral rectitude. I suspect it's the Welsh background.'

'My first wife was Welsh,' George replied. 'She didn't have any moral rectitude.' There was a light knock and the elegant figure of Charles Trottwood, the *Gazette*'s chief lawyer, entered.

'Ah, Charlie,' Meadows said returning to his expansive mood. 'What a splendid suit. Tell me, where do you get your clothes made?'

'Corn and Hay, Savile Row,' he replied with a slight nod to Sarah and Conway.

'You must give me an introduction.'

'That won't be necessary, Brian. These days they'll drag you in off the street if you're passing.'

Meadows laid aside his cigar for a moment and laced his hands behind his head. 'I want you to draw up a contract for a

Miss Doreen Clay,' he began. 'It's for a series of articles she will write about her life and times. Got that?'

Trottwood nodded.

'Miss Clay will have all her expenses paid during the duration of the work in hand, but her fee of £15,000 will be donated to the HAND charity. Got that?'

'I think so,' Trottwood replied.

'Sarah will take it with her when she calls on Miss Clay later this morning. Got that?' Meadows now turned to Sarah. 'Incidentally, they're booked into the hotel under the names Higgins and Pickering, got that?'

'By George, she's got it!' Conway said quietly.

When they'd left the office, Sarah arranged to meet Trottwood later, then paused to have a brief conversation at the head of the newsroom with George.

'I thought you said he was in a bad mood?' she said.

George scratched his head and the motion caused even more of his shirt to billow from his waistband. 'I think he's going balmy,' he answered. 'I promise you, five minutes before he was acting as if he were Jehovah – and we were the population of Sodom and Gomorrah.'

'Well, he'd certainly changed by the time I got there. He even asked me to call him Brian!'

Just then, the swing doors that led from the stairwell opened and a slim, beautiful woman entered and stopped to look about her in a decidedly imperious manner. Sarah thought she must be in her late thirties and noted the expensive scent, and jewellery that matched her clothes.

'Where am I?' the woman loudly demanded of George, in a tone of voice that expected cowed obedience.

He looked at her coldly and replied, 'Are you speaking philosophically, or is it a matter of geography?'

'I don't understand what you mean,' she said. 'Are you attempting to be impertinent?'

'I mean are you questioning your place in the greater context of creation, or are you merely lost, and unable to ask directions in a civil manner?'

'I am Lady Amanda Hall, and who are you? I wish to report your behaviour to my husband.'

Sarah swiftly stood between the two of them and said, 'You must have got off at the wrong floor, Lady Amanda, please allow me to show you the way.' She pushed open the doors again, and the woman followed her on to the landing.

'Who was that appalling man?' she demanded. 'I intend to have him dismissed immediately.'

Sarah banged the button on the lifts and then turned to her. 'His name is Walter Burns, Lady Amanda. I must apologise for his rudeness. We have to employ him, you see. It's government regulations.'

'Why?'

Sarah prayed for the lift to appear. 'The Disabled Persons Act,' she improvised. 'Every company of our size must employ a certain percentage of disadvantaged personnel, otherwise we fail to qualify for the government grant.'

'And what was that creature's disability – terminal rudeness?'

Sarah lowered her voice. 'He's a registered manumationist.' Lady Amanda didn't understand the word, but it sounded unpleasant to her. In answer to Sarah's prayer, the lift arrived. She ushered Lady Amanda in and said, 'Sixth floor.'

'Walter Burns,' Lady Amanda repeated to herself as the doors closed.

The Honourable Anthony James Howard Glendowning poured the necessary amount of washing powder into the machine and then sat back on one of the plastic chairs provided while the various items began to revolve in the soapy water. The clothing was not his own. It belonged to a young girl they had taken into the hostel the night before. She was practically in a state of collapse, having spent the previous six weeks dossing in doorways and existing on a diet of dustbin scraps gleaned from the restaurants around King's Cross. He did not mind performing the menial task; his priorities had altered a great deal in the time he had been with HAND. In fact, Tony Glendowning had discovered some very old truths about the satisfaction to be earned from humbling oneself in a good cause.

Around him, the usual collection of humanity he found at the launderette conducted their lives without thought or interest in the heir to one of Britain's largest distilling fortunes. And that was just how he liked it. While he watched the spinning clothes he daydreamed of what he was going to do the day he got his hands on the money.

In his mind's eye, he saw visions of the farms, villages and workshops that his plans would bring about. Tony Glendowning had long ago abandoned the idea of distributing largesse like some pantomime prince scattering coins to the masses capering in his wake. His time with HAND had caused him to formulate another plan. It had first come to him as no more than an exercise to ease his mind when he was confronted by the misery and squalor of his nightly rounds. But gradually he had begun to believe that it could work in reality.

It started when he began to realise how important work was for people. Many of his own family didn't do a stroke; his uncles and cousins were perfectly happy pottering about the various estates Glendowning Malt Whisky had provided for them. It had never occurred to him that for most human beings, 'what I do' is a declaration of 'what I am'. A sort of binding that holds the personality together, something essential to an individual's self-regard. No job, no real existence. It was as simple as that. And that was why so many of the young people he had encountered in his work over the last couple of years had been without hope. Usually, after a time they would confess to him that their lives had no meaning. At first he thought they were talking in a spiritual context. Some, of course were naïve enough to believe that just escaping from their backgrounds would ensure a more desirable existence. But for many it was the deadening prospect of unemployment that ate into them like a cancer.

He had tried to talk to his father about it, but he had been scornful of their desires.

'It's only a few years ago they were all constantly on strike because they didn't want to work,' his father had replied crisply. 'It seems a bit late to complain now – after they've destroyed the industries that used to employ them.' It was about the last conversation they'd had; now intercourse was reduced to monosyllables.

Slowly, Tony learned that nearly all the ones who missed work in their lives came from families that had once earned their living in industries that had suddenly, in a generation, passed into mythology: spinning cloth, shipbuilding, coal mining, steel making. Clearly there was something bred into them that needed to be fed by work. An identifiable job that would again involve them in something coherent. Once this was fixed firmly in his mind, the solution seemed simple: he would reverse history. He had read that millions of acres of farming land were to be returned to nature because Europe was bulging at the seams with food.

Fine – with the Glendowning fortune he intended to build villages all over England and equip them with workshops, staffed with redundant craftsmen, who would teach their skills to the lost boys and girls who now haunted the streets of London.

'New Pioneering', he called the plan. It had worked in America and Australia, he told himself, why not in Britain? The part he enjoyed most of all was how much his father would hate the idea.

His mind still turning pleasurably, like the laundry in the washer, he watched as an old man vacated the seat next to him. The shambling figure had left a newspaper on the chair. Glendowning glanced down and recognised the face of Polly Weaver. He picked up the copy of the *Gazette* and saw that it was dated the day before. Examining the features more closely, he was now sure he knew the girl. There was a number to ring. He found a coin and went to the pay phone at the doorway.

At certain times, Tony knew how useful it was to have acquired the manners of his old school. 'Glendowning here,' he barked authoritatively when the call was answered. 'Put me through to the man in charge.'

There was a short pause and a respectful voice said, 'I'm sorry, sir, Superintendent Greaves has just gone out.'

Tony hung up and stuffed the page into the pocket of his overcoat before he returned to his washing.

Thursday, October 29 9.30 a.m.

From his armoured observation point overlooking a Protestant section in the ancient city of Belfast, Lance-Corporal Peter Tree scanned the narrow streets through powerful binoculars.

Private Graham Booth, who accompanied him and was rarely silent, said, 'Here, Corp, you're from Kilburn, aren't you?'

'That's right,' Tree replied, still watching.

'Did you hear about the shootings in the boozer last night?'

'Yeah, on the news.'

'Did you ever use that pub?'

'No, it's a Paddy pub.'

'Here, do you know the one about the Paddy who goes home from Kilburn to his village in the bogs?'

'Go on.'

'He goes to mass on Sunday morning and the priest says to him, "So, Michael, how are you getting on over there in England."'

Lance-Corporal Tree picked up a small red car in his binoculars and followed its slow journey along one of the narrow streets.

' "Oh, grand, Father," says Michael. "I live in a boarding house with a lot of decent Irish fellas, and every day I go to work on a building site in Waterloo with a lot of Irish fellas." '

The red car was now approaching a woman who was guiding a pushchair while another child toddled at her side. Tree couldn't tell if it was a boy or girl.

' "And in the evening, I go drinking in a nice pub with me same mates, and the place is run by a great fella called O'Reilly." And the priest says, "So tell me, Michael, what do you think of the English?" '

A hand threw something the size of a paperback book towards the walking woman, then the car accelerated away. Tree noted its number.

'And Michael says, "Sure, Father, we never talk to those black bastards." '

The sound of the explosion reached them as Private Booth spoke the word 'English'.

Thursday, October 29 11.00 a.m.

Although they drove west from Victoria, in the opposite

direction to the heavier traffic coming into London, it took Greaves and Holland nearly an hour to reach the network of narrow Victorian streets that lay between Bedford Park and South Acton. Earlier that morning they had visited the scene of the public house shootings. None of the officers present had been able to find a witness to the event, and so far there was no identification on the two bodies.

For most of their current journey, Holland had been attempting to speak to Belfast, with a sergeant in the Royal Ulster Constabulary who was telling him what he knew about Andrew Muir. It was a frustrating business; reception on the car telephone kept breaking up, so every few minutes Holland had to redial the number.

There was a sudden clarity on the line, and the RUC sergeant said: 'OK, we'll fax you a picture of him.' Another burst of static, and Holland waited in frustration for the line to clear. 'Well, here's a strange coincidence,' the sergeant said when he could speak again. 'We haven't heard anything of Muir for weeks, then you ring up about him and as we're talking one of the lads tells me Muir's daughter has just been killed by a bomb … hang on a minute.' There was a pause and then he came back on the line. 'Did you get that: Muir's daughter and two grandchildren, a boy and a girl.'

'When did it happen?' Holland asked.

'Just over an hour ago.'

Holland hung up. He did not have to repeat the sergeant's words, Greaves had heard the conversation quite clearly. 'I don't like coincidences,' Greaves said softly, as the car slowed to a halt.

It must have been a long time since Hope Parade lived up to its name, Greaves thought, as they scanned the dreary flight of shops that ended in a row of terraced houses to the right. To the left, detached form a dry-cleaner's, Number 19 stood rather grandly alone, apart from the parade. Nor did it bear any relationship to the terrace. It was a large detached corner house, lying well back from a sagging fence of rotting boards that was overhung with hawthorn and laurel bushes. A sign next to the gate proclaimed: THE FAIRWAY SCHOOL OF DANCE AND DRAMA.

When Graves and Holland walked up the pathway, they could hear youthful, tuneless voices, singing, 'I'd like to be in America, OK by me in America … '

The door was open at the top of a flight of stairs and they entered a wide hallway, their feet sounding on the bare, dust-impregnated boards. Despite the chipped paintwork and cracked plaster, there was feeling of life and vitality about the place. No matter what the surroundings, hope obviously still lived on in the Fairway School of Dance and Drama. Thankfully, the song came to an end, and a clear voice called out, 'Superintendent Graves, I presume.'

They looked towards the wide staircase and saw the youthful figure of a woman, dressed in a leotard, outlined against the tall window on the landing. She descended with the curious, waddling step ballet dancers use when they are not on points. When she stood before them, Graves could see that she was older than the impression given at his first glance. Early forties, he guessed, but still beautiful. Blonde-streaked hair gathered up from a long neck, and no make-up.

'I'm Georgina Hemp,' she said. 'Let's go to my office.'

She led them along a corridor to the back of the house and into a small, gloomy room, filled with filing cabinets, where a young woman in jeans and a sweater sat at a desk piled with paperwork. The walls were covered with timetables and old theatrical posters. In the distance the youthful voices began again, this time in a hearty rendition of, 'Oh, what a beautiful morning'.

'Coffee?' Georgina Hemp asked.

'If it's not too much trouble,' Graves answered.

'Would you be so kind, Pam?'

'How would you like it?' said the girl in jeans. They gave their orders and she left the room. Georgina took her place while Greaves and Holland sat on two wobbly, bentwood chairs beside the desk.

'I'm sure this is Polly,' Georgina said when she studied the glossy blow-up Holland had brought with them.

'Tell us what you know about her,' Greaves said.

Georgina looked up again. 'There's not much, I'm afraid. She had a good speaking voice, not much of a singer, but her dancing was excellent. She was a pleasant enough child, but she did have a bit of a problem ...'

'That was?' Greaves prompted.

'About her looks,' Miss Hemp said hesitantly. 'Actually she resented looking ... well, black. Or negroid, to be more precise. Her mother, Anne Weaver, is beautiful, quite a lot of white blood I would say. She had very fine features, like an Ethiopian. A lovely woman, she worked as a nurse at Ealing Hospital.'

'And her father?'

Georgina shrugged. 'He's white, so Anne told me, but he left them before Polly came to the school. It must have been a struggle to pay our fees.'

'She was a good mother?'

'Devoted, never missed an open day or a concert, she adored the child.'

'And you say in your letter she went back to Jamaica.'

'Yes. I don't think Polly was too keen, but there were urgent family reasons.'

'Did Polly have any special friends when she was here?'

Before Georgina could answer, the girl returned with the coffee. 'Do you remember if Polly Weaver had any particular friends, Pam?' she asked.

'Emma Howarth,' she replied, passing around the cups. 'They were inseparable.'

147

'Do you have an address?'

Pamela went to one of the filing cabinets and after a brief search produced a brown folder.

'Here we are: 28 Kendal Street, Turnham Green.' Georgina looked towards Pam with a smile, 'I'd quite forgotten Emma's mother.'

Greaves found it difficult to believe Georgina Hemp's remark, when he and Holland stood twenty minutes later outside a trim, semi-detached house and Mrs Howarth answered the door. The figure that confronted them was at least six feet tall, and wore only dark glasses and a white bikini that barely covered a few inches of her impressive body. Both men had to avert their gaze from the narrow line of pubic hair showing above the briefs that confirmed she was a natural redhead.

'Christ, I thought you were my husband,' she said in a throaty voice. 'He's always forgetting his keys.' She vanished for a moment and reappeared instantly, wearing a man's trench coat.

'We're police officers, Mrs Howarth,' Greaves said. 'May we speak to you for a few minutes?'

'You don't sound like a policeman, darling,' she replied, but she opened the door and led them past a pile of luggage in the hallway and into a living room that was decorated in the style of a Spanish holiday villa. A sunlamp on an onyx coffee table threw its intense glare on to a sofa under the bay window. Mrs Howarth turned off the lamp and sat down.

'Now, what can I do for the law?' she asked, but before Greaves could speak a sudden spasm of coughing caused her to lean forward, the coat opened, and one magnificent breast jerked free from her bikini top.

'Damn this bloody cold,' Mrs Howarth said, unconcerned about the breast, which she casually replaced in its tiny harness and covered with the coat.

148

'It's about your daughter, or to be more precise an old school friend of hers called Polly Weaver,' Greaves continued.

'Haven't seen her in a couple of years,' Mrs Howarth replied with a sniffle. 'Polly, that is. Emma lives here, but she's at work now. At least I imagine she is.'

'Aren't you sure?' Holland asked.

Mrs Howarth shook her head. 'We only got back from tour this morning. Emma doesn't know we're home.'

'Where have you been on tour, Mrs Howarth?'

She looked up at the ceiling and spoke as if the names were written there: 'Let me see, Wolverhampton, Leeds, Manchester, Blackpool, Scarborough, Brighton and Watford. We should have done Luton but we had to cancel because of this bloody cold.'

'What sort of tour were you on?' Holland asked.

Mrs Howarth reached down beside the sofa and produced a large roll of paper. She opened it to reveal a poster that showed a man in evening clothes and silk-lined cape, taking a white rabbit from a top hat. Mrs Howarth stood beside him, glorious in a spangled costume.

'The Great Marvello and Ginger,' Holland read aloud. There was the sound of a key in the front door and Mrs Howarth called out, 'Quick, I'm in here, flashing my tits to a couple of coppers.'

A tall, puzzled man came into the room holding a large bottle of dark liquid. He was slim with blue-white hair and dressed casually in clothes of the sort golfers wear.

'This is Superintendent Greaves and Sergeant Holland,' Ginger said. 'Gentlemen, The Great Marvello – otherwise known as my husband Jack.'

'What's up?' he said.

'They're looking for Emma. Or Polly Weaver, to be more precise. I was just telling them we don't know where Emma is.'

'I do,' he replied, passing her the cough syrup. 'She's at the Drury Lane Theatre, I just saw Jenny next door in the chemist's. Emma's in a new show that's opening next week.'

149

'The West End!' Ginger exclaimed with notable envy. 'And she's only seventeen – lucky little cow.'

Harry Porter stood, loaded with two heavy bags full of photographic equipment, in the entrance hall of the *Gazette* building with Sarah Keane. Harry was an impatient man at the best of times, but the wait for Charles Trottwood was making him even grumpier than usual. Only his fondness for Sarah kept him from loosing a barrage of obscenities at the delay. He wore his customary heavy overcoat and brown racing trilby, pulled down so that the rim touched the frame of his horn-rimmed spectacles. Bright blue eyes glared from a round, beefy face that was the colour and texture of a pink house brick.

'Bloody lawyers,' he muttered finally. 'I suppose his fee goes up every minute he keeps us hanging about.'

Sarah was not bothered by the wait. She did not relish working with Cat Abbot, and there was no urgency about the story.

'He doesn't work for a fee, Harry,' she said soothingly. 'He's on a salary like the rest of us.'

'Not like my bloody salary,' Harry continued. 'I haven't had a rise in two years.'

Sarah decided to change the subject. 'Why do you always dress as if you're going to the Antarctic for three months, Harry? And all this equipment. We're only going to the Savoy to take pictures.' She tapped the case of a long-range lens that dangled from his shoulder. 'You could do the job from the roof with this.'

'Derby Day 1949, that's why,' he answered enigmatically.

'What happened?'

Harry lit a small cigar and fixed a withering stare on one of the commissionaires who was about to tell him that Sir Robert Hall had banned smoking in the building.

'It was sunny in the morning and I'd come to work in a new lightweight suit. Nat Goldman was picture editor then, the bastard. He sent me to Trafalgar Square to snap some pigeons sitting on a film star's head. I only took a Rolliflex camera and five rolls of film in me pocket. Well, you would, wouldn't you? Nice day, sun shining, job just up the road. Bang off a few and back in the pub by lunchtime.'

Trottwood arrived with a smile. 'Sorry for the delay,' he said smoothly. 'A new girl in the office, she didn't know the form for contracts.'

'Anyway,' Harry Porter continued as they walked to an office car waiting in the vanway, 'I'm there in Trafalgar Square taking the snaps and an office dispatch rider, Eddie Burke, rides up and says: "Mr Goldman's ordered me to take you to the Derby on the back of the bike. Bill Flaxman has phoned in sick and you've got to cover the runners at Tattenham Corner. Then I'm to bring you back with the film." So I leaves the film star, still covered with pigeons, and gets on the back of the bike. By the time we get to Epsom it's pissing down with rain. I have to stand at Tattenham Corner soaked to the skin with one roll of film left, and I've got the wrong camera for the job. The rewind jammed and all I got was the last three runners passing me.' He slapped the bags around him. 'Since then I've always been ready for anything. You never know how a day is going to turn out.'

'No matter how bright the morning, there will be darkness at noon,' Trottwood said from his seat next to the driver.

'Darkness at noon,' Harry repeated with gloomy relish, 'that's the story of my life.'

The car dropped them at the Strand entrance to the hotel. Entering by the revolving door, they crossed to the right of the hushed foyer. 'My name is Mrs Keane,' Sarah told the duty clerk at the reception desk. 'And this is Mr Trottwood and Mr Porter. We've come to see a guest: Mr Henry Higgins.'

'Yes, madam,' the clerk replied. 'Actually Mr Higgins has gone out at the moment, we're moving him from his room into a suite. Would you care to wait?'

'May we wait in his suite?' Trottwood asked.

'I'm afraid that's not possible, sir. Had Mr Higgins given us instructions … I'm sure you understand.'

'Of course,' Trottwood replied. 'We'll hang on until he comes back.'

They crossed the foyer and sat down in deep chairs. The peaceful atmosphere of the great hotel seemed to soothe Harry. 'Nothing's ever easy when Cat is involved,' he said cheerfully, while he arranged his coat and bags about him. 'He breeds trouble like my brother-in-law breeds rabbits.'

'We used to breed rabbits during the war,' Charles Trottwood said dreamily. 'We had a cook who made wonderful pies.'

I wonder if Colin likes rabbit pie? Sarah thought. I must ask him this evening.

A few minutes later, Cat Abbot entered the hotel, his face riven with worry. He scanned the foyer anxiously and saw them. 'I can't find Doreen Clay anywhere,' he said when he stood before them.

'It's going to be one of those days,' Harry Porter said with satisfaction, from the depth of his armchair. 'Darkness at noon again.'

CHAPTER
EIGHT

Thursday, October 29 11.55 a.m.

Lily Doyle was enjoying her morning. She had taken her regular minicab to Brent Cross shopping centre to buy a new outfit. Then she continued to her regular hairdresser in Willesden High Road. The cab waited while the owner gave her his personal attention, and now she returned, in regal splendour, to the Brent River estate. Where another treat had been promised. She loved living on the estate. Danny had offered to buy her a house anywhere she chose, but she always refused. They all knew her here – and they looked up to her. Lily was shrewd enough to realise that the stares would come from another direction, were she to take up residence in some respectable suburb.

Lily was a tall, bony woman of fifty, with a strong body and large powerful hands. As with Danny and Fergus, there was no family resemblance. Her short yellow hair was swept away from a face that over the years had turned from a sensuous sort of beauty into stone-like hardness. Her once soft skin was now pitted and rough and, despite heavy make-up, it still resembled photographs of the cratered surface of the moon. Constant smoking had yellowed her large prominent teeth, but a fear of dentists had caused her to refuse Danny's offer to have them capped like his own.

Unlike her brothers, she did not speak with the harsh cutting Belfast accent. Odd words bore the same inflections, but Lily Doyle had spent the early part of her life in other places.

Her brothers had been too young to remember their parents clearly, except for Danny, and he'd only been snot-nosed and barefooted then. Never playing with the other kids in the camp, Danny had always been on his own. Their father had called him the stoat because of his liking to snake about in the shadows, quick and nervous, ready to prey on anything weaker and slower than himself.

Their family name had been Smith then, like many of the travelling people who roamed England in convoys of motor-hauled caravans. Outcasts, loathed by the indigenous populations of towns and villages, who suffered the blight they brought to the landscape and the squalor left behind when they passed on. Some people referred to them as gypsies, but in fact they were descended from the dispossessed families who had taken to the roads of Britain in the wake of the Irish famines during the early half of the nineteenth century.

Although they were not Romanies, travellers had assimilated many of their superstitions and beliefs over the generations, and they often passed themselves off as gypsies to the unknowing. It was in their camps that Lily Doyle learned to respect and fear those with the Gift: old women who could put the evil eye on you, tell of your life to come from the lines in your hand, or read the future in a strange pack of cards.

When Lily Doyle was thirteen, her mother and father had been killed. The car that hauled their caravan had broken down and they had pulled out of the convoy into a lay-by to make repairs. In the night, a lorry hit them both as they stood by the side of the road. Lily was in the caravan with her brothers. The police took them to a children's home in Liverpool but Lily had escaped with the boys and they roamed around the docks, sleeping rough for three days, until she found Joe Doyle, a merchant seaman from Belfast. Joe was a big, dim man, already middle-aged, and Lily got to him before the prostitute he was seeking.

Doyle took them all back to Belfast with him because he had never before known the sort of pleasure Lily provided. He owned a little brick box of a house inherited from his parents and the whole gaggle moved into their new home and adopted Joe's name. Lily had lived as Joe's wife until he died when she was in her late twenties. Since then no other man had touched her. The early years had been harsh, until Danny made his reputation. It wasn't that he had been stronger than others; it was a pitiless quality he had possessed, even as a child, which perversely commanded loyalty. Lily could remember quite clearly the day he had won over the Bradys. The boys in the street had found a cat with newborn kittens. The Bradys had dared each boy to kill one of them. When it came to Danny's turn, he looked the Bradys in the face and, without taking his eyes from them, picked up a kitten and slowly bit it to death. From that day on, they had followed him.

When he had brought them back to England, Lily finally came into her own. In Belfast, she had known the respect that comes from fear, but Danny had only been one of a number of gang leaders. On the Brent River estate he was Chief of Chiefs, and she was treated like royalty.

When she had dismissed the cab driver Lily entered her flat, which always smelt of cooking fat. Despite the expensive furnishing there was no extractor equipment, and Lily's diet consisted entirely of fried food. Leaving the front door open, she unpacked the carrier bags and banged on the wall of her bedroom three times with a clenched fist. Moments later, in answer to her summons, two women appeared in the living room, where Lily now sat, shoes kicked off, in a deep armchair upholstered in purple Dralon. Although each item in the flat had come from one of London's smartest department stores, Lily had somehow managed to assemble a décor that was much the same as the interior of a traveller's caravan. Colours were harsh and clashing, with a predominance of engraved glass, mirrors, bowls and ornaments, all glittering reflected light from every wall and surface.

There was a deep contrast between her two visitors. One was middle-aged and stout, almost cringing in her flowered apron. The other was young, swarthy and unafraid, with black hair that had been oiled and a long dress of scarlet silk and black velvet that showed off her straight, willowy figure. She would have been beautiful but for an extra heaviness about her features.

'This is her, Lily,' the elder woman said proudly. 'The one I told you about. Rose Tancra, she's a real gypsy.'

Lily got up and stood close to the girl. She smelt like a gypsy; it was a musky, perfumed body odour Lily could remember from the fairgrounds and camps of her childhood, when the travellers made contact with the other people who lived on the road.

'Where are you from?' she asked.

'Neasden,' the girl answered in a nasal north London accent.

'What about your parents?'

'They was moving about, till my mum went in hospital for an operation when I was little. Me dad works in a restaurant now.'

'Betty tells me you can read palms.'

'S'right, me mum taught me.'

'Would you like to read mine?'

The girl nodded towards Betty. 'She says you'll pay me.'

'Do you know who I am?' Lily asked. She was a little annoyed that the girl lacked the usual servitude shown in her presence.

'Everyone around here knows who the Doyles are,' Lily replied flatly.

156

'But you're not afraid.'

The girl studied her face with dark, unblinking eyes until Lily lowered her gaze first.

'I know what's going to happen in my life,' Rose said without emotion, and with such utter conviction that Lily Doyle felt an involuntary shudder ripple through her body.

'Betty, make us a cup of tea,' Lily ordered and the elderly woman hurried to carry out the order.

Rose Tancra looked about her, then pointed to the kitchen table. 'In here,' she said. 'The light's better.'

Lily followed her instruction and sat opposite the gypsy girl, who took her outstretched hand and curled it slightly, to better reveal the indented lines.

'You became a woman when you lost your parents – they died together,' the girl began immediately, in a matter-of-fact voice.

'Yes.'

'You did not love the man who made you a woman. You have never known love.'

'Yes.'

'You have a dead brother. He died across the water.'

'Yes.' Lily's voice was hushed now.

'You will live a long time, but you won't know that you're alive. The others in your family are in danger, they could die soon. There is an enemy at the gate. A powerful enemy. If your brothers go far away they may be safe, but the angel of death is hovering. I see nothing but darkness, darkness of spirit, darkness of the heart and of the mind.'

The girl suddenly released Lily's hand so quickly it knocked over the teacup that the elderly woman had placed beside her. Lily looked at her, her features transfixed with fear.

'I don't want to do any more,' Rose Tancra said with less confidence than she had shown before.

'What did you see?' Lily asked in a voice so soft it was barely audible.

Rose shook her head so that her oiled hair swung before her face. 'Something … I don't know … something that can kill without touching … just with the power of a thought.'

'The evil eye?'

'More, much more … ' she stood up. 'I want to go now. I don't want any money.' Although the old woman tried to restrain her, she hurried from the flat. Lily Doyle remained seated at the table, her body chilled to ice and her irregular breath catching each time in her throat.

Rose Tancra walked swiftly from the estate. After about five minutes she reached a main road and continued along it at a slower pace for some time. Then after a glance behind her, she turned into a side street. Looking back once more to be absolutely sure she wasn't being followed, she crossed the road to a large parked car and got into the passenger's seat, next to the driver.

'How did it go?' the man asked in a Belfast accent.

'Just like you wanted. Screaming Jesus, I thought she was going to die of fright,' Rose Tancra answered with a laugh. 'So that was the great Lily Doyle.'

'How did you get to know the old woman?' the man asked.

'Betty? I just waited behind her in the post office where she gets her pension. She can't stop talking. I told her a couple of things I knew about her kids, it was easy. She'll spread the word to everyone on the estate the Doyles are finished now.'

'What did you tell Lily?'

'Everything you said.' Rose paused to touch the polished wood of the dashboard. 'Funny thing, though, it really was in her palm. If you believe that sort of thing.'

'Don't you?'

'Nah, load of bloody rubbish. Mind you, my mum does.'

Andrew Muir smiled. 'Is she really a gypsy?'

'Oh, yes,' she held her hand out. 'And she taught me how to

put curses on people. So you'd better cross my palm with silver like you promised.'

Muir handed her a thick wad of banknotes and she got out of the car. He switched on the radio when she was almost out of sight; a newsreader began to tell about the latest bombing outrage in Northern Ireland.

It was Greaves's turn to use the telephone when he and Holland were back in the car. It took two calls to get the man he wanted. After a brief conversation he instructed the driver to head for Holland Park Avenue. When they arrived, the driver parked on the north side of Bayswater Road, near Lancaster Gate. Greaves left Holland in the car and strolled across into Kensington Gardens, taking a footpath that led to the statue of Peter Pan. The man was already there, a plain, unremarkable figure wearing a fawn-coloured raincoat and seated on a park bench, watching the still waters of the Serpentine.

'Curious name for a pond,' Robbie McNeice said, when Greaves sat beside him. 'I suppose it relates to the shape rather than the content.' There was no trace of a Belfast accent.

'How are the serpents you're watching?' Greaves asked.

'Thriving at the moment. But they haven't got their hands on what they want yet.'

'What are they hoping to achieve?'

McNeice smiled. 'In general, McNally wants to take over the entire Doyle operation: drugs, extortion, whores – everything. But at the moment the Doyles have lost something that McNally also wants to get his hands on. McNally has tried subverting the pimps and the drug suppliers. That's why the girl was murdered; Danny Doyle was teaching them a lesson. Stay in line, that sort of thing. Seems to have been effective.'

'Do you think Jill Slade had what it is they're after?'

'Looks like it, old boy.'

'But we don't know what it was?'

McNeice looked towards the statue of Peter Pan. 'That's right. Real Neverland stuff, isn't it?'

'Do you know where McNally is based?'

'Yes, I do.' He gestured across the park. 'Over there, actually. In the Kensington Gardens Hotel. I thought that was quite smart of him. Right side of town for the airport and he's got half the royal family as neighbours. I can't see Danny Doyle starting a gang war in that part of the metropolis. McNally's got Muir and a few others with him. The rest are scattered about town. They're using the club where you call me as one of their rallying points. McNally moves them around, in case Fergus comes gunning for them.'

'Muir killed the Slade girl, and the family.'

'Yes, it looked like his work. Are you going to pick him up for it?'

'Not just yet.'

Greaves got up and looked south-west to where McNally was. 'Does it ever seem odd to you that our masters make us operate in separate compartments?'

'Conquest's Law, old boy.'

'What's that?'

'Every organisation appears to be headed by secret agents of its opponents.'

Greaves smiled. 'Take care, Robbie,' he said and walked back to the car.

Thursday, October 29 12.25 a.m.

Sometimes, Big Davey McNally felt as if he carried the cares of the whole world upon his stooped shoulders. He had spent the entire morning making arrangements to protect the families of his people in Belfast, even though he knew it meant diverting precious manpower from their usual duties at the betting shops. In other times the task would have fallen on the capable shoulders of Andy Muir, but at the moment his Chief of Staff was unable to function. It had taken all his authority to stop Muir from returning home on the next plane. He had been close to his daughter, and the grandchildren were as precious as his heartbeat.

Usually McNally liked to spend at least a couple of hours each morning studying *Sporting Life*. Today he'd had to forgo that pleasure, and there was racing on the television that afternoon. Softly, he cursed again: the operation he had planned so carefully was coming apart, like a barrel with the hoops sprung. Only McNally's iron grip was keeping all the staves in place.

'What's wrong with this fucking tea?' he said to the nervous youth who was acting as his aide.

'It's called Earl Grey, Big Davey, don't you like it?' the youth replied.

'It tastes like a tart's bathwater, get me something decent.' The youth moved towards the telephone.

'Do it in the bedroom, and send that useless piece of shit in now,' McNally ordered.

The aide went to a door in the suite and said to Eddie Page, who waited in the hall, 'You're to come in now.'

The young man who entered was fair, with the sort of skin that showed every blemish, delicate compared with his thick, brutal frame. He stood to attention and watched David McNally, who now stood at the window looking towards the distant towers of the Brent River estate. McNally was not a big man, but he frightened Eddie Page. All his life, Eddie had heard stories of what Big Davey McNally had done to his enemies. Page didn't want to add his own name to the legends. Not that McNally looked dangerous, thinning grey hair and a hatchet face were common enough characteristics in half the old men in Belfast, but then a blowlamp didn't look dangerous, until it was turned on somebody's face.

'Sit down, Eddie,' McNally began in a soft enough voice. 'How's your daddy? We used to play football together when we were boys, did you know that?'

Page licked his lips. 'I did, Big Davey. He used to tell me about it when I was a wee lad.'

McNally scratched an armpit. The heating in the hotel was too high, it made him sweat, something he preferred others to do. 'Now let's go over what happened the other night. Slowly, take your time and don't leave anything out. I want every detail, understand? Begin from when you met the girl.'

The youth sat on the edge of his chair. 'I went to King's Cross like Andy said. I had the money, he told me I was to guard it with me life. He said if anything happened to it I would answer to you.'

'Go on.'

'It was raining, the traffic was bad and it took longer than I thought it would to get there.'

'You went by car instead of the underground?'

'I had all the money, Big Davey. I didn't want my pockets picked.'

'So you were late?'

'Only a few minutes. She was waiting among all the tarts, they'd come in from the rain. I says to her: give me the package, and she says, the money first.' He looked up, pleading, 'So I gets hold of her and says: give me the package, you fucking bitch.'

'Why didn't you give her the money first?'

'Jesus, Big Davey, I told you about the warning Andy Muir gave me.'

McNally sighed. It was as simple as that: the stupid little bastard had been more worried about losing the money than getting the package. 'So what happened then?'

'I had her by the throat, when this big black bastard, one of the pimps, takes hold of me. "Take your hands off the merchandise" he says. He must have thought she was one of his girls. I let go of her to give the blackie a smack and the girl buggers off into the station.'

'Did you follow her?'

The youth nodded. 'After a couple of minutes, I saw her watching these two fellas who were talking to some kids. Then one of them goes into a burger bar and she follows him.'

'Did she pass the package to him?'

'I don't know, I didn't see any contact.'

'You're not sure?'

Eddie Page shook his head.

'Would you know the man again?'

'I think so.'

McNally smiled. 'OK, son. Now you go and wait next door. I'll tell you what I want you to do in a wee while.'

Eddie went to the door and turned. 'I brought the money back, Big Davey, all £10,000, just like Andy told me.'

McNally watched the door close. 'Ten thousand pounds,' he said softly. 'He wrecked it all for that. When it's over, I'll make the little bastard eat that amount.'

After a few minutes he went to another room where the curtains were drawn. Andrew Muir, a man so similar in appearance to McNally that people often took them to be brothers, was lying on the bed in his shirt-sleeves, one tattooed arm thrown over his eyes.

McNally sat beside him. 'How are you feeling, Andy?' he asked.

'Bad, Big Davey,' he replied. 'I've never felt this bad before.'

'We'll get them, Andy. I promise you that, but first there's a fella we need to find.'

'Just give me a few hours, Davey. Then I'll be with you again.'

McNally reached out and patted his shoulder. 'Good man. I'm just going out for a bit, see you soon.' He left the room and found his jacket draped on the back of a chair. After carefully straightening his tie, he combed his hair and left the suite.

Kensington High Street was filled with pedestrians. He crossed to the south side of the road and pushing past two strolling Arabs, whose eyes flashed at the insult, entered a department store. McNally wanted to be sure the call he was about to make would not be overheard. One of his informers in the RUC had recently described how sophisticated electronic eavesdropping equipment had become, and since then Big Davey had been obsessed with the possibility of being bugged.

Without any evidence to support his fears, he had begun to suspect that communications in the hotel were not secure. Just a hunch, but hunches had kept him alive in the past. Now he was taking no chances. The woman already speaking on the public telephone he wished to use was impervious to his hostile stare. She continued her conversation at a leisurely pace, but at last hung up.

The number he dialled was answered at the second ring by an English voice, cultivated and petulant. 'I was expecting you to call earlier, I have an urgent appointment.'

McNally didn't bother to apologise. 'The girl definitely had it, and I'm fairly sure she's passed it on to someone else.'

'Who?'

'I'm not sure yet, but I'll find out.'

'This is ridiculous. I hand everything to your people on a plate and they bungle it. This whole business defies imagination. I provide you with of one of Doyle's top-of-the-range tarts, so you can sample the merchandise, and what do you do? Fill her head with such big ideas about her future she boasts about it to Doyle's organisation. Now she's dead. Have you any conception of the time and money that's spent on those girls? All wasted. And what was that little episode last night suppose to mean? London's not like Belfast, you know. People aren't used to gang fights on the streets.'

McNally scratched his nose. 'That was Andy Muir just trying his luck. He thought a quick hit might knock over Doyle and cut out a lot of waiting.'

There was a sharp intake of breath. 'I tell you how to seize Doyle's organisation, I infiltrate the girl, Jill Slade, and arrange for her to steal the material at the perfect time – all it takes is one simple transaction on your part and you bungle it. Then you allow your thugs to go rampaging around like Al Capone's boys. I'm simply speechless.'

'Listen, you primping little shite,' McNally growled, his patience exhausted. 'You weren't always so fucking efficient yourself – just remember what you owe me, and think yourself lucky I haven't ripped out your kidneys. All I want to hear from you is what Doyle's plans are, not any fucking lectures, understand?'

The voice changed instantly: there was now conciliation in the tone. 'Forgive me, it's just we were so close. I'm sure you'll recover it. I have every confidence – obviously Danny's looking as well but so far they have nothing to go on.' There was a moment's pause, then the voice said, 'By the way, there's a good thing running at Chepstow this afternoon, owned by a chum of mine.'

McNally didn't hesitate. 'I wouldn't listen to you if you told me which end of a horse the shit came out,' he answered. He hung up.

Thursday, October 29 1.12 p.m.

Cat Abbot had always wanted to stay in a suite at the Savoy, but the experience was proving to have all of the flavour of Dead Sea fruit. Now he sat sprawled in an armchair, his back to a

165

magnificent view of the Thames, while Sarah and Charles Trottwood fired questions at him in an attempt to jog his memory.

'Has she left the hotel before?' Sarah asked.

'No.'

'Does she have any special friends or relatives she may have slipped off to see?' Trottwood added.

'None that I know of,' Cat answered and the telephone rang. He snatched it up, but hope left his face at the sound of the voice on the other end.

'Yes … I see … sure, that will be fine … I understand … OK, see you then.' He turned to the expectant faces. 'That was Barry Quick in publicity. There's a big rush on, it seems Sir Robert is keen on the story. Apparently his wife is fascinated by Doreen Clay. He's extended the advertising budget. They want to make a television commercial this afternoon. Barry's bringing a limo round with black-out windows, so we can go to a studio in Covent Garden without being seen. They want to use me in it,' Cat said miserably. 'Talking to camera. They'll only film the back of Doreen's head.'

In normal times the news would have made him ecstatic with joy, but now, remorse had tranquilised his spirits. Nobody spoke for a while. The only sound in the suite was a soft whistling from Harry Porter as he made fiddling adjustments to his photographic equipment. Then there was a click as the door in the outer passageway opened and a voice called out, 'Cooeee! It's only me.'

'I doubt if that's the maid,' Trottwood said drily and Doreen Clay entered the room.

'Where in God's name have you been?' Cat barked, leaping from the chair.

Doreen looked at the room full of strangers and said, 'I was feeling peckish so I popped over the road for a bite to eat. Nobody would recognise me, Raymond, it's you they all know.'

Cat held his hands up in the air, then began to tug at his hair.

'This hotel has one of the finest kitchens in the world. Why would you want to go out to eat?'

'Well, I didn't want to be any bother,' Doreen replied quietly.

'Bother? … bother?' Cat repeated, his voice rising on each syllable. 'That's what the staff are here for – so that you can bother them – they like being bothered, it's the way they earn a living.'

'There's no need to shout,' Doreen said with a slight break in her voice.

Cat reached out and embraced her. 'Forgive me,' he apologised, his own voice filled with emotion. 'I thought something had happened to you.'

When he had released her, Sarah stepped forward. 'My name is Sarah Keane, Miss Clay. I'm very glad to meet you. This is Charles Trottwood, and Harry Porter. We're all from the *Gazette* as well.'

Doreen took her hand. 'Ah, yes, I've been expecting you,' she said. 'I'm glad to see you're better now.'

'I'm sorry?' Sarah said puzzled.

Doreen gave a little laugh. 'It's all right, I got a picture of somebody else for the minute and I confused her with you. A fat girl, she was very unhappy.'

'I used to be fat,' Sarah said. And unhappy, but that thought remained unspoken.

Doreen was about to speak again but Charles Trottwood interrupted. 'Forgive me, Mrs Clay, but I'm in a fearful rush. I wonder if I might ask you to sign the contracts I have with me? Then I can leave you in peace.'

When the paperwork was completed, Harry Porter took over.

'You know I don't want my face in the paper,' Doreen said.

'It's all right, my dear,' Harry reassured her. 'I only want to take a picture of one part of you.'

'Oh, my eyes,' she said, smiling.

'That's right,' Harry said. 'How did you know?'

'Make sure you touch out the bags,' Doreen replied obliquely.

'Will you be long?' Trottwood asked anxiously. He had agreed to share a taxi back to the office with Harry Porter.

'Two minutes,' Harry said, leading her to the light from the window.

He was as good as his word. As they were preparing to leave, Barry Quick knocked on the door.

Thursday, October 29 1.35 p.m.

Detective-Sergeant Holland was pleased to find that everything backstage at the Drury Lane Theatre was how he had always seen it portrayed in the cinema. Scenery, ropes, sudden dazzling lights and a stern choreographer putting the chorus line through its paces. Real life was rarely depicted with such accuracy, especially police work. He watched from the wings as the dancers completed a complicated series of steps, then he waited for Emma Howarth to leave the stage. It was easy to spot which one she was: there was no mistaking the red hair of Ginger's daughter.

'May I have a word, Miss Howarth?' he asked, showing her his warrant card.

'Do you know me?' she replied.

He shook his head. 'No, but I met your mother this morning.'

'Ginger?' the girl said quickly. 'What's the matter, is she all right?'

'Everything's fine. I just want to ask you some questions about a friend of yours.'

'What friend?' she asked, her voice now full of hostility.

Drugs, Holland thought. She thinks I'm going to question her about drugs. She looks so young, she shouldn't be frightened by the police.

'It's about Polly Weaver, she is a friend of yours, isn't she?'

'I haven't seen her in ages.'

'Do you have an address for her?'

'No.'

Holland knew she was holding something back. 'You saw her picture in the paper, didn't you?'

Emma looked away, 'Polly got mixed up with some bad people, we didn't keep in touch.'

'But you've got a telephone number, haven't you? Just give me that and I won't have to bother you any longer.'

Emma hesitated for a while, then made up her mind. 'Just a minute,' she answered. She went and picked up a bag from a pile on a table.

'That's all I have,' she said when she'd read out the number. 'She was there some time ago. She might have moved since then.'

'Thanks,' Holland said and the choreographer called for her to return to work.

Catchy tune, Holland thought, when the music started up again as he walked from the theatre.

Brian Meadows was escorting Fanny Hunter up the stairs of the Reform Club when he remembered that he was wearing a Garrick tie. She saw him hesitate on the last step and said, 'What's the matter with you? Women are allowed in here, you know, it's not a fucking monastery any more.'

Meadows smiled weakly. There were times when he wished Fanny were less robust in her choice of adjectives.

'It's not that, Fanny,' he replied. 'It's just that I'm wearing my own club tie, it's a bit … '

'Bad manners, eh?' she said when they stood in the imposing marble atrium that lay at the heart of the building. 'Don't worry, I'm not wearing any knickers, I expect that's against the rules as well.'

The heads of two men standing with drinks beneath a portrait snapped around at her last remark and Meadows hastily ushered her towards the staircase that led to the gallery. Geraldine Miller raised a hand to attract their attention. Meadows saw that Jeremy Blakestone, Geraldine's other guest for lunch, had already arrived at the little table where they had arranged to meet for drinks.

'Hello, Geraldine,' Fanny said as she sat down, 'I was just telling Brian I'm not wearing any knickers.'

'Is that oversight or anticipation, darling?' Geraldine replied, determined she would not be wrong-footed by Fanny's usual vulgarities.

Fanny snapped a suspender that now showed quite clearly through her silk dress. 'I suppose it must be anticipation, otherwise I would've put on tights this morning.' She turned to Blakestone and smiled sweetly. 'Forgive our little game, Jeremy. Geraldine and I are old mates, we always joke like this.'

Meadows raised his eyes to the glass roof for a few seconds and offered a silent prayer of thanks that this wasn't happening in his own club. A steward took their order and Fanny leaned towards Blakestone. 'Did anyone explain to you why I came along, Jeremy?' she asked.

Blakestone looked towards Geraldine. 'No, neither of us knows. We were speculating on the reason when you arrived.'

'Hasn't Brian said, Geraldine?' Fanny chuckled. 'I thought there were no secrets between the two of you these days.'

'Why don't you enlighten us,' Geraldine replied with a poisonous glance.

'Let's do it over lunch, shall we? I'm so hungry I could eat one of these leather chairs. Mind you, they look as if somebody's already been chewing on them.'

When they were seated in the dining room, Geraldine passed the wine list to Meadows and turned to Fanny. 'Now, what brings you here today? I must confess I was surprised when Brian's secretary rang. I'd always thought you preferred more – informal places for lunch.'

Fanny looked to her right and said, 'That man over there.' They followed her gaze and saw the portly figure of Lord Glendowning at a far table, accompanied by a senior civil servant from the Treasury.

'Glendowning?' Blakestone exclaimed. 'He's got nothing to do with us.'

'What about his son?'

'I'm afraid it's out of the question. Tony only works for us on the strict understanding that it's his own private business. He's most insistent on that point.'

'Bollocks,' Fanny said cheerfully.

Meadows noticed that Blakestone had dropped the affectation of his disc jockey vocabulary while he was in the hallowed surroundings of the Reform. He wished fervently that Fanny would do the same.

'What do you mean by that remark?' Blakestone asked.

'Oh, come on, Jeremy, you know what the word signifies. I mean you're talking bullshit.' She leaned closer. 'The *Gazette* is putting £15,000 your way. All we want is a little co-operation. Glendowning hasn't spoken to the press about his son since he got him off the drugs charge. It's great stuff, even the mightiest in the land suffering the setbacks that thousands of poor families know. I want an interview with them together, pouring their hearts out to me.' She poked him in the ribs. 'You can fix it, I know you can, and think of the great publicity for HAND.'

And for Fanny Hunter, Geraldine thought.

'I'll give it a try,' Jeremy sighed. 'But I really can't promise anything.'

'Good boy,' Fanny said, and dug into her egg mayonnaise with relish.

Blakestone made his excuses as soon as he'd finished his meal, pleading another appointment. Fanny announced she

171

would go with him, as she wanted to do some shopping in Jermyn Street. 'Must buy Osbert a new tie at Turnbull and Asser,' she said. 'Toodleloo.'

'She ought to buy some socks to stuff in her mouth while she's about it,' Geraldine said when she had left the dining room to a turning of heads from other tables. 'How can you bear to work with that creature?'

'I suppose one gets used to a hair shirt,' Meadows answered philosophically. 'I hardly notice any more.'

'It's a good job you didn't get used to it on Monday,' Geraldine said, brushing his trousers leg beneath the table.

Meadows glanced around before he spoke. 'I wonder what she's up to?' he said slowly.

'Surely it's obvious,' Geraldine said in a low voice. 'She wants to get Blakestone into bed.'

'Blakestone? How do you know?'

'All that stuff about not wearing any panties. He's a typical member of the English upper classes underneath all that nonsense. Didn't you notice how he changed the way he spoke while he was in here, it must have reminded him of his public school, all these prefects about.'

'Wouldn't Fanny be a bit crude for him in that case?' Meadows asked. Despite his years of privilege, he was still a provincial grammar school boy at heart.

Geraldine laughed. 'If you think that about the upper classes you're making a big mistake. A bit of the rough cuts both ways, you know. Blakestone was twitching so much I thought he was going to put her to the knicker test before we got to the table.'

Meadows felt a moment of self-doubt in the light of Geraldine's sophistication. 'Is that what I am for you?' he asked. 'A bit of rough on the side?'

She leaned forward. 'There's nothing rough about you, darling,' she answered softly. 'Actually, you're a perfect gentleman, but that's not always the same as being a member of the upper classes.'

Meadows felt a sudden warmth at her compliment, until he recalled that he was sleeping with the wife of another member of the Garrick Club. Is that the act of a gentleman? he wondered, while Geraldine stood in line to pay the bill.

*   *   *

A few streets away, Blakestone and Fanny Hunter grappled eagerly with each other, while another squall of rain lashed at the fogged windows of the taxi they shared. Fanny gave a sighing little gasp of pleasure when Blakestone discovered that she was telling the truth about her underwear. Hands and tongue working frantically at her wet, available orifices, Jeremy redoubled his efforts.

'Harder, harder,' she urged, as they turned from St James's Street into Piccadilly. His wrist was beginning to ache by the time they reached the entrance of the Royal Academy. But Fanny began to mutter soft obscenities which renewed his strength of purpose. He was lost in his endeavours all the way along the broad highway, until with a series of shudders and convulsive moans outside Simpson's, Fanny stilled his hand with her own.

'Wait until we're in Shaftesbury Avenue,' she said huskily, as he guided her hand beneath the raincoat he had spread over them both. Then she began to return the compliment; it only took her as far as Wardour Street to release his pent-up emotions.

'Darling,' she whispered at the traffic lights before Cambridge Circus. 'You will get me the interview with the Glendownings, won't you?'

CHAPTER
NINE

Thursday, October 29 2.00 p.m.

Greaves was waiting for Holland in St James's Square. The rain pounded on the roof of the car and washed through the trees with a tropical intensity: it reminded him of days long ago in China but he did not want the memories they brought. Instead he turned his mind to the traffic swishing past, until he saw a taxi drop Holland on the east side of the square. The sergeant ran through the downpour, dodging the cars that splashed his flannel trousers.

'Did they trace the address?' Holland asked as he got into the car.

'Just around the corner,' Greaves said when Holland sat next to him, wiping his face and short hair with a handkerchief.

The driver dropped them in King Street and they hurried to the doorway they wanted. The flat was on the ground floor, next to an art gallery. They entered a marbled hallway that smelt of fresh paint. Holland pushed the bell on the only door and studied the elegantly carved plasterwork on the ceiling. It was a profusion of cherubs and fruit-ladened vines. 'Doesn't look the sort of place a working girl would live, sir,' he said softly, but the marbled hallway still seemed to amplify his voice.

The door opened after a short delay and the spare figure of a man, with sharp blue eyes and a clipped moustache, stood before them, holding a silver-framed photograph of a smiling woman. Greaves thought that the picture must have been taken some time in the Forties judging from the woman's hairstyle. Although the man's bearing was upright, and the flesh on his face taut and wind-burnt, it was clear from the white hair that matched his moustache that he was no longer young.

'Yes?' he said tersely. It was not the bark Holland had expected from his appearance, but it was a voice that was used to being obeyed by others, not one that sought approval. The man wore a charcoal-grey cardigan over a blue shirt, fawn cavalry twill slacks and highly polished brown brogues.

'We're police officers, sir,' Greaves began, then looked at the man more closely. 'Aren't you Brigadier-General Wescott?'

'That's right. Who are you?'

'Superintendent Colin Greaves. This is Detective-Sergeant Nicholas Holland.'

'You're a bit senior to be banging on doors, aren't you?' Wescott asked, a hint of interest in his voice.

'Not when the occasion warrants it, sir.'

'How do you know me?'

'I heard you lecture on anti-terrorism – and I've read your books.'

'Well, you'd better come in,' Wescott said, and they entered the apartment. It was compact and comfortable and, as Holland had remarked, not the usual sort of place where a working girl would live. The furniture was leather and the walls hung with military prints. Two tea chests in the centre of the room were half filled with books, a few had already been placed on the shelves either side of a small marble fireplace and part of the mantle was arranged with silver-framed photographs, mostly black and white, but a few in colour. Somehow the coloured ones looked wrong to Greaves. Clearly they had interrupted the Brigadier in his task. He placed the picture he held among the others and studied it for a moment. Then as if he had read Greaves's earlier thought, he said, 'Why do modern photographs look so garish and cheap when they're framed. It's a curious phenomenon.'

Neither Greaves nor Holland answered. He turned to them and said, 'Fancy a drink? I was just about to have a beer but there's gin and whisky – and some sherry, I think.'

'Thank you, Brigadier,' Greaves replied. 'Beer would be fine.'

'Same for you, Sergeant?' Then he clicked his fingers. 'I've seen you play at Rosslyn Park, haven't I?'

'Not for a few years, sir, a leg injury,' said Holland. 'Beer suits me too.'

'My son was still playing about the same time as you, he's given it up now. My God, you know you're getting old when your son's too old to play rugby.' Wescott went to a small kitchen off the living room and returned with a silver tray and three crystal glasses filled with ice-cold lager. 'Now, what can I do for you?'

'It's really about the previous occupier of the flat,' said Greaves. 'Tell me, how long have you been here?'

'Since Saturday,' Wescott answered. 'I was rather lucky, it's just what I was looking for. Handy for my club, and just round the corner from the London Library. I lost my wife last year, so I don't need much space these days.'

'How did you come to find it?'

'I was on Harrods's list. They rang me on Friday to say the tenant had gone abroad suddenly and the rest of the lease was available.'

'Do you have the name of the person you dealt with?'

'Certainly,' Wescott walked to a small writing desk and picked up a card, which he handed to Greaves.

'May we use your telephone?'

'Help yourself, it's in the bedroom.'

Greaves passed the card to Holland, who went to the room indicated by Wescott.

'Beastly weather,' the Brigadier said, as a flurry of rain rattled against the windows.

'Must remind you of Borneo,' Greaves answered.

Wescott smiled into his beer. 'You are familiar with my record. Do you know that part of the world?'

'Hong Kong and Singapore, not so far south as your territory.'

'Hong Kong?' Wescott repeated. 'Are you related to Sir Edmund Greaves?'

'He was my father.'

'Good Lord! Teddy Greaves's boy. What on earth are you doing in the police?'

Before he could answer, Holland returned. 'No luck, sir,' he said glumly. 'They were only acting as an intermediary. They say the money is paid into some property company registered in Gibraltar.'

Greaves nodded and sat deeper in the little leather sofa. There was no obvious sign of his disappointment. Then there was the soft tinkling of a bell and a Siamese cat stalked into the room and leaped up to sit on a table at Greaves's elbow.

'My lodger,' Wescott said. 'He turned up on Sunday. Must have belonged to the previous tenant. Bloody unpleasant thing to do, just to go away and abandon a pet like that. Mind you, it's a pampered brute, he'll only eat jellied chicken from Fortnum's. I found some tins in the kitchen cupboard, everything else was cleaned out.'

As if sensing his despondency, the cat reached out a paw and began to claw gently at Greaves's arm. He tickled the cat's ear and it pawed even more. Greaves examined the collar with the little bell, while the cat gazed at him with hard blue eyes. There was a small silver plate set in the leather, engraved with the words: 'Love, G.'

When they'd finished their beer, Wescott showed them to the door. 'Good to meet you,' he said in the hallway. 'Drop in whenever you're passing, I shall be here most of the time.'

Greaves gave a half-salute in farewell, and once in the street they sprinted through the rain to where the car was parked.

'Dead end,' Greaves said when they pulled away.

'No, it's OK, sir,' the driver replied, misunderstanding his words. 'I can get into St James's Square again.'

Thursday, October 29 2.30 p.m.

Andy Muir was still thinking what Christmas would now be like without his family, and the pain clawed at him like a beast trapped in his body. But with each passing hour he grew stronger, as if he had transmuted the grief into a fuel that fed his anger. Now his emotions were composed of pure hatred as though he'd been able to fashion some malignant force in the terrible moments of his rage. What they had done to him would seem like nothing, he vowed, when the time for judgment came. Andy Muir swore to have his revenge in full measure.

He sat now, on the Circle Line, next to Eddie Page who had made one attempt at conversation, before Muir cut him off with a curt, 'Shut your mouth.' When they emerged from underground in the interior of King's Cross station, Muir led him to a nearly deserted platform. When he was sure no one was in earshot, he leaned so close to Page's face that the youth could feel the heat of his breath. 'When will you learn to keep that trap of yours shut over here?'

'But they're Protestants, like us, Andy,' Eddie said plaintively.

Muir shook his head in disbelief. 'Next time you're in a crowd, take a good fucking look around. There's Muslims, Jews, Catholics, Buddhists – only a few of them are Church of England, and that's about as Protestant as the fucking Pope anyway. Remember, they're the English! That means they hate you as much as the Fenians back home. They don't want you as part of their country. As far as they're concerned you're just another pig-Irish Paddy. Every time they hear that accent of yours their skin crawls. It makes them look around to see if you've stuck a bomb up their fucking arse. So keep your trap shut. When they can't hear you they think you're one of them.' He turned to look around. 'Now keep moving, and tell me what the two fellas you saw were like.'

Eddie Page concentrated. 'The young one was thin, he was good-looking, but he'd had a spotty face when he was a lad. You can see the scars. Black hair, and a long black overcoat.'

'Did he look rich or poor?'

Eddie thought again. 'He sort of looked poor, but when I was up close he talked like a British officer. Not the words; the way he spoke them.'

'And the other, the one who talked to the girl?'

'He was older, wearing a scruffy raincoat, but his shoes were expensive and he wore a dicky bow.'

'How did he sound?'

'I didn't hear him, the young one did all the talking. He was asking these two kids where they were going to sleep the night. He gave them some money, just change and a wee card.'

'Is that all you saw?'

'Yes, Andy, honest to God. I didn't want the girl to spot me.'

Muir thought for a time, his head forward and chin buried in his chest. Eddie watched him as they paced slowly about the station concourse. Then Muir's head snapped up and he said, 'We need to find the worm.'

180

'What sort of a worm, Andy?' Eddie Page asked, like a child asking his father how long a journey would last.

Muir looked up at the glass and iron roof while he answered: 'This place is like an old sow, every little pig sucks at her tits, but there's got to be a worm inside her, living off the leavings of the others. The worm will know everything that happens here, night and day. Find him and he'll lead us to our man.'

Smokey had new shoes. He'd found them, still in their box, inside a carrier bag on the floor at the bookstall. Someone had put the bag down to browse through a magazine and walked away. He got rid of the packaging quickly and scurried to the far side of the station to examine his prize. They were trainers, in two shades of blue, padded like carpet slippers and with thick rubber soles. His grime-encrusted fingers moved slowly, threading the white laces, then he discarded the cracked shoes he had worn for the past months and slipped into his new footwear with a satisfied smile. They were a nice fit, room to wriggle his toes; this was going to be a good day.

Smokey lived in King's Cross station, but it was more than just a home, it was the entire limit of his existence. Even St Pancras, the other station just across the road, was like another continent to him. But inside the boundaries of his own world, Smokey felt free. He didn't know how much time had passed since he'd found his refuge. Seasons were easier to measure than days.

If he'd been able to read the discarded newspapers so frequently littered about him, they would have explained the economic policies of the nation. And then he might have been able to understand why they had seen fit to close the mental hospital where he had spent his youth. As it was, all he could remember was that one day, a long, misty time ago, when he had been released from its comforting confinement – like a bird that had never known any life but that of its cage.

Although Smokey had the mental age of a small child, he was not stupid; in fact he possessed a great deal of cunning that enabled him to survive. But the workings of the world were a mystery to him. In some more primitive circumstances he would have been looked after by the tribe, maybe even considered special by the gods who had chosen to keep him innocent, even though his body had aged to that of a man. But the rulers in his own society had decreed that he should stand on his own two feet, and Smokey was doing that – as best as he knew how.

Ironically, the most useful asset in his struggle for a day-to-day existence was the very factor that caused him to be such an outcast among his fellow human beings. His foul smell: a stench so daunting, others shied away when he was close, as though he bore the stigma of some dreadful plague. People had to wait in stations; queue for tickets, and for trains. They could not hurry past his outstretched hand. When he was hungry he would sit next to someone eating and they would invariably abandon their food to him. When the weather was really harsh he would allow the Salvation Army to lodge him through the worst of the cold. But they always demanded a price in cleanliness that was bad for business.

So Smokey lived out his life in the great hallways of the station, always wary, never still. The usual needs of humanity – such as love, self-respect, comfort and companionship – were as alien to him as the light from the stars.

Muir knew he'd found his worm the moment he saw him. A stooped, shuffling figure in ancient jeans and army anorak, the filthy, stained clothes in curious contrast to the brightly coloured trainers that flopped on his feet. Muir smiled at the shifting eyes set in a grey-skinned, sunken face, and Smokey stopped warily, sensing the man might give him something, but ready for flight. People who smiled were not always kind. One night the previous winter two shaven-headed youths had smiled at him – before they kicked him unconscious.

182

Muir walked closer, rattling change in his hand. The smile shifted slightly when he was near enough to catch Smokey's odour, but he persisted.

'I'm looking for a friend,' Muir said. 'Maybe you know where I can find him. He comes here a lot.'

'Friend?' Smokey repeated. He didn't like this man, or his companion. They emanated danger although they offered him money.

Muir smiled again. 'He talks to kids, gives them handouts – money. A dark lad in a black overcoat. Do you know him?'

'Might do,' Smokey said cagily.

Muir let the change cascade from one hand to another. 'Tell me where I can find him and I'll give you this.'

For the first time in his life, Smokey sold something. He reached into his pocket and produced a grubby card, which he held towards them. Muir took it quickly and let the change fall into Smokey's hand, making sure he didn't touch the grimy flesh.

The two men made their way to a row of seats and examined their purchase. 'Pentonville Road,' Muir muttered. 'Where the fuck is that?' He pushed Eddie on the arm. 'Go to that bookstall and buy me a London Street guide,' he ordered.

Eddie returned a few minutes later with the book.

'Look up Pentonville Road,' Muir said.

'How do I do that, Andy?' Eddie asked nervously.

Without bothering to answer, Muir snatched the book from him. 'Just over the fucking way,' he said after a quick examination, then got up and walked swiftly away.

Eddie Page caught up with him: 'Where are we going now Andy?'

'To the pictures,' Muir replied. 'I want to wait till it's dark before we talk to this fella Glendowning.'

* * *

Sarah sat next to Doreen in the vast motor car that was taking them on the brief journey to the studio. 'I must say,' Doreen said after a few minutes, 'this doesn't seem like work at all.'

'What's your work like usually?' Sarah asked. She had begun to warm to Doreen's unaffected qualities. After glancing about the plush interior, Doreen reached out to touch the smoked glass of the window next to her. 'A bit like this,' she said. 'All one way, really. They can see into our world, but it's very hard for it to happen the other way round.'

Sarah smiled at the comparison, and remembered Greaves's not unfriendly comments about her. 'I understand you met ... ' Sarah paused for a moment: 'boyfriend' sounded slightly ridiculous for a woman her age. Lover? No – although it was true – and she couldn't call him fiancé, they hadn't yet finally agreed on marriage.

'Yes,' Doreen answered, rescuing her, although Sarah hadn't finished the question. 'What a lovely man. He's very old, you know.'

Sarah glanced at her quickly. 'Only in his early forties.'

Doreen laughed. 'No, I mean an old spirit, he's been on earth many times before. So have you.'

'Me?' Sarah exclaimed.

'Oh, yes. Old souls are by far the nicest people, they care more about others, see. The young ones are only concerned with themselves, it makes them dreadfully unreliable.'

'Are they always unpleasant?'

'Oh, dear me no, some of them can be the loveliest people you'd want to meet, but self-centred.'

'What about twins?'

Doreen looked at her. 'Twins can be interesting, sometimes, they're the same soul. That's when you can prick one and hurt the other.'

The limo stopped in Wardour Street and Barry Quick ushered them down into a basement studio before sending Cat and Doreen off to be made up.

'I only want my hair done, dear,' Doreen explained to the young girl who was looking at her face with professional detachment. 'They won't be filming my face.'

Cat leaned back in the chair and waited for the full treatment with a sigh of deep contentment.

Sarah was shown into a darkened director's booth that overlooked the studio. There was a plate of fresh sandwiches there and a jug of orange juice, for which she was grateful, as she hadn't had any lunch. A young assistant called Trixie asked if she wanted anything stronger to drink, but she refused.

It was the first time she had seen what Barry Quick actually did for a living; before that she had only known him as one of the crowd in the Red Lion. A pleasant, stocky, middle-aged man in a good suit. Now, on his own territory, he set about his task with impressive competence. There was a director present, but he played only a nominal role; it was clear that Barry Quick ran the show.

After about twenty minutes they had already begun working. An actor whom Sarah had seen a couple of times on television was there to read the voice-over. He had done similar jobs many times before, so Barry was satisfied with his third attempt. Then Doreen and Cat were seated in the studio and she could watch the proceedings on the monitor screens, before which Quick now sat with the director.

'Let me hear the music selection before we start,' Barry said into a microphone, 'It'll get us all in the mood.'

'This is the first one,' the director said and the booth was suddenly filled with the ominous opening chords of 'Mars', from the Planets suite.

Barry waved his hand to cut. 'This isn't for *The War of the Worlds*,' he said with just a touch of impatience. 'It's about a lady from Camden Town who happens to have second sight. What else have you got?'

The director played several other snatches of music but Barry

185

was dissatisfied with them all. At last he looked up at the clock, then clapped his hands together. 'Trixie,' he called out and the assistant came running. 'Get me an old-fashioned clock – hands set at … ten minutes to midnight. Film it going forward fast … about half a dozen revolutions. Then run the film in reverse so the hands go backwards. Right?'

'Right,' she answered.

'Then I want some stock footage of fast-moving clouds, you know the sort of thing. Spielberg stuff.'

'Yup.'

'Superimpose the two images. I know it's a bit of a cliché but we haven't got any time.'

He turned to the director. 'While Trixie's doing that we'll shoot the studio stuff. We can put it together later.'

'What about the music?'

'We won't use music, just the ticking of a clock very loud, and fade it when we go into the studio shot.' He leaned to the microphone again. 'Jerry,' he said and the actor looked up. 'Will you be able to pace the voice-over to the time of the ticking clock?'

'No problem.'

While they continued with various technicalities, Sarah began to feel bored. It was not the first time she had been on a film set and she knew there was nobody more redundant than an uninvolved observer. There would be at least another hour of this, she told herself. Finally she got up, left the director's booth, walked to the ground floor and out into Wardour Street. The rain had stopped so she decided to take a stroll in the fresh air. London always felt better after rain. She walked to Berwick Street Market and bought some fruit from a barrow, stopped at a book shop for a time, then made her way back to the studio. It was pretty much all done by the time she returned. There was no sign of Doreen in the studio, but when she went to the Ladies' room she found her sitting on a stool before the mirror.

'Are you all right?' Sarah asked. Doreen was not looking at her reflection but staring down at her hands. She looked up with a smile. 'Yes, my love, I just had to sit down quietly for a minute.' She reached out and took Sarah's hand. 'That man of yours, do you think there's any chance he would come here and see me? Barry says we've got to wait until the whole thing is completely finished in case he needs to reshoot anything. But I would like to see Mr Greaves. It might be urgent.'

'Why do you want him?' Sarah asked.

'I don't really know, to be honest,' Doreen answered. 'I keep getting his name. I expect it will become clear when he gets here.'

'I'll do my best.'

'Good,' Doreen said with a squeeze of her hand.

Sarah found a telephone in reception and dialled Greaves's mobile number.

'Where are you?' she asked.

'In a pub in Soho with Nick.'

'Good Lord, so am I – in Soho, that is. Look, do you have time to come to the studio in Wardour Street? I'm with Doreen Clay – she says she wants to talk to you.'

'Why? Has she remembered something?'

'I don't really know. But she says it's important.'

'We've got nothing else to do,' he said. 'Give me the address.'

When they arrived at the studio they were directed to a little windowless reception room, where Sarah sat with Doreen and Cat Abbot. There was barely space for Greaves and Holland to squeeze in.

'Would you mind if I was alone with Mr Greaves?' Doreen asked. The others began to rise and she added, 'Oh, you stay please, Raymond.'

Mystified by her request, Sarah and Holland stood in the

narrow corridor outside. Doreen shut the door and then asked Greaves and Abbot to hold hands with her. Greaves did so, feeling rather foolish.

'Now I'm not going to go into a deep trance, I'm going to try something I don't usually do – stay conscious when I make contact.' She closed her eyes. Still feeling distinctly foolish, Greaves watched her face in the silence that followed.

'I've got someone,' she suddenly said in a normal voice. Then: 'Oh, dear, it's a child, I think. Ah, yes, showing me her letter blocks … will you speak, dear? … no, what a shame. Yes, I can see them. You're going to spell something. I understand.' There was a longer pause, and then Doreen smiled: 'Cat, yes, I can see that. Now the next word. Cat knows. That's the message? Thank you, dear.'

She released their hands.

'I don't know anything,' Abbot said apo! getically, in the following stillness.

'Cat,' Greaves repeated slowly. Then: 'CAT!' in a much louder voice. He pulled open the door. 'I've got it, Nick,' he said in sudden elation. He turned to Sarah. 'Where's the telephone?'

Fortnum and Mason were a bit sticky about releasing the information Greaves wanted; they regarded any dealings with their customers as confidential. Holland noted that the secrecy of the rich's personal business was maintained – even when it came to the purchase of their groceries. But Greaves used his authority, the accounts department checked with dispatch and discovered that a weekly order for jellied chicken breasts was sent to the flat now occupied by Brigadier Wescott. The bill was settled monthly by a Mr Gavin Stuart De Courcey-Beresford of 16 Corton Mansions, South Audley Street, W1.

It was growing dark when they arrived at the address. An open-cage lift took them to the fourth floor, where they could hear the sound of a string quartet playing Vivaldi as they rang the bell. The door was answered by a slight figure, dressed exquisitely in a pin-striped, three-piece suit, fine gold watch-chain across the waistcoat and a white carnation in the button-hole. A soft hand wearing a heavy gold signet ring on the little finger fluttered towards them.

'If you're the caterers, it's far too early. I told Mr Mitchell you were to come at seven, you'll have to come back,' he said in a petulant, high-pitched voice.

Bonnie Prince Charlie, Greaves thought, as he looked down at the pink and white, pop-eyed features surmounted by a mop of curly hair that had been dyed to preserve the gold.

'We're police officers, sir,' Greaves replied. 'May we have a word with you?'

De Courcey-Beresford sighed. 'You'd better come in.' He led them into a wide entrance hall. Through one open door, Greaves saw a group of young women seated on upright chairs listening to the music.

'We'd better go in here,' De Courcey-Beresford said, and ushered them into a gloomy bedroom. It was dominated by a vast four-poster bed draped with extravagant swags of material emanating from a large coat of arms. A large bowl of white carnations stood on the bedside table and the walls were covered with dark portraits and a collection of ancient weapons, fans of pikes, claymores and muskets. De Courcey-Beresford took the only seat in the room, a large throne-like chair, with lion heads carved into the handrests.

Greaves studied the man for a while without speaking; it was obvious that he was not disturbed by their presence. 'Are you by any chance descended from the King across the Water?' Greaves asked in a friendly, respectful tone.

De Courcey-Beresford gave a little squirm of pleasure and lowered his gaze like a girl. 'How did you guess our little family secret?' he said in a more friendly voice.

'The resemblance to the prince is remarkable.'

The old man fluttered his hand again. 'Yes, the face pops up every few generations. Now, how can I help you?' He reached out and rang a bell while he spoke. A dark-haired woman limped into the room so quickly Greaves did not have time to begin. She had obviously been listening at the door; she moved awkwardly and leaned on a thin walking stick. Greaves noticed that she was elegantly dressed and quite beautiful despite the misshapen leg.

'Arrange for some chairs for my guests, please,' De Courcey-Beresford ordered.

'Do you want me to dismiss the class?' she asked.

'Yes, but tell Caroline, Alexandra and Elizabeth it's their turn to eat dinner with me. They can study the book on the Post-Impressionists while they wait.'

Greaves did not speak until the chairs were brought in by another pretty, nervous girl. Then he began: 'Do you know a girl called Polly Weaver, sir?'

De Courcey-Beresford shook his head.

'She lived in King Street, just off St James's Square. I believe you gave her a Siamese cat.'

His face cleared. 'Oh, you mean Cressida.'

'Cressida?'

'Yes, Cressida Paradine, delightful girl. She went to Mustique last week. Why should you think her name is Polly?'

Greaves did not answer the question, but asked another instead. 'How did you come to meet this Cressida Paradine, sir?'

'The usual way,' he answered. 'She was enrolled in my classes.'

'What exactly do you teach?'

De Courcey-Beresford waved a hand. 'The social graces, of course. I suppose you could call this a finishing school.'

Greaves produced a picture and handed it to him. 'Is this Cressida?'

He glanced down. 'Yes, rather an odd photograph. What's the matter with her?'

'She's dead, sir,' Greaves answered flatly.

'Oh, my good heavens,' he said. 'How terrible, she was such a sweet girl, such fun. Much more *élan* than the others. Even when she left us she would come and call on me. That's why I bought her the cat.'

'Tell me, sir, do you ever watch television, or read the newspapers?' Greaves asked.

'Certainly not,' De Courcey-Beresford replied. 'They're filled with vulgar rubbish, what could one possibly learn from them?'

'You would have found out about the death of this girl, sir.'

'That would not have improved my life, Superintendent.'

Greaves thought he heard the front door open before he asked the next question. 'And who paid Cressida's fees?'

'Miss Newburn will know.' He rang the bell again, but this time no one came.

Greaves glanced towards Holland. 'I believe I heard the door a moment ago, I think it was Miss Newburn leaving. Bring her back.'

A few minutes later, Holland returned with the woman. She was dressed in street clothes now.

'May we have a word in private with Miss Newburn, sir?' Greaves asked.

'As you wish,' De Courcey-Beresford replied, and he rose from the throne-like chair. 'I shall be with my pupils, instructing them in the mystery of pronunciation,' he announced. 'I wonder why the rich are so neglectful of their children's upbringing these days? Some of these girls can hardly speak English at all.'

Miss Newburn was frightened. Greaves could see her hands trembling and she kept glancing nervously towards the door, as if expecting another visitor. In the silence they could hear De

Courcey-Beresford's high-pitched voice in the other room quite clearly, urging someone to speak from the diaphragm: 'Place your hands above your tummy and feel the vibration when the word is pronounced correctly.'

For a moment, Greaves thought of the man's ancestor leading his wild army of Highlanders. Then he turned to the woman before him. 'Who brought Polly Weaver here, Miss Newburn?' Greaves asked, and his voice was cold and hard.

The woman made a slight adjustment to her dress, to conceal her deformity.

'She just rang up and enrolled herself,' she answered, but the words were spoken in barely a whisper. It was like listening to someone who was drowning and trying to call for help.

'I thought she was known as Cressida Paradine here?'

'That's how she introduced herself.'

'But you saw her picture, didn't you?'

Suddenly all attempts to hold back collapsed and she covered her face with her hands. 'Oh, God, they'll kill me. What can I do?'

Greaves got up and walked to a small table where there were decanters of drink set out on a large silver tray. He found some brandy and poured a glass. She took it and drained the measure in one swallow. But no colour returned to her pallid cheeks.

Greaves was gentle now. 'Don't worry,' he said softly. 'Nobody is going to hurt you, I promise. Just tell me who they are.' He nodded, and Holland poured her more brandy.

'I only have a telephone number,' she said slowly. 'When the girls are ready, that is when he says they've passed, I call it and they take them away. They ring me when they have another enrolment.'

'And the girls live here during their instruction?'

'That's right.'

'Why do you think they'll hurt you?'

She did not answer immediately, but instead stretched out the malformed leg. 'They did this to me because I didn't tell them when one girl ran away.'

Greaves could see how brutally the bone had been smashed. He forced his voice to be calm. 'Give me the telephone number, Miss Newburn,' he said gently. 'They'll never hurt you again.'

CHAPTER
TEN

Thursday, October 29 6.35 p.m.

Despite his terse, rather austere manner, Richard Gibson, the managing director of Gazette Newspapers Ltd, was in reality a rather cheerful, carefree sort of individual. And the reason for his inner peace of mind was simple. Although his title sounded imposing, he actually had few real responsibilities. Sir Robert Hall, the chairman, had chosen him for the job because, over the years, Gibson had developed a technique in his dealings with Sir Robert that had proved foolproof. While other members of the board merely agreed with the chairman's decisions, Gibson had added a dimension of his own which his fellow directors secretly referred to as 'aggressive creeping'.

Gibson had perfected the technique some years before, when he was first seconded from the accounts department to act as a temporary personal assistant to Sir Robert. At first he had appeared to make no impression at all on the chairman, who barely seemed to acknowledge his presence, no matter how deeply he grovelled. Then, one Saturday afternoon, with only another week to go before he returned to his usual post, he watched an old movie on television called *The Mudlark* and it changed his life.

The film portrayed the relationship between Queen Victoria and her manservant, the gillie John Brown, with such insight that Gibson had immediately been able to translate it directly from the screen into his own world of bondage to Sir Robert. The film showed Brown as being gruff, upright and plain-speaking – a man of enormous personal dignity, who nonetheless slavishly carried out the wishes of his monarch to the obvious satisfaction of them both. Gibson instantly saw how he could duplicate the relationship, but he had to wait until the following Wednesday to put his plan into action.

On Sir Robert's instructions, he had prepared the contract of a new union agreement with the journalists which had given them a 5 per cent pay rise. Sir Robert had concluded the deal reluctantly. Only a last-minute loss of nerve had caused him to crumble in his original intention of sticking at 3 per cent, and he was still feeling sensitive about being bested in his encounter with the negotiators. Few people knew that beneath his spiky exterior Sir Robert was in fact a timorous soul. He owed his original success to one aspect of his personality: he had no feelings about human beings at all. His childhood had been friendless, and he had been unable to form relationships in his youth. Then he discovered accountancy, and fell in love for the first time in his life. A world where people's lives could be controlled by simply altering numbers seemed perfect. But faced across a table by angry individuals, Sir Robert invariably folded his hand. When Gibson laid the surrender document before Sir Robert, he said, reluctantly, and with just a trace of a newly acquired Scottish accent, 'Well, I suppose I'd better congratulate you on this one. The gamblers in the office were betting you'd come a cropper for certain.'

'What did you say?' Sir Robert asked incredulously, not quite sure if the remark had been insult or praise.

Gibson took a deep breath before he continued. 'I said, I suppose you should be congratulated. When I saw what you were doing, I'll confess I had the deepest doubts, but now I've got to say, in all honesty, it was a brilliant piece of work.'

'So you approve?' Sir Robert asked, with a grim little smile of pleasure.

'Approve? Man, it was a work of genius. None of us dreamed you'd get them below 7 per cent. That's the figure I would have settled for.'

Sir Robert looked at him more closely. 'So you would have settled at 7?'

'Aye, and proud of it.'

'Well at least you're honest.'

'It seems to me you could do with some honest speaking around here,' Gibson said, plunging further. 'There, I've said it, but I'll not be afraid of telling you the truth.'

'What other truths do you have in mind?' Sir Robert asked, beginning to enjoy the conversation.

Gibson drew himself up. 'If you don't mind plain speaking – you work too hard. Slow down, man, you'll burn yourself up, and without you this whole place will go down the pan.'

'And what are my other faults?'

'You're too generous, and you suffer fools too gladly. You're carrying an awful lot of men about on your shoulders. Pass some of the load.'

'Any other suggestions?'

'Remember others don't have your gifts. You look at a problem and you see straight to the heart of it right away. That's why you're often misunderstood. You need someone steady who can follow through your orders. You throw off ideas like a

Catherine wheel. The sparks lie on the ground because they're just not quick enough to catch them in the air.'

Sir Robert had began to nod. Everything this stern young man said was true. In a few minutes he'd heard more common sense than in all of the usual sophisticated blather he got from his other directors in a week. In a sudden moment, he had decided it was better to listen to the plain unvarnished facts, spoken from an honest heart, than waste his valuable time seeking understanding from those who wished to use his broad shoulders only as a prop for their own inadequacies.

From then on, Richard Gibson's rise had been as swift and sure as a kite in a strong wind. And each twitch on the strings had sent Gibson dancing in the direction Sir Robert required. The only difficulties he ever encountered in his day-to-day duties occurred in his dealings with the editor.

It was a common fact in all newspaper offices that the line of control between management and the editorial department was blurred. Although the journalists worked within the financial constraints imposed by a business plan, the policy of the paper was in the hands of the editor, who reported directly to the chairman. All other departments took their instructions from the managing director – and that was the cause of the present problem.

Richard Gibson had never seen Brian Meadows so angry. A red flush suffused his features and he banged his fists down on the bleached-wood surface of his desk so hard that an overloaded in-tray spilled its contents on to the fawn carpet.

'You're telling me that you're putting a television commercial about Doreen Clay out tonight!' he shouted.

Gibson wrung his hands as he answered. 'That's right, Brian, the chairman agreed to the extra cost, in fact it was his idea. I thought you'd be pleased. You keep going on that you need more money spent on television promotion.'

Meadows stood up and glared across the desk. 'I'll tell you why I'm not pleased,' he said in a low voice. 'We haven't got any bloody copy yet – the readers are going to watch the television advertisements tonight, rush out to buy the paper in the morning and find nothing about Doreen Clay except a puff on page one saying read the *Gazette* tomorrow. I think in those circumstances they'll be justified in feeling more than a little pissed off. They may even sue us under the Trade Descriptions Act, I know I would.'

Gibson reached out to support himself on the edge of Meadows's desk. 'But I thought you had the story,' he bleated and there was no trace of his Scottish accent. 'I've already signed the cheque for £15,000.'

Meadows held a hand to his brow. He told himself it was useless to shout at the quivering figure before him. 'Look Gibby, all we've got is Doreen Clay's agreement to tell us her story, nobody has written a bloody line yet. The advertisements should go out tomorrow night; you'll have to re-book the slots and pay the penalty.'

'I can't,' Gibson said miserably. 'There's no way I can get in touch with the chairman, and he's ordered them to go on tonight, the time spots were specially chosen. We had to pay a premium.'

'Where is he?' Meadows demanded, snatching up his telephone. 'I'll talk to him and explain the cock-up.'

'You can't,' Gibson wailed. 'He's out of touch.'

'Nobody's that out of touch, Gibby. Now where is he?'

'I can't tell you,' Gibson said and he slumped down in an easy chair. 'Security. I swore I wouldn't.'

'Gibby,' Meadows said softly. 'I'm the editor. If you don't let me know where Sir Robert is right now I shall lock you in your office, rip out the telephone and cancel the advertisements myself.'

Gibson looked at him warily. He had known reckless behaviour by members of the editorial department on other occasions, and despite Meadows's senior position, he was still a journalist at heart. Reluctantly he owned up.

'He's on board a nuclear submarine. No civilian messages can be received,' he said finally.

Defeated, Meadows sat down. 'What, in the name of Judas Iscariot, is he doing on a submarine?' he asked after a moment of despair.

Gibson looked up. 'It's been planned for months; I've been working with the publicity department on a need-to-know basis. He's the personal guest of the Admiral of the Home Fleet. Remember how we backed the keeping of Trident during the election campaign?'

Meadows nodded: the chairman had insisted on that one item of policy above all others. Meadows had gone along with the order for the sake of a quiet life.

Gibson continued: 'This is why, apparently, he's always wanted to go on a submarine. He gets off in Portsmouth Harbour at nine o'clock and goes straight on board Nelson's *Victory* for dinner. Publicity have spent all day arranging for a giant television set to be installed on board so they can watch the commercial that goes out in the 9.30 slot. Imagine what he will do if the whole thing is a flop.'

Meadows said nothing. He just sat for a moment with his head in his hands.

'Don't worry, Brian,' he said. 'There won't be any comeback tomorrow, you know he never reads the paper. Only the readers will notice.'

The editor still said nothing. He had swivelled his chair to look out of the window into the dark sky. Gibson got up and quietly sneaked away.

Meadows swung around at the sound of the closing door and looked up at the clock – there was just time for what he now had in mind. He told his secretary to get Sarah Keane on the telephone, then called the back bench on his hot line. Reg Stenton, the night editor, answered. Meadows was relieved it wasn't Frank Corby.

'Reg, hold out the feature about the gnome craze on page seven and make it your last forme to go … yes, even after page one. Tell Features I want them to re-do the page on the edition. They can use a large blow-up of Doreen Clay's eyes, the one in the puff on page one, oh, and alter the puff to cross-refer to seven. Tell them to use the headline: THE MOMENT I KNEW OF MY STRANGE POWERS. They're to set it all up and allow for 800 words, and I want a big tomorrow line: HOW SEX PUTS OFF THE SPIRITS, got that? OK, get moving.'

He caught Sarah in Cat's suite at the Savoy; the three of them were sharing a bottle of champagne while they discussed the shape the series would take.

Sarah raised her eyebrows to Cat when Meadows came on to tell her about the piece he wanted for the edition, but she did not protest. 'Well, I did think it was odd, Brian,' she answered, using the editor's Christian name for the first time. 'But I imagined you'd written an extended introduction for the series in the office. That's all right, we'll manage to get something together.'

She hung up and turned to Cat again. 'They want 800 words right now.'

Cat did not flinch at the prospect. Panic was not an unusual state of affairs on a newspaper, in fact it sometimes simplified things – if one could avoid seizing up under stress. There was no time to agonise, just bash it out and hope for the best. And if anyone said it was rubbish, there was always the answer: that's what you get when you ask for the impossible.

'I've brought a Tandy,' Sarah said. The portable lap-top terminal could be attached to a telephone so that the copy would be sent straight into the *Gazette*'s computer at Gray's Inn Road. Cat nodded. 'OK, we both ask questions, I dictate and you type, clean it up as we go along.'

Sixty-five minutes later they'd finished writing. Doreen's story told of the day at her primary school when she'd warned a teacher that two children, who had not returned to the classroom after the lunch break, were trapped in an abandoned refrigerator at the back of a local butcher's shop in the High Road. The teacher couldn't understand how she had known where the missing children were; Doreen had been kept in the classroom throughout the break as she'd come to school with a bad cold.

Once the copy had been sent, they sat back again and finished the champagne.

'Funny that,' Abbot said in a satisfied voice, as he poured the last dregs into Doreen's glass. 'When I was a kid something odd happened to me at school.'

'What was that, Raymond?' Doreen asked.

'I'd forgotten it until now. A mad dog got into our playground. Bloody great black thing. All the kids were terrified, including me, I can tell you.'

'What happened?' asked Sarah.

Cat shrugged. 'The others all buggered off, but it trapped me in a corner against one of those chain-link fences. I tried to climb up but I was too frightened, I kept slipping down again.'

'So? Did it bite you?' Sarah asked.

He shrugged again. 'No, I turned round to face it and it just dropped dead. Bit of an anti-climax really. At least for the other kids. They were expecting it to tear me to pieces.'

'Did you touch it?' said Doreen.

'No. One minute it was snarling at me, the next it was as stiff as a board.' He got up. 'Come on, let's go and eat. It's all right for you two, I haven't had a mouthful all day. We can come back later and watch the commercial on TV.'

It was dark when Andy Muir and Eddie Page emerged from the cinema. Page had enjoyed the double feature they had sat through: the first film had been a comedy set in Los Angeles where rival gang leaders fell for the same girl, the second was set in a fantasy-world of questing knights and magical creatures with cosmic powers.

Andy Muir had barely glanced at what was happening on the screen before him. He had been planning what to do about Glendowning. When they came out of the theatre, Eddie Page cursed softly, but Muir was glad to see that the rain had started again: people didn't notice what went on around them in bad weather. 'Let's find a pub,' he said and to Page's growing bewilderment they tried three, which Muir explored inside and out, until he settled on the one he wanted, close to Pentonville Road.

It was a great empty, decaying barn of a place that smelt like a midden. They settled in a corner, close to a door leading on to an alleyway, then Muir explained his plan. 'I want you to go along to this address,' he said softly, handing Eddie the card Smokey had given him. 'Find this fella, Glendowning, and tell him you've come over here to bring back your sister who's run away from home. Say she's a junkie. Say that you've found her and she's with your uncle – that's me. Tell him we've got her out the back here – ' he nodded towards the alleyway. 'But say she won't come with us until she's spoken to Glendowning because he's helped her. Say she's only agreed to come home if he thinks it's a good idea. Understand?'

Eddie smiled. 'And you'll be waiting out there?'

'That's right. Send him around the back, not through the bar. Then you keep watch at the head of the alley. I'll make the bastard talk.'

'How will you know it's him?'

Andy Muir considered the question and then smiled at his solution. 'Tell him to whistle: "When Irish Eyes are Smiling", every fucking Englishman knows that. Tell him it's the girl's favourite song.'

'Won't he be able to describe us to the police when you're done with him?'

'You just go and do what I tell you. Don't worry about that.'

When Page had gone off into the night, Muir slipped into the alleyway. The rain was still heavy, but he didn't mind. He reached into his pocket to check on the plastic syringe he'd brought with him; it contained enough pure heroin to kill a charging rhino. Once he had talked, Glendowning wouldn't be recalling any lads with Belfast accents.

While Muir waited, a single swaying man came out of the pub to relieve himself against the wall, but he ignored the hunched figure of Andy Muir. It was the sort of area where people did not inquire into the behaviour of others. The rain had soaked through the shoulders of his overcoat by the time he saw a man coming towards him, outlined by the street lights at the end of the alley. Muir could not make out the face that approached him along the narrow cobbled walkway – but the tune he whistled was familiar enough. When the man was a few feet away, Muir leaped forward, seized him by the lapels of his coat and banged him with such force against the wall, he could hear the crack of his head against the blackened bricks.

'Jesus, Andy it's me!' Eddie Page cried out.

'You fucking idiot,' Muir hissed. 'Where's our man?'

Eddie rubbed his head. 'There's no need to question him. I know who the other fella is.'

'How?'

'It was just amazing. Like something out of that film we saw. There I was, talking to this Glendowning fella in some shit-heap of a little office, and there's a television switched on in the corner. I'm just about to tell him the tale, when this fucking tart comes barging in, saying he's expecting her. I nearly punch her in the tits, I'm so bloody angry. Just as I'm going to give her a mouthful, the very man we're looking for suddenly appears on the TV screen. I tell you, I could hardly believe it.'

'On the television, you say?'

'Honest to God, Andy. He's in a fucking commercial for the

204

Gazette newspaper. Some crap about ghosts or something. Anyway his name is Raymond Abbot.'

'You're sure?'

'As sure as I'm standing here. They even put the name on the screen.'

Muir shifted his shoulders under the wet overcoat. 'A newspaperman,' he said softly. 'Big Davey's not going to relish killing a reporter.'

Fanny Hunter and Tony Glendowning disliked each other on sight, but they made an effort to conceal the fact for differing reasons. Fanny because she wanted the joint interview with his father, and Glendowning because he possessed inherent good manners, a trait his expensive education had been unable to eradicate, and would always treat women with respect. He had agreed to see her only because Jeremy Blakestone had pleaded it would be good for HAND, now his worst suspicions were confirmed by her domineering manner.

Fanny told herself that her antipathy to the young man was caused by her loathing of inherited privilege, an attitude that had made her one of Margaret Thatcher's most devoted admirers, but in reality she knew instinctively that Tony Glendowning would not be susceptible to any of the techniques she usually employed when dealing with the opposite sex.

She realised, in the moment they shook hands, that he did not find her attractive. He had no reason to fear her, and he wasn't of the generation who would warm to her coarse, no-punches-pulled evaluation of life. This young man, who had been given on a silver platter everything she'd had to strive for, was exactly the kind of wet, bleeding-heart liberal whom she had counted as the enemy since the day she had begun her column.

'I thought we might go somewhere else and have a drink, I've got my chauffeur outside,' Fanny said, when the other young man who had been hanging about the office departed.

'If you like,' he replied, and he took his overcoat from the coat-rack. When he put it on he felt in the pockets and produced a sheet torn from the *Gazette*. He hesitated, then said: 'Would you mind waiting while I make a quick telephone call?'

Fanny stood in the doorway while he dialled the number and saw that he was unable to speak to the person he wanted. 'What's all that about?' she asked.

Glendowning passed her the sheet of paper. 'I think I know this girl,' he answered. 'I've been trying to talk to the man in charge of the case all day, but he's been busy every time I've rung.'

'Where do you know her from?' said Fanny, as they left the scruffy premises of the hostel and entered the warm interior of Fanny's car.

'We have a rehabilitation centre near Guildford. I think I saw her there, but it was a long time ago, I could be wrong.'

'And Superintendent Greaves has refused to speak to you?'

'Oh, I don't think so. They tried to put me through a couple of times, he just wasn't available.'

'What was the girl's name?'

Glendowning thought for a while. 'I'm pretty sure it was Polly Weaver,' he answered.

'Did you talk to her?'

Glendowning nodded. 'Actually, we spent part of the afternoon together. We went for a walk in the woods around the home. I wanted to ask her out again, but when I rang the following Saturday they said she'd gone to another job.'

'So she wasn't one of the waifs and strays?'

'No, she was organising a disco for the other kids. All sorts of people give up their spare time for us. She was a professional dancer.'

Fanny sat in silence for the rest of their journey to a wine bar near Hatton Garden. She was beginning to sense that Glendowning's conversation held the seeds of an opportunity to harm Colin Greaves, and the prospect was deeply appealing.

When Glendowning was seated at a little candle-lit table Fanny went to the telephone near the entrance and called Scotland Yard. After a few minutes she got the duty officer she wanted. 'No, madam,' he replied in answer to her question. 'We don't have the name of the murdered girl yet. Do you have any information that might be of assistance to us?' Fanny said no and hurried back to the table, the idea of an interview with Tony Glendowning and his father no longer foremost in her mind.

'Tell me more about Polly Weaver,' she said as she picked up her glass of wine.

Thursday, October 29 10.05 p.m.

Kevin Sinclair sat at the news desk and drummed his fingers while he listened to Andy Muir once again pleading to speak to Cat Abbot. It was the third time he had called. 'I'm sorry, Mr Pearse, Mr Abbot is out of the office at the moment … As I explained before, sir, we can't give his number to you, but the second he's in touch I'll give him your number and he can ring you back … yes, sir. I promise I'll do it as soon as he calls us … yes, sir, he's still out on the same job.'

Sinclair replaced the receiver and redialled Cat's suite at the Savoy. The number rang for a time without an answer. Sinclair hung up and turned to his computer terminal. He called up Cat Abbot's personal file and typed in: A Patrick Pearse wants you to call him urgently. Says it's a big story. He added the time and the telephone number and sent the message into the electronic bowels of the machine.

The task completed, he listened once again to the conversation that was taking place a few feet away on the back bench. Reg Stenton was talking to Fanny Hunter, who was not usually seen so late about the office. Clearly Stenton had reservations about something and Fanny was bullying him into letting her have her own way.

'Are you sure you wouldn't prefer to wait until tomorrow, Fanny?' he pleaded. 'The early editions have gone now. We've just about missed everything but London.'

'Who the fuck cares about anywhere but London?' Fanny replied. 'Come on, Reg, how often do you get a belting story handed to you like this? Scotland Yard will probably release the name tomorrow, they must have it by now. You'll have beaten the rest of Fleet Street out of sight.'

Reg Stenton turned to the screen of his terminal again. He had to admit, it was bloody good copy. He would've preferred to consult with Brian Meadows, but the editor had gone off duty an hour ago and he wasn't going to disturb him now. Not after what he'd said about being glad he could leave the paper in his hands rather than that little prick, Corby. Reg had been feeling his age recently and the devils of self-doubt had begun to whisper to him that he might be past it. Well, he'd show them. There was no point in pissing about when you had a good one. He pulled a layout pad towards him and scrawled:

> EXCLUSIVE by Fanny Hunter.
> *Gazette* beats Scotland Yard
> to identify murder victim –
> PEER'S SON DATED DEAD GIRL
> POLLY WEAVER.

Fanny leaned over and slapped Stenton on the back. 'That's brilliant, Reg,' she said with deep satisfaction.

Jamie Lambert loved his own body so much he liked to look at himself at every available opportunity. To his own great good fortune, he lived in a world that allowed him to spend his days wearing only the minimum of clothes and surrounded by mirrors that reflected his long, muscular form. Whenever he wished, he could gaze upon his body and admire skin the colour of polished mahogany, streaked blond hair and a face that many women found devastating.

The health club that Lambert managed for the Doyle organisation was the last link in the arduous programme of training that Doyle's most expensive prostitutes underwent before they were ready for the market-place. After their schooling in the social graces, Lambert concentrated on their bodies. Each was under his personal supervision for six weeks. And in that time, he saw to it that they worked. Of course, if the basic material hadn't been there, the task would have been impossible. But Lambert only got the cream of the crop, so his task wasn't that difficult. And there were plenty of perks attached to the job.

Some women thought his finely formed features at their best when he smiled, but he had practised and perfected a little-boy-lost glance that often had more success than the grin which revealed his perfect teeth. Lambert's only real passion in life was his body, but his hobby was hurting women. He could only enjoy sex when his partner was in real pain. Out of every group sent to him, he selected one particular member whom he would subject to his own special preference. It had always worked, with the exception of that little black bitch with the nose job, but he'd even made her pay in the end.

He used the little boy look now as he gazed down at the girl who lay naked on the massage table before him. He could tell she was young; her breasts still had the full firmness that lasted only for a few years. The little bitch had been watching him for five weeks now. Every day she'd come with the rest of the intake and he'd trained her to be as supple as a seal. He knew Fergus Doyle was interested; he'd hung about the club a lot over the last weeks, talking to her. But Fergus didn't have what he, Jamie Lambert, had: the little boy look. It was so easy: all he had to do was smile and they begged for it. This one had stayed behind as soon as he'd asked. He knew what he was doing was dangerous – Fergus was not someone to cross lightly – but the need was greater than the fear. And when he was finished with her, she wouldn't want to tell Fergus Doyle what had happened.

When the others had left, he'd turned out the lights in the rest of the club, and she'd gone into the massage room as instructed. Then he'd set to work on her with his hands covered in warm baby oil and she'd responded, like they all had. When he judged that she was ready, he whispered for her to turn over onto her stomach and close her eyes. She did as she was told and her heavy blonde hair fell forward to spill from the edge of the table. He raised her buttocks with a gentle lifting motion, and muttered some endearment. Then he reached beneath the table to the ledge below and took hold of the carved ivory phallus, thick as his wrist, that he had concealed earlier. With the first thrust, her body had contracted in agony and the scream had been so satisfying he'd felt his own penis rising in anticipation. She squirmed now, like an impaled butterfly, as his muscular arm moved like a piston. Later, he would take his own time, slowly, while she was still wide-eyed with the pain, and there would be no comment about his inadequacy.

Winner's Health Club had closed at 10.30 p.m. Greaves and Holland stood before the row of darkened shops in Maida Vale and looked at the notice that declared the premises open for business again at 7 a.m. the following morning. The rain still fell,

210

but with a monotonous weeping now. Since they had traced the telephone number given to them by Miss Newburn they had door-stepped the empty flat in St John's Wood, until a neighbour entering the next apartment had told them that Lambert often worked late at the health club. But there was no sign that the premises were now occupied.

'Let's call it a day,' Greaves said. 'We'll come back tomorrow.'

They had turned to walk away when the sound of a distant scream from inside the building reached them.

'Can you break it down?' Greaves asked. Holland looked at the door. It had recently been given a fresh coat of paint, but the original woodwork was old and did not look too strong. He took a short run and hit the spot next to the Yale lock with the upper part of his right shoulder. One hundred and ninety pounds of bone and muscle, concentrated like the blow from a sledge-hammer, smashed into the spot and the door shattered from the frame like a crust of bread. As they entered the darkened hallway they heard another scream, and hurried forward along a corridor towards a glimmer of light at the rear. When they entered the brightly lit room, they found the naked figure of Jamie Lambert crouching towards them, holding the ivory phallus like a cosh. The girl had fallen from the table and now lay huddled in a corner like a wounded animal.

Lambert swung the phallus at Holland, who avoided the blow and caught hold of his other arm, but Lambert's oiled body was too slippery to hold and his next blow caught Holland above the left eyebrow, causing him to stumble and fall. Lambert now advanced towards Greaves, who backed into the corridor. Launching himself forward, Lambert raised the phallus again, but Greaves did not retreat any further. He lifted his left arm in a blocking motion and thrust forward his right hand, palm cupped, to catch his assailant under the chin.

Lambert's head snapped back, jarring the spinal cord and transmitting the shock to the nerves in his cerebral cortex,

211

causing him to black out. He fell, like a half-empty sack of potatoes, at Greaves's feet and the phallus rolled from his hand.

Holland had handed the girl the towel from the massage table and she sat huddled now, in shock from the bewildering events she had witnessed, and the assault she had endured.

'It's all right, Miss, we're police officers,' Holland reassured her.

'I don't want to bring any charges,' she said in a gasping voice, 'I just want to go home.'

'Are you sure?' Holland asked.

'Quite sure,' she answered. 'I know my rights, I'm a law student at London University.' She looked around her, and Greaves could see that she was gradually recovering her composure. 'I just want to find my clothes and go home.'

'We'll take you,' Holland said.

She shook her head vigorously, stepped over the still supine body of Lambert and entered another room.

A few minutes later she appeared once again, fully dressed, and with a muttered farewell fled from the premises. By now, Lambert had recovered somewhat and was sitting in a chair in the massage room. 'You've got to let me see my solicitor,' he insisted, while Greaves and Holland glanced around the room. Holland saw it first: a Polaroid camera on the ledge beneath the table, half covered by a towel.

'You like to take pictures of them, do you?' he asked. 'So where do you keep your album?'

'Look, just fuck off, will you,' Lambert replied, but Greaves noticed in which direction his eyes had flickered. He stood on the massage table and reached up to the panels in the false ceiling. The second one he tried was loose. Reaching into the recess, he withdrew a cardboard box.

Inside was a collection of pictures Lambert had taken of girls when he had finished assaulting them. The first in the pile was of Polly Weaver.

CHAPTER
ELEVEN

Thursday, October 29 11.20 p.m.

Fanny Hunter sat in her office, still gloating over the story that was now being prepared for publication, but at the same time feeling a little flat. She didn't want to go home after her evening of triumph, because her husband, Osbert, would be sitting in his room, reading some interminable tract on theology; or if he were in a lighter mood, German medieval history. Osbert Hannay, a devout Catholic, was some years older than Fanny, who was his second wife. They had first got to know each other when he taught her at Cambridge. Later, when he was a widower, they met again and married.

It had hardly been an ideal match for Fanny, because she always thought of herself as being in love with Jack Keane. As with Cat Abbot, Jack had affected her life more deeply than she ever wanted to admit, and still represented something to her that was unattainable.

The fact that he had loved Sarah and chosen to make his life with her represented a failure that Fanny found intolerable, and the daily presence of Sarah in the offices of the *Gazette* served as a reminder of that failure. As it was now impossible to win Jack, the next best thing would be to drive Sarah out of her life; and one way of bringing this about was to destroy the base of her power. The editor was a supporter of Sarah Keane, therefore the editor must be undermined, and tonight's story would help. Fanny remembered her creed: My enemy's friend is my enemy.

She could hardly tell all this to Osbert, knowing that he would find her motives sinful and would consider it his duty to explain why. Fanny did not relish the prospect of a lecture on ethics and morality from a man she despised. Still charged with the adrenalin of malice, she was in the mood to gossip. A sudden series of sounds from her secretary's office interrupted her train of thought: soft bumps and intermittent giggling.

Fanny opened her own door and in the gloom of the outer room, found her secretary, Jackie, swaying in the embrace of Ted Bolt, one of the features subs. Both of them looked towards her like guilty children caught stealing biscuits in the dead of night.

'It's two fucking months until Christmas,' Fanny said belligerently. 'No leg-overs in the office until then.'

'I'm ever so sorreee, Miss Hunter,' Jackie answered. 'I didn't know we were disturbing you. I only came back to get my shopping.'

Fanny was about to let them go on their way, when she remembered something. 'By the way, Ted,' she added. 'Why the fuck didn't you put a picture of the Princess of Wales in my column?'

Emboldened by the pints of draught lager he had consumed in the Red Lion for the greater part of the evening, Bolt attempted to demonstrate his independence to Jackie.

'She was only a digression in the piece, Fanny. The main thrust was about life on the Brent River estate.'

Fanny advanced towards him, like a battle cruiser descending on a rubber dinghy.

'Don't tell me about main thrusts – save that for Jackie, if you can still get it up,' she hissed. 'I mentioned Princess Di in the piece so that we could get her picture on the page, not some depressing fucking snapshot of buildings in the rain. One more cock-up like that and I'll have you checking car competitions for the rest of your life. Now piss off.'

Jackie tugged him from the room and Fanny stood victorious, her spirits restored by the encounter. She glanced at her watch and wondered if there was a congenial companion in the office who felt like a late-night drink. Her wish was answered when she looked along the newsroom. The bulky figure of Geoffrey Walker was standing at the back bench talking to Stenton. She hurried over and linked arms. 'Hello, you old bastard, how about taking me out on the town?' she said playfully.

Walker turned with a smile. 'Fanny,' my darling, what a pleasant surprise.' He pecked her on the cheek and added, 'I should be delighted.'

Fanny collected her coat and linked arms once again when she rejoined him. 'It's good to see you. What are you doing here so late?' she asked, as he escorted her from the building. Although they had known each other for many years, they did not meet a great deal. Walker seldom came into the office; most of his time was spent at the House of Commons.

'My weekly ritual,' he replied. 'I creep in like some creature of the night, leave my expenses as proof of my existence, and then slip back to the Palace of Westminster and my bed of native earth. Count Dracula had the right idea. Daytime is impossible in London. Much better to move about when the traffic is light.'

He saw that Fanny's chauffeur-driven car was still waiting in the vanway. 'What pleasures the company of the rich bring to we lumpenproletariat,' he sighed. 'And I thought I should end the evening in a taxicab.'

Fanny laughed. It was well known that in addition to his substantial salary, Geoffrey Walker had married money. The family of his American wife were reputed to own every fifth gallon of oil that was pumped out of Texas.

'How is Margot?' she inquired.

'Still in the forefront of the class struggle,' he replied when they were seated in the car. 'She was convinced Labour lost because they had drifted too far to the right.'

Although Geoffrey's own political convictions were of the deepest shade of blue, his wife was a fiery radical, who continued to preach for the redistribution of wealth, secure in the knowledge that the covenants of her trust fund could never be breached.

'Take us to Annabel's,' Fanny instructed her driver, and the car moved off in the direction of Berkeley Square. She leaned back and said, 'So tell me what you hear, Geoffrey. What news on the Rialto?'

'Politics, you mean?'

'Fuck politics, tell me what you know about Brian Meadows and Geraldine Miller?'

Walker glanced up to make sure the glass panel behind the driver was closed before he spoke. 'You know about that?' he said easily.

'Only that they're going at it like a pair of sumo wrestlers.'

Walker nodded. 'Yes, apparently the grunts are beginning to reverberate around Whitehall – to the accompaniment of much tutting from the grandees in her party.'

'Christ, that's fast.'

'Small world, you know. Ministers live in a goldfish bowl.'

'Will it do her any harm?'

Walker patted her leg. 'My dear, sex is always harmful to a political career in Britain; far better if she were suspected of treason. It could be bad for Brian as well. Sir Robert is entering one of his periodic bouts of moral fervour, I understand.'

'So you think he'll object?'

Walker smiled again. 'Sir Robert is quivering to get his peerage, how do you think the Conservative party will react when the news comes out that his editor is boffing the Virginia McKenna of the Tory shires? Good Lord, you must know the image Geraldine has in the country: faithful British blonde, waiting while her hubby comes back from flying his Spitfire against the enemies of capitalism. They don't know that she's a highly effective politician, as far as they're concerned, she spends her time rolling bandages at Central Office.'

The car drew up at Annabel's and Fanny swept in. It was crowded but she could see the person she now wanted. 'Fix us a table, my old darling,' she called out to Walker. 'I just want to powder my nose.'

Walker pressed on towards the restaurant, but Fanny went to the bar first, where Jonathan Gaunt, a freelance diary writer, was buying an extremely expensive bottle of champagne.

'Hello, Fanny, good to see you. What are you doing here on your own?' he asked when he saw her standing next to him, glancing anxiously about her.

'Oh, hello, Johnny,' she answered in a distracted fashion, 'Geoff Walker and I are looking for our fucking editor, I don't suppose you've seen him?'

'No, why?' Gaunt replied, his nostrils flared and quivering from the scent Fanny had just sprayed.

She leaned closer. 'Listen, Johnny, this is strictly off the record but he's gone missing with Geraldine Miller. If you see him for Christ's sake give me a ring. I'll put a decent credit through for you, OK?'

'Anything for you, Fanny,' Gaunt said blithely.

Fanny smiled her thanks and passed on to catch up with Geoffrey, who was just being shown to a table.

Walker waited until she was seated and he had ordered drinks, then he rose again, 'Sorry, darling, I should have gone with you,' he said.

Slipping back into the bar, after a moment he located Gaunt, who was leaning against a pillar overlooking some friends. In the years he had reported the machinations of politicians, Walker had developed a sixth sense when it came to the art of treachery. He had noticed Fanny talking to Gaunt and intuition had told him of her purpose. Now, in a moment of improvisation he leaned towards Gaunt.

'Any luck, old boy?' he muttered.

Gaunt shook his head. 'Not yet, but he's hardly likely to bring a junior minister here, is he, even if he is in love?'

Smiling grimly at this confirmation, Geoffrey patted him or the shoulder and passed on to the public telephone. He was fond of Fanny in a strange sort of way, in the fashion that a collector of insects might admire a scorpion.

The editor was different; he was a close friend.

Friday, October 30 1.05 a.m.

Bridget Gillespie was paid to sing Irish folk songs in the pubs of Kilburn, but when it came to listening, she preferred old Hollywood musicals. They allowed her to escape into a world of make-believe, where a young Fred Astaire vied with a boyish Peter Lawford for her affections. In truth, Bridget didn't much like being who she was. She had spent the whole nineteen years of her life in London, but it might just as well have been County Kerry – the birthplace of her parents. The youngest of eight children, Bridget had known only church, poverty and hand-me-downs until Danny Doyle had chosen her as his consort. But that had extended her world only as far as the penthouse suite in which they lived, at the top of the Shamrock Building in Covent Garden. He insisted that she stayed there when she wasn't singing, not that he cared much for her voice, it was just a way of demonstrating his property. The redhead with the big tits –

great to look at but keep off, or the Doyles would turn you into dogfood. The night he had brought her here, he'd told her he had selected her because it was well known she was a virgin. Everything Danny wanted had to be brand new; he wore his clothes only a few times before he bought more.

At first she'd been excited by the prospect of getting away from her parents, seeing a bit of the world. She thought she might travel: even the rest of England was as foreign a place to her as the fabled country her parents reminisced about. But Danny had kept her locked up, like the piles of clothes that lay in the fitted wardrobes, still in their cellophane wrapping. So, with the help of her videos, Bridget created a fantasy world, home was now a Metro-Goldwyn-Mayer sound stage, and her new family the ancient stars who peopled her dreams.

She thought she resembled Judy Garland, except for her carroty hair, pale skin and freckles. My nose is definitely like hers, she told herself, and my legs; the same long, slim legs. Danny had promised to take her to Hollywood – one day. She knew when she got there, that would be it. The stars would know their own. Like a long-lost daughter, they would gather her to them and they would all sing and dance together for the rest of her days. Not songs about dead gunmen and meaningless anniversaries, they would be happy songs, about falling in love.

She lay now, on the wide sofa in Danny's penthouse, watching *Easter Parade*, a movie she knew by heart. Suddenly there was a hard grip on her arm and she saw that Danny had returned. 'Turn that fucking rubbish off and get in the bedroom. I want to work in here,' he ordered.

Bridget was wearing an old blue shirt of Danny's. She pulled it closer about her and glanced around: Fergus and the Brady brothers stood in the centre of the room.

'Your sister's been ringing all day, Danny,' Bridget said. 'She wants you to call her right away.'

'What did she want?'

'Christ, she wouldn't tell *me*,' Bridget replied. 'She hates my guts. All she'd say was tell him to ring me. She won't even speak my name. But she sounded frightened.'

'Just get in the fucking bedroom,' Danny ordered.

Bridget did as she was told. She didn't bother to turn on the lights or draw the curtains at the massive windows. The rainclouds had finally rolled away, leaving a night sky filled with stars, bright as a million chips of glass. A Hollywood sky, she told herself, and she began to cry as she lay on the wide bed.

In the next room the four men sat around a polished table and Fergus passed the bottle of whiskey.

'So what have we found out?' Danny Doyle asked.

Fergus answered: 'McNally is in the Kensington Gardens Hotel, with Andy Muir, Eddie Page, Craig and Buchanan. The others are all over the place, but they meet at the Tartan Club. We've bought one of the waiters at the hotel. He tells me that they're still looking for something, but Muir and Page came back earlier tonight and they've made some sort of progress. They seem to have a name. The waiter doesn't know what it is.'

Danny Doyle got up and paced the room for a time, then he turned back to the table. 'Who looks after McNally's car?'

'Usually Eddie Page drives, it's a Jaguar.'

'Where do they keep it?'

'There's an underground car park beneath the hotel.'

Danny turned to the Bradys. 'Go to the hotel. Ring up Eddie Page and tell him you work in the car park and you've seen that there's something wrong with the Jaguar, an oil leak or a flat tyre. When he comes down, snatch him. I don't want him hurt – we'll leave that to Fergus.'

The two men left and Fergus sat with his drink in silence. 'Are you going to ring Lily?' he asked after a time.

Danny looked at his watch again. 'No, I'll leave it until morning now. But put some men on the estate as guards. McNally might try something after the bombing.'

Friday, October 30 1.35 a.m.

Sarah knew Colin wasn't at home when she paid the taxi in front of her house. There was nothing to show that he wasn't there, she just had a feeling. Weariness seemed to cling to her like moss on an old tree as she climbed the stairs. But the evening had been fruitful. The long conversation with Doreen over dinner had gone on so long that to Cat's dismay they had forgotten to watch the television commercial, but it had given her a pretty good idea of the shape the series would take. In actual fact, the material was pretty thin. Doreen had spent most of her life telling unhappy people that their loved ones on the other side were still thinking of them and they would be hard put to get three instalments out of that, but that was somebody else's problem. She would do her best – it was all Brian Meadows could expect.

As she passed Emily's room she thought she heard a gentle noise. She opened the door softly and the sound of crying was unmistakable now. Sarah sat down on the bed and laid a hand on her daughter's shoulder. 'What's the matter, darling?' she asked, already knowing the answer.

Emily turned and Sarah held her in her arms.

'Oh, Mum,' she said brokenly. 'Ric and I have split up.'

'When did this happen?' Sarah asked wearily.

'This evening. I tried to ring you, but they said you were out.'

'Tell me about it.'

Emily continued to cling to her while she spoke. It made her seem very young. When she had been a little girl she had always been so self-possessed; funny old world, Sarah thought.

'He says we're just not getting anywhere,' Emily began, 'the relationship isn't developing. He says, if I don't want to take it any further then it's best to end it now – a clean break, before we hurt each other any more.'

Sarah rocked her back and forth. 'There, there,' she said

221

soothingly, wishing she could heal her daughter's aching heart, and thinking at the same time she'd like to kill Ric Daggert. Poor Emily, she told herself. Where academic subjects were involved she had a mind like quicksilver – any problem could be analysed, dissected and ultimately solved – but when it came to emotions she was a dunce, just like the rest of us.

'I know it's not much help now,' Sarah said softly, 'but in time it will get better.'

'No it won't,' Emily said. 'I shall feel like this for ever.'

'No, no,' said Sarah. 'Life's not like that.' She lay down beside her and began to stroke her daughter's head as she spoke. 'When something happens that hurts you, you think: I'll never get over this – but you do. Everyone does.' Sarah remembered something her father had told her when her mother died. Strange, she had not recollected it before this moment. 'Human beings are made to forget things, otherwise they couldn't tolerate the pain of life. They say that time heals, but it's not time, it's some inner power all people have. You think you can't bear to be without Ric, but one day you'll see him again and you'll think: did I really feel that way about you? It doesn't seem possible now, but it will happen – I know.'

Emily's breathing was regular now. Sarah made a move to leave, but her daughter still clung to her. Sarah lay back and rested her head on a pillow.

Friday, October 30 2.05 a.m.

Brian Meadows and Geraldine Miller still lay awake in the darkness of the bedroom on Half Moon Street. The call from Geoffrey Walker, warning that their affair would soon be made known to the public, had come like the last act in a Greek tragedy:

expected, but nonetheless painful to contemplate. Both of them had known that the euphoria they had enjoyed in the last few days couldn't last. Now the painful consequences of their actions were about to unfold.

'It's not fair,' Geraldine said, in the tone of a schoolgirl who had watched her hockey team suffer an unwarranted defeat.

'Life seldom is,' Meadows answered, then added, 'It's going to make things bloody awkward at my club.'

'Oh, bugger your club,' Geraldine said bitterly. 'What about us?'

'You could always divorce Charles and marry me,' he ventured after a few minutes.

'Are you asking me?' Geraldine answered after a long pause.

'Well, yes, I suppose I am,' Meadows replied. 'If people heard about it before the gossip, no one would care. Affairs are a juicy read, engagements don't raise much dust.'

Geraldine sat up, suddenly alert. He could practically hear her mind racing. 'Could we announce it before the gossip columns get their teeth into us?' she asked.

Meadows thought for a while. 'If we move quickly, maybe we can get it into the *Evening Standard* by tomorrow night.' He paused again. 'Of course, your husband will have to agree.'

Geraldine settled down in the silk sheets once again. 'You'll have to talk to him in the morning,' she said. 'Thank God, that's settled.'

Meadows lay looking at the ceiling for a time and considered her last statement. How like a politician, he thought, to imagine that the intention to embark on a certain course of action would automatically lead to the desired result.

Friday, October 30 2.05 a.m.

Jamie Lambert felt as if the walls of the interview room were closing in on him. Everything was like a bad dream, and his solicitor was no comfort. Lionel Baston, a weak-faced pudgy individual, sat beside him, long streaks of thinning hair falling over spaniel eyes that were fluttering with fatigue. There was no sign of tiredness – or impatience – in the two men on the other side of the table; they just kept asking the questions over and over again.

Lambert had been good at only one thing in his life: gymnastics. His father, a moderately successful builder in Petts Wood, had wanted him to be an architect, but the reports from the private school he had attended ruled out that particular dream. Although he had the physical build for it, he hadn't liked rugby, or any of the other sports that required bruising contact and possible danger. In the gymnasium, he was in control. 'It's all a matter of timing and balance,' the instructor, Mr Reynolds, used to tell him. 'When you can feel your timing and centre of gravity, you can do anything.'

Lambert looked around at the cream-painted walls. The hard, bright lights made his eyes ache, and his mouth felt dry and sour. The nightmare had embraced him so totally, he felt drained of the strength he usually possessed. It seemed to take an enormous effort even to slide his hands on the cheap, veneered surface of the table. Whichever way he answered he was in danger. Balance, he kept telling himself, hold your balance. But the wrenching sensation in his stomach felt as if he were coming out of a triple somersault that had gone badly wrong. Everything was off. Any moment now his head was going to smash on to a solid wooden floor.

If he told them part of what he knew, he would go to jail, and the Doyles would be able to reach him there, hurt him terribly, scar and maim his beautiful body. But if he said nothing, then they would nail him for the murder of that cheap little bitch Polly Weaver. Why had he bothered to bring her back to the club first? If he'd done what Fergus had instructed and taken her straight to the house in Kilburn there would have been no evidence to connect him.

It had been her fear, it always worked on him like an aphrodisiac. He'd caught a hint of the scent on entering her apartment. When he told her that the Doyles knew she'd been talking to McNally she'd started to tremble. Then the smell increased and he couldn't resist: the sharp, slightly acid scent that started from every pore of her body. He'd had to have her, and Polly Weaver had recognised his need. As always, it was over for him in a moment, the second he had entered her. Then Polly Weaver had made the mistake of smiling. So he'd taken her to the club on his way to Fergus. When he'd used her in his customary way, she thought she'd paid her price in full, that the ordeal had come to an end, but then he'd delivered her to Fergus – and Polly Weaver had never smiled again.

He'd been in the police station a long time now and he wanted to sleep. It was important to him; rest was necessary if he was to maintain his skin tone. A beautiful body didn't last long without constant vigilance. A police constable entered the room and whispered something to Greaves, who nodded and turned to him again.

'We've just had the laboratory report, Mr Lambert. The semen found on the towel used by the girl you raped this evening matches that found in the body of Polly Weaver.'

'You don't have to say anything,' Lionel Baston said in his prissy voice.

Lambert shook his head. 'I fucked her but I didn't kill her. I swear to that.'

'Who killed her?'

'Fergus Doyle, I suppose. I just dropped her off at the house in Kilburn.'

'Did you see Doyle?'

'No, just Terence Brady, he took her from me. I went home after that.'

When the last of the paperwork was completed, Greaves and

Holland stood on the wet pavement outside the police station and breathed in the clean night air.

'Shall we go for Fergus, now?' Holland asked.

'No,' Greaves replied, 'he'll keep. Let's get some rest.'

They walked to the car and Holland looked back at the police station before he took his seat. 'There's one thing that puzzles me about Lambert,' he said as he stretched out his weary frame.

'What's that?' Greaves replied.

'Lambert's in love with himself, body beautiful and all that. I bet he's a health freak.'

'Yes.'

'Why would he screw a prostitute and not bother about wearing a French letter? He didn't with the other girl either. It doesn't make sense. A bloke like that would be dead scared of catching something these days.'

'You're right,' Greaves replied with a yawn. 'Ask him about it tomorrow.'

When he got home to Hampstead, Greaves walked as silently as he could to the bedroom. Emily's door was open as he passed and he saw that Sarah still lay curled on the bed, holding her daughter in her arms. He covered them both with a duvet and softly left the room.

Friday, October 30 6.35 a.m.

Although it was still dark outside, Eddie Page was awake. He found the hotel room uncomfortably hot and hadn't discovered how to regulate the thermostat that controlled the temperature. He was watching the weather report on breakfast television and thinking of his mother's cooking. Eddie was homesick and missing the great mounds of fried food with which he customarily began the day. He was contemplating calling room service when the telephone rang. The accent of the man who spoke caused him no surprise. Apart from television, Eddie had hardly heard any other voices in his life except those from Belfast, so he accepted the familiar sound, never pausing for a moment to wonder at finding a fellow countryman in London and working at the hotel.

'I'll be right down,' he answered when the voice had explained about the oil leak.

Eddie dressed quickly in the new suit he had bought especially for the trip. Bloody good job the man had spotted the trouble, he told himself. Big Davey would not have been pleased to find the car out of action if he'd suddenly required it.

The lift took him down into the still basement, where only the sound of his own echoing footsteps broke the silence. Eddie Page was not very bright. At school Eddie had been classified below average intelligence. Maybe because of that he possessed certain animal instincts that might have been buried deeper in someone of greater intellect.

Now Eddie's primeval senses warned him of danger with every step he took closer to the Jaguar. But it was too late. As he reached for the gun tucked into his waistband, Terence Brady took two swift paces forward from his hiding place and hit him on the crown of the skull with a length of lead pipe. Eddie crumpled to the ground and the two brothers quickly lifted his body into the boot of a parked car.

The attendant at the pay booth on the ground floor did not give them a second glance when they paid the bill and drove off along Kensington High Street.

Sir Robert Hall had spent a troubled night in his Belgravia flat. Despite the previous day's diversion beneath the surface of the Solent and the consequent pleasures of dinner on board *Victory*, a problem nagged at him like the nerve in a rotten tooth. He'd had the dream again. Each time it was the same. Now he sat in his study, still dressed in his pyjamas, looking up at an artist's sketch of the new headquarters of London and Overseas Communications PLC: a glass stump that was already rising above Docklands in glittering splendour. This was only part of an ambition that he had nurtured for so long.

The completion of the building in the new year was to coincide with the peerage that was so nearly in his grasp. Then, as Lord Crannock, he would supervise the opening ceremony of Amanda House – and his wife would be kind to him again.

Although Lady Amanda was civil enough in public, when they were together in private she maintained the icy distance that had gone on since she had discovered the facts about his brief affair with Fanny Hunter some months before. Sir Robert had offered to fire Fanny, but Lady Amanda was shrewd enough to realise that the dreadful creature would immediately let it be known why she had been dismissed, and Lady Amanda would become a laughing stock among her friends.

That was why the new building was so important to him. He would lay it at Amanda's feet as a peace offering. What woman could resist such a gesture?

He had always worshipped his wife, the second daughter of an earl, since they had been introduced at his first hunt ball. To the new young lion of the City, she had possessed all of the qualities that he admired and desired in life: snobbery, selfishness, great wealth and a total disregard for the feelings of others. Attributes that Sir Robert considered the true marks of an aristocrat.

To be fair, Lady Amanda had not objected to his relationship with Fanny on moral grounds; she had been conducting a liaison with a young Guards officer at the time. It had been a question of judgement. In Lady Amanda's view, Fanny Hunter was a tart, and therefore her husband was guilty of poor taste: a crime, in her eyes, far greater than adultery.

Sir Robert now rested all his hopes on Amanda House, which was why the dream was so unsettling. It began at the opening ceremony. A band played and sunlight drenched the scene as the member of the Royal Family, who had cut the tape, led the assembled dignitaries into the great foyer for a champagne reception. But the doors closed on Sir Robert when he tried to enter the building and he stood on the forecourt banging hopelessly on the glass walls, where the blazing sun reflected as though the whole edifice was on fire. Inside, the guests ignored his muted cries, while his wife mouthed something to him that he could not hear, through the burning window.

What did it mean? he asked himself. Why should such a dreadful omen present itself to him? Like all people with a sense of destiny, Sir Robert was deeply superstitious. What else could explain his countless victories in the City but divine providence? Some guiding supernatural force that smote his enemies and laid bare the simple secrets of high finance so that the chairman of LOC PLC prevailed above all others. He even saw a measure of fate in his stature. Throughout his boyhood in Croydon he had been mocked for being short, and then on his nineteenth birthday he had discovered that he was exactly the same height as Winston Churchill. There had been other signs as well: a car crash where all had been killed but himself, and that business of the Crow Mountain Mining Company last year. For a few months his fellow directors had trembled, but all had gone quiet, and any day now they would be out of it for good. He pushed the thought aside and looked at the artist's impression once again. Then he decided to call Gibson.

Friday, October 30 6.55 a.m.

Sarah came to at the sound of the telephone. It took a few seconds for her to realise that she was still in Emily's room. She hurried to the extension in the hallway, not wanting to disturb Greaves, and found it was George Conway on the line. 'Can you get around to the Savoy right away?' he asked.

Sarah looked at her watch. 'I wasn't planning to start until about 10.30. We worked until late last night, Doreen will be tired.'

'This is top secret, Sarah, and I'm afraid it's a bit of a problem,' George said urgently. 'The chairman wants Doreen Clay to give him a private consultation. But if it gets out, it's the chop for everyone.'

'George, this isn't fair,' Sarah protested. 'Cat Abbot is there. You might as well give a handout to the Press Association.'

'I've already warned him.'

'What about Brian Meadows? Can't we stop this? For God's sake, we're supposed to be writing a series.'

'Brian's not available today. He's out of the office on personal business. Richard Gibson rang me. Now get your glad rags on and shoot off to the Savoy. It's important.'

Sarah hung up. Was it important? she asked herself. Not to the rest of the world, only to the employees of Gazette Newspapers, who had to suffer the personal whims of Sir Robert.

When she got to the suite, she found Doreen and Cat Abbot still eating breakfast.

'He's due here in fifteen minutes,' Abbot said while he chewed on a piece of toast. Doreen poured her a cup of coffee and Sarah sipped it appreciatively.

'Now, tell me about Sir Robert,' Doreen said cheerfully.

Cat held up a piece of paper. 'Born May 14, 1935. Educated, Croydon Secondary School. Married 1972 Lady Amanda, daughter of Lord Crowley. No children. Hobbies: collecting silver. That's all the library has on him.'

'Well, it's not much to go on,' Doreen said. 'But I should be able to manage something.'

'Aren't you going to give him the real thing?' Cat asked.

Doreen shook her head. 'Oh, I don't think so. It usually turns out so upsetting. I thought I'd just give him the same sort of thing I do for my old dears at the Institute. A few messages he'll want to hear, and let it go at that.'

'Is that wise?' Cat asked, biting into another piece of toast. 'After all, he is paying the bill and I'm told he's pretty shrewd. I don't know if it would be a good thing to risk a lot of old Egyptian rubbish on him. He's not like one of your old ladies. This man was taking over companies in the City of London when he was barely old enough to vote. I think he'd rumble the truth and send us all packing. Better play straight with him.'

'As you wish,' Doreen said. 'But I think you'll be taking a risk. You can't tell what will come out, and I won't be there to help you.'

'You want us to be there?' Cat said, and it was clear from the tone of his voice that the prospect did not make him happy.

'Certainly,' Doreen replied briskly. 'I shall insist on it.'

Cat digested this piece of news along with his toast, until there was a sharp knock on the door. When it was opened, a short upright figure stood before them, light gleaming from the silver-topped cane he carried like a Field Marshal's baton. 'I am Sir Robert Hall,' he announced in a voice deeper than Sarah expected.

'Lovely to meet you,' Doreen said, holding out her hand.

CHAPTER
TWELVE

Friday, October 30 6.55 a.m.

The house in Kilburn was unremarkable, except for one particular feature: the alterations to the cellar that the Doyles had made. Once, many years before, it had been inhabited by a prosperous shopkeeper called Bayliss, who'd owned grocery stores all over north London, but the area had gradually declined after the First World War and the houses in Lakeland Avenue were, one by one, converted into flats. After the Second World War they became bedsitting rooms. Unloved by a succession of landlords, Number 1, which was next door to a builder's yard on the corner of the street, began to fall into decay. Just enough money was spent on maintenance to keep out the rain, but the inside rotted like a windfall from an apple tree. In 1981 Danny Doyle bought the house, along with the yard, and reconverted it into flats for a handful of specially selected employees. These men were the blunt instruments of his trade, enforcers, who would respond to his instructions with ferocity but without thought. He had four other houses, similarly occupied, in north London.

When he chose his thugs, Danny Doyle made sure they were men of limited intelligence, creatures who would not display curiosity when called upon to hurt people. So none of them questioned the work that went on in the cellar of Number 1. Danny Doyle wanted it done; that was enough for them. The shabby, peeling paintwork on the outside of the property did not offend them; they had spent all of their lives in mean surroundings.

The car that brought Eddie Page to the house parked in the builder's yard. The Brady brothers shut the tall wooden gates from prying eyes before they took the still stunned body of their captive from the car boot and hustled him down a short flight of steps. They passed a basement office and entered a brick corridor that stopped at a double set of doors leading into the cellar of Number 1.

To Eddie Page's first bleary glance, the cellar room gave the impression of being a workshop, but he had no illusions about the purpose of the equipment scattered about him. There was a carpenter's bench fitted with a heavy vice and piled with tools; next to it, an old-fashioned iron bathtub stained and streaked with lime-scale. The floor and walls were tiled, and there was a drainage outlet set in the centre of the room, so that the whole area could be hosed down.

Eddie knew what was coming, and hatred for his captors welled up inside him like black bile. He was quite sure he was going to die, and he knew they would break him, but before that time came he would show them his defiance, let them see what 400 years of bitter loathing for their kind had bred into him.

The Bradys strapped him into the a heavy wooden chair and left the room by another door that he guessed led up into the house. When it closed behind them the light clicked off.

He seemed to wait for an eternity in the inky darkness; he may even have slept. Suddenly the lights snapped on again and this time the Bradys were accompanied by Fergus Doyle. 'Why don't you scream now, Eddie?' Fergus inquired mildly. 'I want you to use all the facilities we have on the premises. This room is soundproofed, did you know that?'

'I thought it was just a pigsty,' Eddie replied hoarsely, when they removed the handkerchief that had been stuffed in his mouth. 'It smells like you Fenian bastards have been living down here. We know you murdered Andy Muir's wee ones. When Andy gets through with you, you'll wish your mother'd fucked a dog instead of giving birth to you.'

Fergus studied his man dispassionately for a time, like a sculptor preparing to release the inner form from a piece of stone. The infliction of pain was a fascinating business for him. He had found that human beings reacted differently to torture. For some, the idea alone was enough to take them to breaking point. Just the sight of a pair of pliers or a bare electric terminal would bring about complete collapse. Then they would babble anything to avoid the moment when metal touched flesh.

Others could tolerate extraordinary suffering. But each dreaded a particular instrument above all else. One thing that imagination told them would inflict the ultimate agony. It was all a question of knowing your subject and the purpose of your task. Occasionally torture was an end in itself, punishment as a prelude to the death that would follow. Such work was also important as a deterrent to others, like the black tart he had burned in such a decorative fashion. In those cases, it didn't matter if the victim was conscious or not: others would see the mutilations on the body and dread a similar fate. People who didn't know the business imagined that those who talked under torture did it because they wanted to live. That wasn't so. When you wanted someone to talk, the secret was to bring the subject to the point where death was preferable to the agony of existence, and telling their secrets would end the pain of living.

What would Eddie Page dread most? Fergus asked himself.

Fire … water … the needle … the knife? It had been a while since he had used the knife. He went to a peg on the wall and began to put on a set of long rubber overalls.

As requested by Superintendent Greaves, the police had begun a surveillance of Number 1 Lakeland Avenue, but there had been an administrative delay; so the two officers, parked in a plain grey Bedford van, had not been there to see the arrival of the Bradys with Eddie Page. In the early light they watched a tubby figure in a brown overall coat who had arrived in a little red Toyota a few minutes before. He opened the gates of the builder's yard and after spitting carefully into the gutter, backed the motor car into the premises.

Ten minutes later a large dark car parked in the forecourt of the house. The Bradys, accompanied by Fergus Doyle, got out and entered by the front door. The officers recognised the three men and one of them used his mobile telephone to call Greaves at home.

'I'll be thirty minutes, or so,' Greaves said. 'Ring Sergeant Holland and tell him to meet me there. If Doyle moves make sure you follow him, and keep in touch.'

When he had showered and dressed he stood in the bedroom for a moment, making up his mind about something, then went to a small safe concealed in the bottom of a large wardrobe and took out a Walther PK automatic and a shoulder holster. He was just snapping in a full magazine when he caught a movement at the doorway and looked up to see Martin, who was gazing at the scene wide-eyed with interest.

'I've got to get some target practice in today – regulations,' Greaves said quickly.

'I only came to ask if you wanted some of the coffee I've made – I didn't know you had a gun,' Martin said. 'Can I have a look?'

'*May* I have a look,' Greaves corrected him. 'It'll have to be quick, I'm in a hurry.' He ejected the magazine and worked the action to make sure there was no round in the firing chamber before handing it to Martin.

'Wow!' the boy said, levelling the gun towards the window with both hands, as he had seen demonstrated so many times on television. 'If Mum could see me now she'd kill me – and you.'

'That's enough,' Greaves said. 'I must go.'

'Are you a crack shot?' Martin asked, following him down the stairs.

'I can hit the proverbial side of a barn.'

'Colin's got a gun,' Martin called out to his brother when they entered the kitchen.

'Really?' Paul answered. 'Let's have a look.'

Feeling like a character in a bad movie, Greaves opened his jacket, then reached for the coffee pot. He managed a few mouthfuls of the awful brew and left the house to the sound of Martin boasting that he'd actually been allowed to hold the gun.

Forty minutes later, Greaves was waiting at one of the support cars in the adjacent street when an unshaven Holland arrived. Heavy morning traffic was now moving through the area.

'You can go in now,' Greaves told the sergeant who was standing next to him holding a radio handset.

'OK, all units,' he muttered. 'Go now, repeat: go now.' On the instruction, four police vans drove to their appointed positions, two before the house and two in the street at the rear of the property.

The police officers who came from the vehicles were dressed in blue combat overalls and heavily armed. The first team broke down the door with a sledge-hammer and fanned through the building. But the first blows on the door had triggered an alarm in the basement. When the door leading to the cellar was smashed open, the Brady brothers were waiting, armed with Browning automatic pistols. Their opening fire forced two of the police

237

assault team to stand back from the cellar steps and cover their faces with gas masks. Then, in unison they threw tear gas grenades into the darkened stairwell from where the shots came.

Greaves and Holland had moved up to stand by the Bedford van, watching the front of the house. After the sound of the shots fired by the Bradys they heard the flat bangs of the gas grenades, followed by three distinctive blasts from a shotgun somewhere higher in the house. Then there was the crashing splinter of glass and a man, dressed only in a pair of underpants, threw himself through a closed window on the first floor and landed on the roof of the car parked in the forecourt. He jumped from there to the pavement but Nick Holland moved swiftly across the street and caught him before he managed to get more than a few paces.

The silence that followed was broken by the sudden crash of tearing wood. The tall doors of the yard smashed open and the red Toyota roared into the street swerving to narrowly miss an electric milk float that had just turned into the avenue. Greaves saw Fergus Doyle at the wheel as the car hurtled past. Cursing softly, Greaves rapped on the window of the van. 'Did you get the number?' he asked.

'Yes, sir.'

'Get it out right away. I want him picked up. Top priority.'

Greaves slowly walked across the street as the first of Doyle's enforcers was being escorted out.

'Anyone hurt?' he asked the officer in charge.

'No, sir,' he replied. 'Sorry about all the gunplay, couldn't be avoided.'

Greaves could smell the sharp peardrop scent of the tear gas now. Two officers appeared escorting the Bradys, and Greaves noticed that their footsteps all left smears of blood.

'Better call for an ambulance, Sarge,' one of the officers said. 'There's a body down there – I think it's still alive.'

'Man or woman?' the sergeant asked.

'I don't know – it's hard to tell.'

Friday, October 30 8.00 a.m.

Sir Robert Hall entered the suite at the Savoy and stood for a moment, looking at the remains of the breakfast with an expression of slight distaste. Then he glanced up at Sarah and Cat Abbot. Although he had been informed that staff members of the newspaper were with Doreen Clay, he had no idea who they were. Sir Robert's policy was always to keep employees at a distance. As Amanda's father used to say, 'It's easier to shoot the rabbits you don't know.'

'You are … ?' he asked coldly.

'Sarah Keane, general news reporter on the *Gazette*.'

'Cat Abbot, Sir Robert. I'm also a reporter on the *Gazette*.'

Sir Robert kept his distance: he did not like subordinates to tower over him and Abbot was nearly six feet tall. He chose an upright chair near the fireplace and rested his gloved hands on the top of his cane.

During the years he had controlled the *Gazette*, he had absorbed fragments of journalistic jargon, and in his rare encounters with members of the staff he liked to use them in conversation, thinking his expertise would impress.

'You're news reporters,' he began sharply. 'Why aren't feature writers working on this buy-up?'

'It started out as a news story,' Cat explained.

Sir Robert nodded. He began to look about him, into all corners of the room and then at each piece of furniture, as if he were seeking something. 'Why did you choose such an expensive place to work? Have you any idea how much this suite costs each day?' His voice was querulous now, like the miserly baron in a child's pantomime.

'That was my idea,' Doreen answered, realising that Sir Robert was seeking a victim. 'I've always wanted to stay at the Savoy and I thought: Doreen, here's your big chance. But if you're dissatisfied and you want to end the contract … well, I understand other newspapers will offer a lot more than the *Gazette* for my story. I'll be happy to go to them.'

'I thought you hadn't spoken to the other papers,' Sir Robert said suspiciously.

Doreen's eyes did not leave Sir Robert's. 'Mr Abbot, get my coat and bag from the bedroom, I'm leaving immediately,' she said. Her mood suddenly changed from warm friendliness to ice-cold formality.

They could see that the little man was disconcerted. He began to rap his cane on the carpeted floor. Cat stood rooted to the spot, paralysed by the sudden turn in the conversation.

'Please, Miss Clay,' Sir Robert said after the merest hesitation. 'I meant in no way to impugn your honour. Forgive my clumsy words.'

'Well, that's better,' Doreen said, clearly now in charge of the situation. 'Much nicer if we're all friends, isn't it?' She sat down on a sofa next to Sir Robert's chair and patted the place beside her. 'Now you come and sit here, so we can hold hands.'

'Hold hands?' he repeated cautiously, not sure if he cared to adopt such an undignified posture in front of inferiors.

'Yes,' Doreen replied. 'I want to find out all about you. We won't need this,' she said, taking Sir Robert's silver-topped cane and handing it to Sarah. They sat in silence for at least a minute and then Doreen said, 'Fine, now I think it would be better if we all went into the little bedroom.'

'All of us?' Sir Robert said. 'I was expecting something more … private. I'd hoped that what you might tell me would remain in confidence between us.'

Doreen slowly shook her head. 'No, Sir Robert, it will be absolutely necessary for all of us to take part. You're a very important man and the spirits will sense that. If I were to conduct the seance with only the two of us – well, anything could happen. All the psychic energy released would concentrate on you, it would be like the power of an electrical storm being caught by a single lightning rod. We wouldn't want that to happen, would we?'

Sir Robert considered the point about his importance. It seemed understandable enough, but he hated the idea of these other two listening in. 'So you're quite sure these other people should be there?'

'Quite sure.'

Sir Robert stood up stiffly. 'In that case,' he said to Cat and Sarah, 'I must warn you that everything that takes place here, and anything you learn, is in the utmost confidence. Any transgression of the trust I now place in you will bring about the gravest consequences. If you do not honour this agreement, you will both have breached the terms of your contract of employment and will be liable to dismissal without recompense. Do you understand?'

Sarah found his pompous little speech deeply offensive and was half inclined to walk from the room, but curiosity to see Doreen exercise her powers held her back, so she muttered, 'I understand,' and folded her arms.

'I think it would be better if we're not interrupted,' Doreen said. 'Raymond, will you telephone down and tell them not to put any calls through until we ring them again. And a "Do not disturb" sign on the door might be a good idea – just to stop the maids walking in on us.'

She led them into the bedroom she had designated, selected a small table and asked Cat to bring chairs from the sitting room. When the curtains were drawn, Sarah suddenly had to repress an urge to giggle like a schoolgirl. Standing in the gloomy room with such an unlikely selection of people, it was as if they were at a children's party and they had been told to go and prepare for a charade.

Before they were seated, Doreen looked around. 'I wish I had my stone,' she said to herself. She picked up a heavy crystal ashtray and held it in her hands for a few moments. 'This will do,' she said, and placed it in the centre of the table. She smiled

241

in the half-light and said, 'I would like you all to relax. If you want to go to the bathroom, now's the time … All right, everybody set? Now let's sit down and all hold hands. And I must warn you, when I go into a trance don't speak unless you're asked a question, and don't let go of each other's hands under any circumstances, do you understand?'

They answered 'yes' and Sarah took the hands of Sir Robert and Cat Abbot. Immediately she was surprised at the contrast. Sir Robert's was small, like a child's; Cat's enveloped her hand completely.

'Silence now, please,' Doreen said, and there was no sound in the little room apart from her deep, regular breathing. Gradually the noise quietened and she slumped back in her chair, head lolling on to her chest and her eyelids beginning to flutter. Sarah was sure the room had suddenly become colder. She could feel goose-flesh on her bare arms.

There was nothing for at least a minute, then suddenly a deep masculine voice emerged from Doreen's still form, saying, 'So you want to know, do you?' Loud, booming laughter followed.

'Yes,' answered Sir Robert, assuming this was a question for him, in which case he could break Doreen's rule about not speaking.

There was another long silence, and then a soft muttering as if from a long way away. Sarah leaned forward, straining to listen, and the voice grew louder. It sounded like an old woman speaking in German. It stopped, and Doreen's shoulders began to turn from side to side. This time the voice was younger: another woman, cultivated and English. There was deep distress in the tone: 'Keep away, you can see the fire,' the voice commanded.

'Why?' asked Sir Robert. 'Why can't I come in?'

'You mustn't,' the voice continued, and it sounded almost angry. 'There's danger. Nothing you can do. I know you want to come in, I know you love me, stay out. For my sake, stay out.'

Sir Robert broke free and stood up. 'Why can't I come in, I

demand to know?' he shouted angrily. Prompted by his outburst, Doreen Clay seemed to float to her feet, her body twisting from side to side as if two great hands held her like a child's doll. Her hair whipped across her face and a moaning sound came from her half-open mouth. Suddenly she collapsed into her chair, followed by a sound like a loud crack, as if a pistol had been fired in the room. Sarah looked down, and saw that the heavy crystal ashtray had snapped in two.

Sir Robert hurried from the room and Sarah went to Doreen's side. She reached out and felt her forehead: the flesh was very cold. Cat drew the curtains and Doreen blinked awake in the strong light.

'Everything all right?' she asked softly.

'We're fine,' Sarah answered. 'But I'm not sure about Sir Robert.'

Doreen rose unsteadily and they walked into the next room where Sir Robert had recovered his cane. He did not look at them when he spoke. 'I must go now. Please remember what I warned you of earlier,' he said in a shaky voice, and with a vague nod towards Doreen, he left the room.

They sat down once again and Doreen looked at each of them in turn. 'Did he get any sort of message?' she asked.

'It seemed so,' Sarah answered.

'No,' Cat said slowly, 'He thought he did. But actually it was for me ...'

'How do you know?' Sarah asked.

Cat sat hunched forward, staring at the carpet. 'I recognised the voice,' he said after a time.

'Who was it?' Doreen asked.

'My mother.'

'Did you understand the message?'

'Yes,' he answered and he covered his face with his hands for a moment. When he looked up again his features were furrowed with pain. In all the years she had known him, Sarah had never seen Cat Abbot like this. She was used to his expression of self-pity, but this anguish was unexpected.

'My mother was the daughter of a musician,' he began. 'She met my old man when her father took her to Dublin for a concert. My dad was poor, didn't have two ha'pennies to rub together. All they had was kids. I was the youngest – her favourite. She was killed when I was just little,' he continued. 'They blame me for her death.'

'Why?' Doreen asked softly, and he looked down as she took his hand.

'We lived in a flat then, after my dad was killed, just a couple of rooms – the six of us. The place was like a bloody zoo. I always wanted to read. My brothers thought there was something wrong with me.' He looked around the room. 'Imagine what it was like, growing up in those sort of surroundings ... One day, my mother was ill with pneumonia. It was winter and we only had an oil stove to heat the place. I just couldn't stand to be in there any more. I said I was running away. My brothers didn't take any notice, but my mother sent them to look for me. They tried everywhere but the most obvious place. I was in the public library. When it got dark I went home.

'My brothers were still on the streets. When I got to the flat it was on fire. They said she knocked over the oil stove.' He stopped and looked at each of them. 'I tried to get in but the neighbours stopped me. I could hear her screaming.' He stopped and Doreen reached out to hold him. When he started to speak again his voice sounded very tired. 'My brothers blamed me – they said I might as well have killed her with my own hands. I was sent away to school after that – I never saw any of my family again.'

A long silence followed; eventually Cat got up. 'I think I'd like to go for a walk for a bit,' he said.

Sarah was about to rise, but Doreen held out a hand to restrain her. When Cat reached the door he remembered something and turned. 'By the way, the other voice – the German woman – she said: "The Man from the East must beware of caritas." '

'Caritas – what does that mean?' Sarah asked.

'It's Latin,' Cat replied. 'It means charity. The Man from the East is Colin Greaves. I know that for sure.'

'How do you know?' said Sarah.

He shrugged. 'I just do, like I know my name, or the day of the week.'

When he had gone, Doreen said, 'Well, that story explains a great deal. He'll be a different man from now on.'

Sarah wasn't so convinced. 'Do you really think he'll change?'

'Oh, yes,' Doreen answered with certainty. 'I understand now. You see, the shock of losing his mother like that blocked his powers. Since then he's been like some sort of television set that could only receive odd fragments of programs because the aerial was disconnected. Only a little part of him was working, and that caused mischief more than anything else. I shall have to stay close to him for a time. All that power suddenly being switched on – anything might happen.'

Sarah got up. Despite the disturbance of recent events, duty still called. 'I think we really must make some sort of start on your story,' she said. Then she remembered something. 'What about Sir Robert?' she asked. 'He didn't seem to get any joy at all.'

'Oh, that silly little man,' Doreen answered with a smile. 'He's a very new soul. I think he's here this time to learn humility. He's certainly riding for a fall; I could tell that when I held his hand.'

Sarah sat at the table, and recalled Cat's parting words. 'I think I'll just give Colin a call,' she said, and went to the telephone in the bedroom.

Friday, October 30 11.30 a.m.

Brian Meadows was attempting to do two things at the same time: write a note to Reg Stenton, and telephone Geraldine's husband, Charles Miller. He was calling on his private line, and Miller's secretary had put him on hold. Now music was being played to him. 'Moon River', performed by the Boston Pops Orchestra, was not the best accompaniment to his attempt to compose an angry memo.

Stenton would not be in the office until 2.30 p.m. and Meadows wanted him to feel his full anger about Fanny Hunter's story on that morning's page one. Having given an undertaking to Sir Robert Hall that the paper would be careful in handling any mention of Tony Glendowning, they had practically accused the youth of consorting with a prostitute.

The music clicked off and a young woman with a singsong voice said: 'I'm connecting you with Mr Miller now, caller.' Meadows screwed up the note and threw it into the wastepaper basket. Then he took a deep breath.

'Miller here,' the voice said in a neutral tone.

'Brian Meadows – we've met a couple of times at the Garrick.'

'Yes.'

'I think you may have some idea of what I'm calling about,' Meadows said, trying to keep his voice even.

There was a longish pause, before Miller answered. 'Yes, I suppose I do,' he said.

Meadows breathed deeply again. 'I know it's short notice, but is it possible for us to meet today? I really do think it would be best if we thrashed this matter out in a civilised manner.' As he spoke, Meadows remembered that Miller had been a boxing blue at Cambridge; he hoped he wouldn't take the word 'thrashed' too literally.

'Actually, I'm free for lunch today,' Miller replied. 'Why don't we meet at the club?'

'Isn't that a bit ... well – public?' Meadows said hesitantly.

'Not if we book something away from the common table,' Miller said briskly. 'I always find that the more intimate the subject, the less people believe you would discuss it in the open.'

'Very well,' Meadows said. 'Shall we say one o'clock at the bar?'

'Fine, I'll get my secretary to arrange a table for two.'

When he had replaced the receiver, Meadows tried to begin the memo to Stenton once again, but he couldn't concentrate. The only time he could recollect feeling so jumpy had been during his last year at Oxford, when he had been swotting for his finals. A friend had given him some pep pills so that he could work through the night. But the amphetamine had charged him so much, he had resembled some demented jack-in-the-box. Instead of applying himself to his books, he had chain-smoked and chatted like a myna bird for twenty-four hours.

He got up from his desk and paced about the office. It was more than an hour before he was due to meet Miller. Perhaps a walk would do him good, help calm his nerves, he thought. He looked from his window. The weather seemed bright enough, although there were dark clouds moving across the hard blue sky. He decided to risk it.

After looking in on his deputy, Gordon Brooks, to tell him that he would be out for a good part of the day, Meadows set off at a brisk pace across the Gray's Inn Road and into Bloomsbury. Despite his apprehension about the meeting to come, the unaccustomed activity began to make him feel virtuous. Although he had been a fairly keen tennis player in his youth, it had been a long time since he had taken any regular exercise, and in recent years the constant use of a chauffeur-driven car meant that he was hardly ever called upon to walk more than a few hundred yards.

By the time he reached Russell Square, he was beginning to feel his breathing, and his left foot hurt. It started to rain as he entered Montague Place. Resolve abandoned, he decided to seek refuge in the British Museum and ring for his car. There was still plenty of time to kill and it had been many years since he had entered the museum. The last time had been with his son, Renfrew, when he had been a schoolboy. 'Renfrew,' he thought. He still didn't care for the name – but Valerie had insisted. She'd insisted on so much over the years that Meadows had ended up quite a different person from the one he had intended to become.

He'd expected to give up journalism by the time he was thirty and write. He'd always imagined living simply, on a houseboat somewhere on the Norfolk Broads, watching the seasons change, close to nature. And as his reputation grew, young men and women would come to interview him in his lonely retreat. After tea, he would row them through secret channels in his wildfowler's punt, and pause in the reed-fringed waterways while they questioned him deeply about the profundity of his latest novel.

But Valerie had wanted another life, and gradually the comforts of Highgate had enveloped him. I wonder if Geraldine has a dream? he thought. He told himself it would not be for a houseboat in East Anglia. It was raining quite heavily now; he was glad to get into the car when it arrived.

Miller was not yet at the bar of the Garrick Club but there was a convivial group of barristers that Meadows knew. They were talking to an actor who was appearing in a successful television series. Meadows had never actually seen the show, but the reviews were good and the young man had a reputation for brilliance. The barristers invited Meadows to have a drink and he listened to the actor's long anecdote about the late Sir Donald Woolfit performing Hamlet. Meadows was slightly disappointed: he had heard the story many years before in El Vino's and had expected more from this young man.

One of the barristers continued with the story of an old judge who had always donned the black cap with enthusiasm during the days of capital punishment. Meadows half listened, smiling when he thought the occasion demanded, and watching the doorway.

' ... so he woke up and said, "If I can't hang him or flog him, how will he remember me the next time he commits a crime?" '

Meadows forced a laugh, and just then Charles Miller entered the room. Glancing around, he recognised Meadows and joined the group and accepted a glass of sherry. He seemed rather flattered to be greeted warmly by the actor. Once again, Meadows was bemused by the priorities of powerful people. Successful actors carried more social weight than archbishops these days, he reminded himself.

After a time, Miller suggested that they go into lunch. They nodded to various people in the crowded dining room as they were shown to their table. Miller assumed the role of host. He hardly glanced at the menu, but took longer over the wine list.

Meadows selected artichoke as a starter, followed by grilled fish.

'Do you like artichokes?' Miller asked, sounding mildly surprised by Meadows's choice.

'Actually, no,' he replied. 'But I'm trying to lose a little weight.'

'Well, you bloody well deserve to lose something after eating one of those,' said Miller. 'They always taste to me like cardboard dipped in vinaigrette.'

Meadows noticed that Miller ordered the wine without consulting him, but he was happy when it was served. A cold Sancerre. He took a deep draught.

'Have you tried the Hay diet?' Miller asked when the food arrived.

'No I haven't,' he replied, looking at the potted shrimps before Miller with a jab of envy.

'Supposed to be extraordinarily effective,' Miller said, his mouth full of buttered toast. 'Quite simple to follow. You don't eat carbohydrate and protein in the same meal. It's something to do with the way the acid in your stomach breaks things down. That's all there is to it. The best part is, you can eat as much as you like.'

'You don't appear to have trouble with your weight,' Meadows answered.

'No,' Miller said. 'I play squash every morning and I swim afterwards in the pool at the RAC club.'

'I've been thinking of doing that.'

'You ought to, best thing in the world.'

When the main course came, Miller tried the burgundy he'd ordered to go with his steak. 'Do you want some more white with your fish?' he asked.

Meadows shook his head. 'No, I don't mind the red.'

Miller smiled. 'Quite right. All this wine snobbery is bloody absurd. It's what it tastes like that counts.'

He ate very quickly. It seemed only a few minutes until his plate was bare. He pushed it aside, rested both arms on the table and lit a cigarette. 'You don't mind, do you, it's after two o'clock?'

'Not in the slightest,' Meadows replied, pleased about anything that might delay the inevitable conversation.

'Now,' Miller said briskly. 'Let's get on with it. I must say I'm a little surprised at you approaching me so early.'

'You are?' Meadows replied faintly.

'Yes. Of course, I knew it would get out. You can't keep a bloody thing secret these days. I think it's because of the drugs young people take. Our generation drinks, but we can hold it. Cocaine is the curse of the discreet.'

'I hadn't considered that.' Meadows nodded to the wine waiter who hovered to fill their glasses.

'So how does Sir Robert Hall feel about it all? Pretty jumpy, I should imagine?'

Meadows blinked. 'I don't think he actually knows yet.'

Miller laughed briefly. 'So you're acting purely on your own initiative. Tell me, how do you feel about loyalties in a situation like this?'

'Loyalties can change,' Meadows said cautiously.

'Very good,' Miller said with a broad smile. 'I like that. You know, of course, I want you to carry on exactly as you are now?'

'You do?'

'Absolutely, I don't intend to interfere. It's not my style. When a man's giving his all, I prefer to keep out of the way and let him get on with it. Anyway, I've got my plate full as it is.'

Meadows drank some more wine and suddenly let his shoulders relax. 'Well, I must say you're taking a very ... sophisticated approach to the whole business.'

Miller waved a hand. 'It's much better to be civilised, don't you think?'

'I couldn't agree more.'

'Well, that's settled then.' Miller waved to the wine waiter. 'I'm going to have a large brandy – will you join me?'

Meadows nodded. 'Better make mine a small one. There'll be a lot of calls today. I'd like to get an announcement into the *Evening Standard* tonight.'

Miller paused. 'That's a bit premature, old boy. I think it will have to remain a secret for a bit longer yet.'

Meadows glanced around. 'I'm afraid it's too late. The gossip columns will have it by tomorrow morning if we don't act quickly.'

Miller shook his head, 'Not the gossip columns, old boy. This is a City page story.'

Meadows was beginning to feel as if the whole conversation was slipping out of true. Like an aircraft out of control.

'Have you actually talked to Geraldine?' he asked.

'Geraldine?' Miller said puzzled. 'What on earth has

Geraldine got to do with me taking over London and Overseas Communications?'

Meadows's head began to whirl, but he was in too deep now. 'I've asked Geraldine to marry me,' he said faintly.

'What?' Miller exclaimed so loudly that several heads nearby turned towards them.

'I thought that's what we were talking about,' Meadows said miserably.

Miller's head had suddenly slumped down so far that Meadows could only see the top of his crown. Slowly his shoulders began to shake, and for one terrible moment Meadows thought he was about to burst into tears. Then he heard rumbling laughter and Miller looked up, his face wreathed in a happy smile. 'This must be my lucky day,' he said eventually. 'I've been wondering how the hell I was going to tell Geraldine my girlfriend is pregnant.'

CHAPTER
THIRTEEN

Friday, October 30 9.30 a.m.

The chairman, three main board directors, and the company secretary of Shamrock Circle PLC sat in silence around the long cherry-wood table and waited until the uniformed security guard completed his electronic sweep of the room. Each man who sat before him had been selected by Danny Doyle because of the particular expertise he brought to one of the various divisions that made up the parent company. Danny did not believe in appointing non-executive directors.

'All clear, sir,' the guard said finally and Danny Doyle nodded. 'Thank you, Roger. Please tell my secretary that I don't want to be disturbed until the meeting is over.'

When the guard left the room, the company secretary read the minutes of the previous meeting and it was agreed they were an accurate record of the proceedings. The financial director,

Matthew Prewitt, then gave a concise report on the current trading position and a few questions were asked, which he answered in his usual precise manner. Danny Doyle nodded to the company secretary, who laid down his pencil and closed his minute book.

Doyle took a sip from a glass of mineral water and rapped lightly on the table. 'First, I must apologise for the absence of Fergus Doyle. He has been unavoidably delayed. Now, as you all know,' he continued, 'this board came to a vital decision, nearly three years ago, that was to have a profound effect on the future of the company. We agreed then that the way ahead was to go up-market with our products and services. The decision was a simple one, based on the self-evident fact that the rich are less liable to feel the restraint of recession. So our markets, which are based on the cash flow from discriminatory incomes, would be less vulnerable to fluctuations in the economy as a whole.' He paused to sip from the water again and there was a murmur of assent.

Doyle put down the glass on the blotter, careful to avoid the beautiful surface of the table, and began again. 'But there was, of course, another vital element in our thinking, and that went to the very heart of one of our core businesses. I refer, gentlemen, to Aids. Despite the precautions our girls always took, street trading took an appalling loss. It was clear we were suffering from a credibility gap. No matter how much we assured the customers our girls were safe, we had a major problem of perception. It was then that our marketing director, Bertram Giles, came up with the quite brilliant idea of executive sex. A new concept, where only the richest clients, after careful screening, would be allowed access to our specially selected and trained girls. And only when they themselves had undergone a stringent medical examination and exhaustive blood tests.' The board muttered its approval once more.

Doyle acknowledged their support with a smile. 'Along with

that decision we also decided it would be a matter of simple synergy to market our supplies of quality drugs to our new range of customers. At the same time, so as not to overstretch the performance of our own best men, we decided to franchise the street dealing of drugs and girls. I think I can say that our efforts met with unqualified success – but like all new ventures, it brought problems. Recently, our decision to franchise the street operation gave certain rival companies the idea that we had gone soft – that we no longer had the stomach for the rough and tumble end of the trade. So it was necessary to demonstrate our resolve by making an example. The opportunity presented itself when one of our executive girls got out of hand. Somehow, our chief rival, David McNally, had made contact with her and promised that she would have a better future with his organisation.' He paused and smiled. 'I think we dissuaded her from that particular folly – and the display of her body on the Brent River estate reminded others of the underlying strength of our company.' The other members of the board nodded.

'This appeared to be effective,' Doyle began again, 'but our rivals then had an extraordinary piece of luck. As you know, recently we began to put all the records of the company's special operations on computer, thus eliminating the need to keep books, which are always a security problem. All our suppliers, contacts and customers were so recorded, and as each piece of information was entered, the relevant paperwork was destroyed.

'The normal practice in such an operation is to back everything up on copy discs, in case the master is damaged. This was done. Unfortunately one of our employees, a girl called Jill Slade, was greedy. We now know that the McNally organisation bribed her to steal the master disc and destroy the back-up copies. She did this just before the close of business on Monday night.'

Doyle held up his hand to silence the mutterings of dismay. 'We also know that the master disc was not handed over to our rivals as planned, and my brother is, this morning, expected to report to us where it is located. I hoped he would be here to tell you himself, but so far we haven't heard from him. However, I'm sure we are all confident that he will be able to obtain the information, and quite soon the master disc will be back in our possession. Meanwhile I will keep you all informed through the usual channels. Thank you for your attention. Good morning.'

They were about to rise, when the telephone in front of Doyle rang.

'It's Mr Fergus, sir,' the secretary said nervously. 'He says it's urgent.'

Doyle smiled. 'It's Fergus now, I'll put him on broadcast.' He pushed a button so that the whole room could listen to the call.

'Danny,' Fergus said urgently, 'we've got trouble. The police raided the Kilburn house this morning. They picked up everyone. I only just managed to get away.'

Danny Doyle closed his hands into fists and leaned towards the telephone. 'Did you get Eddie Page to talk first?'

'Sure. The man who's got the master disc is some fucking reporter on the *Gazette* called Raymond Abbot. The girl passed it to him at King's Cross.'

'How did the police find the Kilburn house?'

'It was that cunt, Jamie Lambert. The police picked him up last night.'

'How do you know that?'

'I'm at Angela Grant's flat, she told me.'

'Who the fuck is Angela Grant?'

'The wee girl who's supposed to be a law student. I've been seeing her.'

'How the hell does she know?'

'Lambert screwed her last night, at Winner's. I always said he was cock happy. He's been doing it to a lot of the girls he trained for us. When he was on the job, Greaves crashed in.'

Danny thought for a moment. 'When Lambert screwed her, did he use a French letter?'

There was a pause while Fergus consulted the girl. 'Angela says no.'

Danny banged a fist down on the table. 'Lambert picked up that black bitch, didn't he? If he screwed her without a French letter the police will be able to match his sperm. They'll have levered that against him. I bet he's talked. They'll be able to implicate you now. The rest of us are safe.'

'That's why I'm getting out of the country,' Fergus answered.

'How are you going?' Danny asked.

'From the Enstone airfield. Max King is flying me to Amsterdam. I'll be in touch.'

Danny Doyle switched off and looked at the rest of the board, who were shifting uneasily in their padded leather chairs. He could see it was a time for leadership.

'Gentlemen, we're all right if Fergus gets away. The trail stops with him. Now just relax and let me take care of this Mr Abbot.' He nodded to the company secretary, 'Meeting adjourned.'

They got up and filed from the room, with the exception of Robin Congreve, the legal representative on the board. Both sat in silence for a while and Danny looked from the smoked glass window towards west London. 'What do you think, Robbo?' he asked finally.

'You know what I think,' Congreve replied. 'We've got a leak at the top. McNally has been getting his information from someone powerful, not just some file clerk.'

The telephone rang and the secretary said, 'Your sister is on the line, Mr Doyle, she says it's urgent.'

'Tell her I'll call her right back,' he said in a distracted fashion.

When the rest of the board left the premises, one member walked into Covent Garden Market and browsed among the stalls for a time. When he was sure he was not being followed, he made his way to an outdoor café and used the public telephone.

Big Davey McNally answered his call.

Friday, October 30 4.00 p.m.

Greaves was finally contacted by Sarah on his car telephone. She had tried several times to get him throughout the day but he had been on the move, trying to locate Fergus Doyle after questioning the gang members picked up in the raid in Kilburn. More recently, he had visited the hospital where they had taken Eddie Page and had a brief conversation with the consultant who had spent most of the morning sewing the flayed body back together again.

'Good practice,' he had said to Greaves. 'An excellent lesson for the students who observed the exercise. The body of a human being is an extraordinary thing. Sometimes it seems so fragile that the slightest blow will finish it off and then along comes something like this, and the bloody thing seems indestructible.'

'When will he be able to talk?'

'Never, old boy. His last surgeon slashed the vocal cords. He must have been tired of listening to him complain.'

Greaves gave a wintry smile at the man's sepulchral humour, but Holland winced.

Now there was little they could do but wait and see if Fergus tried the unlikely move of trying to leave the country by the conventional routes. Meanwhile, Greaves was pursuing another line of inquiry as he sat back in the car and began to read Fanny Hunter's page one story again.

'Are you all right?' Sarah asked, when the driver passed him the telephone.

'Yes,' he replied. 'Why do you ask?'

Sarah told him about Cat's warning.

'Caritas,' he repeated. 'I shall bear it in mind.'

'What are you up to?' she asked.

He looked through the window at the Albert Memorial awash with rain in the afternoon twilight. 'Actually, Nick and I are meeting someone for tea at the Natural History Museum. A policeman's life isn't entirely sordid. How about you?'

Sarah rubbed the back of her neck. 'I've spent the whole day writing Doreen Clay's story.'

'How is it going?'

'I've got the first part done and filed, read it in tomorrow's *Gazette*.'

'I may give your paper up. Did you read what Fanny Hunter wrote about police incompetence this morning?'

'Don't take it personally. It's just her way of getting at me.'

'What are your plans later?'

'I want to get home as early as possible. Emily's upset. I'd like to spend some time with her.'

'Ric?'

'That's the one. I've been considering castration.'

Greaves laughed, 'Remember, boys are only half the problem. I'll see you when I can.'

It was almost dark when they reached the museum. In the cafeteria they found Tony Glendowning reading a paperback at one of the tables. Greaves noted that it was Orwell's *Animal Farm*. 'I hope you don't mind meeting here,' Glendowning said. 'I find the atmosphere at home a bit oppressive.'

'You still live with your parents?' Greaves asked, mildly surprised.

Glendowning nodded. 'By order of the court. Actually it expires in a few weeks' time. I shall get something of my own then, a bit closer to work.'

Glendowning noticed the copy of the *Gazette* that Greaves still carried. 'I see Miss Hunter did us both proud this morning. I suppose it was my own fault. I was beginning to trust the *Gazette*. That fellow Abbot wrote quite a nice piece about us.'

'It was this I wanted to see you about,' Greaves said and he glanced up as Holland brought cups of coffee. 'I'd like to know a little more about Polly Weaver.'

Glendowning looked at each of them. 'There's nothing to tell. I met her one afternoon at the hostel in Guildford. We didn't have any sort of romance. Mind you, I did fancy her. We spent some of the afternoon together. I never saw her again.'

Greaves tapped the newspaper. 'You say here, she was instructing some of the others at the hostel in modern dance.'

'Yes, that part is correct. At least that's what she told me. I had no cause to doubt her word.'

'Tell me about the hostel at Guildford. What part does it play in the work of HAND?'

Glendowning spread out his hands on the table. 'Guildford is just one of our centres. We have ten others.'

'Isn't that very costly?'

'I suppose it is, but that's how Jeremy wants it, and his theory seems to work.'

'What theory is that?'

'It's all based on peer group pressure. When the kids come to us they're interviewed, evaluated and then placed in tightly graded sets.'

'What determines their membership of a particular group?'

'The individual's strength of character.'

'Why?' Holland asked.

'So that Jeremy can decide who dominates the set.' Glendowning waved a hand in the direction of a gaggle of schoolboys who were noisily occupying a corner of the café. 'Most young people only respond to their peer group. It's what the pack says that counts. Parents, teachers, social workers, newspapers, policemen, leaders of the church, politicians, all traditional sources of guidance and authority are ignored nowadays. They're just seen as self-seeking fat cats – liars. The kids say the only thing you can rely on is your own circle. Jeremy's theory is that young people look to certain dominant members of their immediate group and take their behaviour patterns from them. If Charlie is the most charismatic person around, what Charlie says goes, as far as sex, music, drugs or crime is concerned.'

'This all sounds pretty basic,' Holland said. 'Kids have always played follow my leader.'

Glendowning smiled. 'Yes, but eventually kids mature and begin to choose their peer leaders from the adult world. For a whole section of society, this isn't happening any more. They just go on locked in their own section. And if that section is bad, they're pretty much doomed.'

'Go on,' Greaves said.

Glendowning flicked the pages of the newspaper before he continued. 'We isolate them for a while and then give them a new peer group leader. Someone who isn't so ... shall we say, anti-social.'

'And it works?'

'It seems to.'

Greaves thought for a minute. 'So who actually does the evaluation?' he asked finally.

'Jeremy, he's a genius at it. He also trained the original peer group leaders. Now they do it themselves, a sort of oligarchy.'

'And these centres, are they boys and girls mixed together?'

Glendowning shook his head. 'No, and that's created some controversy. But Jeremy insists. Mix boys and girls together at that age and it would create more problems than it solves. They're allowed to see each other on social occasions, but under supervision. That's what I was doing at Guildford when I met Polly Weaver. During the week it's girls only.'

Greaves rolled up the *Gazette* and rapped once on the table with it. 'Thank you, Mr Glendowning. You've been a great help to me. Can I give you a lift anywhere? We've got a car outside.'

Glendowning shook his head. 'No thanks. I'll get the tube later.'

'It all seems a bit simple to me,' Holland said when they'd left the museum. 'Rather like the Boy Scouts and Girl Guides.'

Greaves looked down at the newspaper he still held. 'Be Prepared,' he said softly, and the rain beat on the roof of the car.

Friday, October 30 5.34 p.m.

Max King had long retired from the Fleet Air Arm. Now he and his wife, Dottie, ran an arts and crafts shop in Chipping Norbury and lived at Duns Tew, a pretty little village in the Cotswolds. But Max still liked to fly. He kept a two-seater Piper Cub Trainer at Enstone airfield in north Oxfordshire, an old wartime base that was now given over to recreational pursuits. Microlights mostly, which he regarded with the sort of contempt a genuine biker reserves for the riders of motorised scooters. Max's passion was for stunt flying: hurling his tough little machine about the sky in gut-wrenching acrobatics was his idea of a good time.

Occasionally, Max would do a favour for a friend. The money was always good and he got a charge from the danger that sort of flying entailed. It was nothing compared with landing a jet fighter on the pitching deck of an aircraft carrier, but fun was fun wherever you found it.

The evening was wet and dark, filthy weather for flying, but he whistled happily as he pulled on his flying jacket. 'I might stay over in Amsterdam and come back tomorrow,' he told his wife, who was busy bottling plums in the kitchen. She kissed him good-bye absentmindedly and went on labelling the fruit bottles.

A car followed him out of the village but he paid no attention to the way it stuck to his tail. Once they were on a long, deserted stretch of road, it flashed for him to let it pass. Max eased as close as he could to the ditch and slowed down; he was in no hurry, he wasn't due to meet Fergus Doyle for nearly an hour. The car overtook but instead of continuing on its journey, it pulled up, blocking the narrow lane.

Max was irritated. He opened his car door as a figure walked towards him in the headlights.

'What sort of a silly bloody game … ' he began, but before he could complete the sentence, the right side of his skull was caved in like a broken eggshell from the weight of the blow Andy Muir delivered.

Satisfied that he was dead, Muir quickly dragged him away from the car, stripped off his flying jacket and rolled his body into the ditch. He got into Max King's car and after flashing the headlights to the vehicle ahead, both cars set off for the airfield.

Fergus Doyle was fairly relaxed now; he was only a few hundred yards from his destination. He knew the route to the airfield well. Max had taken him on several runs when he and Danny had first set up in business and they'd had to do the menial work themselves. The headlights of his car played on the concrete runway which led like a road to the hangar where Max's Piper Cub was kept. There was no one else on the airfield. He could now see a small light illuminating the apron before the hangar doors.

When he got out of his car, a figure stepped from the pitch darkness and held a sawn-off shotgun at his stomach. The blow to his head was not intended to kill.

He regained consciousness a few minutes later and found himself sitting in the cockpit of the aircraft. His wrists were tied with wire, and a young man he did not recognise was binding his body into the seat. The upper part of his torso was still free. In the confined space, Andy Muir was wiring two terminals to a cheap alarm clock.

'Oh, you're with us again,' he said cheerfully. 'I'm glad. I suppose you can work out for yourself what I'm doing. I'm going to set this for seven o'clock, so you'll be able to sit here for the next half an hour and think of all the things you'll never do in your life, while you watch the big hand getting closer to the hour. When that happens, a charge is going to ignite the petrol in the tank and you're going to burn, Mr Doyle. So prepare yourself. I'm sorry I couldn't bring a fucking priest with me, seeing as this is a two-seater, but then, nothing is perfect in life, is it?'

Fergus Doyle did not hesitate for a moment. As the youth holding the wire passed another loop across his chest he struck out like a snake. Catching the hand in his teeth, he rammed his head forward and the splayed end of wire the youth held made contact with the two terminals. An electric charge was conveyed to the pool of petrol Muir had prepared on the floor of the hangar. There was a curious whumping sound as the aircraft was enveloped in a fireball that roasted the three men writhing at the centre, like meat thrown on to a barbecue.

In the nearby village of Enstone, a husband and wife on their way for an early drink in the pub saw the dark sky suddenly illuminated as if a giant firework had been discharged.

'Probably some kids buggering about,' the husband grumbled as they walked on.

Friday, October 30 7.05 p.m.

Brian Meadows was suffering from a crisis of conscience; and his dilemma was not made any easier by the presence of a young designer from the publicity department who had come to discuss the redecoration of his office. The youth, who was dressed in jeans and a baggy blue denim shirt and wore his hair pulled back in a ponytail, was now showing him a swatch of material.

'This will be painted the colour of burgundy, it will look marvellous with this sort of sacking texture.'

'Sacking?' Meadows repeated, only half listening to the youth's comments. 'You're going to put sacking on my wall?'

'It's not really sacking,' the youth pouted. 'It's hand-woven linen. It just has that nice rough texture.'

Meadows looked at him with dislike. 'How will people know it's hand woven? A few ignorant fools, like myself, may actually think it's just a few old potato sacks.'

'We can use something smoother if you like.'

'By all means.'

The young man slapped his sample-book shut. 'One more thing. Is it absolutely necessary for you to have a computer terminal in here?'

Meadows leaned across his desk and cupped his chin in a hand. 'That's how I know what's going in the paper,' he said mildly, deciding sarcasm would be utterly wasted. 'But why do you ask?'

'The whole theme of the room is going to be Victorian. A plastic terminal will hardly be compatible with the rest of the décor.'

'Why don't you put it in a brass-bound mahogany box?'

The young man sniffed. 'Umm ... I suppose that *could* work.' He began to make a little sketch on a pad.

Meadows could no longer tolerate his presence. 'If you'll excuse me now, I really must get on,' he said.

The youth left and Meadows went back to the problem he had been wrestling with since lunchtime: what to do with the information Sir Charles Miller had given him. Meadows was an honourable man, and although he detested Sir Robert Hall, in the deeper recesses of his heart he still believed he owed him a loyalty as an employee of the company. In his view, signing a contract involved more than a legal obligation; there was a moral one too. Granted, he had learned the truth in the most exceptional circumstances, but that didn't discharge the problem. Meadows knew that a takeover bid was going to be made for LOC PLC, and one that would be to his personal advantage. Miller had indicated there would be splendid rewards if he were to stay on as editor, and was obviously delighted about the path being cleared as far as Geraldine was concerned. But conscience still dictated that he must inform the chairman of the coming storm. At least everything had gone smoothly on the other front. The *Evening Standard* Londoner's diary had been pleased to use the engagement story he had given them. He expected it to be displayed prominently in the late edition.

With a heavy heart he reached for the telephone, but before his hand came in contact it rang.

'Come up immediately,' Sir Robert snapped, replacing the receiver before Meadows could answer.

Meadows made for the executive lift and a few minutes later was shown into the chairman's office. Richard Gibson, the Managing Director, stood with Sir Robert in front of a fake Georgian fireplace where gas burned through artificial logs.

'Sit down, Meadows,' Sir Robert said. The editor noticed that Gibson would not catch his eye.

Meadows took the chair indicated and waited for Sir Robert to speak.

'I want you to fire Stenton today,' Sir Robert said flatly.

Meadows slowly folded his arms. 'I'm sorry, I can't do that,' he replied easily.

'Why?' Sir Robert asked. 'I understand he put that disgraceful piece on page one. It has deeply offended Lord Glendowning. And that's after I gave my word his son would be treated with discretion. And another thing. I understand you're conducting a sordid affair with a prominent member of the government. That really is intolerable. It could do the *Gazette* untold harm.'

'That's my private life, it has nothing to do with you,' Meadows answered. 'The Glendowning story was an error, but it was my responsibility. If you want to fire anyone, let it be me.'

Sir Robert exchanged a furtive glance with Gibson. 'If that is the case, I'm prepared to offer you two years' salary.'

Meadows shook his head. 'When I was induced to come to this company, I was given a five-year rolling contract. Pay that, and I'll be happy to go.'

'Ha,' Sir Robert said quickly. 'Tell him what they say in the City about five-year contracts, Richard.'

Gibson cleared his throat. 'They say: a five-year contract means two years. That's as much as anyone gets if they go to law, regardless of the piece of paper.'

'You hear that,' Hall said. 'Five years is two years.'

'I'm familiar with the expression,' Meadows said. 'But I expected more.'

'More money?'

He shook his head. 'You wouldn't understand – it has to do with honour.'

'Honour … honour? What about my honour? You made me break my word to a valuable friend … Where are you going?'

'Have the cheque for two years' money made out immediately,' Meadows said from the doorway. 'I want to take it with me when I leave the building tonight.'

After they'd watched him go, Sir Robert turned to Gibson. 'Why do you think he was smiling?' he asked, with just a hint of worry in his voice.

Danny Doyle had had a man in the Red Lion since Fergus had told him that Cat Abbot possessed the master disc. By six o'clock it had paid off. An overheard conversation between two reporters at the bar told his man that Cat Abbot was in a suite at the Savoy hotel, registered in the name of Henry Higgins. On receiving the information, Danny made his plans.

Cat Abbot had been walking for hours. He had not returned to the hotel suite during the afternoon because, as Doreen had predicted, he had much on his mind. During the day he had thought through all of the various periods in his life: boyhood, youth, marriage, and the years since he had been divorced. It was as though he were examining events that had happened to somebody else; examining his own past as if it were a tragedy that he had never been able to understand – until now. The trust people had placed in him, which he had never been able to return; affections that had gone unreciprocated; friendships that he had always exploited rather than cherished. Finally he'd come to understand Jack Keane completely. It was so bloody simple. People had loved Jack because he had loved them; it had nothing to do with 'special gifts' or 'getting the right breaks'. For all those years, Cat had got it the wrong way round. Now he desperately wanted to put things right – reshape his life. Live like a man.

In his journey he had walked all over the City. Now, he suddenly found himself at Chancery Lane tube station and he slowly became aware of his surroundings. Deciding to look in at the office, he set off up the Gray's Inn Road. A few minutes later he was at his desk in the newsroom.

'Bloody good stuff on Doreen Clay, Cat,' a passing features sub said.

'That's Sarah Keane,' he replied, suppressing his first impulse, which was to take the credit offered. 'She's written it all.'

After consulting his contact book, he dialled a number in Spain. The voice that answered was the one he wanted to hear. 'Debbie,' he said hesitantly. 'It's me.'

'Sorry,' his daughter said after a moment. 'I don't recognise your voice.'

'It's me, your father.'

'Dad ... is it really you?'

'How are you?'

'I'm fine. What's the matter, why are you calling?'

'No reason – well, I just wanted to speak to you. It's been a long time. When are you getting married?'

'I got married last year, Dad. I had a baby in August.'

'A baby! Why didn't you tell me? Is it a boy or a girl?'

'A boy. I didn't think you'd be interested.'

'I know, Debbie,' he said, his voice trembling slightly. 'I've not been much of a father. But that's going to change. Something's happened to me ... I've found out something about myself. I'll tell you about it when I see you.'

'Are you coming over?'

'As soon as I can. How's your mother?'

'She's fine, the bar's doing well. She's so suntanned you wouldn't recognise her.'

'Give her my ... best regards. I'm glad she's happy.'

'Good-bye, Dad.'

'Good-bye, Debs. I'll see you soon, I promise, and my grand-son.'

He sat back for a minute, then switched on his terminal. The message Sinclair had left the night before appeared on the screen. Intrigued, he rang the number and asked for Patrick Pearse. As soon as Big Davey McNally spoke, Cat could feel danger: not for himself, but for Doreen and Sarah.

'I'll come directly to the point, Mr Abbot,' Big Davey said. 'You have something I want to buy. I'll give you £20,000 for it. Just name a place to meet and the money's yours.'

McNally's voice seemed to activate something in Cat's head. Pictures began to form in his mind, pale and monochromatic at first, like a photograph in a developing tray. Then stronger and flooded with bright colour. He saw Danny Doyle, surrounded by the carcasses of dead animals, then Lily, standing in her flat in the Brent River estate. Without understanding why, he knew where the places were and recognised the people. Then he saw McNally, his face wreathed by darkness, like the Angel of Death. All these people were evil, Cat knew. He had to guide them away from Doreen and Sarah, he could still feel the terrible danger threatening them.

'Did you say £20,000?' he asked quickly.

'That's my price.'

'I didn't know it was worth that much. I've already sold it.' He could hear an intake of breath on the line. 'What will you give me if I tell you where it is now?'

'That could be worth, say, £10,000,' McNally said. 'If it can be recovered.'

'I delivered it to Lily Doyle this afternoon.' Cat said. 'It's in her flat on the Brent River estate.'

'Thank you, Mr Abbot. If we find it there, you will receive full payment in due course.'

Cat hung up, and the pictures returned to fill his head once again.

He could see Sarah and Doreen in the suite, and there was still a terrible threat to them. His forehead was covered with sweat now and his heart palpitating.

'Are you all right?' Pauline Kaznovitch said as she paused at his desk. He looked up and tried to smile.

'I think so, just a bit faint for a moment.'

'Must be the drink,' Pauline said. She looked at him again. 'Are you sure?'

Cat reached out. 'Will you hold my hand for a second?' he said.

'Is this some kind of trick?' she asked suspiciously.

He shook his head. 'No, really, just a favour.'

Hesitantly, Pauline reached out and felt a flow of energy pass through her in a sudden jolt. It was as if her entire body had been warmed momentarily. For Cat it was like a powerful electric current being grounded. Gradually, his heart returned to its normal pace and, without thinking why, he got up from his desk and walked towards the features department.

'What's the matter with you?' Mick Gates asked Pauline, who was still standing in bewilderment.

'You're not going to believe this,' she answered. 'But Abbot has just given me an orgasm.'

Cat reached the coat rack in the features department and felt in the pockets of the old mackintosh that hung there. He withdrew a flat plastic disc.

Friday, October 30 6.40 p.m.

Greaves and Holland left Companies House in the City Road, long after it closed to the public. They hurried to the car, where the driver was holding out the telephone. 'It's a Cat Abbot, says it's urgent.'

'Yes,' Greaves said, 'how can I help you?'

'I've got something important for you. I'll meet you in the suite at the Savoy, hurry. I think Sarah and Doreen are in trouble.'

'What kind of trouble?' Greaves asked, but Cat had rung off.

There was a knock on the door of the suite and Sarah continued to speak as she got up to answer it. 'So when did your husband actually leave?' she asked.

Doreen was about to tell her not to open the door but she was too late. The three men who entered the room worked for Danny Doyle; to Doreen, they had auras like wild beasts.

'Who are you?' one of them asked in a flat, emotionless voice.

Doreen answered quickly. 'I'm Mrs Raymond Abbot and this is his sister, Sarah.'

'Where's Abbot?'

'He won't be back until later this evening.'

Sarah looked bewildered but Doreen gestured for her to be silent.

'Search the place,' one of the men ordered. He walked up to Sarah and took a cut-throat razor from his pocket. He laid it against her cheek. 'So you're Abbot's sister. Tell me, do you love your brother?'

'Yes,' Sarah murmured, transfixed with fear.

'Well, I tell you what's going to happen,' the man said quietly. 'You're going to leave a note for your brother telling him to ring a certain number. Then you're going to come along with us. Any trouble and you die, understand?'

Cat got to the suite first. He found the note Sarah had written, and sat down in a chair. 'Where are they?' he said aloud, and closed his eyes. Instantly, the image of Danny Doyle surrounded by the carcasses of dead animals came to him. Concentrating, he discovered he could alter the scope, as if using a film camera, but he still maintained the peripheral vision as in ordinary sight.

Pulling back, he passed through the roof of the building and looked down from the night sky on to the rooftops of the surrounding buildings. Then he swooped down, like a bird in flight, and found the name of the road. He got up and was about to add the address to the bottom of the note left by Sarah when Greaves and Holland entered the room. 'I know where they are,' he said. 'But they're in terrible danger.'

Greaves took the sheet of paper from him, then glanced around the room. On a chair near the door was a new coat and hat that Abbot had bought Doreen from the shop in the hotel. His mind filled with a numbing dread for Sarah's safety, he picked up the wide-brimmed hat and saw that there were two long hat pins thrust through the finely woven straw. He pulled one out: it was about seven inches long, and wickedly pointed. For a moment his thoughts flashed back to the garage in Belfast.

CHAPTER
FOURTEEN

Friday, October 30 6.45 p.m.

Big Davey McNally sat at the desk in the main room of his suite with a sheet of the hotel notepaper before him. He felt like the commander of an army who knows that one more push against the enemy will see the war won. A mood of exaltation filled his being with such swelling pride that he felt pressure on his breastbone, as if the organs inside his chest had expanded. He knew he had to act quickly now, but he missed his right-hand man; Andy Muir had not yet returned and he could wait no longer. Throughout the afternoon, when it was clear to him that Eddie Page had been taken, he had called his best remaining men to the hotel: Prentice, Buchanan and Franklin. They sat before him now, ready for his instructions.

Buchanan had drawn a rough map of the Brent River estate

on the sheet of paper, and indicated where the guards on Lily Doyle's flat were located.

'You're sure of this?' McNally asked.

Buchanan got up from his chair. 'Definitely, Big Davey,' he replied. 'I've been there myself. There's two on the balconies of the facing block and one on the door. If the weather's bad like now the one on the door sits in a car they keep parked there.'

'What are they armed with?'

'Impossible to see, but if I was doing the job I'd have rifles on the balconies and something small and handy in the guard car.'

McNally nodded his agreement. 'How would you hit them?'

Buchanan tapped the map with an index finger. 'Take out the balcony positions first.'

'What with?'

Buchanan smiled. 'We've got a beautiful piece for the job. An Armalite with night sights.' He pointed to the map again. 'Prentice is the best shot. We drop him here, out of sight, and he goes to the landing on the second floor of this block. From there he's got a clear shot at both positions.'

'Can he hit them both? He won't have much time for the second shot.'

'I can do it, Big Davey.'

'How do we get the one in the car?'

Buchanan put his hands in his pockets; it was clear he was confident. McNally was pleased by the quality of his work. He didn't feel so badly about missing Andy Muir now.

'We've stolen one of the niggers' cars, it's got smoked windows and a sound system that can knock your head off at twenty paces. Lily Doyle hates nigger music, so we draw up close to the guard's car and play the system at full blast. That will cut out the sound of the Armalite and draw the other bastard out of the car. Then I hit him.'

'Good,' Big Davey smiled. 'Let's go now.'

* * *

Greaves's car was stuck in the rush hour traffic. He did not want to use the police siren until Cat Abbot had made his call. Danny Doyle lifted the receiver on the second ring.

'Do you have my property?' he asked, when Abbot identified himself.

'Yes,' Cat replied.

'You know I have your wife and sister. I will exchange them in two hours' time. Go to the Shamrock Meat Company, in Braysfield Road, Kilburn. The yard gate will be left open. Park there and wait. Do you understand ?'

'Yes.'

'If you do anything silly, like call the police, I will butcher your women. You do believe that, don't you?'

'Yes.'

'In two hours, Mr Abbot.'

Danny Doyle replaced the receiver and looked at Bridget who was, as always, lying on the sofa half dressed, watching a musical. Her sloth usually annoyed him, but being close to action always aroused his sexual needs. Without speaking, he removed the minimum amount of his clothes that was necessary, and pulled her on to her back as though laying a side of meat on a butcher's block. Grunting with satisfaction, he entered her without any effort at foreplay or tenderness.

'Oh, that's lovely, Danny,' she moaned, but her head was turned away from him to watch Gene Kelly and Cyd Charisse dance romantically through Central Park.

The telephone rang again, when he had readjusted his clothing. It was Lily. 'Jesus Christ, Danny, I've been trying to get hold of you for ever,' she said. He could hear from her voice that she was close to hysteria.

'Calm down,' he answered. 'Just tell me what it is.'

'I've had a warning, something terrible … oh, God, I've been going out of my fucking mind. Where's Fergus?'

'He's gone away for a few days, he's fine. Now what kind of warning is it?'

'A wee gypsy girl, she told me we're all going to die … I tell you, I've been going fucking crazy. There's someone real bad, someone with power who's after us, it's greater than the evil eye. For Christ's sake, come over here. I've got to talk to you.'

'Who's this girl who's been filling your head with this shit? There's nothing anyone can do to us. I'll crucify any man who tries.'

'You don't understand,' Lily moaned. 'You and Fergus and Liam were too young. I remember what Ma told me. The gypsies know … I tell you they fucking know. I've seen it happen. People are fine one day and the next … oh, Jesus, I'm scared so much I can hardly stand.'

'All right, all right – now just take a hold of yourself. I've got to go over to Kilburn on business later. I'll call in on you, so stop worrying.'

'You will?'

'Sure, now that's a promise.'

'Are you hungry, Danny? I know that bitch never feeds you properly. Let me do you a fry-up.'

'When I get there. Now just relax; nothing's going to happen to us. That's a promise.'

Doyle hung up. He looked at his watch: it would be some time before his men got the women to the abattoir. He might as well take up Lily's offer, a bit of home cooking would be a treat. He rang down for his car and added that he wanted an escort of three men. Ten minutes later he was heading for north London in the rush hour traffic.

Greaves's car pulled up before New Scotland Yard. Abbot waited with him in his office, while Holland took the disc to be copied.

'So you invented everything about Doreen Clay seeing the body of Jill Slade in the seance?' Greaves asked.

'Yes,' Cat replied. 'I needed a big story. It seemed harmless enough at the time. The girl was already dead.'

'What about the rest of the things she said?'

'That was all true.' He looked up. 'Did you ever know anyone German?'

Greaves shook his head. 'My great-grandmother was from Munich but I never knew her, she was dead before I was born.'

Abbot changed the subject. 'Do you think Doyle will let them go if I give him the disc?'

Greaves looked from the window into the night, which shimmered with coloured lights in the falling rain. 'There's not much chance,' he answered eventually. 'Doyle likes killing people. It's anyone's guess how he will react.' He turned back. 'But the only ace we hold is the disc. It's obviously very important to him. Enough for him to risk everything.'

'Do you have a plan, some course of action?'

Greaves moved to a large-scale map of London that hung on the wall, and indicated the Kilburn area. 'This is a warren of old streets. The abattoir stands on a crossroads, next to the main junction of a sewer. God knows how many ways out there are. The best we can do is hold back and mount as many marksman positions as we can. But there's a vast refrigerated basement under the building. There could be exits all over the shop. You'll have to bargain with him.' He waited for a few seconds, then said, 'If he lets the women go, he will probably hold on to you. Are you prepared for that?'

Cat Abbot tried to smile. 'Yes. I'd already worked that out for myself.'

'I can't make you do this.'

Abbot got up. 'It's all right, I want to.'

Holland entered the room. 'We've copied the disc and there's a compatible system in the next room. I can show you what's on it now.'

They moved to the terminal and Holland tapped in the instructions. Names and addresses filled the screen, each of them accompanied by a set of initials and numbers.

'Try one of those,' Greaves instructed. Holland entered the code, and information was revealed about invoices and monies paid. There were also faces of the girls available for executive sex.

Holland whistled softly. 'No wonder he wants this, it's his whole bloody operation. We can crack him wide open with this.'

'Thank God,' Greaves said quickly. 'It's worth a lot to him, maybe two lives. I want you to stay here and work on this, Nick.'

The rain fell with steady intensity on the Brent River estate, puddling the muddy expanses between the tower blocks into a quagmire and overloading the inadequate drainage system, so the gutters of the roadways turned to running streams thick with garbage.

It was good weather for the job McNally had in mind. The high floodlights mounted on the tower blocks shone down on the deserted wasteland. They parked the car out of view and waited until Prentice took his rifle, carefully wrapped in two plastic carrier bags, and made for the landing to take up his firing position. When he was ready, he signalled with the flame from a lighter.

'Tell them to go,' McNally ordered and the car with the smoked windows drove slowly forward, with music blasting into the night.

Everything went smoothly. McNally could see the flashes from the muzzle of the Armalite, and no sooner had the stolen car come to a stop near the entrance to Lily Doyle's flat than a man emerged from the parked Ford Granada and moved towards the source of the music. Buchanan shot him at close range and dragged his body into the shadows.

'Hide the others before we go in,' McNally said. 'We don't want any good citizen calling the police.'

But the events had already been observed from the tower block from which Prentice had fired. At the sound of the music, WPC Janice Woods had turned out the lights in her flat and opened the door on to the balcony. Her husband, Alistair, was not at home; he was drinking in one of the local pubs. Janice Woods also noticed the muzzle flash from the Armalite and recognised it. Then she saw the killing of the guard outside Lily's flat.

Slipping back into her living room, she prised up a floorboard and removed a Smith and Wesson .38 calibre revolver, a box of ammunition and a mobile telephone from the recess. She snapped open the chamber of the revolver to check the load and took a handful of spare cartridges, which she placed in the pocket of her denim jacket.

The rapid-response unit she called took her message that there was gunfire on the Brent River estate and told her a team was on the way. Janice Woods replaced the telephone receiver and left the flat.

Lily Doyle had gone to the window with a frown of annoyance the moment she'd heard the pounding music. She saw her guard get out of his car, so she let the curtain fall again. A few minutes later the noise stopped and she turned to Betty, who was working at the kitchen table. 'Those fucking blacks never learn. I suppose Michael's had to give one of them a good hiding.' She watched Betty slicing bread and shook her head in disapproval. 'Here, give me that,' she said. 'Danny likes it thinner than that, so as it's crisp all through.'

There was a tap on the door and she turned to Betty. 'Get that, it'll be Michael telling me about the niggers.' The elderly woman wheezed her way to the door. She turned the lock and when the door burst open she was sent staggering across the room.

Lily spun round with the carving knife in her hand, but Big Davey McNally was levelling a large semi-automatic pistol at her face.

'You,' she hissed, the venom in her voice causing her vocal cords to contract so she could only speak in a whisper.

'Hello, Lily. I've no time for small talk – where is it?'

'Where's what?'

He walked over and hit her across the face with the gun barrel. The impact split open her lip and broke two front teeth. She crumpled to the floor, but remained conscious. 'Danny's coming,' she whispered through her damaged mouth. 'He'll cut out your fucking heart.'

'Just tell me where it is.'

'I don't know what you're talking about.'

'Get her up,' he ordered Buchanan. 'Sit her in a chair.' He looked around in agitation and saw Betty, who was still cowering on the floor.

'Bring the old woman over here and tie her in this.' He indicated another of the chairs at the kitchen table. Buchanan used the lead from the television aerial to tie her up.

McNally opened the kitchen cupboards and swept items aside until he found two that he wanted: a large plastic funnel and a full container of household bleach. He walked over to the old woman whose face was now mottled with terror, casually pulled back her head by the hair and thrust the funnel down her throat. Then he began to pour the bleach. A dreadful gagging sound came from her and after a few more moments' struggle, her body gave a convulsive heave and she was still, sightless eyes staring at the ceiling. The funnel still protruding from her throat, she was a figure of comical horror.

'Tell me where it is, Lily,' McNally said quietly. 'Or you'll be wishing I'd finished you as quick.'

'Honest to God, I don't know what you're talking about,' Lily answered, but the defiance had gone from her voice.

282

'A man called Raymond Abbot delivered something here today. I want it.'

'No one's been round here today. They lied to you.'

McNally's face contorted with rage. Knowing she spoke the truth, all control left him and he began to advance on Lily, who tried to drag herself away across the floor of the room.

He raised the gun again and Lily looked up into his face. There was a sudden crackle of shots from outside, as she cringed, expecting the blow. Then two deafening reports from close by, and before McNally could bring the barrel down on her face, his forehead exploded. The 9mm bullet from Danny Doyle's Browning had entered the back of McNally's skull and flattened against the frontal lobe before tearing a large piece of the bone away and splashing brains and blood over Lily's dining table.

McNally's body fell half over Lily. She screamed as more contents of the skull poured into her lap.

Buchanan was finished too, she could see that now, and her lovely flat smelt of death and cordite. Danny dragged McNally's body off her and pulled her to her feet. There was the sound of more shots from outside and one of Doyle's men ducked into the room. 'Someone's still shooting at us,' he gasped. 'Murphy and Callaghan are down.'

'I thought you got them all?'

'So did I,' the youth replied.

'Turn off the lights,' Doyle ordered.

In the darkness he peered from the window. Outside it looked like a battlefield, with bodies scattered about the parked cars.

'We'll make a run for the Mercedes,' Danny said. 'I'll bring Lily. You go first … ready now.'

The youth ran from the doorway and a woman's clear voice called out: 'Police, lay down your weapons.' Janice Woods stood in a half-crouch, twenty paces from the Mercedes, both hands levelling the Smith and Wesson revolver. The youth fired wildly in her direction and a random shot hit her in the left thigh. She went down on her stomach, but still managed to get off two rounds. The first hit the youth in the throat and the second was dead centre. He was thrown back against the brick wall in a crumpled heap.

Holding Lily by the arm, Danny sprinted forward and managed to get to the Mercedes. Janice Woods fired again but this time her shots were wide.

She lay face down in the mud as the car roared away. Not bad, she thought through the pain. She'd hit all three of Doyle's henchmen.

It was pitch dark and icy cold in the vast echoing room where they had put Sarah and Doreen.

'Are you all right?' Sarah said softly.

'I think so,' Doreen replied in the same tone. 'Where do you think we are?'

'Some sort of storage warehouse, an abattoir I think. It's refrigerated.'

They had been forced to the floor of the car throughout their journey, with their heads hooded.

'What in God's name is this all about?' Sarah asked as they stood close together in the icy blackness.

'Cat has something they want – they'll do anything to get it. That's why I told them we were related to him.'

'I don't understand.'

Doreen put her head close to Sarah and whispered, 'I was bargaining on the possibility that if they thought Raymond cared for us, they'd keep us alive as hostages. Otherwise they would have killed us out of hand. I could feel it when they entered the room.'

Sarah thought for a time. 'I don't give much for our chances if we're relying on Cat's good nature to see us through,' she said after due consideration.

'Don't despair,' Doreen answered. 'Remember he's a changed man now.'

Sarah still had her reservations, but she did not voice them. The cold was beginning to numb them as they stood together in the darkness.

When Danny Doyle arrived at the abattoir, the men who had brought Sarah and Doreen were waiting in one of the deserted offices as instructed. Lily, in a state of near collapse, was given a hot drink from a vending machine and Doyle broke open a locked cabinet, where he knew the manager kept a bottle of whisky. He took three long pulls straight from the bottle, then added some to Lily's coffee.

'We'll be all right soon,' he said. 'The gypsy curse didn't come true, did it?'

Lily looked down at her dress, still encrusted with the remains of McNally. 'I hope that's the end of it, Danny. Jesus Christ, I can't take any more. Did you see what that bastard did to Betty?'

'Just take it easy,' he said. 'I'm going to see our guests. What are these?' he asked, pointing at two handbags lying on a desk.

'They belong to the women,' one of his men answered.

Doyle tipped the contents of both on to the desk top and ran his hands through the jumble. Then he stopped. There was a snapshot of Sarah, taken with Colin Greaves in the garden of the Hampstead house.

'Greaves,' he said softly. Then he held up the picture to the nearest man. 'Is she here?'

'That's right, Danny,' he answered.

'Greaves,' he repeated. 'He's coming too, I fucking know he is.' He took hold of Lily. 'He's the one who shot Liam.' He turned to the other men: 'All of you, go and check on those bitches. I don't want them hurt yet. I'll make sure they die of broken hearts.'

When they were alone, Lily said, 'Are you planning to kill a policeman, Danny? Christ, you'll never get away with it.'

Danny took hold of her shoulders. 'Yes I will. Fergus and I have been planning a get-out for a long time. This man Abbot who's coming here has got a disc loaded with information. There's a Dutch organisation that wants to buy us out, lock stock and barrel. I've been offered five million dollars for everything. Fergus is already in Amsterdam, we go there and meet him as soon as this is done. It's all worked out. Now listen,' he said urgently, 'when I've exchanged the women, I'll have Abbot and Greaves in here. We'll take them down to the basement and kill them there. The other lads can go out the front door and face the police snipers. There's a way from the basement that comes out in Ramilles Street. Have you got that?'

Lily held on to his sleeve and pleaded, 'Let me kill the one who shot Liam.'

He patted her shoulder. 'You've got to do something else first,' he said, then he took a piece of paper on the desk and drew a hurried diagram. 'We're here, and here's Ramilles Street. The tunnel runs alongside the main sewer. Go out and take the little red car you'll find next to the Mercedes. Drive it round to Ramilles Street and park it on the forecourt of Number 18 so we can use it later, then get back here as quick as you can.'

'All right, Danny. Number 18 Ramilles Street,' Lily repeated.

'And wear this,' he said taking off his white trenchcoat. 'Your dress is a mess.'

Lily did as she was told and was back with Danny within ten minutes. The first police began to arrive as she closed the door from the street behind her.

It was now time for Cat's appointment; everything was in place. Greaves had watched as the experts positioned marksmen, but in his heart he did not believe they would affect the outcome.

Danny Doyle would call the tune; and madmen did not necessarily follow the patterns of logic. Rage alone might cause Doyle to start a bloodbath. Cat Abbot now sat in a car, with Greaves concealed in the rear, watching the forecourt of the factory that loomed above the rain-drenched suburban street. A chain-link gate was open, leading into a loading bay that was bathed in sallow light from a lamp set above steel roller doors. A panel opened and Doyle appeared. Cat got out of the car, leaving the driver's door open, and walked forward a few yards.

'Have you brought the disc, Mr Abbot?' Doyle called out.

Cat held it up in his left hand. 'What about the women?'

'All in good time,' Doyle replied. 'You can tell the Superintendent to come out from the back of that car and bring his pistol, I want him in here as well.'

Greaves slowly got out of the car and walked forward to join Cat.

'Now I would imagine all sorts of sharpshooters will be aiming guns at me now,' Doyle said, 'so just bear it in mind that if anything happens, my lads are going to cut the women's throats.' He leaned back into the doorway and called, 'Aren't you, boys?' Then he turned back to them. 'And just remember, I've got my own guns trained on you, so don't try any fancy moves.' Doyle held out a hand and beckoned. 'When you two get in here, they come out.'

Cat slowly reached out and lit a throw-away gas lighter, which he held close to the plastic disc. 'Send them out now, Doyle. If they're not freed, I've only got to touch this with a flame and it's useless to you.'

Doyle grinned. 'Send them out,' he shouted.

Blinking in the light, Sarah and Doreen appeared.

'Keep walking,' Greaves called out. The two women came forward hesitantly. Now they were all at the point of no return.

'Keep going,' Greaves called out again. Then he and Cat passed them on the forecourt and moved to block any line of fire from inside the building.

Doyle stepped back into the darkened doorway. 'Come in, Greaves,' he called out, 'or my lads will kill you where you stand.'

'This way,' Doyle muttered, when they had crossed the threshold, and he reached inside Greaves's coat to remove his pistol. 'Search them,' he said to one of his men, and hands were run over their bodies.

'Is this the gun you used to kill my brother?' Doyle asked softly, looking down at Greaves's Walther.

'That's the one,' Greaves answered.

'Did you hear that, Lily?'

'I heard,' she replied. 'Remember you said I could open him up?'

Doyle jacked a round into the firing chamber of the Walther and handed the pistol to Lily. 'All you have to do is point and pull the trigger.' He gestured with his own gun: 'Down here, and keep your hands on the top of your heads all the time.'

They descended a spiral staircase and found themselves in a network of whitewashed brick tunnels that radiated in all directions. Doyle indicated they should follow one that led to heavy insulated doors. Beyond was a vast refrigerated store, where rows of shrouded meat hung beneath harsh neon lights.

Doyle directed them to stand against a wall, where there was a long butcher's table and racks of saws, cleavers and knives. 'Give me that,' he said reaching out to take the disc Cat held. He remained standing close to them.

'Now let me tell you what I'm going to do to you,' he began. 'First I'm going to break your legs, because I don't want you to move about too much, and then I'm going to show Lily how to dress you both like sides of beef.'

He held out the automatic and quite slowly aimed at Cat's thigh. Greaves slid Doreen's hat pin from where it was secured beneath the strap of his watch-band and in the same movement thrust it into Doyle's extended hand. Doyle screamed at the sudden pain. The gun clattered on to the brick floor, but Doyle managed to kick it out of Greaves's reach. Turning swiftly, Greaves was trying to grasp for the nearest butcher's knife when all the lights above exploded in a shattering display of pyrotechnics. The vaulted space above them was filled with tiny shards of reflecting glass that fell like silver rain. But instead of the expected darkness, a soft new light glowed in the air about them.

Lily fired one wild shot and the bullet creased Greaves's head, just above the right temple. He did not black out, but it felt as though he had been pole-axed. Now, semi-conscious in the strange subaqueous light, his ears were filled with an intense sound, as if a hive of giant bees had been opened. He reeled against the hanging carcasses, fighting to remain conscious; and from the impact of his body the carcasses began to turn and swing on their hooks, as if the stunted limbs were reaching out.

Still half-stunned, he watched Lily and Doyle hold up their arms, their faces contorted in fear, as if they were fighting off some unseen horror; and the source of the new light appeared to emanate from Cat Abbot, whose whole body seemed to pulsate with energy.

Lily Doyle began to scream: 'It's him! It's him … ' Then Greaves began to hallucinate. The swaying carcasses about him turned into shrouded corpses, holding out their arms to embrace Danny and Lily. Through the pulsating noise that filled his mind, Greaves imagined he could hear a tumult of voices like the screams of a multitude begging for an end to their torment; and the rank smell of corrupting flesh came to him … It was as though he were standing at the gates of Hell. A darkness opened about the brother and sister, who were writhing as if caught in a snake-pit, and to Greaves the shrouded corpses seemed to be dragging them towards the centre of the darkness. Greaves felt as if he too were being pulled by an unseen tide. But from somewhere, he could hear a voice that was calling to him alone. 'Stop! Go back, go back,' it commanded. His fuddled mind told him that the voice spoke in another language.

'I don't speak German,' he said quite distinctly. Then he blacked out.

*   *   *

When he regained consciousness, he was sitting in a chair in the offices of the abattoir. Sarah was holding a handkerchief to his head. 'I don't speak German,' he said almost angrily.

'I know you don't, darling,' she replied.

He jerked his head around. 'Where's Cat?'

'He's fine,' she said soothingly. 'Look, here he is.'

Greaves held a hand to his throbbing head. The sound of giant bees still echoed distantly.

'What happened to Doyle?' he asked.

'Dead,' Cat replied quietly. 'A massive stroke, probably brought on by too much excitement.'

'And Lily?'

'She appears to have gone right off her head, keeps babbling about a gypsy's warning. Looks like a complete breakdown.'

'In there,' Greaves said after a moment. 'What actually happened?'

Cat explained: 'The main circuit blew out and when the emergency lights kicked on it seemed to frighten Doyle to death.'

Greaves shook his still pounding head. 'I thought … other things happened.'

'You were nearly killed by that bullet. It was a nasty crack on the head. You probably imagined things.'

'I've got something else to do,' Greaves said trying to get to his feet. 'Where's Nick Holland?'

'That can wait until tomorrow,' Sarah said firmly. 'I'm taking you home.'

'The same goes for you,' Doreen said to Cat. 'I'm not letting you out of my sight.'

290

'I've got to go to the paper,' Cat said. 'This is the biggest story of my life.'

'Well, I'm coming too,' she said.

He didn't argue.

Greaves slept on the way to Hampstead. Sarah refused an offer to help get him into the house. Together they climbed the stairs, suddenly exhausted by the events of the day. But as they came close to Emily's room they heard a man's voice mumbling. Sarah pushed open the door and in the light from the passageway, saw the naked torso of Ric Daggert sprawled over her daughter's bed. Drawing back in shock, she continued to her own room, her footsteps now feeling as heavy as her heart. She opened her bedroom door, and had just managed to get Greaves to the leather sofa when she heard another sound. Turning, she saw Emily sitting up in the bed.

'What's the matter, is Colin drunk?' she asked.

'No, darling,' Sarah replied in a flood of sudden relief.

'Ric is,' Emily said. 'He came round earlier. He was out of his mind. He begged me to forgive him and said he couldn't live without me. I had to put him in my room.'

'The end of a perfect day,' Sarah said wearily.

Saturday, October 31 10.50 a.m.

Sir Robert Hall was on the telephone – dictating instructions to the deputy editor of the *Gazette* who was sitting, in a state of misery, amid scenes of chaos. Since the evening before, when Brian Meadows had told him of his dismissal, Gordon Brooks had felt as if he were marooned at the bottom of an ocean inside an old-fashioned diver's suit, being squeezed by the tentacles of a giant octopus. The paper that morning had been a disaster. Despite the fact that the *Gazette* had had two members of its own staff at the centre of events, they had been cleaned up by the opposition. Brooks had failed to grasp the connection between the Battle of Brent River estate and the Kilburn meat works siege until the last edition, when Cat Abbot had finally arrived at the office and sorted it out.

Luckily, Sir Robert was not particularly interested in the story, but Brooks had felt the scorn of the other executives at morning conference, and he was a sensitive soul.

'I want you to drop the Doreen Clay series,' Sir Robert said.

Brooks looked up as yet another piece of reproduction antique furniture was manhandled into the office. 'One moment, Sir Robert,' he said and he covered the telephone mouthpiece with his hand. 'I told you not to bring any more of that in here,' he hissed.

'Sorry, guvnor, we've got our orders,' the bigger of the two men said dismissively, and walked from the room.

Brooks returned to the call. 'But why? We've told the readers it's going to run for another two days, Sir Robert,' he asked plaintively.

'Lady Amanda doesn't think it's very interesting, in fact she says it's very dull, just some common little woman telling us about her dreary life. End it. Good God, man, you'll have to use your initiative if you want to be editor.'

Brooks would have liked to tell him that the last thing he wanted on earth was the editorship of the *Gazette*, but Sir Robert was speaking again.

'My press conference is the big story of the day. I want you to boom that, understand?'

'Yes, Sir Robert. We're sending three reporters and three photographers.' Brooks did not want to mention that as it was a Saturday: there would be no edition of the *Gazette* that day.

'The work of HAND is vital to the people of Britain,' Sir Robert continued. 'I want my appointment as President of the charity to be recognised as a turning point in the awareness of the nation.'

Brooks made a careful note. The line went dead. When he looked up again, Brian Meadows was standing at the doorway with a sympathetic smile. 'How do you like the seat?' he asked.

Brooks squirmed uncomfortably. In the last two hours, he had spoken more often to Sir Robert Hall than at any other time in his two years as deputy to Meadows.

'Sorry about all this,' Meadows said, waving at the disorder in the room, 'I was having the place redecorated.'

'Oh, Christ, Brian, how am I going to cope?' Brooks said, with sudden emotion. 'I can't manage the little prick like you can. He'll drive me out of my mind.'

'Do what I'm doing, old boy, ' Meadows replied. 'Take a couple of weeks' holiday in the West Indies. Everything will look different when you get back. I can guarantee it.'

Brooks sighed. 'If only I could. I've got to go to this bloody press conference now. You know he wanted me to put the whole staff on to cover it?'

'I'll come down with you,' Meadows replied. 'I only dropped in to pick up my cigar case. In the rush of things I left it here last night.'

The two men walked to the executive lift. Meadows inserted his personal key, then he handed it to Brooks. 'Here, you'll need this.'

Brooks accepted it with a groan. 'You know I only took this job on the understanding I wouldn't have to deal with him. Maybe I can sue for breach of contract?'

Meadows laughed all the way to the ground floor.

When they got out of the lift, they saw that the front entrance hall had been transformed with screens to create a meeting place. There was a raised platform covered with green baize and rows of chairs before it, already half filled with lounging journalists from other papers. Members of the publicity department moved among them, distributing press handouts, and television crews were busy setting up their positions.

'I'll stay at the back, old boy,' Meadows said.

Brooks groaned again and made his way to the top table where Sir Robert was already talking to Jeremy Blakestone and two other members of the HAND committee. Meadows recognised them: they were the two titled fellows who had shared Sir Robert's table on the night of the charity dinner.

When the great were finally seated, Barry Quick tapped a microphone to test if it was live, then began to speak: 'My lords, ladies and gentlemen, thank you for coming here today. Although this event is taking place on the premises of the *Gazette*, I'm sure you will appreciate that it is an event which transcends media rivalries. It is to celebrate the appointment of Sir Robert Hall, Chairman of London and Overseas Communications PLC, as Life President of HAND.

'Now I am sure you are all aware of the wonderful work Jeremy Blakestone, the chairman of HAND, has performed since he founded the charity just a few brief years ago, so I will now call on him to expand on the vision he and Sir Robert Hall have for the future of this great organisation. My lords, ladies and gentlemen, Mr Jeremy Blakestone.'

But before Blakestone could rise, Meadows was aware of another figure who now stood on the platform. It was Detective-Sergeant Nick Holland, leaning over the chairman of HAND. Holland's words were clearly picked up by the microphone. 'Mr Jeremy Blakestone, I arrest you for complicity in the murder of Polly Weaver. You don't have to say anything, but …' The rest of his words were drowned in the commotion that erupted. Meadows felt a moment of pure pleasure when he watched the expression on Sir Robert's face, as Blakestone was led from the platform. He followed the two figures as they walked from the building and saw Superintendent Colin Greaves standing by a police car parked in the Gray's Inn Road.

Saturday, October 31 7.05 p.m.

Nick Holland manoeuvred his father's Mini into the last vacant space of the car park at the Bull and Bush, and picked up a brown paper parcel from the seat next to him. The evening was dark and the air chilled to a misty stillness; but the bright lights of the public house looked inviting. He was a few minutes late. He hoped Lucy Patterson wasn't on time, but when he entered the crowded room he saw her at the bar talking to a group of young men and women. She spotted him and broke away before he could join them.

'Friends from my nursing days,' she said. 'I hope you don't think I'm rude not introducing you – but I wanted to get you on my own.'

Nick raised his eyebrows questioningly as she took his arm and led him to a quieter part of the bar.

'I know what you policemen are like,' she said softly. 'You wouldn't tell me anything in front of the others.'

'Why do you think I'd tell you anything on your own?' he asked, smiling as he handed her the parcel containing the blue sweater.

'Copper's daughter; copper's sister. I'm one of the family.' Nick knew she was right in her assumption. Although policemen tended to keep the more gruesome aspects of the job from their families, they were still more open than with members of the general public.

'Sorry I'm late,' Nick said as he ordered a drink. 'I thought we could have an hour together before we went on to Colin and Sarah's.'

'I saw you on television.'

Nick smiled. 'It should have been Colin making the arrest, but he doesn't care for publicity.'

'You like him, don't you?'

'He's the best,' Holland replied.

'What else do you like?'

Nick grinned. 'Coppers' daughters who work for plastic surgeons.'

'I had a feeling you were going to ring. Why did you take so long?'

'We had a busy couple of days,' he said drily.

'Well?' she said, punching him on the arm. 'Are you going to tell me all about it?'

Nick related the events that had taken place since Monday and she listened without interruption. Then she asked, 'So how did you finally tie Blakestone in with it?'

'Companies House,' Holland said. 'We checked on the board members of Doyle's firm. The only name we didn't know was Bertram Giles. Then we did a cross-check and found that a Bertram Giles had also been chairman of a racehorse-breeding syndicate that went broke a few years ago. Davey McNally had invested heavily in the syndicate and lost all his money. Another policeman, McNeice, who was concentrating on McNally's gang, told us that Bertram Giles was actually Jeremy Blakestone. He'd come across him in connection with McNally a few years ago. It wasn't the first time Blakestone had changed his name. He's been doing dodgy deals for years, using different aliases. One deal was the string of health clubs he helped Doyle to set up. They used them to push drugs originally. Blakestone came unstuck when he got involved with McNally – McNally was going to kill him when he lost all his investment in the racing business. Blakestone wriggled out of it by selling him the idea of taking over Doyle's operation – he'd already begun HAND to find a supply of young girls for Danny Doyle. When the operation was working smoothly, the idea was that McNally would take it over for himself. McNally couldn't resist the chance to harm Doyle.'

Nick drank some more beer. 'Brilliant man, Blakestone. He could have made a fortune without being bent. I suppose it was just in his nature.'

'And what about Doreen Clay? Can she really read minds and tell the future?'

Holland put down his beer and studied her. 'You can judge for yourself. She and Cat Abbot are going to be there tonight.' He glanced at his watch. 'Time to get moving.'

It took them only a few minutes to reach Sarah's house. The mist was thicker further down the hill from the Heath and the night air seemed even more chilled. Nick rang the doorbell while Lucy admired the handsome proportions of the house. Suddenly the door was thrown open and two hideously shrouded figures stood before them, their faces like melted wax. 'Aghaaaaa!' they shouted, and Lucy reeled back in shock.

'Trick or treat?' Paul and Martin demanded.

'How much is a treat?' Holland asked, when they entered the hallway.

'Oh, that's all right,' Martin replied as he took their coats. 'Mum says we mustn't take anything, we're only allowed to scare people.'

'You must be Nick Holland,' Paul chipped in; he turned to Lucy. 'Father Robson says he would have played for England if he hadn't damaged his knee.'

'Does he?' Lucy replied. 'Well, a priest isn't supposed to lie.'

'They're all in there,' Martin said, nodding to the living room. 'Getting plastered.'

When they entered, Cat Abbot was just saying, 'Doreen's coming out to Spain with me next week, to meet my daughter.'

Introductions were made, then Lucy sat on the wide sofa next to Colin Greaves. 'What a lovely house,' she said to him as he handed her a glass of wine. 'Have you lived here long?'

'Not long,' he replied, with a glance at Sarah. 'But I intend to.'

'Best place for boys like those,' Doreen said. 'Plenty of room. I was talking to them earlier. They don't seem the types to be doctors, do they?'

Sarah laughed. 'No – it's my daughter, Emily, who's going to be the doctor, she's out with her boyfriend.'

'Silly of me,' Doreen said. 'I thought she was the one who was going to be a musician.'

They finished their drinks and Sarah announced it was time to begin dinner. When the others had left, Greaves remained in the room to poke the fire and take a record off the turntable. Cat Abbot returned and began to look about him. 'Doreen left her handbag,' he explained. 'Can you see it anywhere?'

Greaves smiled. 'Surely it's easy for you to find – with your new-found gifts.'

Cat stopped searching and shook his head. 'No, that's the damndest thing. When we were in the abattoir something odd seemed to occur, like a massive surge of electricity – afterwards it was as if I'd blown a fuse. Now, whatever power I did possess appears to have gone.'

'Can't you remember what happened?'

Cat looked down into the fire. 'Not clearly, just snatches, as if I were recalling a nightmare.' He looked up and saw Sarah standing in the doorway. 'Doreen says it's because of the way I feel about her,' he continued. 'She says, for everything you gain you lose something.'

Greaves glanced towards Sarah and said, '*Nunc scio quid sit amor.*'

'What does that mean?' she asked.

Cat smiled: 'Now I know what love is,' he translated.